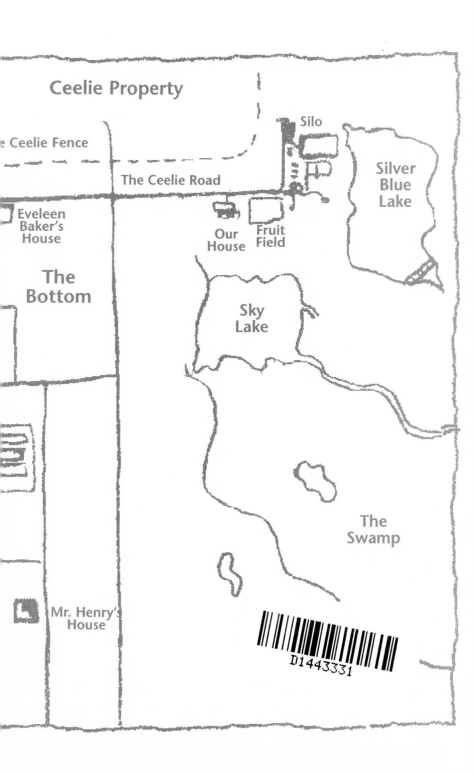

The Thang That Ate My Grandaddy's Dog

A Novel by

John Calvin Rainey

 PINEAPPLE PRESS, INC.
Sarasota, Florida

To Grandma, who fussed and cussed.
And did the best she could.

I would like to thank Rick Wilber, editor of the Fiction Quarterly, supplement of the *Tampa Tribune*, for promoting my work. And Loukia Louka, for taking the time to fool with me. And Pineapple Press, for taking the time to fool with me. And all the people who, at one time or another, restrained themselves, for one reason or another, from killing me, in one way or another.
—*John Calvin Rainey*

Copyright © 1997 by John Calvin Rainey

Inquiries should be addressed to:
Pineapple Press, Inc.
P.O. Box 3899
Sarasota, Florida 34230

Library of Congress Cataloging in Publication Data
Rainey, John Calvin, 1951-
    The thang that ate my grandaddy's dog : a novel / by John Calvin Rainey. — 1st ed.
        p.   cm.
    ISBN 1-56164-130-8 (hb : alk paper).
    I. Title.
PS3568.A4238T48   1997
813'.54—dc21   97-4447
                                                                      CIP

First Edition
10 9 8 7 6 5 4 3 2 1

Design by Carol Tornatore
Printed and bound by The Maple Press Company, York, Pennsylvania

Contents

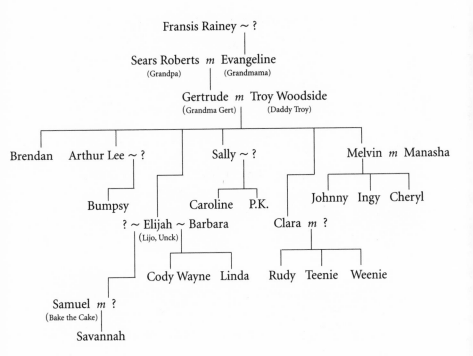

Fransis Rainey ~ ?

Sears Roberts *m* Evangeline
(Grandpa)   (Grandmama)

Gertrude *m* Troy Woodside
(Grandma Gert)   (Daddy Troy)

Brendan   Arthur Lee ~ ?   Sally ~ ?   Melvin *m* Manasha

Bumpsy   Caroline   P.K.   Johnny   Ingy   Cheryl

? ~ Elijah ~ Barbara   Clara *m* ?
(Lijo, Unck)

Cody Wayne Linda   Rudy Teenie Weenie

Samuel *m* ?
(Bake the Cake)

Savannah

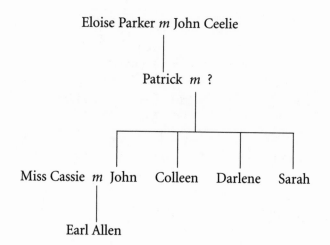

Be sober, be vigilant, because your adversary

the devil, as a roaring lion, walketh about,

seeking whom he may devour.

–1 Peter 5:8

1

Boggy

A Damn Fool

Rudy saw him first.

"Johnny," he cried, "here comes that man again."

He was just a figure in the distance, riding a horse down a little rise at a slow and measured pace. I got up from the marble game and watched him. I wasn't sure whether Grandma Gert saw him, so I relayed the warning.

"Grandma Gert," I called, "here comes that man again."

Grandmama and Grandma Gert looked up from the porch and stared across the pasture that used to be ours. Grandmama just stared, but Grandma Gert sucked her teeth and sighed in vexation. I thought she would get up and go, like she did each time he appeared, but she didn't. This time she watched him.

Even at a distance we could see there was something different about him. He was wearing the same black outfit and riding the same black horse, but somehow it wasn't the same sameness.

In the eight or nine appearances he'd made, he had never come close enough for us to recognize and identify him. We could only speculate; we suspected it was Mr. Ceelie.

Who else could it be? Who else wanted our land?

He rode the horse down the rise and onto the little road that started in front of our house and snaked across the field. The first time he appeared we didn't pay any particular attention to him. We thought he was just another rider out watching the sunset. But we soon realized he was watching us, and the closer he came, the more sinister he appeared.

To Manasha, my mother, this solitary figure atop the black horse was a lurking evil that had her more than afraid. Manasha believes we are not that far removed from the lynchings, murders, and terrors of days gone by. Since Manasha is from New York, she only has a vague understanding of what a lynching actually is. But not Grandmama. And not Grandma Gert. Their understanding of such things is clear. They lived and witnessed these things, and the appearance of the rider conjured up bad memories of things past. Ghastly remembrances of a history that is not fit to repeat itself.

The rider brought these memories back for me to hear. Sometimes they allowed me to listen, with the benign hope that, by listening, that particular history would not repeat itself. So quietly I would sit and listen and learn the confused heap of facts, follies, crimes, and misfortunes that were the history of this squabble, these people, and this place called Boggy.

It began like the Book, with a man and a woman in a garden. Not the Garden of Eden, but a garden of hell called Georgia. He was black. She was white. He was running north. She was running south. Two people running in opposite directions, trying to get the hell out of Georgia.

By time and chance, Fransis Rainey and Eloise Parker met on the banks of the Ona River. He was an escaped slave desperately seeking the Union Army. She was a frantic and distraught woman who had lost her family. Both were directly in the line of march of

General William T. Sherman's Army of the Tennessee, as it cut a wide swath of destruction through the state.

Her mother had died along the way. Her father and a brother had been killed in an ambush by Union bummers. In a desperate effort to escape the scavengers, she and the surviving brother tried to bring the cattle across the river at night. She and some of the cattle made it across, but her one remaining relative, caught in the swift running current and a hail of bullets, perished in the darkness.

Fransis Rainey, hiding in a tree, had witnessed the massacre and was no longer certain about the Union Army. The next morning, as he was burying the brother, he and the bereaved woman were discovered by the Confederate cavalry, which had been shadowing the Union force, killing stragglers, and seizing runaway slaves.

The whole state was fleeing Sherman's Army, and a grieving white woman was nothing out of the ordinary. But there was a bounty on runaway slaves, and Fransis Rainey was being eyed with a great deal of suspicion. Saving him from reenslavement, Eloise Parker claimed the slave as hers. So, the cavalry satisfied itself with the remaining cattle and galloped away in the very direction Fransis Rainey intended to take.

By virtue of her being white, she declared Fransis a free man, then hired him, as a free man, to take her somewhere, anywhere, away from Georgia. Since portions of Wheeler's Cavalry were between him and where he wanted to go, he agreed, as long as somewhere, anywhere, was not Alabama, Mississippi, or Louisiana.

Olustee, Florida, is not very far from the Georgia line, but it was a long way from Sherman's Army. Far enough away for Fransis Rainey to stop and raise hogs, and for Eloise Parker to meet and marry a Confederate captain named John Ceelie, who commanded the cavalry that patrolled the road between Jacksonville and Tallahassee.

The capital city of Tallahassee is the only capital city of the entire South that was not captured by Union forces—which does not mean they didn't try. Unfortunately, the little town of Olustee sat directly in the line of march of the Union forces bent upon capturing the capital. It was there, amongst the piney woods, palmetto brush, and sandy soil, that a small Confederate force halted the Union advance, and young Eloise Parker became a grieving widow.

Rapidly she was becoming a woman of many sorrows, a woman well acquainted with grief. In the wisdom of her new solitude, she decided there was no grief that time and distance could not lessen. Fransis Rainey agreed. He'd lost all the pigs to foragers, so he, Eloise Parker, and a group of war refugees—runaway slaves and deserters from both sides—packed up and moved further south into a world unseen and unknown, trekking for months with only a dim, but determined sense of where they were going.

Where they ended up was not what they had in mind, but it was where they were stopped, suddenly confronted by a vast, steaming wasteland that was not all water and not all land, but a dark and desolate cypress morass filled with poisonous snakes, poisonous plants, disease-carrying insects, alligators, and a variety of savage predators slinking beneath a dismal, never-ending canopy of strangling vines and suffocating vegetation. A primal hell where time stood still and death awaited them if they dared go further.

With the Oklawaha Swamp in front of them, Sherman's Army and Wheeler's Cavalry behind them, they stayed where they were and offered their prayers to the mysterious God. Here there was nothing to squabble about. These were the first settlers in the central part of the state. Their survival and well-being depended on the total cooperation of all.

In the years following the war, the state of Florida held a deep appreciation for these early settlers, more so for some than for others. But all were awarded squatter's rights, and all they had to do was carve out forty acres, put a cabin on it, and live there for six months.

Because she was a widow of a Confederate officer who was killed defending the state capital, Eloise Parker received a land grant of one thousand acres. A lot of this land, swampland, or what they call "bottom land"—was offered by the state at ten cents an acre. All you had to do was drain it. Fransis Rainey never bothered to drain any of the land he was buying. He said that was the work of the next generation, to keep them from going soft.

Grandmama could not tell us anything about her mother. No one ever talked about her except to say she had died. Grandmama can only tell us about a woman named "Berjie," who she said cared for her when she was young.

When my great-great-grandfather Fransis died, my great-grandmother Evangeline inherited a shack, two mules, and eight hundred and sixty acres of swamp. She was fourteen years old. Sears Roberts, the gardener, was fifteen. On the advice of Berjie and Miss Eloise, for whom they both worked, the two young people were married.

Eloise Parker lived long enough to see her children found a city in her name. They were among the movers and shakers in the state, and Fransis Rainey was not forgotten. At the insistence of Eloise Parker, Grandmama and Grandpa were invited to sign the original city charter of "Eloise."

My great-great-granddaddy had planted cotton for Eloise

Parker, but her son Patrick wanted citrus. Grandpa planted the seedlings and took care of their groves. But for himself, he planted three hundred acres of hardwood pine, the kind that takes forty to fifty years to mature. In this they were devising their own future. Their eyes were always on the future.

But Patrick Ceelie's eyes were on the future too, and the future required him to have more land. So he conspired with the other movers and shakers to accrue hundreds of thousands of acres at such cut-rate prices that the stink of these deals reached all the way up to Washington. The scandal ultimately led to the creation of the Oklawaha National Forest and the Oklawaha Wildlife Preserve. Thwarted in their land-grabbing schemes, Ceelie and his cohorts flat out began to steal the land of the homesteaders.

They never pressed Grandpa for his land. We were too well acquainted, and there was always help for the son of a widow. Patrick Ceelie took it for granted that once Grandpa died, the land would pass to him anyway, since Sears and Evangeline had no boys, just one daughter, Gertrude.

But Patrick Ceelie died first and left behind one boy and three girls for Grandmama to nurse and nanny, and for Grandma Gert to play with while she grew up. And all the while she was growing up, Grandpa supervised the Ceelie groves.

The generations were coming, children in whom there was much faith because the trees were still standing. Troy Woodside worked for Grandpa, and, on the advice of Grandpa, married Grandma Gert. But they would have to produce a generation far wiser than the vipers of Patrick Ceelie, for Patrick's son John had a strong desire to raise cattle and he needed pasture land—our land.

John Ceelie wistfully explained his dreams to Grandma Gert,

and the price he offered was fair and even generous. But Grandma Gert asked him what would she have for her children if she did that, and John Ceelie was insulted. He'd grown up with Grandma Gert. Her mother, father, and husband had been no more than nursemaids and field hands. *How dare she!* Her grandfather had been his grandmother's slave! *What impertinence!* The Ceelie family had always taken care of *them!* The Ceelie family felt responsible for *them!* The Ceelie family wanted that piece of land and intended to have it.

Grandpa knew enough to know that the Ceelie family had to be appeased, so he leased the land to them. He allowed them to use two hundred of his acres to begin raising cattle, an arrangement that would eventually lead to trouble because it was all done on a handshake and good faith. It called for them to pay us a nominal fee and buy our hay. It was an arrangement they all felt they could live with.

As Grandma Gert's children became adults, they were given small parcels of land. It was a mistake she would come to regret.

My uncle Arthur Lee was the first to sell his land and leave.

Then my Uncle Elijah, or Lijo, whom I call "Unck," sold his.

Then my Aunt Sally.

Then my Aunt Clara.

Then my father, Melvin, sold his fifty acres of land to Earl Allen, John Ceelie's son.

And all Grandma Gert and Daddy Troy could do was thank God they had never drained the cypress swamp or cut down the pine forest.

It didn't matter. Earl Allen Ceelie made Grandma Gert and Daddy Troy an offer they both refused. Not long after that they lost their homestead tax exemption and the property was reassessed for taxes.

For more than three generations, our family had been joined to the Ceelie family in a friendship born of pain and blood on the banks of an obscure river in Georgia. The overwhelming forces of a hostile society dictated this. To serve their interest was to serve our own. But as their interest became our land, they became our enemy. Despite Earl Allen Ceelie's smiles of assurances and feigned civility, battle lines were drawn.

We were up against the premier family of Oklawaha County, one of the most powerful citrus and cattle families in the state. Finding an attorney to accept the case was an effort in itself, much less finding an effective one. Three private attorneys had dropped the case. The legal-aid lawyers abandoned it. The ACLU refused to accept it, and the NAACP was completely stymied in their efforts. The search for an attorney would have gone on forever if "Bake the Cake" had not kidnapped Savannah and come south.

Wealth and power betrayed Earl Allen Ceelie into arrogance. The two hundred and fifty acres he had gotten from my aunts and uncles were really our front yard. The road ran from Boggy right up to our house. There was no other access. One morning we awakened to find it blocked by a yellow-and-black wooden barricade, with the word "HALT" stenciled across the front in bold black letters. It made no sense, because all you had to do was drive around it. Daddy Troy didn't even bother to do that, but drove straight through it, smashing it to smithereens! Two days later Earl Allen began building a fence that, in effect, hemmed us in.

Earl Allen Ceelie said it was his property, his road, and he was perfectly within his rights, and everybody we complained to agreed. He had the right to put a fence anywhere he wanted, and his cows had the right to graze anywhere they wanted. For some strange reason, they took to grazing right in front of our house.

To everyone else, it appeared that our struggle to hold on to the land was a struggle in vain. To some, it was a struggle to swell the heart. To others it was an unpitied, contemptible struggle because of the amount of money that was rumored to have been offered to us. The generations, it appeared, were gone, lost, so why struggle? Unlike their forefathers, they were a faithless, stubborn, selfish generation, so why fight?

They're gone; gone far away into silence. Gone in haste into the world of night. Gone into tomorrow. Your children are gone. Your great spirit is gone. Not dead, but gone. Not lost, but gone. Gone to the dogs. Gone with the wind. All your generations are gone forever, and what's gone is gone.

But a funny thing began to happen. That gone generation began drifting back. All the gone souls, with nowhere else to go, feeling the oppression of their prodigal weight, returned to the house from which they came. My mother and sisters and I were the first to come.

After my father was sentenced to ten years for drug trafficking, the state of New York and the IRS conspired to confiscate what they called our "ill-gotten gains." They closed both vegetable markets and took our house, our cars, our furniture, and all they could lay their hands on under the law, which was everything we had. Life became a struggle and sometimes desperate.

Manasha's parents are dead. I have no grandma and grandpa in New York City. We were living in a welfare hotel until we moved into a project in Brooklyn. My father, from a prison cell, urged Manasha to go to his people in Florida, but that was three thousand miles away from New York, and New York was all my mother knew. She knew Unck, but the Feds were looking for him too. Manasha would never have left New York if my father had not insisted she bring me and my two baby sisters to visit him in jail.

Manasha emphatically believes that her children should

never see the inside of a jail, not even to visit one. She sent him pictures instead.

My father fumed! The lawyer insisted! Social workers implored her, but Manasha was adamant. So, my father wrote her a letter threatening to petition the court to have custody of his children granted to his mother. Manasha wrote him a letter back saying, "Fine, I'll deliver them myself."

And that is how we came to Boggy.

We came by bus—the four of us and twenty-two cardboard boxes. A man who knew Unck gave us a ride from the Greyhound station. Grandma Gert's first words to us were, "Now where y'all goin' wit all them boxes?"

And Manasha explained.

And Grandma Gert moaned about how she wasn't about to raise any more children.

And how she didn't have no room.

And, "Y'all gotta learn to take care of ya own children."

And, "Y'all gotta learn to take care of y'self."

And, "Oh Lord," this!

And, "Oh Lord," that!

And, "Oh Lord, why me?"

And that was my Grandma Gert.

I loved this place the moment I got here. There was dirt, a lot of dirt. And cow shit, and horse shit, and pig shit, and dog shit, and chicken shit too. But nobody worried about it but Manasha. She said the whole place smelled like shit, which was a wonder, since Manasha went no further than the fruit field, certainly not down to the Silo, where all the shit was. It was a while before she ventured down to the lakes or through the long, dark, leaf-carpeted forest. All she did was cry. There were mulberry trees, pecan trees, almond trees, berry trees, cherry trees, orange trees, tanger-

ine trees, grapefruit trees, lemon trees, lime trees, Spanish lime
trees, Japanese plum trees, and mango trees, all conspiring to
make this place a storybook of exquisite beauty and wonder. But
all she did was cry. Manasha was homesick.

She was from New York. What did she know about outhous-
es and pitcher pumps? For one whole week Manasha would venture no further than the porch because she was terrified of scorpi-
ons, cow-ants, and snakes. And boy, have we got some snakes for
your ass! King snakes and coral snakes and rat snakes and chicken
snakes! Rattlesnakes and joint snakes and hog snakes and wood
snakes! Water snakes, pine snakes, grass snakes, and tree snakes!
Cottonmouths! Copperheads! Blue indigoes, blue racers, black
racers, and coachwhips! Snakes that climb, burrow, swim, and
even glide from trees! Snakes! Creepy-crawly slithering serpents!
The kind that made Manasha often inquire about the next bus
back to New York City.

But there was no way out, and Manasha would hug us and
cry every night, and I would wonder why, because outside of scor-
pions and snakes, it was a wonderful place.

Perhaps it had something to do with loneliness. I could
understand that—loneliness. After the novelty of Silo City wore
off, I quickly became a lonely and forlorn little boy in desperate
need of a friend. *It is not a good thing that a boy should be alone.*
Sometimes I cried more than Manasha, but I would always go off
somewhere alone, because my crying would always upset
Manasha and make her cry even more. Grandmama always knew
when I'd been crying, no matter how much I dried my eyes, and
she would call me and comfort me just like she did Manasha. It
may not have been so bad had I been able to ramble at will; then
my imagination and thoughts would have been my one good
familiar friend. But I was made to stay in the fruit field. I was too

little and too unfamiliar with the place to go gallivanting off somewhere and fall down an old well, or get stuck in a sinkhole, or get bit by a snake. But I was an inquisitive child. There were dangers I couldn't see, and despite the warnings, I would often go rambling down by the lakes.

I never rambled down by Silver Blue Lake, because then I would have to go through Silo, and anytime you, me, or anyone else passed the fruit field, they were met by the dogs.

My Grandaddy's dogs. There were four of them—five if you included Poochie, but I don't include Poochie because she is a house dog. She is a pit bull, but she is female and more of a companion. My Grandaddy's dogs were all male and domineering. That was their whole life. Poochie never growled at me or raised her leg at me. She never gave me a straight unwavering gaze like that big brow mastiff named "Shack." She never raised her hackles at me like the pit bull they called "Ike." She never growled and stiffened her tail, like the blue-tick they called "Blackie." And she never just watched me, like the black dog with one blue eye. No, Poochie is a girl dog. She thought more of protecting us than attacking our enemies—or us. Grandpa said it would take time because the dogs were not used to "chillun." But Poochie was. She picked up right away that "chillun" were her friends.

The house and the yard were her territory, and she was aggressive about her territory. If any of my Grandaddy's dogs came up from the Silo, they were in trouble with Poochie. And if they challenged Poochie and became aggressive toward her, Grandma Gert would blow their heads off!

Silo was their territory, the house and the yard were Poochie's territory, and the fruit field was neutral.

I was an intruder, and my Grandaddy's dogs let me know it. They didn't acknowledge any claim jumpers. Grandpa said I was the one who would be taught how to behave around them, which made them the boss! No, I felt much better by myself, sneaking away to wander around Sky Lake in secret. That was my fun and cured my loneliness. But I was to learn, on one of these clandestine forays, that Grandpa was right—and the dogs were boss.

It was the day I first tried to go all the way around the lake. Each time I came down to the lake, my confidence was boosted. To completely circle the lake would be an achievement not at all unlike finding the source of the Nile. This was a test, to venture far into the unknown and come out whole. Instead, I got lost, which wasn't easy considering all I had to do was follow the shoreline, which was what I was doing until about midway when I came upon a track.

It was just one solitary track at the edge of the water. I don't know what kind of track it was, but it was big and it had claws! I turned around and ran fast and furious, not from my own fear, but from whatever had made that track. I can never forget the taste of fear as I ran, without reasoning or direction, but with fear and panic. I ran to run out of my own skin as if this thing, anything, were directly upon me! I screamed for Manasha, mortal fear becoming a blind desperate fear. I was lost! The lake had always been my guide, but there was no lake and I couldn't find it. There was only a dark, terror-breathing wilderness. And out of it came something even darker—black!

He had a shaggy coat of black hair with a tuft of white that started in the middle of his forehead, streaking down between his eyes to completely encircle his mouth. He had one blue eye and he stared at me. He was my Grandaddy's dog, and I was as much afraid of him as I was of whatever had made that track. With bated breath and streaming tears I grabbed hold of a tree, prepared to go up if he came any closer. But he didn't. He watched me for a moment, then turned and trotted a few yards away, then turned and sat down facing me. Relieved that he wasn't going to bother me, I had a prayerful hope that I could follow him home.

He got up and trotted a few yards, and I came up behind the tree and started after him. He stopped and looked back. I stopped too, and pleaded, "OK, OK." He turned and trotted away, and I ran behind, sometimes struggling to keep him in sight, but all too relieved to have a savior deliver me from such a sorry plight. Suddenly I burst out of the darkness and into an open field and recognized the hog pens. I was home; all I had to do was stay on the path.

I dried my eyes and gathered myself and walked the short distance from the hog pens into Silo. I looked for the dog, but didn't see him. But that was all right because I knew then that I'd found a friend. His name was Lance.

Manasha wasn't so lucky. She needed more than a friend to cure her melancholy. It had more to do with the shack than loneliness. Ingy and Cheryl slept with them in the two-bedroom brick house. Me and Manasha slept in the shack. There were two shacks, and both had been there since World War I. All my aunts and uncles had been raised in those two shacks. Grandma Gert, too. Our shack was set up on cinder blocks. It had no running water and there was an outhouse out back, which only served to make Manasha cry, and Grandma Gert moan each time she did. No one was able to comfort her until the day Aunt Clara arrived and Grandma Gert broke down and cried herself.

I, for one, always thought my grandmother was too old to cry, until the morning Aunt Clara got out of the cab and began unloading her bags. Her jaw was wired shut and her right eye was completely closed. She suffered from an assortment of other bumps and bruises, and she was pregnant. This was Grandma

Gert's baby girl. Manasha had to go and comfort Grandma Gert.

After all the weeping and all the welcoming, the purging and rejoicing, a solemn melting mood took hold and Daddy Troy told me to show my little cousin, Rudy, the fruit field. An evil odor had come with them, and that's what they were discussing. I took Rudy and introduced him to the dogs.

This was a day of adversity, with even more adversity to come. One hour after Aunt Clara and Rudy's arrival, Grandma Gert received a phone call informing her that Alma Edlow had died.

Alma Edlow was Barbara Edlow's mother. And Barbara Edlow was Cody Wayne and Linda's mother. And Unck was their father. No one knew where Unck was, since he was still hiding from the police, and no one knew where Barbara was, since she had long since degenerated into that never-never twilight world of crack. Juvenile and Domestic Services, in cahoots with the county (and therefore with Mr. Ceelie), tried to use the two children to draw Unck out, but the day before they buried Miss Alma, Manasha and Grandma Gert drove home with both Linda and Cody Wayne in tow.

Mr. Ceelie's answer to all these unexpected flowers blooming around the shacks was to build the fence that cut off the access road.

Daddy Troy's answer to the fence was simply to drive through it, but Grandpa's answer was more subtle, yet it demonstrated his great resolve. In full view of Mr. Ceelie, as he was supervising the mending of the fence, Grandpa began surveying the foundation for an addition to the house. The implications were clear, and Mr. Ceelie's answer to this, besides a stream of obscenities, was to call the county building inspectors. It was at this point, one hot afternoon, as two building inspectors were busily examining and explaining nonexistent code violations on the kind of brick we were using, that two more troubles came marching down the road.

I'd first noticed them when I'd noticed that Grandpa wasn't even listening to the inspectors, but instead was looking past them in the distance at two figures walking down the dusty road. As the inspectors rambled, we watched the figures. A man and a little girl. They came between the two county cars parked the other side of the fence, where he lifted the tired child across and then climbed through himself. Without a word, Grandpa walked away from the chattering inspectors and took Savannah by the hand and led her and Bake the Cake into the house.

Samuel Woodside was another one of Unck's children. Unck didn't know him until the day he'd popped up wanting to know his father. He was the reason why Unck had sold his piece of land to Mr. Ceelie, to pay for his son's college education.

He was a commercial lawyer on the legal staff of a large brokerage house in Chicago and was well on his way to a bright future when he was suddenly diagnosed HIV-positive.

This was a misfortune he could not bear with calmness. And there was no one to blame. It had the effect of eliciting certain vices in him that in better times would have lain dormant. For several months he lived in a drunken stupor, cursing life and the world as it is, the shadow of death accounting for his madness. Fate can deal such dirty blows and make life a joke. Or a bottle of whiskey, or an insane dream, or a lost and bitter soul: Life is a fatal disease.

But life is also a sweet little baby girl, and he remembered he'd fathered one. The mother was white and Catholic, and had put the baby up for adoption instead of aborting. The unknown daughter suddenly became the medicine of his life. Tracing her through a succession of orphanages, he wasn't quite sure if the little black girl they'd shown him was his daughter. She was too black to be born of a white mother. But a DNA test proved otherwise, and he tried to gain custody of his only child. Citing his health, the court refused. So Bake the Cake kidnapped her and came south.

Because he was a lawyer, Grandma Gert believed God had sent him. She could not be made to understand it was business law he was trained in, as opposed to civil and criminal law. His purpose, he stated, was to tie up the last loose end in his life, which was Savannah. Grandma Gert told him not to worry about Savannah; she was with family. As for being just a commercial lawyer, she told him law was law and for once we needed it on our side, because the lawyer we had in Bartow wasn't worth a damn. He was a lawyer and he was family, and that's all she needed to know. Never mind HIV. Never mind that he was wanted for kidnapping. And never mind him never having practiced law in Florida, much less civil or criminal law.

"Law is law," she explained to him. "It's like baking a cake. Baking a cake is baking a cake. Damn what kind of cake it is—it's still baking a cake. You gonna bake a cake or what?"

Thereafter, whenever he sat, with furrowed brow, hunched over his quillets, his cases, his tenures, and his tricks, his statutes, his recoveries and discoveries, Grandma Gert would make us be quiet, or go outside, and let him "bake the cake."

It did not take Mr. Ceelie long to find out who he was, what he was doing, what he'd done, and who he was wanted by.

One fine morning, a platoon of law officers swooped down on the house with arrest warrants for Unck and Bake the Cake, and a subpoena for Miss Eva. Nobody knew where Unck was, but wherever he was, you can bet Miss Eva was with him. Bake the Cake had gone into Eloise with Daddy Troy, and Savannah was shopping with Manasha. The whole keystone production was fruitless, except for Savannah, and these people didn't know Savannah from Atlanta. They grabbed Linda by mistake.

When the authorities insisted that Linda was Savannah and took her into custody, there were no hysterics, not even a mild protest from Grandma Gert. Nobody said anything as the last police car drove away with Grandma Gert and Linda in the back seat.

It was a blue-and-gold mistake that allowed us to hide Savannah and warn Bake the Cake. And a fourteen-carat mistake that put the whole county government on the defensive and into litigation.

Despite all his degrees, Bake the Cake did not have a real education. He'd been trained, not educated. He himself realized this while hiding out with Unck, his father, somewhere down in that inscrutable place of mystery and terror known as the Oklawaha Swamp.

Unck came and got him. And, I imagine, it was between there and the Masonic Lodge that he learned of his family, himself, their secrets, their skeletons, and this place called Boggy. And, I imagine, that's where they told him about the guava tree.

Oklawaha County was the only county in this state that still reserved the right to execute its own criminals. Of course, they had not done this in half a century. Like every other county in the state, they shipped their doomed men and women up to Florida State Prison to await execution. But if they wanted to, they legally reserved the right to take a condemned person to the rear of the old county courthouse in Eloise and string him up to a guava tree. This made the old county jail a historic site and a public curiosity. So instead of tearing it down, they tried to strike a deal with the federal government to carry out contract executions. Failing this, they turned it into a tourist attraction.

This came with the obligatory concession and souvenir stand. Plus a guided tour of the 103-year-old courthouse and jail. A view of all the old records. A rogue's gallery of Oklawaha's most celebrated crimes and infamous criminals. "The Hall of Shame" showcased all those who were executed, their history, their pictures, and pictures of their crimes. And then there was the guava tree itself.

With a guava tree as its gallows, the law in Oklawaha County was an exhibition and a stage. It was set in the center of a cobblestone courtyard surrounded by a six-foot-high circular platform with four trapdoors, one at every quarter. It was four feet wide at its base and fifty feet at its highest point. Huge sturdy limbs branched off to correlate with each trapdoor. Secured around each of these limbs was the hang rope tied in the hangman's knot, the lengths having long since been cut away, along with the unfortunate loads they once carried. This grim monstrosity marks an epoch in the county's history. Contemplating it, one becomes quite deaf to the raucous clamor of contemporary life and sensitively attuned to the bugle call of history we know as taps—a cold, clammy, accusing history that makes one look back at things that never came to pass and suffer remembrances of things that never happened. Every piece of rope that was wrapped around a limb was a silent and poignant agony, equated not only with death, but the vulgarity of a dissolute life.

Fifty-three desperate deaths questioning one's conscience in the close of the courtyard: here was the grand and noble character of Oklawaha County. Not grand and noble as in oak, but grand and noble as in guava.

By its very nature it was an aversion. There is something terribly ignoble about meeting one's end in a guava tree. Although public safety is a noble motive, there is little that is noble about a guava tree. Now, don't get me wrong, I like guavas. But I like them a little bit less that sapodillas, and a whole lot more than rutabagas. Being grossly ill-formed, a guava tree seems serenely resigned to the way it has to be. It is the Quasimodo of trees, made to produce the Quasimodo of fruit, and not the strange fruit of Oklawaha County. That is what an oak tree is for.

An oak tree is what Florida's electric chair is made from. An oak tree is what they hanged the wrong men from in *The Oxbow Incident*. An oak tree is what the mob was going to hang Gary Cooper from in *The Hanging Tree*. I don't know what it was those nine just men tried to hang Clint Eastwood from in *Hang 'Em High*, but it sure looked like a guava tree to me. And therein lies the difference: an oak tree is made for hanging. They somehow lend their noble bearing to an otherwise sordid affair, whereas a guava tree emphasizes the sordidness.

The sordid history of the guava tree flooded the American consciousness when a full-color photo of it appeared on the cover of *Ebony* magazine.

The only person who ever bothered to read all those old records was Bake the Cake. It detailed a stupid, brutal, nightmarish history of conduct unworthy of a beast. He did not have to make anything up, or rely on conjecture. All their mischief was recorded, and, with the help of a freelance writer in Chicago, Oklawaha County was made to look like the ass-end of the country.

The article did not focus on what was officially known. Instead, it detailed what was rumored and whispered. All the ones who'd been shot trying to escape. And all the ones who'd committed suicide. And the ones who fell and broke their necks. The men and women who'd been lynched. The man who, after being found not guilty in a trial, was dragged from the defendant's table, taken to the guava tree, and lynched.

The Greek fisherman.

The disrespectful petty thief.

The sheriff who tried to protect a prisoner, but was seized along with the prisoner, taken to the guava tree, and lynched.

The historical exhibit did not mention or even hint about the historical burning of the jail in 1924, probably because a deputy sheriff was shot to death, his family run out of town, and, as the fire raged, two men swung from the guava tree.

People magazine came into the act when the Veterans Administration, which routinely bought tombstones for indigent veterans, announced it was buying a tombstone for Arthur Batts, a World War I veteran who had been lynched in the guava tree and buried in an unmarked grave.

A wave of embarrassment swept the state. A tidal wave of nausea swept the county. We are only seventy miles away from Disney World, forty miles from Gatorland, sixty miles from Busch Gardens. Florida is home to the Miami Dolphins, the Tampa Bay Buccaneers, the Miami Heat, the Jacksonville Jaguars, and the Florida Marlins. Tourism is our number-one industry. And everyone wanted to know, "What kinda damn tourist attraction is that?"

County officials thought it was a good idea and were confounded by all the notoriety. They didn't know what action to take until the County Mayor told the City Mayor, "Cut that damn thing down!" and "Find the sonovabitch who started this!"

To do that, they would have to call upon the ghost of Fransis Rainey.

Instead, they made a deal with Bake the Cake and Unck. After all, they were from one of the pioneer families in Oklawaha. They dropped the dope charges against Unck, and Bake the Cake turned himself in. We, in turn, dropped our suit against the county for false-arresting Linda. They, in turn, caught the sucker who was shooting out the power transformer and cutting our phone lines. And he, in turn, told who'd put him up to it and why. In the midst of all this, Judge Clifford, who was arbitrating the land dispute, handed down his decision. And there was nothing Earl Allen Ceelie could do but wish his father had not waited for Grandpa to die.

All he could do now was sit in the sunset and stew. And pay damages.

But there was something different about him this time. For one thing, he seemed to be coming closer. He was coming down the dusty road straight for the fence.

"Johnny!" Cody Wayne called. "Yo shot." I continued to watch the rider.

"Yo shot!" Savannah cried.

"You lose yo turn!" snapped Rudy.

I glanced at Manasha, who was watching him and trying her best to appear as stoic and unafraid as Grandmama and Grandma Gert, but failing miserably. They noticed the difference too. He was right up to the fence, close enough for us to see the gleam of those black boots, the patterns on that black outfit, the shape of that black hat, and the mystery of that baleful . . . mask? *He was wearing a mask!*

"Somebody please tell me what's wrong wit this gottdamn Cracka!" Grandma Gert hissed.

"Laaaawd," Grandmama cried with a sad shaking of her head, "Earl Allen done lost his mind."

Manasha didn't know what to think, but was depending on

the stalwart sense of the two women to at least clarify the mask.

"He ain't lost his mind," Grandma Gert spat. "He just plain silly! Now he look like the silliest man in the world—a damn fool!"

Grandmama steadied her walker, got up, and went inside. Grandma Gert followed. Cheryl ran up on the porch and climbed up on Manasha.

"Who dat?" she asked. "The Lone Ranga?"

"No," said Manasha, drawing her close.

"Zorro?"

"No."

"Who?"

Manasha didn't answer, but picked her up and took her inside.

"New game!" Cody Wayne yelled.

"Johnny?" Linda called, "you playin'?"

"Yeah," I answered.

For a moment longer I watched him and he watched me, glaring as if he wished he could glare me out of existence. He looked nothing at all like the Lone Ranger, or even Zorro. He looked kind of like "El-Kabong." And the black mask, far from being sinister, was one step beyond the ridiculous. All he needed was a guitar. "Kaboooonnnnggg!"

"Johnny, c'mon!" Savannah called.

And I turned to play.

But every so often, when it wasn't my turn, I would turn and look. And every so often as he rode away into the sunset, he would turn and glare. And when he got back to the top of the rise, he just sat there, atop his black horse, in his black outfit, his black hat, and that black mask, looking like a damn fool.

Prelude to the Gheechie Man

"Hush!" Grandmama hissed and leaned forward with her fingers to her lips to shush us. "Shssssh!"

And only the stillness could be heard above the quiet flames of the kerosene heater, enlivening the narrative. She reached out to grasp at our inflamed imaginations and gave us a clear picture of old Cyrus crouching at the edge of a mysterious waterhole somewhere down in the bowels of the Oklawaha swamp.

"Something was down there!" she whispered with force, "but he couldn't see it clearly. A turtle? Or maybe it was something he'd never seen before."

"Listen!" she snapped and stared directly at me. Then she closed one eye and, with a wave of her hand and in a very hoarse voice, said, "The water began to bubble and turn! Something was moving beneath it. Old Cyrus wanted to run, but he was so scared all he could do was look. And then he saw it! It was a thing! He didn't know what it was; it was just a red thing coming up out of the water. It swam over to the bank and pulled itself up on a rock and sat!

"And Old Cyrus looked at this thing and called Jesus' name! It was blood red! And its two eyes were rollin' round in its head like two black marbles. It didn't have no arms and no legs, it was just a big blob of red, sittin' there, lookin' all around. And when it felt safe it poked out a long black tongue and started lickin' itself like a cat!

"Well, Old Cyrus didn't know what to make of this thing. All he knew was he'd better shoot it quick! He turned to pick up his rifle, but when he turned back to shoot, this thing was staring him straight in the eye! It had him so fascinated he couldn't shoot! He was trying to pull the trigger, but was shakin' too hard. He just kept shakin' and shakin' and . . ."

"Look!" Cheryl screamed.

"The heater!" Ingy screamed.

I thought they were teasing, but then I saw it—fire! A smokeless blue flame licking up the back of the heater. Everyone sprang up in panic, moving everywhere at once! I was the first to reach the front door, only to have to fight with the latch that had suddenly become the most complicated device in the world. It opened and I rushed out into the night, not for safety, but for sand! Not water, but sand! Po Jim had used water, which only caused the fire to spread. So much fire and little Lisa trapped inside. So much fire and Po Jim ran. He ran for water, but I ran for sand. With the thought of that tragedy still in my mind, I ran to the rose bed and scooped up a double handful of soft black dirt. Wild with terror, I raced back into the house and ran into Rudy! The precious, life-saving sand spilled across the living-room floor.

"Now, why you brang that dirt in here!" Grandma Gert snapped.

She was sitting in her big chair next to the fireplace, which couldn't be used until the chimney was extended through the upstairs addition of the house.

Ingy and Cheryl were lying across either side of her. Savannah and Linda were still standing in the corner with a blanket wrapped around them. Cody Wayne was standing in the kitchen doorway. Grandmama was still lying down. The fire was out and everyone was staring at me.

The fire had been put out with two swipes from Grandma Gert's pillow. It was out before I'd reached the door. Now Daddy Troy was out and raging mad.

"This thing ain't nuthin' to play with!" he raged. "This ain't no toy!"

"Ain't nobody been playin' wit that," I said in our defense.

"Don't tell me nobody been playin' wit it!"

Despite the heat, he began dismantling it.

"Don't tell me y'all ain't been playin' wit this!" he roared. "Looka this!"

He pulled out a long, scorched shoestring.

"And this!"

The melted remains of a doll's head.

"And this!"

A burnt clothespin.

"And this!"

Six jack stones.

"And these!"

Six soda caps.

He slammed a pair of pliers down and said, "Don't tell me y'all ain't been playin' wit this!"

Grandma Gert said nothing. She was sitting very still with her eyes closed, her mouth set, and her face flushed with anger.

"This ain't no toy!" Daddy Troy growled. "Y'all wanna burn up, like Lisa?"

Savannah and Linda looked as if they would cry. Lisa was our friend.

"Come look at this!" Daddy Troy called Grandma Gert.

She nudged Ingy and Cheryl up and got up to see what he was talking about. We already knew and stiffened in response.

"Crayon!" she shouted in sudden anger. "Who been meltin'

crayon on the back of this?"

No one answered—a sure sign of collective guilt.

"What the hell y'all wanna do, burn the house down?" she shrieked at us.

Not really, but we did like to see whose crayon would melt the quickest.

"Git over here," she directed Cody Wayne, "and clean this mess up now!"

He wasn't the only one who'd been melting crayons, and he wasn't the only one who had to clean them up, either.

"You too!" she screamed at me.

Very diligently, we began scraping the colorful mosaic of melted wax from the back of the heater.

"If I catch any one of y'all melting crayon on the back of this heater," she declared with her right hand to God, "I swear, and here's my right hand to Gawd, I swear I'll put somethin' on ya ass you'll never forget!"

That said and understood by all, she plopped herself back down in her chair and sat with her eyes closed. Immediately, Ingy and Cheryl plopped across her lap.

Daddy Troy replaced both burners and adjusted the wicks. He replaced the tank and adjusted the drip meter. The floor was swept and mopped, and Grandma Gert still sat with her eyes closed.

"OK," Daddy Troy announced, "it's set. Now if it catch fire again, that's just too bad."

He placed a small pan of water on the top of the heater to help keep the air moist. Then he went out and came back in with a bucket of sand and placed it next to the heater. No instructions were needed.

We drifted back to our spots around the heater. In the time

it took to fix it, the house had gotten cold, and all of us, except Grandma Gert, wiggled for warmth. She just sat there, rocking back and forth with her eyes closed. She made it hard to pretend everything was all right and nothing had happened. So we kept our silence and took the opportunity to appreciate the quiet fire.

The Gheechie Man

Unless we're asleep or dead, it is very difficult for any one of us to stay quiet for long.

"Grandma, make Rudy stop!" Cheryl complained.

"I ain't doin' nuthin'," Rudy lied.

"Grandma, he—stoppit Rudy!"

Grandma Gert jumped from her chair and shrieked, "Now y'all just cut it out! All y'all! That's what's wrong now—ya too bad! And if ya don't straighten up and be good, ahma beat ya butt!"

An ominous silence arose, and we lay beneath the blankets, feigning sleep. Having gotten her message across, she stomped over and slapped out the light, turning the living room into a semi-dark cavern, the warm glow of the heater sending forth a feeling of comfort and security.

"Move!" Grandma Gert towered over me and commanded, "Lemme lay down!"

I was lying at the front of the heater, the best spot, her spot. I'd hogged it for myself, hoping she'd sleep in the chair, or go to her bedroom. But the interior walls were still being insulated, so the house could not hold heat. Grandpa shut the heat off to save oil, so the only heat was the big kerosene heater. It was nice and warm in the shack with Manasha and Aunt Clara, but it wasn't as much fun. I eased back and settled into a spot between Cheryl and Rudy over their half-hearted protests.

The fire killed the first story and left Grandmama and Grandma Gert ill at ease. Another story was not forthcoming. Too bad, because I wondered about Old Cyrus and whatever it was he'd seen down in the swamp. Did he get it, or did it get him? I tried to imagine it. An incognizant mass of red blood. The Blob? A frightening thought.

"Johnny," Grandma Gert called softly, "go bring me them cinnamon rolls."

What! With that shapeless blob of terror lurking about?

"Shoot!" I protested. "Why it gotta be me?"

She sighed long and hard, and then she groaned. "Lawd, lawd, lawd," she groaned. "This the thanks I get. For all I do, this the thanks I get."

"It's cold!" I griped.

"Lawd, lawd, lawd. I ask this child to do somethin' for me and what I get? Back-talk! Lawd, lawd, lawd!"

All the while she was talking and moaning and groaning, she was trying to get a slipper off her foot.

"The thanks I get," she groaned as she struggled with her foot.

By the time she did get it off, I was up and out of range.

The kitchen had been extended and was now twice as large as it once was, and that made it twice as dark and twice as scary.

"Bring the cocoa, too!" she called.

Just after I switched on the light, Savannah and Linda appeared to get the cups. I got the water kettle and the cocoa, and cut out the light as I left.

"Grandmaaaa!" they screeched as they hurried out.

"Now why you did that?" Grandmama demanded.

"I thought they was through," I cried.

"Well, we wasn't!" Linda shrieked.

"Well, I thought you was."

Grandma Gert didn't say anything. Her stare said it all.

"Fix me a cup, sweetheart," she purred to Savannah.

Linda poured the water while Savannah stirred in the cocoa and passed one to Grandmama and one to Grandma Gert.

"Thank you, baby," Grandma Gert cooed. "Least it's somebody around here we can depend on to be of some service."

That said, everybody else made their cocoa and tore into the buns. Then we settled back to gorge and entertain ourselves by watching Grandma Gert eat.

My grandmother had the peculiar habit of slurping her food. No matter what she was eating, she slurped and swilled in a manner we found amusing and fascinating, which is probably why she chewed with her eyes closed.

"Now why the devil y'all staring at me like that!" she would demand, as we sat spellbound.

Daddy Troy was the same way, only he smacked his lips and didn't give a damn what anyone thought. He was quite amused that we should find his eating habits so entertaining. But not Manasha, and not Aunt Clara, both of whom were freaks for etiquette and decorum. Between the two of them, life at the dinner table was a long lesson in how to hold a fork, how to eat soup, how to keep your elbows off the table, how to use a knife, how to chew with your mouth closed, and how not to talk with a mouth full of food. Is it any wonder Grandma Gert and Daddy Troy ate their meals on the front porch? Eating, to them, was a joy and a pleasure.

"Stop lookin' up in my mouth while I'm tryin' to eat my food!" she snapped.

We snickered.

"People can't even eat their food around . . . now, who dat?"

she complained. "Who dat poot 'round me?"

"Hhhhmmm!" Everyone began cringing and complaining, covering their noses and pulling the covers over their heads. "Hhhhmmmm. Hhhhmmmm!"

"Who dat?"

"Johnny!" Savannah accused me out of nothing but spite.

"No it ain't!" I defended myself.

"Why don't you go outside!" Cody Wayne jibed.

"Check ya pants first!" Linda added.

"That ain't me!" I protested again.

"Whoever it is," Grandma Gert warned, "Ahma send 'im t' sleep in the cold if he keep that up!"

Everybody laughed at my expense.

"Smell like the gheechie man," Grandmama quipped.

There was another round of laughter and Rudy asked, "What's the gheechie man, Grandmama?"

"You'll find out," Grandmama said.

It was a warning.

"Keep runnin' down the run with Johnny and Cody Wayne," she warned again, "you'll find out."

We'd never heard of the gheechie man. We'd heard of the 'greasy man,' the 'butt-naked man,' the 'lizard man,' the 'big fat jelly man,' and the 'skunk-ape,' but not the 'gheechie man.' Obviously it was a scare tactic, and quite an effective one at that.

"That's why we tell y'all t' stay from back there," said Grandmama.

"But they won't listen!" Grandma Gert hissed. "They hard-headed and won't listen."

"Well, let 'em keep runnin' back there, they'll wish they hadda!"

Cody Wayne and I exchanged glances.

"What he look like?" Rudy asked hoarsely.

"You'll find out!" Grandma Gert snapped.

I looked at Rudy. He was falling for it.

"If you think I'm foolin'," said Grandma Gert, "ask Troy. He was part of the rescue."

"What rescue?" I asked.

"The plane rescue."

"What plane?" Cody Wayne asked.

"A plane crashed back there?" I exclaimed.

A plane crash excited the spirit of adventure in us both.

"You can go look if ya want, but the rescuers couldn't find it," said Grandmama.

"What that got t' do wit the gheechie man?" Savannah asked.

"'Cause that's how we know about him," Grandma Gert answered. "It wasn't but one survivor, and the gheechie man got her!"

"It was a girl?" Linda asked.

"Yes!" Grandmama said with a great deal of dramatic flair.

"That's how we know what he look like," said Grandma Gert.

"What he look like?" Ingy asked.

"Big, and stink like a grizzly bear!" said Grandmama. "He had so much hair you couldn't see his eyes. The plane had crashed back there on an island, and she was the only one to survive, and he got her and dragged her down in a cave and kept her there!"

Ingy and Cheryl gasped.

"What he do to her?" Savannah asked.

"Everything!" Grandma Gert said.

Linda and Savannah gasped.

"What they eat?" Cheryl asked.

"Whatever he catch," said Grandmama, "crab, crayfish, bird. And they eat them raw! He couldn't stand fire. He had too much hair. Couldn't swim either. He just kept her down there feedin' her raw meat and watchin' her. Everything he catch he tear it in half and share it with her. And he wouldn't let her go nowhere. He'd go out to hunt and he'd block the hole. And when he come back at night he'd tear whatever he catch in half and share it with her. He eat, she eat. He look at her, she look at him. And that's how they live for a long time.

"I guess he say this he wife, so he fool around and fool around until she had a baby."

"A baby!" we gasped.

"Thing look just like him," Grandmama continued. "Had beady eyes and hair all over it. And it didn't cry and it ate raw meat too!"

"How she git away?" Savannah asked.

"Well," said Grandmama, "one day he come back empty-handed. The next day it was the same thing. For four straight days he leave and come back with nothin'. And every night he staring at her. He hungry! He thinkin' 'bout eatin' her—and she knew it.

"So she made up her mind to try and git away. She didn't know where she was goin', but the next day, after he leave to go hunt, she pushed and pushed and squeezed up under the log and got out! When she saw she was on an island, she run to the bank and look for somethin' that float. She see alligata and snake, but she didn't care, she had to git away or he was gonna eat her! And she say to herself it was better to git ate by an alligata!

"So she walked and walked, and she kept looking for some-thing to float. And she look and look, and lawd, if she didn't see a boat! And she screamed, and she jumped up and down and waved until she got their attention. It was two poachers, and they saw her and wondered what she was doin' back there. So they rescue her.

They turn the boat toward the island, and when she see them comin' she fall to her knees and cry cry cry!

"And she looked around and guess who she see—the gheechie man! And he was comin' after her! And let me tell you— she run and jump right in the water! Didn't give a damn 'bout no gata! The gheechie man was comin'! Lord, she swam for the boat! He come in the water after her, but he almost drown 'cause he got too much hair and he couldn't swim. But she swam like Tarzan! And she make it to the boat and they pull her in.

"And these men look and wonder what this damn thing screamin' and ragin'. He run in the water and run back out. He chunk a rock and screamed like a hag! Then it run down to the cave and got the baby! And he brought it back and he held it up and waved for her to come get it. But she don't study no baby, she stay in the boat. And when she ain't comin' back, he took that baby and he held it up in he two hands, and he tore it in half! And he took one half and flung it to her—*that's yo half.* And he took his half and started eating it. Then he waved bye-bye and climbed back down in he hole."

It was very quiet when she finished. And very still. And in the stillness was a fear that would not fade, because we believed in her. To Cody Wayne, Rudy, and me, life was not going to be content until we found where the sweet crystal clear water from Silver Blue Lake flowed. But the tale of the gheechie man made it a different kind of life, a life without contentment, a life where we could no longer give a damn where the water went, because I for one was never going back down there again!

"Grandmama," Rudy asked, "what happened to the gheechie man?"

"Ooooh," she answered, "you'll find out, you'll find out."

When the Devil Comes Calling

The big dummy sailed high into the air then dropped straight down into the center of the circle, busting up the tight cluster of marbles and scattering them every which way. She'd done it to us again.

No one could bust the circle like Aunt Sally, or lag to the lie, or pitch to the gutter, or tip, or tap, or kiss you, too.

"Hilly!" she cried.

She scooped up a little cone of dirt and placed my marble atop it like a little ripe cherry ready to be plucked. Then she took dead aim and knocked it to kingdom come!

"Pay!" she demanded.

I gave her five marbles.

"*Danke shine!*" she sang sweetly. She bagged them, then studied her position.

"Crack 'em!" she cried.

Kneeling down on one knee, directly over Cody Wayne's marble, she took aim at point-blank range, fired, and broke it in three parts!

"Pay!" she demanded. And Cody Wayne gave her five marbles.

"*Gracias!*" she sang sweetly.

She studied the position of Rudy's marble.

"Suicide!" she cried. And from a distance of fifteen feet, she took aim and fired her big dummy at Rudy's little marble. The three of us stiffened, praying to God it would miss and give us at least a fighting chance. But it didn't, and the three of us sighed and sagged.

"Pay!" she demanded. And Rudy passed her five marbles.

"*Merci-boo-coo!*" she sang sweetly. Then, turning her attention to the full circle, she hiked her skirt above her knees, got down in the dirt, and went to work. And it was only a matter of moments before she cleared the circle and stood before us, counting her gains, to the wild cheers and stinging delight of Savannah and Linda, Ingy and Cheryl, and even Teenie and Weenie.

"Wanna play again?" she inquired.

If ever there was a female version of Fast Eddie Felson, she was it. No, it wasn't pool, but even if it wasn't the same game, it called for the same skill, the same psychology, and the same character, because just like Fast Eddie Felson, she talked the same trash while she played.

"Jump back, Jack!"

"Instant replay!"

"Ain't no strain on the crane, 'cause the cable is able!"

And she had the peculiar habit of going "pow" every time she connected.

"This one's for you—pow!"

"Wanna see it again?—pow!"

"See ya' lata 'gata—pow!"

"Chump!"

This was my Aunt Sally.

If Grandmama was the personification of sensitivity, Grandma Gert discipline, Manasha character, and Aunt Clara decorum, then Aunt Sally was the epitome of sophistication. She was a certified public accountant with a degree in business. She had a consulting firm in Eloise, and was the Secretary Treasurer of the local Democratic Party before Eva Horton organized the "Swaggs." She was thirty-eight years old, had two children and two ex-husbands. And there she was, down on her knees wreaking havoc upon her hubristic nephews with all the sophistication of a country girl, too smart to feel any guilt or sympathy.

"Wanna play again?" she asked.

Damn, she could shoot marbles! And once she got inside the circle, she was there to stay, because she used the kind of English only the most prolific pool hustlers would know.

High English to make the marble spin and come back. Pow!

Low English to make the marble spin and stop. Pow!

Left English to make the marble jump right. Pow!

Right English to make the marble jump left. Pow!

And an assortment of behind-the-back, in-yo-face, overarm, underarm, and in-between shots, intermingled with incredible cuts and kisses that conspired to make the marbles go where Aunt Sally wanted them to go, and do what Aunt Sally wanted them to do. And all we could do was watch.

"Pow!"

"Pow!"

"Pow!"

"Cat's eye!" Savannah cried.

"Game's over!" Linda cried.

"Wanna play again?" Aunt Sally asked.

"They ain't got no more marbles!" Linda yelled. "We got 'em all!"

And a great cheer arose from among them. Like Minnesota Fats, she'd had over a hundred shots without a miss. And just like

Minnesota Fats, she played for keeps. She is my Aunt Sally—they call her "Sally-Gal."

Nobody played us for keeps—nobody! They would only play us for fun. And who could blame them? We beat the Boy's Club, the Demolay and anything the P.A.L. could muster against us. We were good—so good no one would play us for keeps. And after a while, no one would play us period, because even if we played for fun, we reserved the right to "crack-'em"—that is, bust the marbles into a bunch of itty-bitty pieces with our big dummies, bummies, and steelies. No one had as many marbles as we had, and therefore they couldn't afford us. Not for keeps, not for cracks, not for fun. We were the marble hustlers of Oklawaha County and proud of it.

So proud, we took a part of our great collection and placed it on display at the Oklawaha County Fair, challenging any and everyone to a shootout. We were proud all right, proud to the point of arrogance, and proud to the point of showing off. And what a show it was. A dazzling display glittering like all the stars in the heavens on some great parade. Twenty-five hundred marbles of all shapes and sizes to buy, sell, or trade. Crystals as clear as air, some with the shadows of crimson eyes glimmering through, some of translucent amber caging flies! Lustrous pearls that excited the senses. Aggies and greenies and bluies and stars. Black beauties, black diamonds, and black hearts so keen they suggested the realization of perfection. This was our great treasure. Our hoarded riches. Greater than the treasure of the Sierra Madre! Greater than the Crown Jewels! Greater than anything Blackbeard ever buried. And it was ours! Ours! All ours!

And then my Aunt Sally hustled us out of it.

Maybe it would not have been so bad if it were boys. It would not have happened because we would have smelled a rat and seen it coming. But here were the sisters of Eve, and all of them, I'm sad to say, are blessed with a con game so smooth and slick that even after a million years, the brothers of Adam are still falling for the okie-doke! They set us up like pros.

Everyone, it seemed, was trying to get her grubby hands on our marbles. Especially Linda and Savannah. They couldn't understand why we turned down the Ladies' Garden Club's offer of three cents apiece for our sacred treasure, and from that day forward they couldn't keep their beady little eyes off them. The day we lost, Linda and Savannah came to us with a little bag of marbles and challenged us to a game. Aunt Sally was with them.

"Wanna play?" Linda had asked.

Who wanted to play them? They were no fun. They offered us no challenge to at least improve our game. We were the best. They knew it, and everybody knew it. At that time, we didn't know Aunt Sally knew how to shoot marbles.

"Just for fun," Savannah said.

"For fun!" Rudy guffawed.

"We don't play for fun!" said Cody Wayne.

"We play for keeps!" I said.

"Why not play us for fun," Aunt Sally said. "Everybody knows how good y'all are."

So we played them for fun. We knew they couldn't shoot, but we didn't know they were that bad! Linda couldn't even hold the marble straight! Each time she took aim to shoot, the marble would fall from the crook of her finger. She had to shoot with both hands, using one to hold the marble in. She was as pitiful as Aunt Sally, whose high heels kept sinking in the dirt. She spent more time worrying about her fingernails and stockings than about beating us, and we spent more time laughing than beating them. When Rudy cracked Savannah's marble, she started crying about how we were only playing for funsies.

"We can crack 'em for funsies!" Rudy told her.

And we could, since they didn't know the rules.

"Y'all cheat!" Savannah screamed, and snatched up her marbles.

"Cheaters!" Linda parroted.

"That's why we don't like to play y'all," Rudy told them, "'cause y'all git mad when y'all lose."

"Let's play for keeps," Aunt Sally said.

"Hah!" Rudy laughed.

"Hah, y'self!" Aunt Sally said.

"Boys against the girls!" Linda cried.

"Hah!" Rudy laughed.

"Hah, y'self!" said Aunt Sally. "What y'all wanna play for?"

Between the three of us we had two hundred marbles. They had about thirty.

"Make it light on ya self," I said.

"We'll play for what we got," she said.

"Y'all ain't got enough," Cody Wayne said.

"We got enough to beat y'all!" Linda said.

"Hah!" Rudy laughed.

"Hah, y'self!"

That should have been the tip-off; instead it was the perfect set-up, and she was the perfect ringer. We should have known we were in trouble when Aunt Clara came out on the porch and hollered back inside, "Manasha, come watch this!"

And Aunt Sally kicked off her high heels and pulled off her stockings. Then, as she walked barefoot across the lawn, she began biting off her nails! But we were too proud to be warned and did not even consider the possibility of defeat. We dared the gods, and lost.

"Here baby." She called to Linda to help bag the first two hundred she took from us. While Aunt Sally did all the shooting, they did all the bragging.

"Wanna play again?" Linda taunted.

"Don't go away mad," Savannah taunted.

"Y'all should quit while y'all ahead," Aunt Clara warned.

"Why quit now?" Aunt Sally said. "I'll give you a chance to win them back."

"Double or nuthin'!" Savannah cried.

That's what did it! Not only were we getting beat, we were getting belittled. They were mocking our greatness, scorning our accomplishments, and utterly disgracing us. And talking shit, too! So we went and got our reserves and talked a little shit ourselves.

And the more shit we talked, the more marbles we played for. And the more marbles we played for, the harder we played. And the harder we played, the harder she played. And the harder she played, the more we lost. And the more we lost, the more shit she talked.

Somebody told somebody else and the next thing you know we had a crowd cheering and hissing in utter delight at what some people said was the most fantastic display of marble shooting they'd ever witnessed. They watched in awe from that morning until dusk, when our chest was empty and our great treasure was gone, and we stood at the edge of the road in the dwindling light in a state of shock, misery, and tears.

"Damn!" Grandpa said in consolation, "she beat the dookey outta y'all!"

"Y'all should know betta than to play marbles with Sally," Grandmama said.

"They know now!" said Grandma Gert.

But nothing they could say could soothe the pain of defeat. I felt like Fast Eddie Felson falling flat on his face the day Minnesota Fats beat the dookey out of him, too.

Such a treasure would make a queen of any woman. Savannah and Linda were treated as such when they offered to sell our marbles to the Ladies' Garden Club for three cents apiece. Our great treasure was gone, destined to become knick-knack, bric-a-brac, and wall plaques.

Most of the week, we staggered around like defeated animals, suffering gross humiliations and outrageous insults. Never did we even consider the possibility of defeat. We demanded a rematch and got laughed at. That served to turn defeat into defiance, if not an education and the first step toward revenge. We had to revenge our honor. It was imperative. We'd lost our rank and distinction. It wasn't the marbles, but the honor. They'd laughed because they thought we didn't have any more marbles, and if we did happen to get some, they said they'd take them, too. So it wasn't so much the marbles, but the honor. The marbles were nothing; after all, there were more where they came from.

Not only did we have more marbles, we had the mother lode! What we'd lost was small compared to what we still had. We knew we could never bring that many marbles home without arousing suspicion. Even the little bit we brought had raised some eyebrows. When they'd asked us where we got them from we replied, "We found them."

"Found them where?"

"Found them at the dump."

That was plausible enough, since we were always scavenging the dump. They bought the dump lie, but Grandpa made us keep them down at Silo since that many marbles around the house were a hazard. It may have been a hazard to them, but it was gold to us. And only we knew where they were.

Boggy is really three different places. First, there is Boggy Bottom, which is everything south of the railroad tracks. Everyone who lives back here has enough land to plant or raise stock. This is where we live.

Then there is Boggy proper, which is above the railroad tracks. This is what's taken as the black subdivision of Eloise. This is where Unck lives.

And then there is Nash. Some people call Nash an industrial area. Maybe so, but, to me, it is just a dead end with a few tobacco barns, warehouses, a pencil factory, and a cement plant. This is where the mango tree is.

It was mangoes that led us to the marbles, mangoes that grew more luscious after Mr. and Mrs. Henry died. It was their house at the end of the Old Nash Road, and the mango tree was in their yard. While they were alive, we would never even consider going near their place. It was a frightening old house. And he was a frightening old man. And she was a frightening old woman, who had once given us a very frightening experience.

Mrs. Henry was an old witch of a woman who'd put the whammy on us. She and her husband operated a small dry cleaners in Porters Quarters. It was a small establishment with a set of landing steps that were its one distinguishing feature. The steps seemed to invite people to it. Customers, wayfarers, the tired, the poor, and the teeming masses had, at one time or another, huddled on the steps of Mr. Henry's shop.

One day, as we tired of rambling through Boggy, we took a turn and rambled up to Porters Quarters. We were going down the railroad tracks when we ran into Charlie Pete sitting on a switching box cleaning two gopher turtles. For no reason that I can think of, Rudy wanted the guts, and Charlie Pete gave them to him just to get rid of us. We placed them in a mayonnaise jar and continued on our merry way.

The first thing we did when we got to Porters Quarters was to rest, and the best place for that was the big steps of Mr. Henry's cleaners. It was also as good a spot as any for Rudy to check out his guts. He was deep into the process of identifying each vital organ when we spotted Nasty Brown zooming past. The three of us took off in immediate pursuit for a ride to wherever he was going, leaving the pile of turtle guts for passersby to contemplate at their leisure. No one would have known we'd been hanging out in Porters Quarters had not a frantic and very frightened Mrs. Henry appeared at the house that evening wanting to talk to Rudy. When Aunt Clara asked her why, she told her that someone told her they'd seen Rudy playing with some guts on the front steps of her shop. What Aunt Clara wanted to know was what in the world were we doing in Porters Quarter? But Mrs. Henry was only concerned about the guts. If we could have lied our way out by stating it wasn't us, we would have, but Mrs. Henry was so distraught that it was best to have Aunt Clara on our side. So we told them about the guts.

"Turtle guts?" Aunt Clara exclaimed.

"You sure they were just turtle guts?" Mrs. Henry questioned.

We assured her they were, and told her to ask Charlie Pete if she didn't believe us.

"Thank God!" she kept saying. "Thank God! Thank God!

Thank God!"

She'd thought someone was trying to put the whammy on her. Turtle guts, or any other kind of guts, especially from the animal you sacrificed to get them, are used to cast spells and "root" people, or at least give the appearance of witchcraft, when left at the door of the intended victim. Mrs. Henry was so relieved to learn it was just us, she was apologetic and couldn't thank us enough.

We thought all was forgiven until the day we were passing by the cleaners and Mrs. Henry hurried outside with a big Bible in her hands. Standing at the top of the steps, pointing her finger and giving us the evil eye, she began reading and uttering dire warnings, dire threats, and dire punishments from the Book of Revelations. She scared the living shit out of us. Apparently, all was not forgiven. We ran straight home to Grandma Gert, who said it served us right because we had no business down in Porters Quarters in the first place. But it scared her, too, because she went to Grandmama and told her Mrs. Henry had put the "mark" on us. Grandmama said if Mrs. Henry could put the "mark" on anyone, she'd put it on herself and do better than she was doing, which did little to comfort us since we were the ones who'd been marked.

Marked for what?

"She's getting even with y'all for scaring her," Grandmama said. "She's scaring y'all back."

That made sense, but what did it mean—"marking" us?

"Marking you for the devil," Grandmama said.

And we all froze. I knew the devil had something to do with this.

"If you're good," she said, "you won't have to worry. But if you're bad, the devil will ride your ass till the day you die!"

Maybe so, but one thing was for certain, Mrs. Henry never lived to see it. She died that year. To our dismay, the curse did not die with her.

Mr. Henry was always an odd old man who got worse after Mrs. Henry died. He never reopened the cleaners, and took to drinking. This probably accounted for his eccentricities, wandering around town, muttering to himself. Most people didn't pay him much attention, but little people, like us, had to be wary. Especially if we were playing marbles. He associated marbles with gambling and gambling with the devil, and was thoroughly convinced his actions were designed to save us from eternal damnation. Every time he saw us playing marbles he would take them. And anytime we saw him coming, we'd haul ass in fear and confusion. So he took to creeping up on us, hiding behind bushes and beneath cars, leaping out and scaring us half to death just to get our marbles. He was worse than the "butt-naked man." At least the "butt-naked man" didn't bother you. All he did was run around butt-naked inviting all those who shared his views about butt-nakedness to follow him. Mr. Henry not only took our marbles, but for some time made the grand game of marbles a clandestine act with us having to post lookouts for the not-so-sound of mind in Oklawaha County.

Eventually they caught the "butt-naked man," and Mr. Henry just sort of disappeared. But not before he'd plundered the county of every marble he could get his hands on.

It never occurred to us what Mr. Henry did with all those marbles. No one ever asked him. And no one ever ventured up to that spooky old house in Nash to try.

We never intended to go there, but that big mango tree was always in the back of our minds. I do believe that was why Nash was one of our favorite rambling places. We roamed the old tobacco barns at will, traversed the mountains of sand behind the cement plant, and piled through the mounds of sawdust at the pencil factory. But never would we venture near that spooky old house at the very end of Old Nash Road. But then mango season came, and Mr. and Mrs. Henry were dead.

It was a very large tree on the east side of the house, which extended over the garage. When it bloomed, it produced big "head" mangoes, the biggest, juiciest, sweetest, most luscious kind. For years, we never ventured to that side of the street, but we did admire them from afar. Mangoes are a very seductive fruit, a rare fruit in this part of the state. You have to go further south to grow mangoes. But Oklawaha County is the state's number-one produce and fruit grower. We have a passion for growing things. A special ability that puts the sun, the wind, and the rain on our side. If we can take the sugar sand of Florida and turn it into gold, we certainly can grow mangoes. At least some of us.

Cracka Bill had sixty trees that produced year after year. They were prized and highly valued, and if you looked like you were going to go near them—well, he had three rottweilers that didn't play.

We had three good fruit-producing trees in the fruit field that were jealously guarded. We could eat as many guavas as we wanted. Mulberries, oranges, tangerines, cherries, and pecans, too. But not mangoes! You had to have permission to get a mango, and permission was seldom granted. Mangoes were meant for cash, and not meant to be eaten away. Of course, if one should happen to fall from the tree, we could have it. And quite a few did fall from the tree, usually with the aid of sticks, rocks, shoes, or whatever was handy at the moment, while Linda and Savannah acted as lookouts and shills to give a collective shrug if Grandma Gert would suddenly ask, "What's that tennis racket doing in the mango tree?"

During the mango season, people often stood guard over their trees to protect them from marauding school children. But there was one mango tree that didn't need protecting, because everyone believed the tree, the house, and the people who'd once lived there were haunted.

Maybe so, but the radiance of all that beautiful fruit was more than enough to add mettle to the spirit in the face of unknown dangers. They were beautiful sirens, luring and enticing us with a sweet song, charming and seducing us ever closer until one day we cast aside our fear and raided Mr. Henry's mango tree as if haints and ghosts didn't exist.

And they were ours! Ours! All ours!

Of course we had to split them with Savannah and Linda in order to keep them quiet. We didn't offer to buy their silence; they solicited it. They assumed we were stealing them from Cracka Bill's grove, and stealing's a major crime, but as long as they were getting something out of the deal—what did they care?

For what we were doing, we saw ourselves as nothing less than dauntless! We considered ourselves bold and audacious! We dared to do what no other in all of Boggy would dare. We weren't afraid because there was nothing to fear. The house was shut up tight. Mr. Henry was dead. Mrs. Henry was dead. And the curse had died with them.

The mango tree was next to the garage, and some of its great limbs extended across the roof. We could climb up and out and onto the roof and pick what we desired at our own leisure.

One day, Cody Wayne and I were atop the roof when we heard a loud and sudden crack! We froze. Before we could move, the whole section collapsed, sending us screaming straight down to crash-land in a dark cosmos of wood and chaos. We'd landed atop a car, and except for the big bright hole in the roof, everything was dark. We were inside the garage. Quickly we scrambled to untangle ourselves from confusion and debris.

"Rudeeee!" Cody Wayne yelled. Immediately I took up the call.

"Rudeeee! Rudeeee! Rudeeee!" we yelled.

By some strange twist of fate, his spot didn't collapse.

"Rudeeee!"

Suddenly we stopped with the realization that we were not only summoning help, but maybe the forces of darkness as well. Fright passed, and fear came on us. Not an ordinary fear of death—but an abject, quivering fear of what we could not see, of what was beyond the darkness, beyond death. It beckoned us.

"Hey!" it cried. It was Rudy somewhere below us.

There was a shaking and a rattling sound. Looking toward it, we were able to distinguish trembling slivers of light shining through the cracks.

"Hey! Hey!" Rudy called. "Where y'all? Where y'all?"

The big double doors rattled and shook. Cautiously, we felt our way along the top of the car and slid along its contours.

"Cody Wayne? Johnny?" Rudy called. "Where y'all?"

"We in here!" I yelled back.

"Ahma go git somebody!"

"Noooo!" Cody Wayne cried.

"Open the doors!" I cried. "Open the doors!"

"OK," he cried.

There was a ghostly silence, then the doors shook.

"I—I—I—can't git it off!" Rudy cried.

"Open it!" we demanded.

"It's got a lock on it!" he cried.

"We know!" we cried. "Git it off!"

We pushed and he pulled, but it would not give.

"Look for somethin'!" Cody Wayne yelled.

"Somethin' like what?" he asked.

"A crowbar or somethin'!" I suggested.

"I don't see none," he yelled back.

"Find one!"

"Ain't none!"

"Well, find somethin'!"

As I peered around, the darkness began to dissipate and I could make out the outline of the car, the walls, and the ground.

"Look for somethin'," Cody Wayne whispered to me.

"You look for somethin'," I whispered back to him.

We stared at the darkness. Then Cody Wayne put his hand up in front of him and began inching forward.

"Look for somethin'," he whispered again.

"Somethin' like what?" I asked.

"Somethin' like a ladder."

I moved along with him, feeling the darkness around me. We stopped. The light shining through the hole in the roof bounced off the car and illuminated one side. Cody Wayne stepped, then jumped.

"What's that?" he asked.

"What's what?" I asked.

"I stepped on somethin'."

I stepped back and kneeled down, feeling for whatever it was. It was all hard and crunchy and—and—and—bones!

"Oh shoot!" I screamed. "Bones!"

Both of us ran back until we ran into the door, beating and screaming.

"Rudy! Rudy! Open the door! Open the door!"

We shrank to the opposite corner trembling in a storm of terror.

"Look!" I cried.

Further down along the side of the wall, I saw a set of small steps and an open door.

"It's open."

We stared long and hard in an effort to determine if this was the gate of freedom that could lead us from the chthonian nightmare or the gates of hell.

"Rudeeee!" Cody Wayne yelled.

After several moments of silence, Cody Wayne eased past me. We were not afraid of the darkness in itself, but of the dark world of the unknown. We hunted at night and knew how to use the night. We knew the night and were not afraid of the night—not even the beasts of the night, for we knew them, too. The night could be your friend and to your advantage if you used it right. We let our eyes wander and adjust to the darkness. Shapes came into focus. A table, a counter, jars, a refrigerator, a faucet, chairs. Gradually it became more gray than dark, and we found ourselves standing in an airless and unused kitchen. A murky glow illuminated another doorway. It was the way out, and we moved toward it. Surrounded by invisible fiends, we moved slowly and cautiously, feeling their presence with every step, expecting him or her to leap out from behind a dusty doorway, with evil intent.

All the windows were boarded from within. So was the front door, but there was light! And the light was our salvation. We rushed to it! Beating on it! Clawing at the boards! Pulling and shouting, "Rudeeee!"

"Where y'all?" came the faint reply. In desperation, I ran to a boarded window and felt the little round ball beneath my foot, but there was nothing I could do to prevent the slip, much less the fall. I landed hard on my butt and found myself staring up at a most unusual portrait.

"Cody Wayne," I cried. "Look!"

It was a portrait of a black man from the waist up, dressed in a black-and-white striped prison uniform. He was carrying a sledgehammer across his shoulders and looking off into the distance. It was a huge picture that struck a note of terror and rekindled fear. It was hanging directly over the fireplace and would have easily dominated the living room if not for what we saw piled high in the fireplace. What I first thought was the glimmering eyes of a thousand cats inexplicably shimmering in the fireplace turned out to be a wonder of pure glory that excited and astonished us by its extraordinariness! Its strangeness! There must have been a million of them! Sensuous and delightful, it was beyond ordinary comprehension. A miracle of rare devise, it aroused in us a great mix of rapturous awe. All we could do was stand there and stare.

"Where y'all?" Rudy called from outside. "I got a pick!"

And the wonder grew.

There were dummies, and bummies, and aggies by the thousand! Pee-wees and steelies, pearlies, and black beauties. We were rich!

Cody Wayne and I stood staring at this great unexpected treasure, totally ignoring the harsh sound of Rudy hacking on the door with a pick-axe.

Such a treasure had to be explained. We could not just walk into the house lugging five hundred pounds of marbles without an explanation. And we could not have just found them either. Then we'd have to explain where we found them. Then we'd have to explain what we were doing down in Nash. Then we'd have to explain what we were doing in Mr. Henry's house. And that was far too much explaining that could not easily be explained away. What we needed was to have "found them" somewhere where it was highly probable for us to find five hundred pounds of marbles, and highly probable for us to be. What we needed was a plausible explanation that had the ring of truth.

"We found 'em," we told Grandma Gert.

"Found 'em where?" she inquired.

"Found 'em at the dump," Rudy lied.

We all agreed that he should be the one to tell it, because Cody Wayne and I were known to lie. Linda and Savannah, too, only they didn't believe they told lies. They fibbed, they were evasive, they misrepresented the truth, but they didn't tell lies—not if you let them tell it. Only Rudy could be depended on for the truth. And when he told them, "We found 'em," it was good enough for them.

To lose the way we lost to Aunt Sally was embarrassing and humiliating. Aunt Clara, being the teacher that she was, said we lost because of arrogance. Manasha said it was because we lacked grace. Grandma Gert said we didn't know when to quit. Well, maybe so. But the loss of some was not as bad as the loss of all. We still had up to three thousand marbles, and the real loss had been our pride.

Over a period of time, we'd gotten them all out of the fireplace, but we never took them home because no lie in the world could explain that many marbles. We'd buried them in the bushes behind Dave's store. This was our secret cache. Like Unck and Red Brown, who had caches of food and water and ammunition buried all over the swamp, or Flynn and Long John Silver, who had their great buried treasure, we had ours, too. They were buried in four large ice chests, and all we had to do was dig one up and we were back in business. But first we brooded.

Everybody knew how Aunt Sally had beaten us. The humiliation was total. They picked at us wherever we went. So for a while we could do nothing but brood and ponder the loss and scrutinize our play. Then we plotted insidious, complicated schemes to cheat. We hatched a campaign of lies and slander to undermine the world as Savannah, Linda, and Aunt Sally knew it. Like Fast Eddie Felson, we were coming back! Defeat was for those who acknowledged it.

Defeat, like triumph, is inside of you. Hubris was our defeat. Aunt Sally had little to do with it. But just in case, we practiced every day, because no matter how much we lied, schemed, and cheated, unless we shot better, she would beat the dookey out of us again. And besides, my Aunt Sally lied, schemed, and cheated better than all three of us put together.

Finally, we set forth our challenge.

"Y'all ain't got no more marbles," she'd snickered over the phone.

"We got some mo'!" I answered her back.

"Yeah, well, not enough to play me."

"Oh, yeah? Well, we got enough to play you and anybody else."

"Oh, yeah? Well, how many y' got?"

"How many you wanna play for?"

"Make it light on y'self?"

"How about one hundred a game?"

There was a slight pause, then she demanded, "Where y'all gittin' all these marbles? And don't give me that 'we found 'em' shit!"

Right away I gave the phone to Cody Wayne, who gave the phone to Rudy, who said, "We found 'em."

"Put Manasha on—where's Mama?"

Mysteriously, we lost the connection. And rightly so, for we were not about to allow Aunt Sally to cross us up. We'd found them and that was that. No one could prove otherwise. No one could prove theft. And no one had reported losing five hundred pounds of marbles. She called back and said the Ladies Garden Club would buy all the marbles she could bring them. The challenge was accepted.

In view of the rematch, we had nothing to do that Saturday morning but sit on the porch and wait. Just as we decided to do one last practice game, we heard an alarming cry come from the back yard. Then came wails of distress and shrieks of grief. Something bad had happened. We ran around back to find Aunt Clara hugging Teenie from behind and alternately pounding her back.

"Teenie swallowed a marble!" Cheryl screamed hysterically.

Savannah had run inside for help. Linda was dialing 911.

"What's the matta? What the matta?" Grandma Gert ran outside shrieking.

"Teenie swallowed a marble!" I shrieked back.

"Teenie swallowed a marble! Teenie swallowed a marble! Teenie swallowed a marble!" Cheryl kept screaming. She was beside herself with hysteria.

Cody Wayne ran to Silo to get Grandpa. I tried to help, but everybody was hysterical and not sure of what to do. The Heimlich maneuver wasn't working. Manasha started pounding her back, and Grandma Gert was trying to dig it out of her throat. Teenie's eyes looked as if they would burst from her head. She couldn't breathe.

Aunt Sally arrived and screamed at me in a panic, "What's wrong?"

"Teenie swallowed a marble!" I cried to her.

She dropped her purse and plunged right into the midst of the hysteria. With a mighty swing of her right hand, she socked Teenie in one side of her chest. Teenie gasped outward and Manasha pushed her head forward. Aunt Clara heaved and Grandma Gert grasped the marble and pulled it out. Teenie still couldn't breathe, so Aunt Clara put her mouth over Teenie's and started breathing for her. I thought she was dead, but she'd only passed out.

Boggy has its own ambulance service, and it was a wonderful thing to hear them arriving, to see the mask over her face, to know she was not going to die.

No one was at fault and everyone was forgiven—that is, until Grandma Gert got back from the hospital.

"Every goddamn one!" she screamed. "Find them, and I mean right now!"

To her, everyone was at fault and no one was forgiven. So we started in the kitchen on hands and knees. In the cabinets, closets, and pantry, we hunted them down, tormented by what happened to Teenie and what could happen to any one of us.

When we got through with the house, they lined us up across the front yard and we policed it foot by foot. Then the roadway, and the driveway, and finally the back yard and the fruit field. For our efforts we found one hundred and twenty-six marbles, seventy-three soda caps, twenty jack stones, eight jack-stone balls, nineteen bullets, and thirty-six cents.

Teenie suffered two broken ribs and a collapsed lung. She remained hospitalized.

There was enough fault to go around, but the biggest fault of all was pride. A criminal pride that was more than a fault—it was a vice. And worse than a vice, it was a curse. It was the very wish for evil that had been heaped upon us by Mrs. Henry before she died. We were marked for punishment and disaster, and now it had arrived.

Our room is upstairs on the south wing of the house, facing the fruit field. Savannah and Linda's room is next to ours. The porch runs straight at a right angle and extends halfway down the side. A roof covers it all the way. From our room, we can swing open the fire screen and sit out on the porch roof. We do this all the time, especially in times of woe.

All of us sat out on the porch roof feeling the pangs of a tormenting conscience. Rudy was worse than miserable; after all, it was his turtle guts that brought about the curse, and therefore he felt it was his curse.

"We gotta take 'em back," he whispered.

Savannah and Linda were leaning out their window pretending they weren't listening, so our anguish took on the air of a conspiracy.

"We can't," I whispered.

"We gotta!" he insisted. "The devil's gonna ride us if we don't!"

It had taken us a whole month to get them behind Dave's store, but no one disagreed they were bad luck. The question was how.

"In the same grocery basket we brought them in," Rudy suggested.

It was Cody Wayne's decision to make.

"OK," he said, after some thought. "We'll do it Monday morning."

"Play hooky?" I asked.

"No—we'll catch the late bus."

"That won't give us much time."

"We'll make it."

"What about them?" I nodded at Savannah and Linda.

Cody Wayne sighed and said, "They won't know."

"That's what you think."

That's what we all thought.

The effect of gloom clouded the weekend. The grownups spent Sunday at the hospital, but we couldn't go. In fact, we couldn't go anywhere further than the yard, so that we couldn't find any more trouble. Mr. Henry was right. Playing for keeps was gambling, and gambling was trouble. But trouble was an ever-present trouble with us, simply because trouble was there. And first thing Monday morning, we went and doubled the trouble.

The problem was how to sneak away from Savannah and Linda. They were watching us like hawks. We thought of bribing them, but that would only cause us to tip our hand. So, as we and everybody who lived on that end of Boggy waited for the school bus, Cody Wayne announced, "We're going to Dave's sto'."

"For what?" Savannah asked quickly, well aware the conspiracy was at work.

"For none of yo' business!" I spat.

"It is my business if y'all playin' hooky!"

Translated, she was soliciting a bribe not to tell.

"You can tell all you want!" said Rudy as we started to walk away. "We just goin' to the sto'!"

"Y'all gon' be late!" Linda cried after us.

"So?" I shouted back.

At the end of Laramie Street, we stopped and looked back. There was no sign of them. We didn't think they'd follow us; they were good girls. We were just paranoid over what we were about to do. Quickly we doubled back between the houses and got on the railroad tracks. The shopping basket was a block away from the bus stop. They were still there. Moving briskly, we ran the three blocks to Dave's store. Using an old pot, we took turns digging up the remaining treasure. We then loaded it into the cart and started up Thomas Road.

The push was easy, but we made an odd sight. I had a nagging suspicion that we were being watched. There was no basis for it, but I found myself looking back over my shoulder.

We went through Boggy hoping no one would see us and call Grandma Gert. It was a bigger job than we thought. Crossing the highway, we kept going until we came into the back side of Nash. Exhausted, we stopped to rest.

"Fuck school!" I exclaimed.

"We too dirty anyway," said Rudy.

"We missed the bus too," said Cody Wayne.

"We gotta git Savannah to write us a note," I said.

"She's gonna wanna know why," said Rudy. "What we gonna tell her?"

"Not a goddamn thang!" I spat just like Daddy Troy.

"All we gotta do is give her some mangoes," said Cody Wayne, "and she'll write all the notes we want."

"Let's go," Rudy said.

Just as I started to get up, I caught a fleeting glimpse of Linda ducking behind a tree.

"Uh-oh!" I gulped.

Since we were up to no good, "uh-oh" meant trouble, and Cody Wayne and Rudy ducked instinctively.

"What?" Rudy asked.

"It's them!" I replied.

"Them who?"

"Them who you think!" I cried. "They followed us!"

We stared hard, as if to make them appear.

"We see y'all!" Rudy hollered.

"Let's run!" Cody Wayne suggested.

Pushing the buggy, we ran as fast as the load would allow us, which wasn't too fast. We stopped and looked back to catch them ducking behind another tree.

"We see y'all!" I hollered.

"We see y'all too!" they hollered back.

"Ahma tell!" Rudy hollered.

"And ahma tell, too!" Savannah hollered back.

We looked at each other and knew we had to come up with something fast.

"We gon' git some mangoes," I cried.

"Mangoes!" Cody Wayne cried.

"Mangoes!" Rudy cried.

They came up from behind the tree and stared. Linda dropped one of her books and bent down and picked it up.

"Where y'all goin'?" Savannah asked as they came up.

"We goin' to git some mangoes," I answered.

"What's in them boxes?" Linda asked.

"Nuthin'!" Cody Wayne answered.

We stared at each other in silence, then Rudy said, "We takin' the marbles back."

"What marbles?" Savannah asked.

Cody Wayne lifted the top of a cooler, and they gasped.

"Why y'all takin' 'em back?" Linda demanded. "We can git paid for 'em!"

63

"'Cause!" Rudy said and nothing else.

They waited for an answer. Three cents apiece was three cents apiece, and they would be in for a cut.

"'Cause we gotta take 'em back!" Rudy insisted.

"Take 'em back where?" Savannah asked.

There was another silence; then I said, "Mr. Henry's house."

They stared at us in disbelief.

"Y'all been in there?" Linda asked.

"That's where we git the mangoes," I said.

"Y'all go back," said Cody Wayne.

"We can't go back," said Linda. "The bus gone."

"Well, go somewhere!" I said. "We gotta go!"

But there was no going back for any of us. We left them watching us pushing the buggy away, but they had come too far and were in too deep to be left standing in the lurch. And this was much too much of a mystery.

"What they doing?" Cody Wayne asked as we ran with the buggy. I looked back.

"Still watchin' us!" I said.

"Let's run!" Rudy screamed.

And again, as much as the load would allow us, we took off running, and so did they.

As we approached the back of Mr. Henry's house, we stopped as always and took a minute to gather ourselves. We were there to remove the curse and get the devil off our ass. It was the only thing to do.

We knew this part was not going to be easy. The doors and windows were boarded from the inside, and the room doors were nailed shut. The garage doors were held shut with a big rusty padlock that we never could break off. We got in and out through a hole in the roof, using a hose we'd tied to a limb. But how to get the coolers of marbles up the tree, onto the roof, down through the hole, off the car, and back into the fireplace was a problem to stump the devil.

"Drop 'em down the chimney," Linda suggested.

A great suggestion it was. Cody Wayne tore loose a piece of clothesline, and we tied it to a bucket. He and I climbed up on the roof as Rudy stayed below to load it up. Cody Wayne pulled it up, while I hauled it over to the little chimney and poured them down.

The click, clack, ping-pong, was very pleasing to the ear. They were bing-banging all over the place! The rush of all those marbles whooshing down the chute was a huge release of all our anxiety about the devil. Our burden of fear was lifted, at least enough for us to laugh, forget, and even enjoy the absurdity of it all.

Linda and Savannah had filled two coolers with mangoes. One was for Cat and Miss Olean, where they intended to spend the rest of the day. They were sitting on one of the filled coolers gorging themselves, as Cody Wayne, Rudy, and me slid down the hole into the garage. By now we were so familiar with the house that we could find our way in the dark. We were not even afraid of old Cyrus.

We knew some of the marbles would spill out from the fireplace, but nothing like the deluge we found ourselves faced with. We couldn't even walk through it, but had to drag our feet to keep from slipping. Marbles blanketed the floor, creating a lumpy carpet of glass.

"Golly bum!" Rudy cried.

"Shit!" Cody Wayne cried.

We should have given it a bit more thought. Instead of solving a problem, we'd only doubled it. Now there was much cause for worry. I was so sick of marbles I wished we'd taken Linda's advice and sold them. They were more work than watermelons! But this was not how we'd found them, and not the way we were going to leave them. Not with old Cyrus up there with that hammer. The riddle of the portrait was unraveling.

Frantically, we began scooping and sweeping the marbles toward the fireplace, but they wouldn't pile up and stay.

"Shit!" Rudy cursed.

And Cody Wayne cursed.

And I cursed.

And the curse came back to haunt us.

"He—he—he—he—he—he—!"

"Huh?" I asked.

"He—he—he—he—he—!"

We looked to where he was looking and met the eyes of old Cyrus staring down at us! Directly at us—as in eye contact! And he'd never looked at us before.

"He lookin' at us!" Rudy screamed.

It was more than looking. It was two hellish moons, glistening like the flaming eyes of a cunning Satan, recognizing and smiling down upon his own.

"Y'all hurry up and c'mon!"

The sudden sound of Savannah's voice threw the three of us into a panic! We broke and ran for the door all at the same time, slipping, falling, and slithering headlong into an undulating wave of marbles that waved and rolled straight down to the end of the hallway where they sat still for a moment, then began rolling back toward us!

"Oh shoot!" Cody Wayne cried. "Oh shoot! Oh shoot! Oh shoot!"

Back they came, rolling past us and on into the living room. Cody Wayne just stood there screaming, "Oh shoot!" But me and

Rudy took off past him falling, slipping, and gliding along, but getting back up to run again. We ran straight through the kitchen into the garage and started straight up the hose without pause or reflection, the three of us shinnying up the hose all at once. It was too much, and the hose broke as we neared the top. The three of us fell into a big heap atop the car.

"Ahhhh!" Cody Wayne screamed. He was hurt.

He was screaming. I was screaming. Rudy was screaming. And Linda and Savannah were screaming, too.

"Cody Wayne hurt! Cody Wayne!" I screamed.

"What's the matta?" they screamed through the door.

"Go git some help!"

They ran for help.

"My leg! My leg! My leg!" he kept screaming.

We tried to comfort him as best we could.

"Johneeee!" Linda yelled from outside.

"Uh-huh!" I answered.

Suddenly there was heavy pounding on the door and we knew they were not alone. The doors swung open, and in a burst of light stood a huge black man wielding a big sledgehammer. Behind him were two white men, with Linda and Savannah.

"Y'all alright?" the man asked.

"My leeeegggg!" Cody Wayne screamed in pain.

He set the hammer down and came around the side of the car.

"Help me slide 'im off," he said to us. The big man cradled him up easily and lifted him up off the car and carried him out to the front of the porch.

"What y'all doin' in heah anyways?" one of the white men asked.

No one answered.

"This ain't y'all's house, is it?"

Total silence.

"I don't think nobody lives here," the other one said.

"Still private property."

Private property or not, they entered the garage and began admiring the car.

The big man came around to the front of the garage and said, "Ahma go call an ambulance. His leg's broken."

"Damn chillun'!" one of the white men cursed, "always gittin' inta thangs they—ahhhh!"

He jumped back suddenly having discovered the old bed of bones we'd long since forgotten.

An ambulance arrived, followed by a police car. There was a lot of explaining to do.

"Lookin' for mangoes?"

"How that hole git in that roof?"

"How that hose git up there?"

"Where all them marbles come from?"

Our hastily contrived explanations were not standing up to the police. He explained to us what trespassing was, and breaking and entering, vandalism, stealing mangoes, lying, and playing hooky. They loaded Cody Wayne into the ambulance and the rest of us into the police car. He was about to take us away when another one drove up.

"Whatcha got here, Clayton?" he asked.

"Buncha young'uns," the first one answered.

"This here's where that crazy old man used to live."

"What crazy old man?"

"Hadda pressin' club over in the quarters."

"What happened to 'im?"

"Kinda lost his marbles after his wife died. I think they committed him."

"Well, that explains it!"

"What?"

"The marbles. He's got a house fulla marbles. I thank that's what them young'uns was after."

The two policemen disappeared into the garage and I looked at Savannah, tear tracks gleaming sadly down her face. I wanted to reach out and tell her everything was going to be all right, but it wasn't. Besides, it was their own fault for following us. The worst was yet to come.

A heavy pounding came from inside the house, and I knew they were pounding on the room doors we were never able to open. Something cracked and split, and a moment later a deputy came rushing out straight to his car. I could only pick up snatches of what he was saying into the mike. Things like, "Code six," and "non-emergency," and "coroner." It sent another round of worry and uncertainty through us. It was something more than marbles.

Another police car came zooming in, then several more. It wasn't long before men in suits were coming in and out of the house.

Now we were very much afraid, but in a different manner, because their manner was different. It was conciliatory, suggesting they'd found something more than marbles, something we'd overlooked, something that had drawn us there and therefore them. Something behind those sealed doors and perhaps even beyond that. Something dreadful, but they wouldn't tell us, because some things should not be known to children until they are old enough to handle it with a certain poise, and able to digest it.

They'd found Mr. Henry—and Mrs. Henry, too.

Instead of jail, we were confined to our rooms. That wasn't so bad. We were long past the stage of bitter reproaches and regrets, and sworn statements and official deposition, and fear. Once again we were proud, because people would come to us and ask about the hundreds of pieces of crystal art she'd created out of glass marbles in her dying days, and did we manage to get any. But most people asked us to describe them, and we would go on to describe how Mrs. Henry was laid out in white and resting peacefully in her gold casket, looking just as she had the day of her funeral. And Mr. Henry, immortal in death, was sitting in his rocking chair, the course of their love still running hand in hand even in death. We never laid eyes on them, but what did it matter.

Some people called us crazy kids. And some people marveled at how brave we were.

Grandmama said it was the devil that called us there for us to find Mr. and Mrs. Henry so they could be laid to rest.

"Maybe so," said Grandma Gert, "but the next time the devil comes calling y'all go the other way! In the meantime, take ya ass straight up to ya room and stay there!"

And, "Take ya ass straight to school!"

And, "Brang ya ass straight from school!"

And, "Hellll no! You can't go!"

And, "No! No! No! No! No!"

Our lives had degenerated into one big "No!"

And parent/teacher conference calls.

And a lot of wishing to God someone would come up with something for us to do so we could at least get out of the room.

Fat chance.

All we could do was piss and moan about how unfair life was and how good we were going to be.

"That's nice," Grandma Gert would tell us. "Go be good up in ya room."

So we sat on the porch roof and contemplated Cody Wayne's broken leg, the mangoes in the mango trees, and the harder lessons in life so that we would be better prepared to resist temptation when the devil comes calling again.

Poochie

Me and Cody Wayne froze. The back door shut. We listened. Were they on to us! Did someone see us crawling up under the sto-house? Whose footsteps were those? Cody Wayne covered the pie with his T-shirt to keep the dirt out. My mouth watered. Someone was coming down the hallway. The front door opened. They were on the porch, standing quiet, standing still. They were on to us. A thump! They were coming down. They were looking— looking—looking—

"What y'all doin'?" Rudy asked. He lay flat on his belly looking down, up under the porch. Cody Wayne grabbed him by the shirt and snatched him down off the porch and up under the house with us.

"Agggghhhh!" he cried. We shushed him.

"What y'all up to?" he asked.

"Sssshhhh!" I shushed.

"Who see you?" Cody Wayne asked.

"Nobody see me," Rudy answered.

"Who in the sto-house?"

"Nobody in the sto-house!"

"Who in the house?"

"Everybody in the house."

"Who in the kitchen?"

"Nobody in the kitchen. They gittin' ready to go."

"Good."

"What y'all got? Gimme some."

"Ssssshhhh!" I shushed.

There was a terse silence as Cody Wayne lifted his shirt and revealed the pie. Pecan pie bordered in whipped cream and topped with crushed pecans. The three of us ogled it in rapturous delight. It was a beautiful and wonderful thing to behold, we hated it eat it—well almost.

"Get a knife!" Rudy cried.

"We don't need no knife!" I cried.

"Just git a hunk!" Cody Wayne cried.

"Whoa—don't git no dirt in it!"

"Ssssshhhh!"

"Yum! Yum! Yum! Yum! Yum! Yum! Yum!"

Ours! Ours! All ours! Had to be. It was the reason why they baked three. One could never be enough. One was for them, one was for us, and one was for us to steal. That's the way they did it. Two of everything. We didn't know what the occasion was, but it had to be a wonderful one for them to bake three pies.

Aunt Clara had called us in earlier and sliced one pie into equal parts, giving each of us a share. The other two were covered and left on the counter to cool. Why? For us to steal, naturally. She had to know that one little itty-bitty piece of pie would not be enough for us. For that reason, whenever there were goodies baked for some special occasion, they always baked enough for us to steal. So we stole it.

"Mmmmm!" And, boy, was it good.

There was a sudden chorus of giggles and laughter. We froze, and peeped out. Little-girl legs, little-girl socks, and little-girl shiny shoes came running by. We watched them and identified them all: Linda, Savannah, Ingy, Cheryl, Teenie, Weenie, Caroline,

Cleo, and Poochie. Behind them came Manasha and Aunt Clara.

"A dozen should be enough," Aunt Clara said.

They walked right between the shacks, and Aunt Clara bent down and looked beneath the one we were under. We squeezed in close and tried to make ourselves unseen.

"After all," she continued, "we've got two pies."

"I want a key lime bad," Manasha said.

"They wanted pecan. See how fast the one they ate went."

"It's a wonder we still got two left."

In desperate haste we began wiping our mouths, faces, and hands. There was still half a pie left, but none of us wanted it.

"We need a sack," Aunt Clara said.

"Van's got a basket," said Manasha. She grasped the pole that was used for hooking fruit from trees and pulled it from beneath the house. She balanced it up and she and Aunt Clara walked from the shacks into the fruit field.

"We in trouble!" Rudy gasped.

"We didn't know," Cody Wayne said.

"Manasha and Aunt Clara gon' be mad," I said.

That didn't mean much in itself, because after all was said and done, Manasha and Aunt Clara were soft, which meant they did a lot of talking. Aunt Clara had actually tried to beat me once. It was after I'd hit Allen Hamil in the head with a rock. She'd declared herself furious, swinging the belt with all her strength, while I just stood there looking up at her until she, too, realized how absurd she looked, and exclaimed, "The hell wit this—Ahma let Mama handle you."

And that put the fear of God in me!

I was lucky it was Aunt Clara who'd answered the phone, and I began begging her not to tell Grandma Gert.

"Please don't tell Grandma Gert! Please! Please! Please!"

So she relented and gave me a good talking to, which was the worst we expected from Manasha or Aunt Clara—unless they got mad; then they called Grandma Gert, and she didn't play.

"Manasha gon' be mad!" I said again.

We didn't know what the occasion was, but it had to be special for them to bake two pies, pick a dozen mangoes, and get all dressed up. Either someone was getting married, or it was a birthday party, or someone had died. That thought started me thinking about death.

We couldn't undo what we'd done. All we could do was wait for the opportunity to crawl beneath the sto-house, haul ass down to Silo, and swear to God we had nothing to do with it. But they were between us and Silo. I saw Poochie coming between the shacks and sniffing at the ground. We tensed. She looked under, saw us, and barked!

"Sssssshhh! Sssssshhh! Sssssshhh!" The three of us began shushing frantically. "Here, Poochie. Here, Poochie. Here, Poochie!"

Cody Wayne held out his hand and tried to wave her under. She had a big ribbon bow tied to her neck and was going to the party too.

Sssssshhh!" we cried. "Here, Poochie. Here, Poochie. Here, Poochie!"

He held out the remainder of the pie.

"Her, girl. Come git some pie."

She stopped barking and came up under the house. We petted her and gave her some pie.

"Let's say Poochie did it!" Rudy suggested.

An excellent idea! Cody Wayne pushed the pie into her face,

so that whipped cream and crushed pecans covered the parts of her head she couldn't lick away. No matter what, they wouldn't be mad with Poochie.

We smeared globs of pie over her ears and neck, and she didn't mind a bit.

"Let's take her inside," I suggested.

They were still plucking down mangoes, so we were able to scoot out the other side and sneak up to the kitchen door of the house.

"Look out for us," I whispered to Rudy.

We are pretty good at things like this. We opened the door and crept in. The house seemed deserted.

"OK!" I signaled to Cody Wayne. He crept in bringing Poochie with him. I held what was left of the pie up in the air and dropped it. All we could do was hope it would work as we beat a hasty retreat out the door and back up under the sto-house to wait for an opportunity to slink down to Silo and pretend we'd been there all afternoon.

The Mulberry Tree

Savannah and Linda held their breath as the mockingbird made another quick dive at the cat. It was funny, the way the cat scooched in its boodie to avoid the bird. Of course, the cat wasn't laughing and neither were the birds. It was a serious game of attack and defend, and all were master players.

The mockingbirds were not a problem until the chicks had hatched. Now they were dive-bombing anything that came near the mulberry tree. The barbecue pit, the swings, and the tables were all right, but if you got a sudden yen for some mulberries, or baby mockingbirds, then you were in for some serious trouble, as the cat was finding out.

As soon as one bird would pass and the cat would straighten up, another bird would come zooming in from another direction. They attacked nothing but its flanks and rear end, sometimes making direct hits. The cat was put completely on the defensive. It could do nothing but twist and turn and scooch in its boodie, until finally it could do nothing at all and took off under the rails toward the truck patch.

Linda and Savannah had observed all this and were quite amused.

I was coming down the path from Silo, blissfully unaware the mockingbirds were on the warpath. Blackie and Shack were with me.

"Johnneeee," Linda sang sweetly, "git us some mulberries."

"Git 'em y'self!" I snapped.

"Aunt Clara said she'd make us a mulberry doobie—if we git some mulberries."

"A mulberry doobie?"

"Pleeeeaaaasssseeee?" Linda begged.

"When?" I asked, suspecting a ruse.

"As soon as we git some," she answered.

"Why can't y'all git 'em y'self?"

"We'll give you some," Linda offered.

"Why can't y'all git 'em y'self—and still give me some?"

"We'll give you . . . half," Savannah offered.

"A whole half?" I asked suspiciously.

A whole half didn't sound right. I looked at the mulberry tree. Then back at them, then back at the mulberry tree. Then it hit me.

"What's the matta?" I asked. "Hmmmm? Scared of a lil' old mulberry tree?"

Both of them cringed and looked fearfully at the tree.

"Aha, ha, ha, ha, ha, ha, ha, ha, ha!" I laughed at them.

"C'mon," Savannah pleaded. "Git us some."

"OK," I said, "but I want more than half!"

"More than half?" they protested.

"Well git 'em y'self!" I screamed.

"We'll give you some," they offered.

"I want more than some!" I demanded.

"Some!" they insisted.

"Go git me a bag."

They took off around the house to the back of the sto-house to get a bag. I called the dogs.

"We ain't scared of no old haint—is we?" I said to Blackie as he came to me. "Ain't no such thang!"

I kneeled down and Shack licked my face.

"It was just an old ghost story—wasn't it?

"And the boy was just a boy like me—wasn't he?

"And the dog was just a dog like y'all—wasn't he?

"And the mulberry tree was just a mulberry tree like our mulberry tree—wasn't it?"

NO!

The boy was a boy who wanted to live a life without any of life's problems. And the dog was nothing like my dogs. My dogs, all of them, were independent, possessing their own spirit and intellect. It was awhile before they would even trust me enough to eat from my hand. And the mulberry tree was not a mulberry tree like our mulberry tree. For one thing, that mulberry tree was haunted. It stood in the graveyard and possessed a spirit charged with guarding the mulberries.

No one dared go up to the mulberry tree for mulberries because of the spirit. For that reason it was a lonely spirit. It knew the boy, and it knew the dog. It saw them every day. The boy always took the shortcut through the graveyard, going and coming from school. And the dog was always with him. The spirit liked this, and it liked the way the boy treated the dog. It did not look like a dog's life at all, but a life of ease and comfort. It certainly was better than a haint's life. Cooped up in a tree all day long, nothing to eat but mulberries, and no friends because everyone was afraid of you. But not the boy. The spirit allowed him to sit beneath the mulberry tree because he liked him. He would watch and admire the boy and his dog. One day he heard the boy complaining about how hard life was and how much responsibility he had. The spirit took it as a plea and an opportunity to leave the tree. The dog got up and peed on the tree. Then it sniffed the tree and fell to the ground and went into a terrible shiver. When it got up, it ran home and left the boy in the graveyard.

The boy knew something was wrong with the dog, but it was not until that night when his grandmother made him take out the garbage that he found out what. The dog spoke to him. It told him he was the spirit from the tree, and promised him great things. But the boy wanted the dog back. The spirit would not oblige him. It wanted to live the good life of the dog. It made a deal with the boy. He promised a life without responsibilities, or work or problems, and if he wasn't happy he could have his dog back. The boy agreed.

What the spirit did was teach the boy how to avoid work, and how to shirk his responsibilities, and how to play hooky, and how to steal, and how to lie, and, most of all, how to take these vices and make them appear as virtues. In turn, the spirit lived a charmed life. He slept with the boy. He ate the same food. He didn't have to guard any mulberries, and, best of all, he could scare anyone he wanted.

People marveled at the boy's great courage. He was the only person brave enough to visit the mulberry tree. It was friendly toward him, for it was now inhabited by the spirit of his dog. And each time he came near it, the tree would shake with so much happiness that mulberries would rain down by the thousands. And the boy would be sad and miss his old friend.

It did not take the boy long to realize that the paradise he'd been offered was a fool's paradise indeed. But to get rid of the spirit, he would have to have as much cunning as the devil. So he began to treat the dog like a dog.

First, he began keeping it on a leash. The spirit didn't like this, so it howled all night. So the boy made it sleep outside in the cold. He put a muzzle on it after it tried to bite him. He fed it dog food and scraps, and he made it take baths. Life for the spirit became so miserable that he begged the boy to take him back to the mulberry tree. The boy refused. The spirit pleaded and begged, and finally the boy relented—but on one condition.

"Anything!" the spirit said.

"You let me come to the mulberry tree and get mulberries when I want."

The spirit agreed, but on one condition.

"What?" the boy asked.

"You bring me some of that good food when you come," the spirit answered.

"Deal!" said the boy.

"Deal!" said the spirit.

And the spirit went back to the mulberry tree. And the dog came home.

"And it was just another one of Grandmama's ghost stories," I said to Blackie. "Ain't no such thang. And anyway, we ain't scared of no haints—is we?"

"Here's a bag," Savannah cried, waving a big plastic bag.

I took it with exaggerated confidence; after all, I was the only one with enough courage to go near the mulberry tree.

"C'mon Shack, c'mon Blackie," I called to my dogs.

I look at the girls and cried, "Boooo!"

They jumped.

"I want more than half! Since I'm the only one around here with any guts! I want a lot! I want a whole, whole lot! I want—Ahhhh!"

The beast gave no warning! It was the sentinel hiding in the cherry tree. It swooped down quickly and silently, attacking with beaks, claws, and bad intentions! I thought it was the devil, or at least that hellish old owl again.

"Ahhhh!" I screamed, flailing at it.

There was a shrill cry and a second attack! And a third! And a fourth!

"Ahhhh! Ahhhh! Ahhhh!"

I fought at them, but wasn't certain of what. A haint?

"Run!" I screamed.

Although it had started as a joke, the fierceness surprised even them. I turned to run, and tripped over Shack.

"Help!" I screamed, crawling through the rails as fast I could.

And the two big bad hunting dogs were about as effective against the birds as was the cat. Even less, for, unlike cats, dogs do not possess that unique dexterity of the posterior anatomy. They cannot scooch in their boodies, or lower their boodies, or hide their boodies. Their boodies were open targets for the birds until the dogs realized the hopelessness of the situation and broke for the rails.

My dogs had sense, too.

Then came the laughter.

"Gottdogitt!" I screamed. "Y'all knowed they was there!"

I turned to the dogs and commanded, "Sic 'em!"

They ignored me and went back down to Silo.

"Ahma git y'all!" I screamed at Savannah and Linda, chasing them all the way up to the house, with the mocking laughter of the mockingbirds ringing in my ears.

The Dirt Doggers

"Ticka, ticka, noby, noby, noby.
"Ticka, ticka, toby, toby, toby.
"All my children—
"Gone to heaven—
"Won't be back 'til June eleven—
"Are you readyyyy?"
"Noooo!"
"Last night—
"Night befoh—
"Twenty-five robbers at my doh—
"Police, police, don't git me—
"Git that nigga behind that tree!
"Are you readyyyy?"
"Noooo!"
"Ready or not—here I come! Anybody round my base is out!"
Why anybody would be around his base is beyond me. Cody
Wayne and Elaine were in the meter room. Bumpsy and Bebe were
on the side of the house. I don't know where Rudy was going. It
depended on where Twala was hiding. One thing for sure, he was-
n't going to find her in the pumphouse, because that's where me
and Janet were.

The pumphouse was my favorite hiding spot in this game
everyone calls hide 'n' seek, but we call "dirt diving" because that's

how we did it: on the ground, and in the dirt, like dogs, which led to Unck to call it "dirt doggin'" and us "dirt doggers."

I imagine so, since he done his share of "dirt doggin'" to be sure. Didn't seem to hurt him none. Us neither. He'd caught us once: me, Rudy, Cody Wayne, and Carmen. He didn't do anything but call us a buncha "dirt dogs." What Grandma Gert called us was something else. How she found out is a mystery to me, but she said if she ever caught us doing something like that again, she would beat the skin off us.

And we believed her, too.

She told Rudy that if he looked at a naked woman he would turn to stone, and he'd know he was turning to stone because the first thing to start getting hard would be his ding-a-ling.

And Rudy believed her, too.

Which is why he was always trying to get into the pump-house with me. "Dirt doggin'" should be done in the dark.

"Close the doh!" I hissed, thinking it was him.

In the rush of light I could see Janet trying to pull up her pants. Before I could stop her, the broom came crashing down upon my head.

"Owwww!" I screamed.

Down it came, again, and again, and again! I tried to run, but tripped over my own pants which were down around my ankles.

"Take ya ass in the house!" she hissed at Janet, smacking her across the shoulder. "Right now!"

It was sad to see her cry, but I had to think about me, because her big sister was about as big as Whoosh, and she was wielding a broom. I attempted to scoot by her, but she tripped me, then stomped her foot on my back and effectively staked me to the ground.

"Didn't I tell you to stay away from here!" she hissed, and hit me again. "And Ahma sho' tell Miss Gert!"

Flat on my face, with a foot on my back, I looked over and saw Cody Wayne easing out of the meter room. Ruby Lee stuck her head out the back door and asked, "What's goin' on out there?"

"Git him!" Brenda shouted, pointing at Cody Wayne.

Fat chance. Cody Wayne took off and ran for the fence, getting up and over with little effort. Elaine ran around Ruby Lee and dashed for the front. From my vantage point, I could see Bumpsy and Bebe crawling from beneath the opposite side of the house.

"That's what y'all come here for!" Ruby Lee shrieked and slapped me atop the head with a spatula. "You nasty thang!"

"Didn't I tell you not to come 'round here no mo'?" Brenda demanded, applying more foot pressure. "Huh?"

"Yeak! Yeak!" I cried.

"And you sneak 'round here anyway?"

"Nok! Nok!"

"Yes, you did, you nasty dog! Everybody ain't nasty like you!"

"I oughta cut it off!" Ruby Lee suggested.

"That's a good idea!" Brenda cried.

Cut what off? I was thinking.

"Yeah," Ruby Lee snickered. "He too mannish as it is."

"Turn me loose! Turn me loose!" I shrieked.

"We gon' turn you loose all right," Brenda said.

"No, girl, we gon' cut him loose!" Ruby Lee laughed.

"Help! Help! Hellllp!" I cried.

"We gon' help you, too," Ruby Lee said, as they dragged me around to the front porch.

"Janet," Brenda called her sister. "Bring me a knife!"

"Don't do it, Janet! Don't do it!" I screamed.

Janet was my girlfriend.

"OK," she cried, and hurried off.

She was back in a moment with a knife—a butter knife. Good girl.

"This ain't shit!" Ruby Lee cursed. "I need somethin' I can work with—the butcher knife."

"OK," she said and hurried off again.

"Hellllp!" I screamed.

Ruby Lee had me pinned by the arms and Brenda had me pinned by the legs, and Janet came running back outside with something that would have sparked the interest of Jim Bowie.

"That's what I'm talkin' 'bout," said Ruby Lee.

She looked down at my works and grinned like a blood-sucking vampire. All seven of her sisters crowded around to watch. She grabbed and hefted the whole package.

"Boy," she said, holding up the knife and examining it, "don't you know this little thing can get you in a whole lotta trouble?"

"Hellllp!"

"Now, do you wanna spend your life in trouble?"

"Hellllp!"

"Me and my sisters don't wanna see you spend your life in trouble—do we sisters?"

"Noooo!" they cried.

"So," she said, "I'll just take this and that way you won't get in no mo' trouble."

And she held up my balls and put them to the knife! I screamed and twisted and shrank from the feel of cold steel against the base of my weenie. She was spiking my guns! Queering my works with the heartless élan of a kill-crazy animal! I kicked and squealed and shouted obscenities, all to no avail.

"You want some mo' pussy?" Ruby Lee inquired.

"Noooo! Noooo! Noooo!" I cried.

"You gon' bother my sisters again!"

"Noooo! Noooo! Nooo!

"I know you ain't," said Brenda, "'cause you ain't gon' have nuthin' to bother with!"

Then she really went to work! Hacking and sawing in earnest. At any moment I was expecting her to thrust forth her grisly trophy for me to witness. *Oh, the blood of human sacrifice!* She was hacking away the very life of me! *Oh, fie—warm blood of slaughtered youth!* I could not bear to look—but I did. She was holding the knife upside down! What a dirty trick!

Janet was holding her mouth with both her hands, eyes wide not in horror, but in mirth! This was funny to her—funny to them all. They were straining to hold in the laughter, lest they give the joke away. I looked for blood, but all I saw was my flaccid phallus pulled taut, the skin wobbling back and forth as Ruby Lee stroked it vigorously, using the dull blunted edge, the sharp cutting edge facing up.

"Stop! Stop! Stop!" I demanded.

And right then a big rock smashed into the wall just above my head, startling everyone. I fell to the porch and saw Cody Wayne, Rudy, and Bumpsy standing at the edge of the street with big rocks in their hands.

"Boy!" Ruby Lee shouted, "what's wrong wit you?"

"You throw another rock up here and I'll come down there and beat yo ass!" Brenda threatened.

And Cody Wayne threw another rock.

And so did Rudy and Bumpsy.

Having pulled up my pants and scooted away, I stood amongst my cousins, armed and ready to do battle. A rock flew past my head—they were throwing back.

"And Ahma call yo Grandmama right now," Ruby Lee screamed, "and tell her just what you been doin' 'round here—you lil' sapsucka!"

"Kiss my ass!" I screamed back, "you big black blimp!"

And stones by the hundreds began raining down upon us! We could do nothing but retreat from the sudden barrage.

True to her word, Ruby Lee had called home ahead of us. Fortunately, Grandma Gert wasn't there, and Manasha had taken the call.

"Where y'all been?" she asked the four of us as we wandered in through the back door.

"Nowhere," Rudy answered.

"Nowhere, like where?"

She was acting very strange.

"Like down at the lake," I cried.

"Like down at the lake, doin' what?" she asked.

"Like down at the lake swimmin'," Cody Wayne answered.

Very casually, she seemed to be trying to maneuver herself between us and the door.

"How come y'all ain't wet?" she asked.

"'Cause we dried off," Bumpsy said.

She was holding her right hand very strangely.

"How come y'all dry so quick?" she asked.

"'Cause—look out, Rudy, she got a switch!" I screamed.

It wasn't a switch, but a belt, and she was trying to catch us all and caught none. Rudy got out through the front door. Bumpsy got out through the back door. And me and Cody Wayne beat a hasty retreat upstairs, opened the screen, and jumped down from the porch roof and hauled ass for Silo. It wasn't Manasha we were afraid of, it was that Manasha was mad enough to tell Grandma

Gert, and only Grandpa could save you from an ass-whipping from Grandma Gert.

We spent the rest of the day lurking around the fruit field, but Grandpa never came up. Around lunchtime Miss Eva came, and we ran to her and surrounded her and followed her into the house. And all Manasha did was glare at us with a steely eye and said, "Y'all go wash them pots!"

The Owl and Miss Eva

"Don't tell me what I saw!" I spat at Cody Wayne.

"OK," Miss Eva said, trying to keep the peace. "OK."

"I know what I saw!"

"You ain't seen nuthin'," Cody Wayne shot back.

"How d'you know what I saw?"

"You ain't seen no owl!"

"I know wha—"

"All right!" Miss Eva shrieked.

We both became quiet. They didn't call her evil for nothing.

"All right," she said again, a bit more calmly. "We'll go and check it out, but I can't see how it can be an owl if it's as big as you say it is.

"I thought it was an eagle at first," I said by way of explanation.

"You don't know an eagle when you see one," Cody Wayne remarked.

I ignored him.

"Well," Miss Eva said, "if it is an owl, we might not be able to see it in the daytime."

"Sho' won't!" Cody Wayne sneered.

I hadn't thought of that, but what did it matter. I had aroused her interest in the owl and, by extension, me.

Miss Eva was as much a relative to us as Aunt Sally, or Aunt

Clara, or Bake the Cake. Savannah and Linda, Ingy and Cheryl, and Teenie and Weenie called her Aunt Eva. But not me, and not Cody Wayne. She was much too beautiful to be our aunt, and we competed for her attention. And we were not the only ones.

Besides beauty, she had money and influence. She owned a packinghouse and considerable property in Oklawaha. She started and funded the girl's academy that Linda and Savannah were now attending. She dabbled in politics, had one son, two adopted daughters, and was twenty years divorced from Rev. Leviticus Keats Jr., and she loved Unck.

Cody Wayne was Unck's son, and she was always admiring him. How fast he was growing. How he was so much like Unck. How much sense he had, and what he was going to grow up to be. Me, I was just Melvin's son—with his bad self! But the owl would change all that. When she saw that owl, she would see me the same way she saw Unck.

It was the biggest owl I'd ever seen, and a frightening thing to see at night. I'd spotted it on the return trip from the reservoir with Tommy Green and Red Brown. It was dark, and we'd stopped along the trail to rehitch the boat, when I heard it rustling up in the trees. I climbed up on top of the cab and shined the spotlight on it. At first I thought it was one of the many unholy terrors from one of Grandmama's ghost stories.

"Ain't nuthin' but an owl," Tommy Green assured me.

Maybe so, but it was the biggest, damnedest owl I'd ever seen, and something I was burning to show Miss Eva.

I told no one else about it, but marked the spot and held my tongue until Miss Eva came to go gallivanting.

Birds. She was a birdwatcher to her heart, and I'd saved the owl just for her. She was in love with birds and would spend whole weeks watching and photographing them. And she wasn't exactly an amateur either. She was as serious about cameras and birds as she was about politics and money. One of her photos, a picture of Ingy and Cheryl feeding the songbirds as they hovered and fluttered directly over their heads, appeared on the cover of *Audubon* magazine. It was a prize-winning photo of a rare and graceful innocence.

Not so the bats! That was another one of her photos that appeared in *Life.* It was a dark and disturbing photo that ranged from grotesque and horrible to fascinating and sublime. And I'd found them for her, too. They were in a den in a dry lake bed beneath the water tower down by Goodbread Alley. Bats by the tens of thousands! Of course, she was afraid of them and would come no further than fifty yards to the mouth of the cave. So we made them come out. We made a smoke bomb, and as she stood behind her tripod, Cody Wayne threw it in. What followed was a wild spectacle of a strange and horrifying wonder, with all the strangeness and wonder that will ever be. Me and Cody Wayne ran like crazy as thousands of aggravated bats poured out of the den ranging for revenge—a dark, unalterable cloud of madness that headed straight for Miss Eva, whose heroically mad photo tickled the editor of *Life.* If they liked those bats, they would love this owl.

"Ain't nuthin' up there!" Cody Wayne snapped, skimming the treetops through the field glasses.

It was dark the night I'd seen it, but I'd marked the spot by a big forked pine that stood out amongst the trees. When we found the tree, we parked the Rover next to it. We found no nest, but I was certain of the tree, and she believed me.

"There is something up there, Cody Wayne," said Miss Eva, focusing. "It might be a nest."

I knew it was a nest and I wasn't even looking at it. I was looking at her instead, as I always did when she wasn't looking.

Her long hair was tied in a top knot, but that only highlighted her beauty. She is blacker than Savannah, and Savannah is as black as coal. So black, it made you think of cotton. An amorous, tender darkness with a graceful delicacy of charm and style. That is what she has above all else—style. Miss Eva has style like no one else. Style like Diana Ross. Style like a black indigo snake moving lazily toward the shade. Style like a pretty little black girl on her way to Sunday school.

"But if it is an owl," she said turning to look at me, "I won't be able to get a picture until night."

At least Cody Wayne wasn't mocking me. We moved around to the other side where we had a clearer view.

"Well," said Cody Wayne, eyeing it through the binoculars, "it might be."

Miss Eva aimed her camera and began snapping pictures. It was not what I had in mind. I wanted her to see the owl in all its feathered glory. I wanted her to see those great wings of unspeakable pomp and vanity. It was nothing short of the vast glory of God. What I really wanted was to experience her little-girl joy and exuberance. I wanted her to hug and kiss me just like she did when I showed her the beehive.

But a big nest was nothing to get excited about. If the owl was out, I could make it come down by flaying a snake and offering it up, just like we did with hawks and eagles. But this was an owl, and, for all its feathers, it did not care to come down and bid the noonday sun g'day.

I would have to make him come down.

As Cody Wayne gawked and Miss Eva snapped pictures, I began shinnying up the tree.

There is not a tree on our property that I cannot get up. We own a forest! All of us, including Savannah and Linda, are adept at climbing trees. Including pine. If I can get my arms halfway around it, I can get up it.

"Hey!" Cody Wayne hollered.

"Johnny!" Miss Eva screamed. "Come down!"

"Ahma make 'im come out!" I shouted back. All it needed was a little prodding.

"Johnny!" she cried. "Come down from there!"

"You gon' break yo neck!" Cody Wayne shouted. That only made me more determined.

"Come down, Johnny!" she cried.

"Come down, Johnny!" he cried.

I kept going. In my mind it only showed how much she cared. Cody Wayne just didn't want me to show him up. It was higher than I'd thought, but soon I was standing on the limb directly beneath it. Viewed up close, a nest of any kind is a curious thing. I was possessed with a sudden inquisitiveness to learn how and why a nest. It was an impertinent curiosity that was none of my business, and the owl made a point of it. Suddenly I heard the flapping of some awful big wings. Then the wings appeared, extending far beyond the borders of the nest.

It was an awesome thing to behold. A sight so touching in its majesty, its beauty, its boldness, it filled the mind with a new and ever-increasing wonder. Nothing on earth arouses so grand a spectacle!

"See it! See it!" I screamed in awe.

It was greater than I'd remembered it. It flew up and out and away from the nest, circling the tree. And Miss Eva was getting her pictures.

"See it!" I hollered down again.

"OK!" she hollered up. "We see it. Now you come down."

"You git a picture?"

"We got a picture—come down!"

I watched it, brooding on a limb in the tree across from me. Up that high, I could not help but admire and envy the bird and its wings. It extended them out in majestic fashion, lifted off, and came directly for me!

"Ahhhh!" I cried as it grazed me.

Suddenly I realized that this was not such a good idea. Its talons were huge, hooked and wicked-looking things that it opened and closed and pointed at me. This was not a happy bird. It looked back sharply, like some masked and inescapable evil, squawked its intentions, then came at me again.

"Johnny, watch out! Johnny, watch out! Johnny, watch out!" they were both screaming.

I wedged myself down between the branches of a bushy limb as it made several passes, then flew up to its nest.

"C'mon, Johnny!" Cody Wayne yelled.

"Where it at?" I called down.

"He in the nest!"

I began climbing down in haste, but halfway down I heard those fierce wings and a hysterical, "Look out!"

It hit once, atop the right shoulder, and I screamed in pain, not sure whether to drop or hold on.

"Cody Wayne!" I screamed desperately. "Help me!"

Cody Wayne had a stick and was climbing up.

"Watch out!" Miss Eva shrieked. "He's behind you!"

I turned just in time to see it and throw up one arm, a paltry defense against talons that embedded themselves deep into my chest and a huge hooked beak that slammed into my forehead like a spiked hammer! We fought. I held on with my legs and fought against its fierce flapping wings in a fight that grew more fierce and wild as I struggled to get it off my chest. It fell away, then whooshed off quickly, the back-draft from its quick departure blowing blood from my head into my eyes.

"Git down, Johnny!" Cody Wayne yelled somewhere under me.

Dazed and scared, I wiped the blood from my eyes and held on.

"Cody Wayne?" I cried. "Where you?"

Miss Eva screamed again and I looked to my left and saw it closing fast.

"Jump!" Cody Wayne screamed. "Jump, Johnny. Jump!"

I let go. I was perhaps sixty feet up and just let go, dropping down to a lower spread of branches trying hard to catch myself and hold on. For a moment I did, landing backwards and holding on, but, extending my shoulder so far back, I heard it pop, forcing me to let go.

Miss Eva either caught me or I landed on top of her, so hard and sudden she yelped in pain. The owl swooped in to attack again and she covered me with her whole body.

"Cody Wayne!" she screamed.

"My arm broke! My arm broke!" I screamed in pain and panic.

"OK, OK," she tried to comfort me. The owl came again.

"Cody Wayne!" she screamed.

From where he was, he dropped the stick and jumped straight down and stood over the both of us wielding the stick like some mad and valiant warrior, poised and ready to strike down the heavens! The owl swooped in low, but veered sharply as Cody Wayne swung the stick as if it were a great battle ax. Thereafter, the owl kept its distance.

Knowing Cody Wayne was there with a stick to keep the owl at bay, Eva did something that jarred my attention away from the pain and gave me some comfort. She lifted me up from the ground, cradled me like a baby, and began to run. It was more than I expected, and everything I'd hoped—to lie within her woman's breast, her hot desperate breath blanketing my face. She was only a woman, so hard a woman—a heroic woman. Her tender fortitude was well worth the hellish torment of a stupid old owl with a wild hair up its ass. That was but a small price to pay.

The Happy Birds

"You ain't got the goddamn sense you was born with!" Grandma Gert shouted.

Miss Eva sucked her teeth, crossed her legs, and looked away.

"You gon' git somebody killed wit all this stupid shit you be doin'!"

Barely able to move, I sat on the sofa in silence and sadness, listening to Grandma Gert and Miss Eva out on the front porch. It had been two days since the encounter with the owl and one of those was spent in the hospital. The final word, besides that it was a stupid thing to do, was that Miss Eva should not have let it happen. Those final words were now being spoken.

"You ain't got no betta sense than that?" Grandma Gert demanded.

"I didn't send him up there!" Miss Eva raged back. "He got up before I could stop him!"

"I don't give a damn! He was out there gallivantin' behind you."

Aunt Clara and Manasha were in the car waiting to take Grandma Gert downtown. She'd been subpoenaed to appear before a grand jury investigating vote fraud in the election of MacArthur Dill. The real focus of the probe was Miss Eva, Michael Cohen, and Julio Sanchez. It was the three of them who spearheaded the drive to oust former sheriff Gil Porter. Julio Sanchez and Michael Cohen hightailed it out of town the minute the opposition party cried "Fix!" And Eva Horton was nowhere where a process server could serve her a subpoena. So they subpoenaed Grandma Gert out of spite. This was her second appearance. The first appearance ended in a two-hundred-and-fifty-dollar contempt fine. After hearing her answer "I don't remember" twenty-seven times, the exasperated prosecutor asked her when her birthday was, and Grandma Gert answered, "I don't remember."

And the prosecutor asked, "Is there anything you do remember?"

And Grandma Gert said, "Not a goddamn thang!"

And as the jurors stared in stunned silence, she added, "And if I did remember somethin', I wouldn't tell a mutha-fucka like you!"

Grandma Gert hated the former sheriff and did not regret working to get him kicked out of office. But all she did was stuff envelopes and bad-mouth him and Judge Shelby. Now she had to go and face Judge Shelby and twenty-three other wicked white faces that always made up an Oklawaha grand jury. She wasn't too thrilled about it, and she blamed Miss Eva.

"Accident my ass!" Grandma Gert raged. "There'll be a lotta accidents 'round here if they keep followin' yo crazy ass!"

Aunt Clara beeped once.

"Clara callin' you!" Miss Eva snapped. "Go on, go some-where—take your old ass for a ride!"

And Grandma Gert said, "Why don't you take yo gut-bucket, sewed-up, tore-up pussy somewhere for a ride!"

Manasha and Aunt Clara looked at each other and laughed. Miss Eva rolled her tongue around her cheek and tried not to laugh. Grandmama said nothing.

"Ooooo Mama," Aunt Clara said, "Please don't take that

nasty mouth 'round them Crackas."

"They gon' lock her up this time," Grandmama said.

Grandma Gert stormed off the porch and got into the car.

"We'll be back," Aunt Clara said and waved to Grandmama.

"Bye, Eva," Manasha said as they backed out the driveway.

Miss Eva sucked her teeth and cut her eyes away from them. She'd comforted me throughout the painful ordeal. So, I went out on the porch to comfort her. All I could do, though, was present myself, since my head was bandaged, my shoulder was bandaged, my right arm was bandaged, my chest was bandaged, and my left arm was in a cast. I could not move without pain.

Although Grandma Gert was long gone, Miss Eva still raged at her.

"She gone, Eva," Grandmama said.

"So?" Miss Eva raged, tears streaming down her face. "Why she blame me? Why she make it my fault, like I was . . . "

Snot ran from her nose as she began blubbering like a child.

"Don't cry, Miss Eva," I said to her.

She turned, reached out, and pulled me to her.

"Owwww!" I wailed in pain.

"Oh!" she cried. "Ahm sorry, baby. OK. OK!"

She embraced me gently and pulled me to her.

Grandmama said, "Y'all should know betta than to go messin' wit an owl. They's worse than eagles once they get riled up."

Miss Eva sniffed and wiped her nose. I looked up at her and she laughed at herself. I did too.

"That's just how the blind man git blind," Grandmama said.

And we both stared at her.

Joe Bird, the blind man, lived in Goodbread Alley. Grandpa visited him often. He played piano and sang the blues at Shadie

Ward's night club. He was a blind man ever since I knew him. I didn't know how he got blind, I just knew he was blind.

"How he got blind?" Miss Eva asked.

"Messin' wit owls," Grandmama said.

"They plucked his eyes out?" I asked, and shuddered to think how close I'd come.

"Worse!" Grandmama said.

"What could be worse?" Miss Eva asked.

"Owl spit."

"Owl spit?"

"I didn't know owls spit," I said.

"Spittin' owls do," Grandmama said.

"Spittin' owls?" we both exclaimed.

"The worst kind," she said.

"I ain't nevah heard of 'em," Miss Eva said.

"That's 'cause you ain't been listenin'," said Grandmama, "and you got a bad habit of hearin' what you wanna hear."

Miss Eva said nothing.

"You gotta go way back there to hear 'em," Grandmama said, "and ain't nobody ever seen 'em except Joe Bird."

"How come?" Miss Eva asked.

"'Cause you go blind lookin' at 'em."

"Grandmama," Miss Eva sighed, "this don't make no sense!"

"Make mo' sense than goin' back there messin' wit 'em. Ask Joe Bird."

"Well, how Joe Bird git blind?"

"Messin' wit them owls."

And Miss Eva sighed again.

"Some people knowed about them," Grandmama said. "Papa knowed. He called them 'happy birds—' 'cause they laughed all the time. You couldn't see them, but you could hear them laughing. Joe Bird is the only man who ever saw one. And that's how I know what they look like.

"They call him Joe Bird because he hunted birds for their feathers. He's the reason why you don't see certain kind of birds around here anymore. But you can't really blame him because people paid a lot of money for feathers. They wore them in hats.

"Joe Bird knew every kind of bird there was. He knew what they ate, where they were, what they did, and where they went. Wherever the birds were, that's where he went. And he always wanted more. More birds, more feathers, more money, and more places to go. He'd been to Africa, South America, New Guinea, and Canada, and bragged that he knew every kind of bird there was. And that's when Ish told him about happy birds.

"Ish was a Micasukee and had been here since God knows when. Him and Sears and Troy were good friends. They'd go huntin' in the swamp and stay for days. And that's how they knew about the happy birds. They never seen them, they just heard them, and only at night.

"Sears said it was the laughter of a man, and the laughter of a woman. He said sometimes he would laugh, and sometimes she would laugh, and sometimes they would laugh together and laugh all night. They were happy at night. Sears say sometimes it would be a lovely laugh from heaven and sometimes a laugh to scorn the bitter soul, like they were laughing at him.

"Ish said they tried to track them down, but they slept during the day and never in the same place. They slept high up in the trees to absorb the sunlight. They had feathers that held light.

"When they flew out at night, you could see the glow, a multicolored hue against the sky, sometimes two, sometimes three, and sometimes a great rainbow of living light blazing across the sky, leaving behind it a long trail of laughter.

"Joe Bird never heard anything like it. If it were true, it would be the world's greatest wonder. But Sears had seen it, Ish had seen it, and Troy had seen it, too. And they took Joe Bird back there to see for himself.

"That was a mistake. This was Joe Bird, the original bird man. Once he saw those birds in all their splendor and all their glory and all their brilliance, he would not rest until he had one.

"No one knew where to look for them in the daytime. They were like owls. But, Joe Bird looked all day and all night. He'd see the light, run to it and follow the light trails, but toward morning the brilliance would fade and they'd go somewhere, build a nest, and hide.

"Joe Bird became obsessed with these birds. They had stolen away his wits and laughed at him. For years he lived in the swamp, chasing them, half-crazed with their spell. People thought he was crazy, but then again, people thought the birds were a myth.

"For years he lived deep in the swamp where the trees are so thick they form a huge canopy over the swamp floor for miles and miles around, making everything dark and comfortless. Dark and terrible beyond any season of hope. It was there, in the dark abyss that he saw a glimmer in the darkness, in the middle of the afternoon. Joe Bird had found his bird.

"In this place of shade and shadow where even the light is dark, the birds still carried a radiant glow, and that is what he saw. High in the top of a cypress tree was a brilliant, many-colored nest of stinging brightness. He'd found one, and he did not intend for it to get away. He fastened his climbing gaffs and, with his net attached to his belt, made the long climb to the top. This was it! Fame and fortune! Such a thing would be new to science. New to man! He threw his net across the top and secured it to the tree. He had it! He raised up and peeked over the top of the nest to look

103

directly into the face of a bright and burning danger!

"And when she saw him, she screamed!

"There was a brightness in her flailing eyes, but that brightness did not belay her beastly stench, or their abominable appearance. He was asleep, but she, poor beast, eyes bright with darkness, leaned on her breast and screamed a strange scream of death, the scream of a wild animal cornered and conscious of capture. She opened her mouth and screamed the scream of a wild witch, which is what she looked like! She had the talons, the wings, the feathers, and the body of a bird, but the hideous head of a woman! A long-haired, long-nosed, long-lipped thing of terror! She screamed and awakened him and he too had the head of a human, with a face so brutish and repulsive it induced Joe Bird to scream in fear and dread.

"And this thing looked Joe Bird up and down, then hawked and hauled up a mouth full of cold and spit it right in Joe Bird's eyes! And Joe Bird fell screaming from the tree! Blinded for life.

"Ish found him wandering around the swamp and brought him out. And that's how the blind man git blind."

Miss Eva was holding me close, with her head nestled to the back of my neck.

"That's a nice story Grandmama," she said, "but that's not how the blind man git blind."

"Don't matter," Grandmama said, "but that's how the blind man git blind—go ask him."

She nudged me, and I eased up.

"We're going to pick some fruit and go see Joe Bird," Miss Eva said.

"Don't take that child down to that bar in Goodbread Alley. Gert find out, we'll never hear the end of it."

"She won't know, and anyway, the bar's closed this time of day."

She lay her hand gently across my head and said, "Let's go git some fruit and go listen to old Joe Bird sing the blues."

A Conversation Among My Aunts

"I heard you can't get a good dick after thirty-five," Aunt Clara said.

"Tell Eva that," Aunt Sally answered. "Lijo's forty-two and she still can't git enough."

"What about Pea-Head?"

"Child, please, that ain't big enough—at least not big enough to give me a thrill."

"How do ya know?"

"'Cause I know!"

"Bigger than Clarence?"

"Girl, don't nobody want that big horse-dick he got!"

"How do you knooooww?" Manasha sang.

"It came to me in a dream," Aunt Sally said wryly, "a nightmare."

"Uh-huh," Manasha signified.

"Yeah, I bet," said Aunt Clara. "Anyway, we heard that dream."

"Heard what?" Manasha asked.

"They didn't hear shit!" Aunt Sally snapped. "Quit lyin'!"

"We heard you!" Aunt Clara laughed.

"We who?"

"Me and Eva."

"Quit lyin'!"

"Heard what?" Manasha asked.

"Quit lyin'!" Aunt Sally shouted.

"Heard her say 'Damn, Clarence, move ya knee—'" Aunt Clara said.

"Quit lyin'!" Aunt Sally shouted.

"And Clarence said . . . "

"Quit lyin'!"

"And Clarence said . . . "

"Quit lyin'!"

"And Clarence said, . . . 'That ain't my knee!'"

And a huge chorus of girlish laughter erupted from the kitchen.

The only way I could sit and listen to such talk was to not be there. To Manasha, Aunt Sally, and Aunt Clara, I was not there, but asleep on the couch—or at least they thought I was. If they knew I was awake, they would have run me upstairs, so they could smoke cigarettes, drink beer, and not feel any guilt about drinking and smoking in front of me.

Everybody else was gone. Grandmama and Grandma Gert were gone to a doctor's appointment in Eloise. Daddy Troy was gone to Canada. Grandpa was gone to Silo. Rudy, Cody Wayne, Linda, and Savannah were gone to school. Ingy and Cheryl were gone to day care. Teenie and Weenie were gone outside to play with P.K. and Caroline. And I had gone to sleep.

Or so they thought. With one arm broken and in a cast, and the other arm bandaged from the damage the owl had done, there wasn't much I could do but sit around and listen to the conversations between my mother and my aunts.

"What about you?" Aunt Sally cried.

"What *about* me?" Aunt Clara demanded.

"What about the nasty shit you was doin'?"

"Like what?"

"Like you and Tommy Tee!"

"Tommy Tee?"

"And Tyrone!"

"Tyrone?"

"And Nasty Brown!"

"Watch yo mouth, girl—the only thing nasty 'bout Nasty Brown is his name."

A child's wailing cry rushed in from outside.

"Now what they doin'?" Aunt Sally growled.

I heard the back door open.

"P.K.!" she shouted, "you betta cut that out before I come out there!"

"I ain't doin' nuthin," P.K.'s little voice filtered in.

"He pushed me down!" Weenie complained.

"I don't know what's wrong wit you," Aunt Sally threatened, "but Ahma come out there and find out. You hear me?"

"Uh-huh."

The door did not close, but I could tell she was sitting down. I couldn't hear them clearly, but they were talking again. A bottle of beer fizzed open. A cigarette lighter scraped and snapped. Were they talking about Miss Eva again? I couldn't tell. With a great deal of stealth and pain, I eased up off the couch and put my ear to the door.

"That wasn't me!" Aunt Clara screeched. "That was Eva—I was just the lookout!"

"The look-in too," Aunt Sally shot back, "'cause you sho' was lookin'!"

"And anyway, what you hear 'bout Eva ain't true."

"Unless you talkin' 'bout Lijo."

"Well, that's a different story."

"Yeah, right, that was a fine choice."

"They're jealous of her."

"Scared of her too!"

Which is exactly what I was wanting to hear.

Eva Irene Horton. The name itself was intriguing. Some people refer to her as "Evil Horton," an unkind or complimentary reference that was part of her persona. She was an enigma, beyond the range of my understanding.

"Now what you hear about her and Lijo," Aunt Clara said to Manasha, "is probably true."

"'Cause after all these years they're still carrying on like a coupla teenagers," said Aunt Sally.

"She know she love her some Lijo!"

"Got to—to be hangin' out round the swamp like they be doin'."

"Why didn't they marry?" Manasha asked.

"Child," said Aunt Clara, "you don't know Eva."

"She bossy," said Aunt Sally. "She think she's the man."

"If they was married," said Aunt Clara, "Lijo would be knockin' 'er upside the head every time you look around."

"And," said Aunt Sally, "Eva wouldn't put up with that shit for one minute!"

"Not like I put up wit it," Aunt Clara said, "fa seven years!"

There was an angry uncomfortable silence, then Aunt Clara said, "They woulda married, but her daddy, Mr. Herbert, was a dickhead!"

"God bless the dead!" the two sisters said and rapped the table with their knuckles.

"Everybody was scared of him," said Aunt Clara, "even the Crackers."

"We was his only friends," added Aunt Sally.

"He was a Mason, like daddy and Granddaddy."

"He was a labor contractor so he stayed on the road a lot and Eva stayed with us."

"She's every bit a sister to us."

"Not to Lijo!"

"They woulda married," Aunt Clara said, "but her daddy wanted her to marry somebody he thought would amount to somethin'—like Leviticus."

This caused Aunt Sally to spit venom. "Hmph!" she spat. "That shit-colored muthafucka didn't amount to dookey!"

Suddenly the chairs screeched and scraped across the floor, and beer bottles rang and clanged with the rushing sound of panic.

"That's them!" Manasha gasped. "She comin'—she comin'!"

Only then did I hear the roaring sound of the engine. "She" meant Grandma Gert.

And she didn't play shit! And she certainly didn't play smokin' and drinkin' and lounging around the house like "a bun-cha sorry ho's," which is exactly what she'd told them the last time she'd caught them smokin' and drinkin' and lounging around the kitchen. Since she was still mad with me over the encounter with the owl, even though I was the one who'd gotten the worst of that deal, I leaped up onto the couch, rolled over, and played dead.

The kitchen door creeped open and Manasha creeped out and over to the front window, easing it aside and peeping out.

"False alarm y'all," she cried in relief and released the curtain. "It's Grandpa with the tractor."

The whole house, it seemed, sighed in relief. Chairs began plopping and sliding back in place, beer bottles popped and fizzed, cigarette lighters snapped and scraped, and the laughter came back. I waited for the talk to get good before I eased up off the sofa and back to the door.

"They think we're their slaves or somethin'," Aunt Clara was saying.

"Even the girls," said Aunt Sally, "and ain't none of 'em shit."

"Colleen wasn't shit either," Aunt Sally spat, "called me a *migger!*"

Aunt Clara giggled.

"A what?" Manasha asked.

"A *migger!*" Aunt Sally said, laughing.

"A *migger?*"

"Yeah. I was over there one day helping mama with the laundry and she and her little friends were out back playing. And I went to hang up some clothes and she pointed to me, talkin' 'bout 'look—look—look at that *miiiiggggggaa!*'"

All three burst out laughing.

"She was only four or five then," Aunt Clara said in defense.

"Made me cry," Aunt Sally pouted.

"Brendan used to beat up Earl Allen all the time," Aunt Clara remembered.

"Melvin beat his ass one day," Aunt Sally remembered, "after he told Melvin, 'y'all my niggas.'"

Somebody giggled, and Aunt Clara said, "Mama said he probably heard his daddy say that."

"Clara," Aunt Sally called, "remember when he caught fire?"

"Aiiiieeee!" they cried in glee.

"He had his daddy pipe," Aunt Sally explained, "and he was hiding in the gazebo tryin' to smoke it and Arthur Lee was cuttin' the grass. All of a sudden he bust out the gazebo screamin' and lookin' like a choo-choo train!"

A round of uproarious laughter filled the house.

"His shirt was on fire," Aunt Clara added, "and he was screamin', 'Nigga! Oh, nigga! Put me out! Put me out! Put me out!'"

There came another round of outrageous laughter that had me holding my mouth.

"But Arthur Lee couldn't put 'im out 'cause he couldn't catch 'im!" Aunt Sally laughed. "And didn't really try." And another lighter clicked and a bottle banged down.

"He used to like Clara," Aunt Sally said.

"Child, please!" Aunt Clara snapped.

"Show me ya pocketbook! Show me ya pocketbook! Show me ya pocketbook!" they sang in unison.

"Child, those were his favorite words," said Aunt Clara.

"But honey, we put a stop to that shit!" Aunt Sally said. "Didn't we, sister?"

"Damn right we did!"

"What y'all do," Manasha added, "cut his dick off?"

"Worse!" said Aunt Sally.

"What could be worse?"

And my two aunts suffered another round of hysterical laughter.

"See," Aunt Clara started, "Grandmama was their nanny. She raised all of them, going back to their great-granddaddy."

"Mama was like their housekeeper since she was a little girl," said Aunt Sally.

"And that big old house was like home to us, 'cause we were over there more than we were here."

"We'd get off the school bus and go straight there 'cause that's where Mama and Grandmama were."

"We'd eat a lil' somethin', do a lil' somethin', then we'd just walk across the fields and come home."

"Half the time nobody even saw us."

"Unless we were playing with Colleen, Darleen, or Sarah."

"And anytime he seen us playin' he'd come sniffin' his lil' ass around."

"Wantin' to play dollhouse!"

"And we didn't play with boys."

"At least we wasn't suppose to."

"Wasn't ladylike."

"Because no matter what we started out playin', we'd end up playin' dollyhouse."

"Well, one day Miss Cassie was having a tea for all these society ladies. So naturally we tagged along to help."

"But we was just goin' to be goin' 'cause wasn't nuthin' for us to do, and we brought our little tea set and sat on the side of the house and had us a little tea party too."

"Me, Clara, and Eva."

"And guess who showed up?"

"The devil himself," Manasha said.

"Come messin' wit us!" Aunt Clara scowled.

"Talkin' 'bout this his house, and this his yard, and this his water, and he could play anywhere he wanted," Aunt Sally said.

"So we packed up and went around back."

"And he followed us back there too."

"Well," Aunt Clara said, "I left them and went inside 'cause I knew he wasn't nuthin' but trouble."

"And you came right back out too!" Aunt Sally snapped.

Aunt Clara laughed. "After he seen we didn't wanna be bothered with him," Aunt Clara said, "he called hisself gittin' slick. He slipped in the house and slipped back out with one of Miss Cassie's dolls."

"Miss Cassie collected dolls. Not just any kind of dolls, but dolls from all over the world."

"And she'd scream like a pig if we went anywhere near them!"

"Child, let me tell you how this little shit tried to play us!"

"Tried?" cried Aunt Clara. "He did—he played you and Eva right out the pocket!"

"You too!" Aunt Sally screeched. "You was right there pullin' up yo dress too, Miss Thang!"

"Well, what he do wit these dolls?" Manasha asked.

"Charmed Eva and Sally into pullin' up their dress," Aunt Clara said.

"You too! You too! You too!" Aunt Sally accused.

"Not me! Not me! Not me!"

"She was right there, Manasha, pullin' up her dress like she was Madonna or somebody!"

"No I wasn't!"

"Yes you was—don't lie! We tried to ignore him, but that doll had our attention."

"Your attention, 'cause I didn't study him!"

"No, but you sure studied that doll!"

Aunt Clara giggled. She said, "It was the prettiest thing you ever seen. It was porcelain and come from China, and I wanted it bad."

"That's why he went and got it."

"Come askin' me if I wanna play with it."

"You did!"

"Damn right I did—but Eva say, 'No!'"

"And he say 'Why?'"

"And Eva say, ''Cause.'"

"And he say, ''Cause why?'"

"'Cause Eva had more damn sense than us—that's why!" Aunt Clara remarked.

"So he say, 'You could have it.'"

"And Eva say, 'For what?'"

"And he say, 'Lemme see ya pocketbook.'"

"And Eva said, 'No!'"

"But you said, 'OK.'"

"No, I didn't!" Aunt Clara shrieked.

"Yes, you did! You did! You did! You did!"

"So what? You did too! He didn't wanna do nuthin' but look and that didn't seem like much. So I said, 'OK.'"

"And he said 'Show me.'"

"And Eva, God bless her heart, said 'No, give her the doll first!'"

"And he said 'Ahma give it to her.'"

"And Eva said, 'Give it to her first!'"

"So, he gave Clara the doll, and Clara got set to give him a peek when Eva said 'Wait a minute—promise you won't take it back.'"

"And that liar promised."

"So, I let him get his look."

"And he act like he didn't wanna stop."

"Told me to hide the doll."

"Then he told me it was my turn!"

"Sally said, 'For what?'"

"And he said 'Yo turn to show me too.'"

"And Sally said 'Well, you gotta git me a doll too.'"

"I wasn't that dumb!" Aunt Sally put in.

"And he say, 'Shoot! I can't give all y'all dolls!'"

"I betcha he went and got one," Manasha put it.

"Two!" Aunt Clara cried.

"But then he got superslick," said Aunt Sally. "Now he wanna do it!"

"And he wouldn't give up a doll unless we did it first."

"Well, showin' him was one thing, but doin' it was somethin' else."

"Just the thought of Mama catchin' us was enough to make me keep my drawers up. I already had mine, so he wasn't talkin' to me."

"Well, I said 'No!'"

"And he said, 'Please—I'll show you mine.'"

"Like that was somethin' we really wanted to see."

"Pulled his pants down too!"

"A curious little thing."

"A little pink one."

"First time I'd ever seen one."

"Since he had it out he said he'd give us each a doll if we just felt it."

"So I looked at Eva, and Eva looked at me and said, 'OK.'"

"So we, uh—"

"Grabbed it and felt it—you know what you did!"

"You too!"

They both laughed.

"And he said, 'Do it again.'"

"And we did it again."

"And again."

"And again."

"And we had all them hot peppers on our hands, too!"

"Hot peppers?" Manasha asked.

And Aunt Clara and Aunt Sally burst out laughing.

"See," Aunt Clara gasped, "we played witches too. We had a little kettle and we'd mix us up a witches' brew."

"We was playin' tea till he started messin' wit us, then we went around back and started playin' witch!"

"We had our witch kettle fulla roots and leaves and cherries and peppers!"

"And I mean the hot kind!"

"And we'd just git a kettle full and just mash 'em and squeeze all the juice out."

"Just like she was mashin' and squeezin' his little thing."

"Gittin' hot peppa juice all over it."

"And he standin' there talkin' 'bout, 'Do it some mo', do it some mo.'"

"Well, I got tired, so he said, 'Do it till I count to ten.'"

"So Eva counted to ten."

"So he said, 'Count to a hundred.'"

"And I said, 'I ain't playin' no mo'!'"

"And Eva said, 'Gimme my doll!'"

"And that little shit talkin' 'bout 'psych'!"

"And then he took back the one he gave me!"

"And Clara started cryin'."

"And then he went round the side of the house and set them up so we could see them."

"Teasin' us!"

"And I just wanted to wring his scrawny neck!"

"But a funny thing happened."

"All of a sudden he started checkin' his self."

"And rubbin' his self."

"Then he pulled his pants off!"

"And we went over and looked and he didn't study us at all!"

"He looked up at Eva and said, 'My wee-wee burn!'"

And the whole house shook with laughter.

"Wasn't funny," Aunt Sally gasped, "and we wasn't laughing." They were dying with laughter.

"We were really scared," Aunt Clara said, "'cause we didn't

know what was wrong."

"He just kept sayin', 'My wee-wee burn!'"

"Then he started screamin'!"

"Then he started runnin' 'round and screamin'!"

"My wee-wee burn! My wee-wee burn!"

"I mean, we didn't do nuthin' but play with him, and now he's screamin' and hollerin'!"

"We knew we did somethin'!"

"We just didn't know what to do."

"Then Eva hollered, 'Put some water on it!'"

"And I ran and got the water hose!"

"And girl," Aunt Sally gasped with laughter, "he slid ten feet on his bare ass tryin' to git up under that water!"

"Like a lil' worm," Aunt Clara laughed, "my wee-wee!"

"I mean he carried on, floppin' round like a fish on the bank—them hot peppas was tearin' his ass up!"

"And he wouldn't shut up for shit!"

"Till finally, all that screamin' brought Mama out."

"Uh-oh!" Manasha gasped.

"And what's the first thing she see?" Aunt Clara asked. "This little half-naked white boy that she's suppose to be takin' care of, screamin' and floppin' around on the ground!"

"And Eva wit the water-hose skeetin' his little thing."

"Mama said, 'What's wrong wit him?'"

"And Clara said, 'He, he, he got, hot, hot, hot peppas on his weee-weeee.'"

"And Mama looked at us and didn't know what to think."

"And Mama say, 'How he do dat?'"

"And the three of us shrugged."

"Mama tried to get him to get up, but he wouldn't come from under that water for nuthin'!"

118

"Then Grandmama came out and said Miss Cassie wanted to know why Earl Allen was makin' all that fuss."

"And Mama told her to tell Miss Cassie that Earl Allen just got his ding-dong stuck in the zipper again."

"Grandmama was the only one who could do anything with him."

"That's 'cause she petted him."

"She got him to calm down, then she took him inside."

"And Mama told us to git our stuff and go home. Then she saw the dolls!"

"Mama say, 'Where y'all git them dolls?'"

"And Eva said, 'He gave 'em to us.'"

"And Mama say, 'What you mean—gave 'em to you? For what?'"

"And nobody said nuthin'."

"She took 'em from us and said, 'Y'all go home, straight home! I got somethin' to give y'all too!'"

A cigarette lighter scraped and I adjusted my position.

"They knew what a little shit he was," said Aunt Sally. "So we made it sound like he made us do it."

"But they wasn't buyin'," Aunt Clara laughed.

"There are some things that just call for a little talkin' to."

"And some things they just send you to your room."

"But for what we did you get an ass-whippin'! Wasn't no two ways about it!"

"That night I learned what a prostitute was," said Aunt Clara.

"And a whore," said Aunt Sally.

"And it was another fifteen years before I dropped my drawers for any man!"

There was an awkward silence, then Aunt Sally said, "You's a fifteen-year lie!"

"Ten!" Aunt Clara shouted over laughter.

"Ten what? Days?"

"Unh-unh, sister. You did it before me!"

"Don't even try it, Clara!"

"What about you and Gort?"

"Well, what about you and Doodie-Poot?"

"What about you and Bay-Boy?"

"What about you and Nasty Brown?"

"What about Nasty Brown?" Manasha asked.

There was another awkward silence followed by a sudden burst of outrageous laughter that went on and on, until we all heard the car door slam and Teenie, Weenie, Caroline, and P.K. scream "Grandmaaaa!"

"Oh shit!" my mother and my aunts cried in unison.

And I jumped back on the couch, feigning sleep to the sound of scrambling feet, scraping chairs, clinking bottles, hissing air fresheners, and disgraceful laughter.

A Good Boy

The wiry old Cracker came into view, and I hugged the limb and froze. Bumpsy and Cody Wayne were suddenly so quiet I could safely assume they'd seen him too. I wasn't so sure about Rudy. He was somewhere near the top where he always liked to be. I could only hope that he'd seen the old Cracker and would do nothing to give us away.

It was a tense and fearful moment, the kind of moment that makes you wonder why you do the things you do and wanna be a good boy, and promise God, on a stack of holy Bibles, that you won't be bad anymore if only he would pluck you from the jaw of death just one more time.

At least that's what I was thinking, and probably what Bumpsy and Cody Wayne were thinking too, since it was so quiet you could hear the cool afternoon breeze rustling through the leaves, birds singing in the distance, and the footsteps of a horrible death walking below us.

They called him Cracka Bill, though not to his face. Slowly he stepped up to the tree, searching it intently. He had a shovel handle and I didn't move except to shudder a faint cold fear. All we could do was remain quiet and still and wait for him to go away.

"Johnny! Johnny!" Rudy shouted from above, "you oughta come up here where the big ones at!"

Up until that moment we had fifty hopes and one fear; now

fear ruled and there was but one hope, and that was to get away in one piece!

"Come down from there!" he screamed in that mean, murderous twang of the Florida Cracker. "Come down from there!"

If they hadn't seen him before, they saw him now. And heard him too!

"Mable! Mable!" he screamed up toward the house, "git the dawgs! Git the dawgs!"

Oh shit! This man had three rottweilers!

"Git the dawgs, Mable! Git the dawgs!"

Fortunately, mango trees are very leafy, long, and colorful, and you can easily hide amongst the branches. So we stayed still. He knew we were there, but he didn't know where. It was no time to panic.

"Git the dawgs, Mable! Git the dawgs!"

Cody Wayne was the first to jump, and suddenly it became a clear case of "abandon ship." Every man for himself!

"C'meah!" the Cracker screamed, raising the stick and moving toward Cody Wayne.

That's when I jumped and drew his attention. Then Bumpsy jumped and drew his attention away from me. The old man didn't know who to catch or how many were still up there.

"Come back heah!" he cried. "Hey you! Git the dawgs, Mable; they gittin' away!"

An eight-foot fence surrounded the grove, which demonstrated the value of the trees. We were up and across it in no time. We heard the dogs, looked back, and saw Miss Mable closing in with all three dogs on a leash. And Rudy was still up in the tree. Huffing and puffing, she stopped about a hundred yards away and unleashed the dogs.

"Jump, Rudy, jump!" we shouted in unison.

"C'mon, Chic. C'mon!" he called to his dog.

"Jump, Rudy, jump!"

"C'mon, Saber!"

"Jump, Rudy, jump!"

"Git 'em, Duke—git 'em!"

It was not exactly a jump, much less a spectacular one. It was more of a fall—no, a drop. Cracker Bill was calling his dogs and Rudy just dropped down out of the tree, directly atop his head.

"Arrrrgggghhhh!" he groaned.

I remember someone saying something about Cracker Bill having lumbago or some strange affliction.

"Oooooh!" he groaned.

He sure sounded like he had something.

"Ummmm, ahhhh, oh! oh!"

Rudy had a good fifty yards on the dogs and made it across the fence with little effort, leaving old Cracker Bill moaning and groaning on the ground and his sorry old dogs barking through the fence.

So much for mangoes.

Raiding is what we called it; stealing is what it was. Larceny if you got caught. Which we didn't, but still, we had nothing to show for our efforts.

"Shoot!" Cody Wayne griped at Rudy. "Why you had to go and open yo big fat mouth!"

"He knew we was up there!" Rudy said in his defense.

"He didn't know nuthin'!" Bumpsy declared.

"Bunk you!" Rudy declared back.

"Bunk you back!"

"Bunk you back on the railroad track!"

"He found our footprints," I said. "He followed them to the tree."

"That means he's on to us," Cody Wayne said.

"No mo' mangoes," said Rudy.

"Oh well," said Bumpsy.

"I'm just glad he didn't start shooting," I said. "Next time he might."

Shooting a ten-, eleven-, or twelve-year-old for stealing mangoes would not sit right with anyone, certainly not us, but those were the rules to the game, and we understood them well. That did not deter us from stealing mangoes; it only made us go to any length not to get caught.

The trees and the land are our livelihood, and trespassing is a serious offense. Thus, whatever we did, it was very important not to get caught. But that only made it all the more fun.

"Let's go git some watermelons," Rudy suggested.

"We got watermelons," Bumpsy said.

"So," I put in, "we got mangoes too."

Besides, there was no fun in watermelons, only some people had better watermelons than others, and Mr. Timmons had watermelons like no one else. We grew melons in the off season, and Daddy Troy ran them up to Canada twice a year. But Mr. Timmons grew watermelons year-round, and several big supermarket chains competed to buy them. He had the sweetest, crispiest, juiciest watermelons anyone ever tasted, and how he did it was a mystery until the day Cody Wayne and I struck out to find out, once and for all, where the sweet, crystal-clear water from Silver Blue Lake flowed.

Silver Blue Lake covers fifty-two acres of our land. It is fed by an underground spring. The run-off from the lake flows out around the swamp and finds a natural course to the Oklawaha

River. It is a twenty-eight-mile journey about as tranquil as a tornado and as safe as a cottonmouth. We are constantly warned to stay from back there. This means anywhere beyond the property line. On more than a few occasions, though, we've struck out to follow the run all the way to the river. The farthest we've ever gotten was about three miles out where we suddenly ran into a mysterious field of black glump.

The day we found the sludge pits was the day we stopped gallivanting down the run. That day, we had to weigh the consequences of being where we had no business and were warned not to go, or reporting something strange and unusual. Something that just wasn't right. We decided to go and tell Unck.

And Unck told Daddy Troy, and he and Grandpa were not all that concerned with what we were doing back there, but instead had us show them what we'd found.

There were eight more fields of this black glump in scattered sites beyond that point where we'd found the first. Some were green glump. Some were blue glump, and there was a bright and glowing field of iridescent glump. None of this strange glump was on our property, but it was much too close to the swamp to be ignored. The Oklawaha Swamp is vital to the lives and livelihoods of the people of central Florida. It is the headwaters to four rivers. It is a twelve-hundred-square-mile recharge area for the Floridan Aquifer, the source of drinking water for much of Florida. Grandpa felt that this pristine, critically important patch of wilderness in the heart of the state was already being contaminated and destroyed by development. He felt the county did not provide enough protection for the swamp.

Grandpa and Daddy Troy took samples of this glump downtown and reported to county officials that a driver of a dump truck, whom they'd cornered, had showed them a county-issued permit. At first the county played dumb. Then they told them it was none of their business. Then they remembered we had a lawyer in the family. So they told Grandpa and Daddy Troy that all the black glump they were so concerned about was just dirt and sediment from the phosphate mines in Bartow. Grandpa and Daddy Troy accepted that answer because they knew it was the only answer they were going to get. So they skinned and grinned and shuffled on out of the county building, came home, and told Bake the Cake to bake another cake.

The Florida Sunshine Law forces government agencies to do the public's business in the light. It was under this law that Bake the Cake found out that Oklawaha County, under the auspices of the Oklawaha Water Commission, had granted licenses to several waste management companies, allowing them to dispose of their waste in Oklawaha County. This was a political hot potato, so naturally, he gave it to Eva Horton. And that's when the shit hit the fan.

Miss Eva Horton began dabbling in politics by doing favors for many of her poor and unfortunate employees. Since she was a businesswoman, she had to walk a fine line between her self-interest and her altruism. That she was able to get what she had was remarkable in itself. That she was able to keep it and prosper was a testament to her intelligence and toughness, for if nothing else, Eva Horton was tough. But the white people ran Oklawaha County, and they weren't shy of letting her or anyone else know it. Now, these white people often had nasty little disagreements over who would run what, but they were never in disagreement when it came to black people, or Mexican people, or Vietnamese people, or any of the other groups of strange people who came to Oklawaha County to pick peppers, oranges, cabbage, strawberries, blueberries, watermelons, potatoes, tomatoes, beans, cucumbers, and what-not.

The white people owned it.
The white people ran it.
The white people controlled it.
The white people ruled.
And there was not doubt about it.

Oklawaha County's black leaders were a group of under takers, Baptist preachers, various criminal elements, Episcopalian preachers, bail bondsmen, bar owners, Methodist preachers, Muslim preachers, labor contractors, and dope dealers. It was against this group of riff-raff (since riff-raff applies even to what is respectable) that Eva Horton formed her own pressure group to counter their influence and the indifference of a self-indulgent majority.

Eva Horton was never understood, even though she was born and raised in Oklawaha County. Her father, Herbert Horton, had been a labor contractor who could always be counted on to protect the interest of the big growers. She was divorced from Rev. Leviticus Keats Jr., another good man who could always be counted on, and had one son by him.

Rev. Keats Jr., and Rev. Keats Sr., and Herbert Horton were considered good black leaders. Eva Horton was considered something else. For one thing, she was a woman, but if that weren't enough, she was an extraordinarily beautiful black woman whom every man wanted, but only two had ever had.

When Herbert Horton retired as a labor contractor, he settled down to manage Ira Mim's packinghouse. Eva Horton came to work for her father as a middleman brokering crops, between farmers and the packinghouse. She earned a broker's license and a reputation as a shrewd businesswoman.

When my Aunt Sally graduated college with a degree in business, and before she could run off to parts unknown, Eva Horton convinced her to come to work at the packinghouse, which by then was carrying a huge mortgage and was not generating much business. When Ira Mims died, the two women took over the mortgage rather than close the packinghouse, and began operating on a true business precept. The two became known as "the two bitch-goddesses." But they were bitch-goddesses of success. If you look at Oklawaha County and call it backward, hook, and redneck, they will point to Eva Horton and tell you how progressive they are.

Even the white people were proud of her—until she began dabbling in politics.

It was some very serious dabbling indeed. It started as a pressure group to get what she wanted, to win small concessions for the black people and aggravate her ex-husband at the same time. It grew into the Swagg Party when her group joined Michael Cohen and Julio Sanchez's group and several other disenchanted self-interest groups to elect a new Water Commission. It was called the Swagg party because Eva Horton said in a speech before the Oklawaha Jaycees, "We don't elect them to be men of integrity, we elect them to send home the 'swagg.'" The Swagg Party, as a whole, was little more than a race of politicians come together, politics being nothing more that a means of rising in the world. By nature Eva was a political animal, adept in the arts of bribery, political villainy, and dissimulation. And Oklawaha politics is an exercise in bribery, villainy, and dissimulation by some of the scurviest politicians in the state. Eva Horton rode among them, loved every bit of it, and no one could rein her in.

The most important and powerful governing body in the county, if not the central part of the state, was the Water Commission. The seven-member governing board was occupied by the cheap relatives of some of the most powerful families in the state. They were the power, a monolithic wall of pharisaical power and organized hypocrisy that believed itself to always be impregnably in the right and its opponents indubitably in the wrong. Too many homes in Oklawaha County did not have running water. If you lived in the unincorporated areas, your water came from an underground well—like ours. In some places, this water was filled with sulfur. Whenever the Swaggs or anybody else tried to pressure the Water Commission to extend water and sewage treatment facilities to outlying areas, they were either scoffed at, ignored, or paid off. The Oklawaha County Water Commission was just another name for absolute power.

The first crack in this wall of absolute power occurred the day Cody Wayne and I decided to find out, once and for all, where the sweet, crystal-clear water from Silver Blue Lake flowed, but instead found a field of black glump.

When Eva Horton got hold of this, the Swaggs were in business and wasted no time firing the first shot.

Not too many people in Oklawaha County were happy to learn their county was a shit dump for the state and a slew of out-of-state industries. The Water Commission said no "out-of-state industries" were involved and it was just wastewater sediments that were perfectly safe because samples of each load were tested and treated before it was dumped.

Everyone knew it was the biggest lie ever told, but here was the Water Commission telling people this stuff was safe and that farmers living on the fringes of the swamp even used it as fertilizer! This disclosure allayed some people's fears and even sent them scurrying back there for sludge by the truckloads.

It was a public relations bonanza that set the Water Commission and real estate developers on the high road to defeat the restrictions proposed by the State Department of Community

Affairs limiting development of the Oklawaha Swamp. But then the Swaggs dropped a bombshell. At a public meeting with state officials, county officials, landowners, homeowners, developers, and environmentalists, they presented the lab analyses of the field of iridescent glump. The report said, in effect, that what Oklawaha County had on its hands was a toxic waste dump!

Oklawaha County is the largest county in the state. We are among the biggest producers of fruit, vegetables, cattle, swine, citrus, poultry, phosphate, and lumber in the country. Buyers and brokers for the U.S. Department of Agriculture and big supermarket chains are stationed here year-round. We are a horn of plenty, but much of that plenty was suspected of being fertilized with some awful stuff. And the Department of Agriculture wanted to know—what stuff? The brokers wanted to know—what crops? And the growers who were once on the side of the Water Commission and had boasted about how wonderful the sludge was, were now asking—what sludge?

But farmers aren't fools; if they were, they wouldn't be farmers—they'd be broke. Some of the sludge from the sewage treatment plant did refortify the soil. To grow something like watermelons, you have to replenish the soil, and you can't grow watermelons there again until you do. Repeated use of chemical fertilizers will kill the soil; all you can do is help nature along.

Mr. Timmons planted sod to replenish his soil. He'd learned about the sludge from one of the haulers who'd broken down on the highway. The hauler told him the stuff was good for grass, so Mr. Timmons took a load and had it spread over his lawn. The results were astonishing. When time came to turn the ground to plant, he sent samples of the sludge in to be tested along with his soil samples. The results showed the sludge to be a mixture of enriched minerals, sediment, and plain old shit.

This was the shit that enabled Mr. Timmons to grow melon crop after melon crop and made him look like a genius.

But who knows what kind of shit people flush down their toilets. If this were all it were, there would not have been any scandal. But waste companies were subcontracting other waste companies from out of state. The sin of all this was that the Water Commission didn't care. They were being paid not to.

Since the sludge he was using was not toxic, Mr. Timmons continued to use it and continued to produce the biggest, sweetest, juiciest, crispiest watermelons in the world. And that's why we loved to raid his fields.

Mr. Timmons was a licensed broker and was therefore able to sell exclusively. When the scandal hit, he swore on his mama's grave that he'd never used the sludge as fertilizer.

But we knew better.

"His watermelons poison!" Rudy said as we came off the railroad tracks and into the woods that led to the backside of Mr. Timmons's field.

"Awwww," I said in defense of watermelons, "he don't use that stuff no more—nobody do."

"How do you know?" Cody Wayne asked me.

"'Cause I know!" I snapped.

"We don't know if he got watermelons!" said Bumpsy.

"I hope so," I said. "I want me a watermelon."

We were pirates on the high seas, bored with inactivity and itching for loot and plunder; we were itching for something to raid. What we had in mind was mangoes. What we were willing to settle for was watermelons. What we did not expect was sorghum, which is what we found in the field where watermelons used to be.

"Shoot!" I cried.

"Corn!" Bumpsy spat.

"That ain't corn," Rudy sneered.

Bumpsy was from Miami; what did he know about sorghum?

"It's sorghum," said Cody Wayne. "It's good if you's a cow."

"We came all this way for nuthin'!" Rudy cried.

"Ahm goin' home!" I cried. "The front way!"

"Somebody might see us," Cody Wayne said.

"So!" I shot back. "We ain't done nuthin'!"

"Let's cut across," Rudy suggested.

"Sumthin' might be in there," Bumpsy warned.

"So!" I shot back. "Ahm ready to go home—let's cut across."

Cody Wayne led the way through what we thought was a field of sorghum, but thirty feet later we stopped abruptly, dumbfounded and mute with wonder. Cleverly camouflaged by the outer rows of sorghum, was the forty-acre field of watermelons we'd raided so many times before. We couldn't figure out whether he was hiding them from field inspectors or us. A person with a one- or two-acre home garden does that, but a big grower like Mr. Timmons hired guards. So the only reason for hiding the field was to hide the fact that he was still using the sludge.

Right away we began snatching watermelons from the vines and smashing them. And when we'd get through with one, we'd go to another, snatching, smashing, destroying, and feasting! Melon after melon, we feasted on those sumptuous centers. We ate nothing but the hearts. In the silence and in the laughter we gorged ourselves like wolves, slurped our pot of honey, swilled up the fat of the land, and could not eat them fast enough. Melons ain't mangoes, but the success of the raid made it a feast of pleasure, a feast of fun, and a feast of pure satisfaction.

"Don't none a' you heathens move!"

When they call you a heathen, it means they don't consider

you human enough to deserve mercy. If it's done in that mean, murderous twang of the Florida Cracker, it means you are not going to get any. And if they're carrying a shotgun, it means you'd better run for cover.

"Halt!" Mr. Timmons screamed as the four of us took off. "Come back heah!"

The blast of the shotgun made me strain to hold my bladder. He fired again. Rudy was the only one with enough sense to hit the ground and stay there. The rest of us ran for the sorghum. So did he. As we burst from the other side, the shotgun blasted again and Cody Wayne screamed in pain but did not fall. The three of us fled back for the watermelon field, but as soon as Bumpsy burst out the other side, the shotgun boomed again.

"Ahhhh!" Bumpsy screamed. "Ahm shot! Ahm shot! Ahm shot!"

"Stay there!" Mr. Timmons cried. "Stay there or I'll let you have it again!"

Bumpsy curled up on the ground screaming, "Ahm shot! Ahm shot! Ahm shot!"

"Y'all come on outta there!" Mr. Timmons hollered to me and Cody Wayne. "Come on out or Ahm comin' in."

"You shot?" I asked Cody Wayne as we cowered in the sorghum.

"Yeah," he whispered back. "He shootin' salt."

He turned his side to me and I saw the blast of white powder, welted and crusted with sweat.

"It hurt?" I asked.

"Feel like a buncha bees stung me," he answered.

"What we gon' do? I don't wanna git shot."

"Run."

That made sense. Rock salt is what they use for chicken-hawks, chicken thieves, and raiders of watermelon fields. It disintegrates into a fine powder on explosion—at least most of it—and doesn't do a lot of damage unless you're a chicken-hawk or they let you have it point blank in the face.

"Ahm shot! Ahm shot! Ahm shot!" Bumpsy wailed.

"Just settle down and be quiet," Mr. Timmons said. "C'meah, Rudy. If I'd a' knowed it was y'all, I won't a' done all that shootin'—who he anyway?"

"He my cousin Bumpsy from Miami," Rudy answered.

"Well, he oughtta know betta."

"I only ate one," Bumpsy whined.

"Was it yourn?"

That settled it.

"I lost six hundred dollars wurf of melons and I been waitin' t' catch the rats been doin' it. Y'all know betta."

We know better than to get caught.

"Ahm shot!" Bumpsy wailed for sympathy.

"Yeah, well that ain't nuthin' like what Miss Gert gon' put on ya ass!" he said.

Me and Cody Wayne looked at each other.

"I know it ain't nobody but Cody Wayne and Johnny in there," Mr. Timmons said. "Call 'em out so's I can take y'all home."

"Johneeee!" Rudy called. "Cody Wayne! We fixin' t' go!"

Cody Wayne and I knew the best thing for us to do was to go too, beat them there, and tell our story first. We had to, because he would be so full of lies that by the time we got there, our side of the story would never be heard. We crawled down the rows and came out running for home, excited beyond all thought and reason. We believed in our cause, and questions like "What y'all doin' over there in the first place?" were of little consequence and reasoned away. The main thing was he shot us, and for nothing!

And he shot Cody Wayne!

And he shot Bumpsy!

And he beat Rudy!

And he called us a bunch of watermelon-thieving niggers!

Manasha was shocked!

Aunt Clara was flabbergasted!

Daddy Troy was incensed!

"Ahm goin' t' go git my shotgun!" he declared, "and go blow his head off."

"And Ahm goin' wit ya," Unck said.

"Y'all c'mon in the house," Manasha called us.

"And rest ya nerves," Aunt Clara said.

"Have a cold soda," Manasha added.

She was leading me by the hand, stroking the back of my head, cooing, "You're a good boy. You're a good boy. You're a good boy."

"Not good enough to suit me!" declared Grandma Gert. "Bring yo ass here!"

She leaped up from behind the door where she'd been hiding just as Manasha threw me in a headlock! Aunt Clara grabbed Cody Wayne but he slipped away and ran right into Daddy Troy. The day we got too big for Grandma Gert would be the day the men took charge. Daddy Troy just looked at Cody Wayne, and he began to whimper.

Grandma Gert held me straight out by the front of my shirt. I tried to get slick and wiggle out of the shirt, but that was exactly what she wanted me to do.

"Wiggle out them pants too!" she said catching me by the arm.

She held me straight up like a plucked chicken. The time for talk was over. There was no explaining. No reasons. No last-minute stay of execution. Only consequences. Mr. Timmons had come and gone. And so had "Cracka Bill" Johnson. Rudy and Bumpsy had already gotten theirs and were upstairs moping. A fiendish joy illuminated her colder-than-a-snake's eyes as she held me at arm's length and delivered some serious consequences with Daddy Troy's strap.

"Grammaaaa! Grammaaaa!" I cried.

"Don't! Gram! Ma! Me!" she gasped, punctuating each word and syllable with a lick.

"Pleeeease! Pleeeease! Pleeeease!"

"Don't! Please! Me! Eith! Er!"

"OK! OK! OK!"

"Don't! O! K! Me! Nei! Ther!"

"Manasha! Manasha! Manasha!"

"Don't! Call! Man! Na! Sha! Eith! Er!"

"Didn't call me when you was out gallivanting!" Manasha said. "Or doin' yo thang 'round Ruby Lee!"

"Unck! Help me! Help me!"

But Unck just watched, stoically amused.

"Oh Jesus! Oh Jesus! Oh Jesus!"

"Don't! Call! Jee! Sus! Eith! Er!"

"He ain't gon' help no way," Unck said.

"Oh God! Oh God! Oh God!"

Because, if God is for you, then who can be against you?

"Grrandmaaaa!"

"You! Gon! Be! Good?"

"Ahma be good! Ahma be good! Ahma be good!"

"You! Gon! Steal?"

"I ain't gon' steal! I ain't gon' steal! I ain't gon' steal!"

"You! Gon! Lie?"

"I ain't gon' lie! I ain't gon' lie! I ain't gon' lie!"

"You! Gon! Be! Good?"

"I swear! I swear! I swear!"

"Don't! Do! No! Swearin! Eith! Er!"

"I won't! I won't! I won't! I swear!"

"Then! Take! Yo! Bad! Be! Hind! Up! Stairs!"

And she didn't have to tell me twice. I flew up the stairs three at a time with Cody Wayne's violent sobs of, "Oh Jesus! Oh Jesus! Oh Jesus!" ringing in my ears.

In times of regret we sometimes recognize the fact that some of our judgments are just plain dumb. That, I imagine, is the purpose of punishment.

Oh the heartache of the dumb! If nothing else, we were not going to mess with any more of anybody's watermelons. Or mangoes. The four of us sat out on the porch roof full of grief and impotent rage. Outcast from God, we were condemned to spend our eternal days in woe and sorrow. And horseshit and hay and watermelons, because six hundred dollars, is six hundred dollars, and since the four of us didn't have six hundred dollars, we were indentured to work it off over a period of thirty days.

Resignation to inevitable evils is the sad fate of us. Unable to have our own way, and unwilling to take advice, and believing sin can blot out sorrow, we suffer the pain of an unwritten code that governs the generations: swift joys and late sorrows: something that really makes you want to be a good boy.

Cleveland?

He thought he was going to sit his big, fat, three-hundred-and-fifty-pound ass in the truck, kick back, swill beer, smoke dope, and just ride. But he had another thought coming.

"You's a big fat lazy piece a' garbage!" Mr. Timmons screamed at his son who struggled to load another seventy-pound bale of hay onto the flatbed.

And this was a man who bench-pressed five hundred pounds!

"Oh shit!" he gasped.

I wiped the sweat from my forehead, looked up at him, and saw his eyes roll back in his head.

"Oh shit!" he gasped again.

He swayed forward, then backward, and continued on down.

"Git 'im!" Mr. Timmons cried.

Git 'im? The big fat mutherfucker weighed three hundred and fifty pounds! What did he mean *Git 'im?* We were too busy trying to git out of the way! He crashed like a giant piece of timber and just lay there. Mr. Timmons stopped the truck and jumped out. The baler kept baling.

"Git 'is head up!" Mr. Timmons told me as he ran back to the truck for water.

I held his head while Cody Wayne fanned him.

"Ahm all right," he gasped, trying to sit up, "Ahm all right, Daddy."

Never in my life have I seen a human head that huge; it resembled a big basketball with hair. It was almost comical the way I struggled to hold it up.

"Christ, boy!" Mr. Timmons cried as he poured water over his head, "you gotta lose weight!"

His life depended on it; the coaches told him so.

He was a rookie defensive lineman for the Miami Dolphins, who'd had less than a spectacular year. He'd reported to camp weighing three hundred and fifty pounds and ended the season weighing three hundred and sixty pounds. Still, he might have been a candidate for rookie of the year if he could have played at least one whole game. But he would come in for two plays, go out and rest for three.

We called him Big Whoosh! His teammates called him Big Tush. His coaches called him something else and pleaded with Mr. Timmons to keep after his son about his weight.

"Ain't nuthin' wrong," said Mr. Timmons, taking a sip of water. "He just sorry as hell."

"Ahm all right," Big Whoosh said, sitting up in a daze.

He sat gazing about as if he were trying to figure out why in the world was he sitting in a field of hay. Mr. Timmons looked at him and sighed.

Some days he would come and get us and some days he wouldn't bother. We owed him six more days, and so far it had all been bliss. It was the height of watermelon season, and watermelon season everywhere is bliss. Everybody makes money. Not everybody as in everybody who grew them, but everybody as in everybody who picked them, packed them, sold and stacked them.

As in everybody who hauled them. As in everybody who had not just a room for rent for pickers, but just a little *floor* space for someone to lie down for the night. Everybody as in everybody who sold ice and food and drinks and dreams and hope and dope and pussy. Watermelon season means money; it is one big Friday night.

Watermelons are America's number-one cash crop because it translates into instant cash on the spot. At twenty to forty cents a pound, you pull in, load up, and pull out. The loading crews are waiting. More often, the buyers are waiting to be loaded up. You can make more than a hundred dollars a day loading watermelons, and that ain't hay.

Since Mr. Timmons had a broker's license, he was also his own middleman, and therefore had contracts with the big buyers. But the big sludge scandal changed everything, at least for a while. Everybody was waiting to see if people began dropping dead from eating Oklawaha watermelons. In the meantime, the brokers weren't buying, hoping to drive the price down, and the growers were storing their melons in refrigerated warehouses all over the state as the price of watermelons steadily rose.

Mr. Timmons had stored most of his melons and was now serving the small buyers, people who pulled up in pickup trucks and bought one hundred to one thousand watermelons. These little buyers are funny. They are always thinking they could save the price of labor by doing their own picking and loading. But the sun changes their minds. The sun, the sweat, the chiggers, the cow ants, the fire ants, the snakes, and whatever else is lurking down there among the vines. With these people, it is never very long before Rudy is up on the truck stacking, Bumpsy is catching, and me and Cody Wayne throwing them up.

You can make a lot of money in the first few weeks of

summer. That is, if you're getting paid instead of working off a debt like we were. But it ain't all gravy, baby. Watermelons will wear your ass out! And some days Big Whoosh would come and nobody would wake up, much less get out of bed. And other mornings we'd look at each other and say, "Fuck him and his daddy!"

Now hay is something else. We first thought we were getting a break from watermelons when Mr. Timmons brought in the hay baler. He had a ninety-acre field of hay. A bale may weigh twice as much as a melon, and you itch like hell, sweat like hell, and cuss like hell. But the baler keeps baling because it is rented and it can bale until doomsday.

"I'll bring the truck around," Mr. Timmons said as Big Whoosh gained his bearing, "y'all unload it, and spread it, then we'll call it quits."

We'd started at five A.M., while it was cool. It was now eleven o'clock, the sun was a killer, and all five of us were worn out.

As soon as Mr. Timmons backed the truck into the hay barn and left, we all lay down in the hay stall on a nice big bed of hay and listened as Big Whoosh swilled beer and entertained us with wild stories about the nightlife and prowess of rookie defensive ends in the NFL.

"Goddammitt!" Mr. Timmons raged, after sneaking up on us. "I need this truck unloaded so's I kin use it!"

The rest of us jumped up and began tussling with bales of hay, but Big Whoosh just lay there and swilled beer.

"Goddernit!" Mr. Timmons screeched. "It's three weeks till trainin' camp and you need t' work off fifty more pounds!"

"I'm down to three-o-six," Big Whoosh declared, "the best football shape I ever been in! And besides, I done enough for t'day."

"Three-o-six my foot! They's gonna run you offa that team!"

"Then I'll go to Cleveland."

"Cleveland?"

"Too hot down here."

"Cleveland—you ain't wurf a shit!"

They were arguing back and forth as we unloaded the hay. We paid them no mind. Rudy was atop the truck, kicking off the bales. The rest of us popped the bales and forked them into the stalls.

We grew hay ourselves—that is another cash crop—but we baled ours and stored the bales in the silos. That is the purpose of the silos and the only reason why they're still standing, and the reason why we call them "Silo City."

We store our hay until the winter months when demand in the northern states is high, so we never bother with unbaling it. We stack it in the silos and ship it out in bales.

Thus, we never have to worry about snakes. Mr. Timmons said something about running the pitchforks through the bales to kill any snake that may have been fortunate enough to have survived the blades of the baler. That, to us, seemed a very unlikely possibility. We'd loaded thousands of watermelons, and snakes, especially rattlers, love to nest down among the vines. But we encountered not one snake in the melons and hardly expected to see any in a bale of hay that had gone through a baler.

Bumpsy popped the string on a bale and Cody Wayne punched his pitchfork into it and watched it collapse in sections. Just as he moved to pitch it up, I saw something that looked to be a very peculiar piece of straw. Then it moved.

"Oh shit!" Bumpsy screamed.

"Look out! It's a snake!" Cody Wayne yelled.

"Yaaaa!"

"Yaaaa!"

"Yaaaa!"

Free at last, it bounded up, coiled, and looked desperately about. It was an Eastern diamondback rattler—the most dangerous snake in Florida! It was at least eight feet long and sounded a dire warning that said, "Look out! I am dangerous!"

And we believed him, too!

Everybody scattered! Rudy ran up the hay, over the cab, and out the door. Bumpsy ran out the side door. Mr. Timmons ran up the ladder into the loft. Me and Cody Wayne climbed up on a stall. And Big Whoosh struggled just to get his big fat self up off the ground. He'd lost sight of the snake, but he could still hear it. We all could. It rattled furiously as if it'd had a massive dose of speed. It did not go anywhere but swayed about as if looking for something to strike. Big Whoosh made it to his feet, saw the snake, and gasped, "Goooodamn!"

He made a quick effort to climb up to where we were, but the stall was not made to hold five hundred pounds and collapsed, and the three of us crashed to the ground, with me and Cody Wayne trapped beneath him and that deadly rattle ringing in our ears!

The mistake the Miami Dolphins made with Big Whoosh was that he was not a defensive lineman at all, but three hundred pounds of personal escort! From a semi-crouch he lowered his head and shoulder and crashed through the stall slats! Like a big pulling guard busting through the line flattening linebackers and defensive backs, he busted through the second stall and the third stall and finally he hit the barn wall, knocking loose two planks. He backed up, screamed like a wild banshee, and ran crashing into the wall again, knocking out three planks and crash-landing outside. And just like a couple of swift scatbacks we scurried through the hole for daylight.

"Shit!" he gasped. "That's one big mutha-fucka!"

"Ain't as big as you!" Mr. Timmons hollered, leaning out the owl hole. "I bet you got your ass up then!" He laughed hysterically. "Damn, boy," he yelled, "ya looked like Reggie White! You musta lost ten pounds gittin' outta there!"

Big Whoosh dropped the potato rake he wielded and started walking away.

"Hey fat boy!" Mr. Timmons laughed, "C'mon back. Do it again and lose ten mo'! Hey, where ya goin'?"

"Cleveland!" Big Whoosh hollered back.

"Cleveland?"

"Cleveland! I'm goin' to Cleveland—ain't no snakes in Cleveland!"

"Ain't no team in Cleveland either!"

"Ahm goin' too," Cody Wayne said.

"Me too," I said.

"Me three," Bumpsy said.

"C'mon back!" he yelled. "Ain't nuthin' but a lil' old snake!"

"Them's the worse kind," Rudy said.

And the four of us followed Big Whoosh to Cleveland, far away from the barn, the snake, and the derisive laughter of his father.

The Greedy Bastard

I know the difference between cows and bulls, stallions and mares, boars and sows, hens and roosters, and men and women. But my cousin Bumpsy is not so sure. If Miss Mable told me to feed the cows first, that is exactly what I would have done, and she would not have had to tell me why. All of us have a big understanding of the what and why of all the things around us. All of us except Bumpsy. To him, a cow is a cow; doesn't matter if it's got a dick—it's still a cow to him. Bumpsy was from Miami; what did he know about cows? If Miss Margarite had told him to go feed the cows, she probably would have explained it to him. But Miss Mable, thinking that he had sense about such things, told him to feed the cows first, and Bumpsy thought she meant cows as opposed to horses.

Even Rudy knew to feed the cows first. Why? Because the males of any species are pigs, and if you feed the bull first, he'll eat all his like the greedy pig he is, then run the cows and heifers off and eat theirs, too.

I like cows. We don't have any, but we do have a few goats and pigs and geese and chickens. We raise fish. That is our primary business, and fish are not as easy to get attached to as cows.

Miss Mable was Cracka Bill's sister, and I liked her cows. Miss Margarite was his wife, and I liked her horses. If you ask my opinion, women do a better job with animals than men do. You have to know how to *be* around animals. They're not as stupid as you think; they sense whether or not you care, and I didn't care for that stupid bull at all.

But to Bumpsy, they were all a bunch of dumb cows; he didn't know that, by feeding the cows first, the bull would eat a little of theirs, then leave them alone when he saw you filling his trough.

He was an aggravating old thing. As soon as me and Cody Wayne came into the shed, all the cows and heifers crowded around us bleating and bellowing. They'd lost their supper.

"I thought you fed 'em," I said to Bumpsy.

Feeding them was the last thing we had to do before going home.

"I did!" Bumpsy cried.

I looked at Cody Wayne and we knew what had happened. All the cows were standing in a pitiful little group expecting us to right a terrible wrong. We looked into the feed stall and there he was, eating his belly full. It made me mad.

"You greedy bastid!" I screamed.

The bull ignored us.

"I'll fix you!" Cody Wayne screamed.

He picked up a two-by-four and, with all his might, whacked it across the bull's rump! The bull let out a loud and protracted wail of pain and rage that reverberated throughout the shed. It frightened the cows so bad they all took off! He leaped straight up into the air, a mad and savage beast, bucking and kicking with such ferocity that even though he missed us, the two of us sailed backward from the sheer force of the effort! With an upward thrust of his powerful head, he sent the feed trough high into the air, then he turned, saw me, and charged in a wild and desperate fury. Quickly I scurried beneath the iron railings to temporary safety. He looked at Cody Wayne, lowered his head, and charged him too!

"Over here! Over here!" Bumpsy waved and called.

He was holding open the shed doors, urging us to escape. Me and Cody Wayne shot out the shed, closed the doors, and tried to hold it shut. Bumpsy was trying to latch it when it suddenly slammed into our faces, knocking all three of us down in the dirt! The brute beast burst out looking for us, but failed to notice us cowering behind the doors. He started after the cows who'd taken off for the rear of the shed. Near the corner of the building he saw us out the corner of his eye, turned, and charged. The three of us hustled ourselves back inside the shed and pulled the doors shut. The bull still crashed into it but we held on to it to keep it from flying open. He rammed into it repeatedly; all we could do was hold it shut and pray for Miss Mable to come and get her stupid bull.

I hate bulls. But bulls are forever. I don't think we should eat cows, but we should eat bulls, like Miss Mable's stupid bull, that kept crashing into the doors, over and over and over again.

Sweet Georgia Brown

"Johnny?" Miss Margarite called me softly.

"Huuuuh?" I answered.

"Did you brush the mare?"

"Uh-huh—all of em."

"No, I mean the Trenton mare?"

"Uh-huh—her too."

"Oh," she whispered softly, and I, too, realized what I'd done.

The Trenton mare. They'd had her for only a month and she'd turned out to be an unexpected problem for Mr. Bill, me, and the rest of our gender. She hated men. I don't mean disliked men, or had an aversion for men. I mean HATE! A deep-seated violent hatred! A murderous hatred that did not suffer me or any man near her.

"She didn't act up?" Miss Margarite asked.

"No," I answered. "She tried to bite some sugar outta my pocket, but she acted all right."

"Hmmmm. Maybe that's all she needed—to get away from Trenton."

Maybe.

"OK," she said, "and you might be what's needed to help her. But let me feed and groom her from now on—OK?"

"OK," I replied.

"She can't help it. She's mostly afraid."

There was no reason to be afraid of me, but I know where she got her fear and her hatred.

The Trenton Horse Farm is located in the northeast part of the county. It is a place for horses and a haven for scoundrels. They train, breed, stable, and auction horses. Thoroughbred and show horses. The majority of these trainers, groomers, and jockeys follow the horse circuit from Florida to Canada. They are a migratory lot, much like farm workers, only worse. They are outlaws—a transient clique of scalawags, assorted vagabonds, rogues, rascals, and miscellaneous miscreants. True rapscallions who plunder the states they travel without prejudice.

We sold them hay and bought their horseshit. Thus, we were pretty much familiar with some of the doings around the stables, the worst of which were dogfights, cockfights, and ratting. None of which we found amusing. Nothing we saw at Trenton was amusing. One day, as me, Cody Wayne, Unck, and Rudy waited for them to unload a trailer of hay, we observed the training that some of these horses receive.

We were lounging on the railing surrounding an exercise track where one particular jockey was having trouble trying to exercise a horse that obviously did not want to be exercised. Each time the would-be rider climbed into the saddle, the horse would sit down on its side and roll over. Unable to get the horse to cooperate, the exasperated jockey consulted another jockey who shrieked, "Oh, he don't wanna work, huh? OK I fix that."

He sauntered over, mounted the horse, spurred it, and drew the reins. The horse stepped forward, sat back, and rolled on its side. He got off and threw a leg across the neck of the horse which restrained and prevented it from rising. Then he proceeded to pummel the animal unmercifully.

"He ain't shit," Unck had remarked.

After making his point, the jockey released the horse and offered the reins to the other jockey.

"OK," he panted. "See if he'll work now."

The first jockey climbed into the saddle and spurred the horse. It trotted off slowly without any trouble at all.

"Anytime he act like he don't wanna work," the little jockey said, "beat the shit outta him!"

This was the Trenton Horse Farm. This is where Miss Margarite's beautiful mare received all her training in hate.

At a glance, you would not think there was anything vindictive in the mare's nature. She reminded me of Linda, chocolate brown with flowing black hair and large intelligent eyes. She had legs like pistons striking the ground in a synchronized four-beat cadence, her body absorbing the shock as she glided along at trot speed in a gait so smooth that Miss Margarite did not even bounce in the saddle.

She was a Paso Fino, whose name means, "fine gait." They are the Rolls-Royce of riding horses. She is a very classy horse, but if a man goes anywhere near her—well, Miss Margarite bought her to keep them from destroying her. She bought the horse believing that by the one word, love, she could get the horse to release all her vengeful and troubling demons, and make everything all right. But I don't know. She'd let me brush her without any sign of resentment, and that was an encouraging sign. But that was also an accident.

I'd forgotten the warning to stay away from her stall. Bumpsy, who was now consciously aware of the difference between bulls and cows and stallions and mares, was showing a certain diffidence, if not obeisance, to any member of the female persuasion. Not only did he feed the cows first, he fed hens, sows, and mares first, too. Thus, he *brushed* the mares first too. Bumpsy was from Miami; what did he know about horses? Especially mares. And mares in heat. When he finally got around to brushing a stallion, it kept bumping and trying to bite him. And that monstrous slong hung so low, it gave Bumpsy the willies. Well, Bumpsy got sick of that stallion soon enough and left the stall in a hurry. The stallion followed him out. He tried to close the door, but the stallion wouldn't let him, nor would he leave Bumpsy alone.

"Lemmee lone! Lemmee lone!" Bumpsy cried and whimpered.

The horse had him jammed against the wall and would not let him escape. It wasn't trying to hurt him, but smell him! It just kept nudging him and making weird whinnying noises.

"He likes you!" Miss Mable laughed and exclaimed.

"Well, I don't like him!" Bumpsy grumbled.

Miss Margarite and I coaxed him back into the stall with a pail of apples and a handful of sugar cubes.

"You smell like pussy," I told him as soon as Miss Margarite was out of earshot.

"You smell like pussy too!" he snapped back. "You smell like dookey! You smell like zoo-dirt! You smell—"

"You smell like that to the horse," Cody Wayne told him.

"What?"

"You brushed the mare first, didn't ya?" I asked.

"She's in heat," Cody Wayne said.

"You're supposed to brush the stallions first!" I said and bopped into the barn to show him how it's done.

Showing off is what I was doing. He was the same age as Cody Wayne, was from Miami, and it was always a pleasure to show him how much he didn't know. I went into the stables and brushed the stallion, cooing to him, petting him, and letting him nibble sugar. In my zeal to show up Bumpsy, I forgot the warning about the mare, climbed over into her stall, and brushed her, too.

It never was Bumpsy's job to groom the horses. He didn't quite know how to be around them—how and where to stand, what signs to watch out for, what not to do around them, and how to minimize the risk of getting kicked, stomped, or bitten. Usually, horses are difficult for me to handle because they are so big. But Miss Margarite's horses are all Paso Finos, smaller than most horses, about thirteen to fifteen hands high, easy to handle and a pleasure to ride. I liked them all, even the Trenton mare, and I believed she liked me too, because of all the men in the world, she'd let me brush her. Not Mr. Bill, not Cody Wayne, not Bumpsy, not Rudy, but me. This solitary feat swelled me with pride. There was indeed something special about me, and I wanted Miss Margarite to know.

I wanted to surprise her. I wanted her to step back in the stalls and see me working with the mare and reinforce her belief in that one word: Love.

The mare saw me climbing into the stall. She knew me; I was her sugar daddy. I was so full of myself I missed all the signs indicative of fear. Her body trembled and she pinned back her ears, like horses do when snakes are close around. It was a sure sign of trouble, an obvious warning, but I thought she was flirting and jumped down into the stall, running my hand along her side. Suddenly she began stamping her forefeet and tried to swing her head, but the narrow stall would not allow her to, so she kept stamping her feet and I knew then to leave her alone. I was starting to climb back up the rails when she suddenly threw her body sideways, pinning me against the stall! I yelled in anguish and tried to squeeze up, but she was pushing her full weight against me. She kept swinging her head, trying to bite me, but there was no room for her to maneuver, so she kept me pinned to the stall, bumping me up against the iron railings in a murderous effort to squash the life out of me! I could barely keep my breath, much less call for help. My head banged up against the rail, and blood gushed out. She was trying to kill me, and only by dropping straight down to the ground could I escape being crushed. She screamed and whinnied like some midnight hag gone berserk, raised her forelegs and crashed them down, scratching them back to spray me with dirt. Unable to kick her back legs, she kicked her forelegs, barely missing my already bloody head. She looked down to see where I was as I inched back out of her vision and away from her hooves.

"Help!" I finally screamed. "Miss Margarite, heeeellllp!"

Miss Margarite came running through the stable doors, calling my name.

"Johnny?"

"Miss Margarite, help me! Help me!"

She saw the mare in a wild and frenzied state of madness, but she didn't see me.

"Johnny! Johnny!"

"Miss Margarite!"

She ran up to the stall and started to open it but stopped.

"Miss Margarite, Ahm down here! Ahm down here!"

The mare was foaming at the mouth! Slamming herself from side to side! Heaving up on all fours and slamming herself down, bucking and kicking in a viperous, frustrated effort to stomp me.

"Miss Margarite!" I screamed. "Ahm here! Ahm here!"

What was she doing? Why wouldn't she open the gate? She'd run into the next stall and I could see her from beneath the horse, but any move by me either way would put me in range of those deadly hooves.

"Ahm here! Ahm here!"

She paid me no mind. Had she gone mad? She was singing! No—humming!

"Miss Marg—"

"Shsssssh!" she shushed, thrusting her hand out, demanding silence. She continued humming.

A soft prolonged humming. Inarticulate in its effort but intense and effective. She hummed some sweet song, purred some soothing words of womankind. She stroked the mare's neck and hummed, soothing her wounded heart, softening the pain, subduing the rage. Her other hand eased down to her side and gestured very subtly. I eased up the other side of the stall, climbing easy, climbing up, climbing out, and running out the door without looking back.

If she had opened the stall door, the mare would have had enough room to get me under her hooves. Instead, Margarite chose to quiet her spirit. She hummed the mare to the quiet of her bosom. She understood the depth of the mare's hatred and the kind of love it takes to calm such hopeless passion. The Trenton mare, in my opinion, was a raging beast that should have been destroyed.

Mr. Bill took care of my head as I related the harrowing experience to him. He understood and was very sympathetic. He said his first wife had tried to stomp him to death, too.

Only Miss Margarite understood. She came in to see how I was, then she left and went back to the mare. After a while, I followed her down.

"She ain't mean," Miss Margarite said. "At least she don't mean to be."

She was standing at the rail when I'd come up, feeding the

mare sugar cubes from her hand. The horse had seen me coming, snorted and trotted away.

"She's just dispirited," Miss Margarite said. "She's like a lovely creature stuck in a desolate mask. I bought her to keep them from destroying her, but she's been so dispirited I can't even name her."

She looked down at me and rubbed the bump on my head.

"You all right?" she asked.

"Uh-huh," I answered. "It's just a bump."

She came through the rail and placed her arm around me.

"I thought she was starting to heal when she let you brush her," she said, then sighed and looked at the horse sadly.

I'd thought so too, but evidently she'd only wanted sugar. She'd seen me giving it to the stallion.

"I was humming," I said.

"Humming?" she asked, smiling. "Humming what?"

Humming what I'd been humming all weekend, ever since Aunt Clara and Nasty Brown had taken us to see the Harlem Globetrotters in Orlando.

"Sweet Georgia Brown," I said.

For a while we watched the mare moving lazily around the corral with her head down, trapped and troubled in a lonely world of hatred.

"What would you name her?" Miss Margarite asked me. "What would you call a troubled spirit?"

I thought and felt of what she was asking me. A wounded spirit we thought love could heal. Sweet love, which saddens and soothes and heals. What I was thinking could not easily or wisely be said, but thoughts are free and easy, and words are images of thought. I gazed at the horse trotting around the field in an exquisite and proper four-beat cadence. In her heart, Miss Margarite knew she had a champion, but would never enter the horse in any of the shows or competitions. She was too unpredictable. And she didn't have a name.

"Sweet Georgia Brown," I responded, still gazing at the mare.

"Georgia Brown?" she asked with a laugh.

"No," I said, "*Sweet* Georgia Brown."

And she looked at her horse, her gorgeous Rolls-Royce of a horse, and mouthed the name to herself.

What Nasty Brown Did to the Mailman

What Joe Head did to Bolita Sam was not a bad as what Nasty Brown did to the mailman—not that the mailman didn't deserve it. He started it. And it's not that we disliked him. He was the mailman, and everybody likes the mailman, especially dogs.

Why dogs follow mailmen has to be a public wonder. Perhaps it is the routine, the regularity with which they appear every day. Or maybe it is the color of their trucks. Whatever it is, you can be sure that whenever the mailman appears each day, a posse of dogs will be following.

We had every reason in the world to like the mailman. The biggest reason was he threw away some good stuff. We found this out one day while scavenging through an illegal dump near Goodbread Alley. Scavenging is our business, but what business does a mailman have at an illegal dump site? At first we thought he might have a girl in the truck or maybe he was there to meet one, but except for all the stray dogs that followed him there, he was alone, and all we saw him do was eat a sandwich.

Our dogs were with us—Blackie, Shack, Lance, and Ike—crouching down as if we were on a hunt. Our dogs are masters of the hunt and know to be quiet when quiet is called for. All we'd wanted to do was spy on the mailman, not get into a fight with the fourteen stray dogs that had come with him. Fourteen against four is an uneven fight, and we tried to remain hidden to avoid one, but the strays were out scavenging also, and one of them saw Rudy.

He was hiding behind an old icebox in front of us and to our right. Shack was with him. He ducked, but the stray had seen him and sounded the alarm. A group of seven or eight charged, and immediately our dogs sprang into action! Four against fourteen is not a good fight—not good for them! They were all a bunch of shiteaters that bit off more than they could chew. Our dogs hunted predators! And the only thing they feared in this world was Grandma Gert. A big ferocious shepherd met Shack head on and a battle exploded with unrestrained fury; it did not take Shack long to kill it.

During the whole raging battle, the mailman smoked a cigarette and enjoyed himself and the wanton brutality with a barbarous pleasure unworthy of human beings. When our four dogs put those fourteen—minus one—to flight, he snuffed out his cigarette and drove away.

Although we were proud of our dogs, we regretted the fight. But not what happened to the shepherd. He'd asked for it. For all we knew, it may have been the same group of strays that had attacked and mauled a little girl and killed her little schnauzer. The little dog was in heat at the time and had unwittingly attracted trouble. When the little girl tried to protect her pet, the strays attacked her viciously. We felt no sympathy for the stray—bunk him! He'd been after Rudy.

Flushed with excitement and victory, we were leaving the dump when we ran across a pile of what appeared to be mail right where the mail truck had been. It was mail! We were flabbergasted! Here was a big pile of U.S. mail! What a find!

What we thought was a fortune turned out to be a crazy-quilt pile of confetti addressed to: Dear Occupant.

And: You May Already Be a Winner!

And: If You're Eighty Years or Older—etc., etc., etc., and all that kind of crock.

No wonder he threw it away. But even junk mail is U.S. mail and is supposed to be delivered. What kind of shit was this?

You would think that a mailman's job is as sweet as it gets. Who didn't think of being a mailman when he was little?

Not me!

Mailmen work their asses off! Oh, it's easy in places like Boggy and Eloise and Railroad Shoppe, where mailboxes are at the edge of the road, but in places like Goodbread Alley, Porters Quarters, and Augustine Quarters, the mailboxes are attached to the houses. This means the mailman has to stop at the end of the street, load up his mailbag, and hump it all the way up one side of the street, then back down the other side, then on to the next street and start all over again. What's glamorous about a job like that? And throw in three hundreds pounds of bullshit like "You may already be a winner," and sweet job becomes hernia city!

We knew there had to be something good in all this, so we kept looking until finally, underneath it all, we found something that at first glance appeared to be good.

What we found was twenty-two cases of soap samples. It appeared to be good because it was some really rank-smelling soap, but they were individually packaged in pretty little yellow boxes that made whatever was inside easily worth twenty-five cents. Or a least a dime.

We lugged three of these cases down to Goodbread Alley, straight to the nearest 7-Eleven store, and set up shop, pitching great sales lines like, "Hey, wanna buy some soap?"

Starting at a quarter a bar, we quickly marked down to

fifteen cents. Then ten cents. Then a nickel. And finally we were down to a penny a bar. An hour later, and down to two for a penny, we attracted one customer who held it up, looked at it, and said, "This shit's suppose to be free."

"Free my ass!" Cody Wayne said.

"Ain't shit free!" Rudy said.

"Well," said the man, "it says so right here on the box."

He pointed out the words "Free Sample."

"That's the name of the manufacturer!" said Cody Wayne.

"Manufacturer hell!" the man said as he slipped the bar soap in his pocket and started to walk away.

"Hey!" Rudy yelled.

Ike growled and Cody Wayne grabbed him.

"Give it back!" I demanded.

Rudy held Shack. Blackie and Lance were standing at alert. The man looked at the dogs and knew they were not ordinary yard dogs and really had no business where they were. Shack's mouth was still encrusted with the blood of the shepherd.

"Here!" he said, grinning a shit-eating grin and shoving the bar of soap back at me. "Go take a bath!"

"Go fuck a duck!" Cody Wayne cussed.

A minute after he disappeared inside the store, the manager came rushing out.

"What the hell's goin' on?" he demanded.

We'd seen him coming and began shouting stay commands at the dogs and gathering up our boxes.

"We ain't doin' nuthin'," Rudy said, hefting up his box.

"Well, go and do it somewhere else!" the manger retorted. "This is private property. Git outta here!"

Luckily we were holding the dogs, but he looked at them and realized we would have to let them go in order for us to pick up the boxes. This completely unnerved him and he turned quickly and hurried back inside.

What we thought was a bonanza was turning out to be just what mailmen all over town were saying it was: a pain in the ass!

"This shit ain't nuthin'!" I grumbled as we started up Fourteenth Street, trying to look as inconspicuous as three boys lugging three boxes followed by four ferocious dogs could look.

"Can't even give it away!" Cody Wayne grumbled.

"I ain't luggin' this shit all over town either!" Rudy grumbled.

He threw his box in the bushes just as the yellow Cadillac zipped passed and beeped twice. It was Joe Head, and Peggy Mann was in the car. Rudy ran back and got his box.

"What y'all doin' way over here?" he asked, peering over her.

"Tryin' t' make some money!" we replied in unison.

"Well I'm all for that. Git in!"

"Un-unh!" Peggy protested to him. "Don't let them in here wit all them damn dogs!"

She refused to open the door, so Joe Head opened his side, and all of us, with all our boxes and all our dogs, piled into Joe Head's canary yellow Lincoln Cadillac over the strenuous objections of the vivacious Peggy Mann.

Joe Head didn't ask, and we had sense enough not to offer information or talk our business in front of people outside our family circle. Joe Head was not kin, but he was just as close.

"What's in all them boxes?" Peggy asked. "What y'all done stole?"

"We ain't stole nuthin'!" Rudy spat.

"We don't steal!" I put in.

"Hah!" She laughed and asked Joe Head, "Ain't these Lijo boys!"

"That one is," he said, nodding at Cody Wayne.

"We his nephews," Rudy and I sang, happy to be identified with Unck.

"All y'all ain't nuthin' but a buncha rogues!" she sneered. "Just like him."

"Yo mammy a rogue!" I snapped, and Joe Head laughed.

We knew more about Peggy than she suspected.

"Which one you?" she asked me.

Not understanding, I looked at Cody Wayne. He shrugged.

"Melvin," Joe Head said.

"Ain't he in jail somewhere?" she asked.

No one answered.

"Hmp!" she snorted and glanced back at me. "Just like 'is old dope-sellin' daddy."

Snide remarks about my father stung.

"Where you takin' them?" she asked Joe Head.

"Y'all wanna wash my car?" he asked us.

"Yeeeeaaaah!" we cried.

"We goin' t' yo house," her told her, "and wash my car."

"Shhhheeeeit!" she cried.

She lived in Boggy on Laramie Street.

We parked in front of her house and she got out.

"Pheeeew!" she gasped. "Y'all need to do somethin' wit them dogs—wash them too!"

She started to say something to Joe Head, but glanced at us and paused. She went around to his side of the car and whispered in his ear. Me and Cody Wayne struggled for the front seat with both of us falling over and landing upside down. Peggy Mann stuck her tongue in Joe Head's ear and laughed.

"OK?" she asked.

"I'll think about it," he said.

"Well, don't bust ya brains!"

"I might."

She sucked her teeth, rolled her eyes, and walked away.

"Bye!" I shouted after her.

She stuck out her tongue and went inside.

"What's in them boxes?" he asked as he started the car.

"Soap!" we all said.

"Soap? What kinda soap? Lemme see."

We showed him a box.

"Where y'all git all this?" he asked.

"We found it," I answered.

He looked at me hard.

Joe Head is as close as family and has as much authority as any relative. That is why he stopped in the first place and why he wouldn't think twice about our dogs in his Cadillac. If any one of us turns out to be a thief or lowlife, it would be of our own undoing to some twisted turn of fate and not because of how they'd raised us.

"We found it," said Cody Wayne in earnest.

And he believed us, because watermelons and mangoes were just devilment. We weren't little thieves, but we were little devils.

"Found it where?" he asked.

And we told him. And about the mailman. And about the dogs. Rudy described Shack's victory over the big shepherd in graphic detail.

"Hey Shack!" Joe Head cheered.

"Jumbo! Jumbo! Jumbo!" we cheered.

And the dogs let loose an explosion of howls.

We drove back to the dumpsite, finding it just as we'd left it. Joe Head opened his car trunk and ordered us to load the other nineteen cases of soap. He rummaged through the piles of discarded mail, selecting various bits and pieces and studying them with great interest. He put a stack in his glove compartment and along with the dogs walked over and viewed the dead shepherd. He came back and we all got into the car.

"Damn," he said, starting the engine, "y'all always finding things."

"That's 'cause we look!" I said.

"Well, I want y'all t' find somethin' for me."

"What?" Rudy asked.

"A snake," he said.

"Oh, that's easy," I said.

"A big snake!" he said.

"We got boo-coo snakes," Cody Wayne said.

"What kind of snake?" Rudy asked.

"A big black snake!" he said.

"A coachwhip?"

"A indigo?'

"A moccasin?"

"Nothin' poison," he said. "Just a big black one."

"When you want it?" I asked.

"Git it and save it for me," he said. "I'll tell ya when I want it."

"What you want it for?" Rudy asked.

"Now you're worrying about the wrong thing," he answered. "I'll tell ya when the time comes."

We pulled out onto the highway and Joe Head said, "I gotta talk to that mailman. Mutha-fucka s'pose to be deliverin' the mail and he's throwin' the shit away! Although I can hardly blame him. I wouldn't tote all that shit around for nuthin' in the world."

"But he's the mailman!" I said.

"That's right!" Cody Wayne said.

"He might be throwin' away my mail!" Rudy said.

"Shoot!" said Joe Head. "I coulda had me a bar of soap!"

"How much y' gon' pay us?" Rudy asked.

"Pay y'all?" he cried.

"Yeah, pay us!" we cried.

"Pay y'all for what?"

"Pay us for our soap."

"Yo soap? This U.S. mail soap!"

"It's our soap—we found it!" I yelled.

"I went and got it!" he bargained.

"We told you about it!" we countered.

"What Ahma do wit all this soap?" he implored.

"Same thang you gon' do wit dat snake," Rudy remarked slyly.

"There you go again," Joe Head sighed, "worrying 'bout the wrong thang—keep quiet 'bout dat!"

"OK."

"OK."

"OK."

"You gon' pay us for that too?" Rudy asked.

"Ahma pay ya all right—pay ya knot upside yo head!"

He paid us five dollars and a slab of barbeque for the dogs.

I think we got the better part of that deal even though Joe Head owned three motels in Oklawaha County and was set for soap for a long time. He convinced us to keep it all a secret with the hope that one day the mailman might throw away something of real value, like whiskey, or cigarettes, or TVs, or meat. All we had to do was keep an eye out on the dumps.

Sure enough, over a period of time, we were to find cases upon cases of cigarette samples, shampoo samples, toothpaste samples, nail polish samples, shoe polish samples, car polish samples, furniture polish samples, and cases upon cases of things labeled "free."

This was some good stuff he was throwing away! Stuff we never heard of, but it was free and of some value. Of course, we couldn't keep all this stuff a secret. There was some concern over us gallivanting in dumps, and a whole lot of concern over the mailman, but Manasha and Aunt Clara, Linda and Savannah, Ingy and Cheryl, and even Teenie and Weenie had cases upon cases of stuff they hoped would not make their hair fall out or their fingernails turn black.

The mailman was all right with us. He was our favorite mailman until he butted into our business and took sides with Mr. Ceelie in our never-ending dispute over land.

In the judgment against him, Mr. Ceelie had to pay the cost of an access road across our property. He'd lost the case; there was no appeal; the road was built. But in all of this, he did obtain one small victory. The County Manager, in deference to him, named it, "The Ceelie Road."

We were not amused.

No road at all would have been better than "The Ceelie Road." It was our property and we felt it should have had our name. So one day after they'd christened it "The Ceelie Road" with freshly painted signs, me and Cody Wayne painted over it, renaming it "The Daddy Troy Road."

And they were not amused.

Mr. Ceelie complained to the County Road Department, and the sign was repainted "The Ceelie Road." Two days later it was repainted "The Grandma Gert Road." Alternately over a period of a month, it would be painted and repainted: the "Road With No Name," "The Ceelie Road."

"The Aunt Clara Road."

"The Ceelie Road."

"The Manasha Road."

"The Ceelie Road."

"The Rudy, Johnny and Cody Wayne Road."

"The Ceelie Road."

"The Linda and Savannah Road."

"The Ceelie Road."

It was the "Ingy and Cheryl Road" until one day the County Manager consulted the Department of Transportation, who consulted the Postmaster, who instructed the postman to warn us that our mail would not be delivered if the street signs were altered.

But that was not why we disliked the mailman; after all, he was just doing his job. It was the way he did it, the way he spoke to Aunt Clara, like he was admonishing an impudent child. He didn't have to be so nasty about it. It was not his fight. Nor was it his affair. And it was Linda and Savannah who'd painted her name up there. She was an innocent in this whole thing and just happened to be the only adult home when the mailman came calling.

He was nasty to the point of being threatening. So nasty that me and Cody Wayne, and Rudy, and Linda and Savannah and Ingy and Cheryl, and even Teenie and Weenie, surrounded Aunt Clara in defense. I don't know who threw the first foul, but he threw the first nasty one: he called Savannah a pickaninnie!

And Cody Wayne said, "Yo mammy a pickaninnie!"

He called Cody Wayne, "Buckwheat!"

And I said, "Yo mammy Buckwheat!"

He called me, "Sambo!"

I said, "Sambo yo mammy!"

This whole affair stank to high heaven. It got stanker when two days later we were informed that our mailbox was three feet too close to the road and our mail would not be delivered until we moved it back.

He'd made it personal, and that's why we disliked him. He

didn't have to be so nasty about it. My Aunt Clara is nice. She can get along with a rattlesnake. There was no reason to insult and humiliate her like that. That's what hurt the most.

When white people, or any other people, in Oklawaha County, or anywhere else, get mean—we get mean. When they get personal—we get personal. When they get nasty—we get nasty too. Real nasty! Down in the gutter nasty! They don't know nasty like we know nasty. And we know *Nasty* personally.

Nasty Brown is Joe Head's younger brother. He is in the same age group as my father and Aunt Clara. In fact, he took Aunt Clara to the senior prom. When she came back home after seven years of a bad marriage, Nasty Brown took her out, even though she was pregnant with Teenie and Weenie. He'd never stopped loving her. She was still his sweetheart and she was still nice.

Nasty Brown was quite amused about the mailman's antics, but not so amused by the manner in which the mailman had spoken to his first love. But what could he do?

"If I'd been there," he growled, "I woulda stuck my foot in his ass."

If he'd been there, the mailman would not have spoken that way. The Culligan Man had gotten that way with Grandma Gert. She didn't argue with him, she just turned and hollered, "Troy, we got a bad one out here!"

Manasha would have said, "Cracka kiss my ass!" and slammed the door.

Aunt Sally would have gotten *siditty* on him, using proper talk and correct grammar and big words whose meaning she knew he'd have no idea of, since she'd be making them up as she went along.

But Aunt Clara had listened to him out of nothing but respect and had gotten her feelings hurt. And when you hurt Aunt

Clara, you hurt us all. She is the best thing about us. A Broward County Teacher of the Year, who'd suffered seven years of abuse because she was too nice to take Rudy away from a father whom he hated. A father who did not exercise his visitation rights because Nasty Brown had put the fear of God in him. When you hurt Aunt Clara, you hurt Nasty Brown.

His name was Nasty Brown, not Stupid Brown. Putting his foot up the mailman's ass would not have been a smart thing to do, especially if the mailman was in uniform and on duty. That was asking for trouble with the federal government. Aunt Clara tried to placate him, telling him it was just one of those things that didn't mean nothing.

But it meant something to Nasty Brown, because he would not forget, and for a long time he stewed about it.

What Nasty Brown did to the mailman was an idea he got from what Joe Head did to Bolita Sam, which was a particularly nasty thing to do.

We were in the car waiting for Unck who was upstairs in Jessie Red's skin-house, taking care of some business. Joe Head saw us in the car and came down.

"Y'all got my snake?" he asked in a whisper.

"No," we had to admit.

"Damn!" he sighed in disappointment. "I thought I could depend on y'all."

"We had it," I told him, "but Pepsi ate it."

"Who?"

"Pepsi," I told him.

"He a skunk," said Rudy.

It took a moment for that to sink it.

"A real skunk?" he asked. "A real live four-legged skunk?"

"Four legs, black fur, and a big white stripe," said Cody Wayne.

"He stank?" Joe Head asked.

"No he don't stank!" I snapped.

"He been deodorized," said Rudy.

Cleo too. We'd found them one day while gallivanting around the reservoir with Miss Eva. We were driving through a patch of tall grass when we came up on the mama skunk lying dead and the three little baby skunks still fretting over her. We stopped and watched them long enough for Miss Eva to begin fretting over them, too. She offered me and Cody Wayne a huge sum of money to get out and get them and put them in a canvas bag so she could save them.

Not me! And not Cody Wayne either.

And not for all the money in the world. She started to do it herself and had gone so far as to open the car door to get out, but skunks have a stink so bad they can move hell, and she immediately closed it back.

There are a thousand men in Oklawaha County that would gladly go a-ting-a-linging through hell for Eva Horton, but there was only one who would go back down the reservoir and save three baby skunks for her.

Not only did Unck save them, but he had them demusked. She had one and we had two, Cleo and Pepsi.

Funny, our big bad dogs were terrified of two baby skunks. Especially Blackie. He was a world-class tracking dog, but a single blast in the snoot from a skunk could kill his sense of smell and render him worthless. So in the beginning, Blackie would hightail it the other way whenever he saw them coming.

But not Poochie!

She took them to heart, like all our sisters. It was Poochie who trained and nurtured and house-broke them. She didn't have pups, but she had Cleo and Pepsi; they were the fruit of her spirit.

You could almost see the devilment bubbling in Joe Head's head.

"A skunk," he mused, "hotdigitty dog! That's even better! Let's go git it!"

Joe Head owned the Hill Top Motel in Railroad Shoppe. This was the flagship of his various enterprises. The previous owners had lost their license when the motel, if not the whole area, degenerated into a morass of sin, vice, and crack cocaine. When Joe Head bought the Hill Top Motel, that marked the end of sin, vice, and crack cocaine not only at the Hill Top, but in the whole neighborhood—which led some people to believe that Joe Head had more than a little to do with sin and vice and crack cocaine. But Joe Head was in good with MacArthur Dill, and under his supervision, the Hill Top went from a whorehouse masquerading as a flea bag to a very nice place to be.

One person who liked to be at the Hill Top everyday was Bolita Sam. And he liked to be there with Inez Eliot, and Joe Head didn't like it one bit. He stewed, watching them sitting by the pool, eating in the restaurant. And smoldered every morning staring at the morning dew on the windshield of her car after it had been parked there all night. He was sick with envy, having to listen to Sam Bolita say things like, "Damn, she got some good pussy!"

And, "That pussy so hot ya can't even stay on it!"

And all what she liked to do, and how she liked to do it.

But what could he do? Bolita Sam had beat his time and there was nothing he could do.

"Now you git under the bed wit the skunk," he conspired as

we sat in the motel's parking lot in his car.

"Why can't Johnny do it?" Rudy questioned, more than a bit reluctant.

"'Cause I can't fit up under there!" I protested.

Joe Head feigned disappointment. With his face all broken down and looking sad he said, "I thought y'all was my boys."

We all hung our heads in shame.

"This man done stole my gal and braggin' 'bout it!" he exclaimed. "And y'all don't wanna help me?"

"How much you gon' pay us?" Rudy asked.

"Ahma take care of ya," he sighed. "Don't I always?"

Me and Rudy looked at each other, trying to decide.

With a heavy sigh, I agreed.

The plan called for me and Rudy to climb up under the bed with Pepsi and wait.

"Wait till she git 'er drawers down around her ankles," Joe Head insisted.

Then we were to simply let Pepsi go.

"What if he see us?" Rudy asked.

"He's hot after her," said Joe Head. "He ain't gon' be lookin' under no bed."

"That's what you say," I quipped.

"And anyway," he said, "Ahma be right next door, in case he start some mess."

We knew he wasn't telling us everything; like, what about the video camera?

Bolita Sam was a "do right man." Not "do right" by the law, but "do right" by his wife, who was a "do right" woman, but her name was not Inez. He was a "do right" man until he started staying up all night with a "do anything" woman, and his wife started staying up all night trying to find out who she was. She never found out because Bolita Sam became at least a "do half-way right" man again and ceased running around all night. He didn't cut Inez Eliot loose, he simply realigned his priorities and began rendezvousing in the afternoon. And the afternoon me, Rudy, and Pepsi waited under the bed for them, they were right on time.

We were far up under the bed all the way over to the wall when we heard them coming in. Rudy held Pepsi and we were both scared to death as the reality of it began to unfold. They came giggling and laughing, but there was little talk, just black high-heeled shoes and brown Ballys and a lot of kissing. Rudy and I blushed, the fear draining away with anticipation of what was to come. He dropped down on the bed, and she dropped down on top of him, and four shoes dropped to the floor. The bed bounced, and one of them went "hissss!"

She jumped off the bed and raised one black-stockinged foot, and stripped off her pantyhose. Both were undressing in a heated frenzy. Keys jingled, and a pair of brown pants, loose change and all, flew across the room and hit the wall. Then came her black dress. Then his yellow shirt. Then her black slip. And his bikini drawers.

Rudy started to turn Pepsi loose, but I stopped him. *Her drawers, stupid!*

"Hissss!" she sighed. Or maybe it was him.

"Gimme that big dick!" she grunted.

"Ooooobaby!" he moaned.

"Ahm ready!"

"Ahm ready!"

"Let's fuck!"

And her drawers came tumbling down. She had one foot up and was stepping out of them when we pushed Pepsi out.

"What's that?" she asked.

"That's the black snake!" he grunted with a lustful guttural tone. "That's the totem pole! That's the magic wand! That's—"

"No—it's somethin' under the bed—it's a skunk!"

"What?"

She turned to run, but tripped over her panties and fell. We thought she saw us as she scooted back against the wall screaming, "It's a skunk! It's a skunk!"

One big black foot stomped down off the bed and jumped straight back up.

"Oh shit!" he cried.

"It's a skunk!" she cried.

She was trying to get up off the floor and pull her drawers up at the same time. Bolita Sam was up in the bed screaming, "Oh shit! Oh shit! Oh shit!"

"A skunk! A skunk! A skunk!"

A pillow sailed across the room at Pepsi. *What if he had a gun?* Pepsi squeezed into a corner and took an aggressive posture, hissing and baring his teeth. Inez, no longer concerned with getting the other leg into her drawers, was frantically trying to get out of the room. In her desperation she forgot to unhook the night chain and at that moment it became the most complicated thing in the world. All she could think to do was scream and holler and yank at it.

Bolita Sam threw another pillow, then hopped down off the bed wielding a blanket as if he were about to engage in a little bit of bullfighting. But Pepsi could make the greatest bullfighter in the world pull up and break camp. Which is exactly what Pepsi did. He turned quickly, tooted up, and fired a great burst of air that Bolita Sam and Inez thought was the real thing.

"Oh shit!" he cried.

"Aggggh!" she cried.

Then Bolita Sam, big time numbers man in Oklawaha County, pulled the blanket up to his chest and held it like a young girl trying to protect her modesty.

"Oh shit! Oh shit! Oh shit!" he cried.

Inez didn't give one whit about her modesty, she was too busy trying to get the door open, something the night chain would not allow her to do. And desperation would not allow her to see.

Me and Rudy strained to hold our laughter. We had to hold our mouths. In one motion, Bolita Sam snatched the door open and Inez out of the way and ran outside butt-naked screaming, "Oh shit! Oh shit! Oh shit!"

And Inez followed him out.

Now what? We strained to hold in the laughter but it came pouring out of our mouths, ears, and eyes, until we couldn't hold it anymore. We laughed loud and joyously. Laughed at him, laughed at her, laughed at that big black-and-white pom-pom tail fluttering and gusting with each burst of empty air.

A muffled voice came through the wall.

"Open up! Open up!"

We froze. The knocking was insistent. We listened. It was Joe Head in the adjoining room. Me and Rudy slid out from under the bed.

"Open it!" I directed him as I picked up Pepsi.

Rudy unlocked and opened the door between the rooms. Joe Head stood in the doorway with a big grin on his face.

"Oh sheeeeiiiit! He mocked Bolita Sam then laughed hysterically. "Sssssh! C'mon."

He hurried us into the adjoining room, started to close the door, then stopped and did a curious thing: he picked up Inez's black-lace drawers and stuffed them into his pocket.

It was a hilarious scene, not at all unworthy of *America's*

Funniest Home Videos, somewhere we considered sending it, because Cody Wayne had videotaped the whole thing.

We watched and rewatched the whole thing at Jessie Red's house. Unck and Nasty Brown watched it too. At one point they played it fast forward, showing Bolita Sam and Inez zipping into the picture and pecking at each other like chickens. Since he'd filmed it from the car, all you could see was the door shut, then crack back open with Inez's desperately grasping fingers, and Bolita Sam, butt-naked, snatching Inez out of the way, his mouth forming the words, "Oh shit! Oh shit! Oh shit!" Over and over again.

No one laughed when they played it in slow motion. Bolita Sam wasn't funny as he eased up, .38 special in hand, and kicked at the door of room twenty-six.

"Fuck 'em all if they can't take a joke," Joe Head said.

"Why you git my boys mixed up in y'all shit?" Unck asked Joe Head. "Suppose he woulda shot through the door?"

"He wanted to shoot the skunk," Joe Head said.

"Yeah. A two-legged one."

Nasty Brown was more than amused. It was something he wished he'd thought of and a dirty trick he wished he could play on the mailman, if only he could trick the mailman into a room at the Hill Top. But what he wanted was a snake. Nasty Brown was feeling nasty.

A snake in a mailbox is not a joke. A plain old green snake can give someone a heart attack. A rattler with its rattle-tail cut off can kill. Nasty Brown asked Cody Wayne to catch him one, but Cody Wayne told Unck instead. Unck must have said something to him about it, because he never mentioned it again.

It is a paltry, feeble, tiny mind that takes pleasure in revenge. We'd forgotten all about the squabble with the mailman; it didn't mean nothing. We were heart-broken because we couldn't find any more goodies at the dumps. All we found were postal supervisors hiding in the bushes, waiting to pounce on any mailman who would throw away the U.S. mail. But Nasty Brown said it was a sorry man that no kind of wrongs could arouse him to vengeance, and he wanted revenge.

He stopped by the house one day to see Aunt Clara. When he got ready to leave, he asked us if we wanted to wash his car. We agreed, but when we got down to Goodbread Alley, instead of washing his car, he told us to find him two cats. Alley cats.

Finding two cats was easy. All we needed was a couple of fish heads and a box. The hard part was getting them out. Two cats in a box are jolly good fun. Imagine two cats in a mailbox. That is what Nasty Brown did to the mailman, and just like Joe Head, he wanted to videotape it.

With two cats in a box and a video camera, we went looking for the mailman and a good place to lay our trap. Stopping at a 7-Eleven store in Lemon City, we bought slurpies and potato chips while Nasty Brown bought a Coke and a bottle of Tabasco sauce. They don't call him Nasty Brown for nothing.

All along the mailman's route, dogs would fall in behind him. Strays, watchdogs, yard dogs, and pets of every stripe and nature. This canine parade would follow him all along his route, so we stayed a block ahead of him, still looking for a mailbox large enough to hold two cats with hot sauce up their ass. We found it at the First Christian Church of Lemon City.

Not even Nasty Brown, for all his nastiness, was comfortable with a church, but it was the only mailbox we could find that was big enough to do the dirty deed. It took a lot of effort to get the cats to cooperate, but we got them in, latched the lip, and raised the little flag that indicated there was mail to be picked up.

"Can't we go to hell for this?" Rudy asked.

It was something we'd not given much thought to, but now that he'd raised the issue we had to consider it.

"Only if we git caught," Nasty Brown answered.

That was good enough for me, but not Rudy.

"Ain't God watchin' us?" he asked.

A very interesting question.

"God's on our side," Nasty Brown said.

And I agreed, but I don't see how.

Rudy started to say something else, but Nasty Brown said, "Ain't he throwin' away the mail? And don't forget how he talked to ya mama."

I remembered, and Rudy remembered, and we didn't want an apology from the devil. We wanted revenge!

"Here he comes!" Cody Wayne alerted us.

We ducked, but Nasty Brown raised the video camera and turned it on. The mail truck zipped up the street, stopping here and there to reach out, flip open a box, and slip in a letter in one fluid motion, then zip away. One thing could be said for him, he was a wizard at delivering the mail.

Then he got to the church.

First he had to unlatch the box, and when he did, the lip fell open and two surly demons from hell shot straight up his arm terrifying him half to death! There came a wild wail from the truck and a mewing screech that rose to a scream from the cats.

Self-control was impossible.

Self-direction was impossible.

They were a cold and entangled trinity from hell! Scratching, scrambling, and wallowing in a hail of packages, letters, and soul-chilling terror. A sight and sound too fearful for even the feel of fear.

And then there were the dogs!

There must have been at least twenty of the sorriest, scurviest, mangiest, most unwanted sooners you can ever imagine. Shiteaters—every last one of them! And when they saw the cats, there was a terrible burst of rage and howls. They circled the truck in wild disorder, scampering in and out and up and over, creating a welter of confusing sounds of uncontrollable fear. The clamor attracted a small crowd, and one of the cats shot out of the truck with a pack of dogs hot on his trail. The other one flew out the window and got in the wind.

In the distance, and growing ever closer, was a wailing of sirens.

"Police comin'," I warned Nasty Brown.

He kept filming.

"We betta go!" cried Cody Wayne.

The sirens grew louder and closer.

"They gon' know we had somethin' to do with it," Rudy said.

Because we were the only black faces around. But Nasty Brown, with the same stolid objectivity Miss Eva had photographing the bats, kept filming, detail upon ghastly detail, until the cumulative picture included curious onlookers, mangy dogs, police cars, dog catchers, rescue squads, chaos, and madness, climaxing, finally, with the mailman crawling halfway out of the truck and collapsing in the doorway. He was the image of a hideous grim-looking thing grinning a strange and ghastly smile.

And the point to all of this was lost on all of us, because the point had gone far beyond revenge and degenerated into nastiness. Nasty Brown was just being his old nasty self.

Another Conversation Among My Aunts

"Stickama trees?" Manasha asked, looking at Cat in a state of bewilderment.

"Or stickama bushes," Cat said.

"Or po' people's barbwire," Aunt Clara said.

"I never understood why Mama planted them," Aunt Sally said, "until that morning Lijo came in all stuck up."

"We had all kinds of flowers planted beneath our window," Aunt Clara said. "Then one day we came home and she had pulled them all up."

"We asked her why, and she said she was planting roses," said Aunt Sally.

"But the next day," Aunt Clara said, "all we saw under our window was stickama bushes."

"I said, 'Mama, what about the roses?'" Aunt Sally said. "And she said, 'They's gotta bloom first.'"

"That's why whenever she runs me a line of bullshit," said Aunt Clara, "I say, 'Yeah Mama, and I'm still waitin' for those roses to bloom.'"

And they all laughed.

"Don't laugh," Aunt Clara said, "'cause one day we gon' plant them too."

"For what?" Manasha asked.

"For Savannah and Linda," Aunt Clara said. "Give 'em a few more years."

"Maybe sooner," said Aunt Sally. "As soon as they start their periods."

"Not Savannah!" Cat cried, "not Linda!"

"Why not Savannah?" Aunt Sally asked. "Why not Linda?"

"As much as I talk to them, I don't think they're going to be like that," Cat said.

"Like what?" Aunt Sally asked. "Girls?"

"What do you think they were doin' sitting on the fence rail when we came up?" Aunt Clara asked.

"Looking sweet and innocent," Cat said.

"Well," Aunt Sally said, "they were looking all right, but wasn't no sweet and innocent in it."

"They were looking out," Manasha said, "for Rudy and Cody Wayne who were up in the tree trying to git some green mangoes."

"That's why they didn't wanna sit out here with us, and them other two went runnin' down to Silo," said Aunt Clara.

"They've got some green mangoes stashed somewhere," Manasha said. "They like to eat them with salt."

"Where's that other knucklehead?" Aunt Sally asked. "I didn't see him, but you can bet he was in the middle of it."

I lay across the limb very still, breathing shallow and looking straight down on them. Occasionally, someone would look up from the table, but they didn't see me. All I could do was lay still and hope they didn't see me. And listen.

"Girls will be girls," Cat said.

"Girls will be women," Aunt Sally said, "as soon as nature gets ready for them."

"I ain't waitin' for nature," Manasha said.

"But they sleep upstairs," said Cat.

"All the more reason," said Aunt Sally. "If those bastards jump out the window, they'll jump right in the stickama bush!"

Cat laughed.

"Like Lijo," Aunt Clara said.

"Aiiii!" Aunt Clara and Aunt Sally squealed.

"Mama thought it was us," Aunt Sally said. "All week she hinted about the dirty dogs that been wallowin' in the stickama bush."

"And how she betta not catch no pisstail boys sniffin' round here!" said Aunt Clara.

"And one morning Lijo had his shirt off," said Aunt Sally, "and he was all stuck up!"

"Aiiii!" they cried.

"And Mama asked him, 'What happened to you?'"

"And Lijo said, 'I ran into a beehive.'"

"And Mama said, 'Oh.'"

"Wasn't nothin' she could do, except make them marry."

"She was fifteen and he was sixteen, and if you think she look good now, you shoulda seen her then."

"All the boys thought we acted stuck-up, but we had to act that way; it was the only way we could look out for each other."

"But Eva had eyes for Lijo and no one else."

"It was always Lijo this and Lijo that."

"And she was the only one who could get Lijo to comb his hair."

"We use to plait Melvin's hair all the time: that's why it's so long. But talk about plaitin' Lijo's hair and sheeeeit!"

"Just like Cody Wayne," Aunt Clara said. "I can plait Johnny and Rudy's hair all day, but if I call Cody Wayne, he'll look at me like I wanna torture him or somethin'."

"Told me he ain't no doll baby," Manasha giggled.

"Just like his daddy," Aunt Sally said, "wouldn't let nobody touch his hair."

"Except Eva," said Aunt Clara.

"That's how Mr. Herbert saw it comin'; she was always plaitin' his hair."

"And eye-ballin' him."

"Then she saw him naked!"

"Aiiii!" they cried.

"Remember?" Aunt Clara asked.

"Do I?" Aunt Sally responded. *"It's an alligata!"*

"Aiiii!"

"Child, lemme tell ya," Aunt Clara gasped. "Mr. Herbert decided to take Eva to Alabama with him. He didn't like the way she and Lijo were gettin' along."

"See, Eva is our big sister, but not quite a sister. So he wanted to get her away from Lijo."

"But Eva had plans of her own, and Alabama wasn't in them."

"Humf! Eva say 'Fuck Alabama!'"

"She pissed and moaned to Mama and Grandmama, and when that didn't work, she got sick."

"Lovesick."

"Precisely."

"It wasn't nothin' but puppy love until the night Arthur Lee and them snuck off to peep at Miss Verdell."

"Wit her nasty self."

"She was always undressin' in the window and walkin' around naked."

"And she knew they use to peep at her."

"That's why she did it."

"Anyway, Mama and Daddy went to a funeral, and told us to stay in the yard and be in the house by dark."

"Well, they stayed in the yard all right, but as soon as it got dark, they snuck off to peep at Miss Verdell."

"And got back one step ahead of Mama."

"And had to bathe in the dark, and in cold water."

"Why's that?" Manasha asked.

"Wasn't no electricity back here when we were little," Aunt Clara answered.

"If you think them shacks were rough when you got here, Manasha," said Aunt Sally, "then you shoulda been here back then."

"No, I shouldn'ta!" Manasha exclaimed.

"Cat know what I'm talkin' about," said Aunt Sally.

"No, I don't," said Cat.

"Yes, you do," said Aunt Sally.

And they both laughed.

"We had to heat water first," Aunt Clara said. "Then we took turns."

"They took theirs outside."

"Because they needed a tub."

"They just threw a sheet across the line and took baths."

"That's why we had to bathe before dark."

"Because wasn't nobody heating up water all night."

"But they'd been out foolin' around watchin' Miss Verdell, so they had to bathe in the dark, and in cold water."

"Well, we took ours, and we were in the house eating dinner while Mama had them outside takin' a bath."

"Mama had a belt and she was makin' sho' they bathe when somethin'—we don't know what it was, or if it was anything at all—hit the fence."

"Wasn't shit," Aunt Sally said.

"But Brendan screamed, 'It's a alligata!'"

The whole group burst out laughing.

"He was the oldest and the biggest and he was screamin' like a little girl!"

"It's a alligata! It's a alligata! It's a alligata!"

"Melvin turned over the tub gittin' outta the way!"

"Arthur Lee ran dead over Mama!"

"Lijo ran through the sheet!"

"And Brendan just kept screamin' 'It's a alligata! It's a alligata!'"

"And ain't nobody seen alligator the first!"

"We didn't see one either, but the minute we heard it, all three of us jumped on the table screamin' 'It's a alligata! It's a alligata! It's a alligata!'"

"All four came runnin' in through the back door butt-ass naked—dicks floppin' all over the place!"

"Mama too! She came runnin' in and slammed the door!"

"And me, Eva, and Clara were up on the table, screamin' our ass off! I mean, it had to be bad if they was runnin' and screamin' and butt-naked!"

In a low voice, Aunt Sally said, "First time we ever seen anything like it. I mean, we seen weenies, but these were dicks! Big swingin' dicks!"

"And that's all Eva saw! Me and Sally were on the look out for this alligata, but Eva couldn't take her eyes off that dick!"

"Mama turned around and looked at her, then looked at them and it made her think: *what damn alligata!*"

"Because none of my brothers were scared of alligatas—they hunted alligatas, and wrestled alligatas for fun!"

"Mama grabbed a broom and went to whackin'!"

"And she whacked their asses all the way outside. Back in the dark, in the cold, with the alligata!"

They were laughing hysterically, when Manasha cried, "Well look who's comin'!"

I looked through the leaves and saw her stoop through the fence and come across the grass.

"Hey y'all," Miss Eva greeted as she approached the table, "talkin' 'bout me again?"

There was a moment of absolute silence before Aunt Sally shrieked, "It's a alligata!"

And the whole table erupted in wild raucous laughter.

Chicken Shit

The minute I stepped into the kitchen I knew I should have turned around. Linda and Savannah glared at me, Ingy and Cheryl frowned, and Grandma Gert stared impassively. I stopped abruptly and knew I was guilty of something.

"Johnny," Grandma Gert asked calmly, "have you been throwin' my eggs around?"

It was a question, a statement, and a judgment of guilt. A trick question if ever there was one. It didn't matter whether I admitted it or not, she just wanted to hear me lie.

"No!" I lied.

"Yes, you did!" Savannah screamed vehemently, which made it more than the lie it already was.

"He was throwin' them like they was baseballs!" screamed Linda, making the deed more dastardly than it already was.

"That's why we ain't got no eggs!" Cheryl whimpered, about to cry.

"We got plenty eggs," I said, by way of explanation.

"We ain't got no eggs for Cat!" Ingy snapped.

I sighed steadily, looked down, and studied my feet. It was true that we had been throwing eggs inside the chickenhouse, but not as many as they were claiming. To let them tell it, I had emptied every nest there. Yes, "we," because Cody Wayne and Rudy threw them too. We were throwing eggs at the post, at the roosters, at the dogs, and at each other, even though each of us knows eggs are a commodity and a blessing to the people we give them to. A dozen or two is just a little bit better than a few kind words. That Ingy and Cheryl should go inside the chickenhouse and find nothing but empty nests was a shock beyond understanding.

"You gone crazy?" Grandma Gert demanded. "You lost yo mind, or is you just plain stupid?"

I squirmed and stared at the floor and imagined myself punching Savannah in the mouth.

"We ain't got no food to throw away!" Grandma Gert shrieked, her voice rising with her blood and anger.

"Like he was in the World Series or sumpthin'!" cried Savannah, throwing fuel on the fire.

"They was throwin' 'em at the dogs too!" Linda put in her two cents.

"They was?"

"Yeaaaah!" they cried in unison.

"And they threw some at us too!" Cheryl had to get in on the act too.

"They was?"

"Yeaaaah!" they cried against me.

"Well, you just keep it up!" Grandma Gert hissed. "You hear me, mister?"

I squirmed.

"You hear me?" she shrieked.

"Uh-huh," I replied in a small voice.

"Now git! And stay away from my eggs!"

Big deal! So I threw a few eggs at the post. So what? It was nothing I'd never done before. We had a-plenty eggs, and a-plenty more chickens to lay more eggs. And a-plenty more eggs to make more chickens. We had twenty egg-laying hens, and each one laid an egg about every twelve hours. They squawked all night and there should always be eggs. But Savannah said there were *no* eggs. Why would there be no eggs?

Nobody gathered the eggs but Ingy and Cheryl. We helped take care of them, but we didn't bother with the eggs. Neither did Manasha. In fact, she hated live chickens ever since the first time she'd tried to gather eggs and had gotten pecked for her efforts. Manasha thought you just walk in, reach under, and get and egg. She thought they were *her* eggs. She came into the chickenhouse, in her little bonnet, carrying her little basket, looking like little Mammy Yokum, and stuck her hand into the first nest she came to, and the hen pecked the devil out of her! It wasn't funny, but hard enough to draw blood. Little did Manasha know that mama hen is not going to let you walk in and just take *her* eggs. Manasha couldn't understand why a chicken would do such a thing. To her it was just meanness. So Manasha showed it what meanness was, and choked the shit out of it!

And that is why gathering the eggs is the province of Ingy and Cheryl. Every morning as we marched to school, they marched down to Silo, fed and watered the chickens, and gathered the eggs. But this morning, they'd gone down to Silo and found no eggs, and no one could understand why.

If it were not Friday, this would have been just another unsolved mystery, but Friday they take eggs to Cat. The only logical explanation to the empty nest was that they'd seen me pitching eggs the day before. A charge I vehemently denied—at least to the extent to which they accused me. I'd thrown three strikeouts—nine pitches at the most—and that is all I would confess to.

"If ya weren't throwin' 'em in the first place," said Grandpa, dropping another hen into the basket, "nobody would be blamin' you."

I sighed in shame.

"Brang that," he pointed and commanded me to bring the basket of dead hens.

I picked up the basket and followed him.

"I don't blame them for being mad," he said as we walked toward the fruit field. "They take them eggs and make theyself a little change. And now you done pitched 'em all away."

"But I didn't!" I pleaded. "Not that many."

"Well, I guess they all just jumped up and left."

I guess.

"My dogs ain't got no taste for eggs," he said, reading my thoughts.

I felt a pang of guilt thinking that about our dogs. It is the worst thing a dog could do, besides turn on you. It is worse than being a shiteater, a disgusting habit *all* dogs must be broken out of. Shit to a dog is a great delicacy: catshit and horseshit is a gourmet meal. But an egg is something else. It is a sorry sooner that sucks an egg, and we were much too proud of our dogs to think they would suddenly degenerate to egg-sucking sooners.

Instead of solving the problem, I was looking to place the blame.

The barbeque pit beneath the big live oak was already fired up. The black cauldron of oil and water was beginning to steam. One by one, I dropped in the seven chickens, then sat down on the counter of the pit. Grandpa pulled a grindstone from his pocket and began sharpening a skinning knife.

"Where them polecats?" he asked. "I ain't seen 'em t'day."

"Up at the house," I answered. "They gave 'em a bath."

"I don't see why, they just git dirty agin."

That was my clue to listen. When Grandpa didn't understand something, he talked the solution out of you. Listening was the key.

"Every time I see 'em," he said, "they's crawlin' under somethin'."

"Lookin' for snakes and rats," I said.

"Well, they sho do a good job of findin' them."

"Chickensnakes!"

"What about 'em?"

"They eat eggs!"

"All snakes do."

"Not chicken eggs!"

He pursed his lips and thought.

"Git them," he pointed to the cauldron.

I lifted a hen out of the water with a pair of tongs and gingerly began plucking it.

"Chickensnakes eat eggs all right—but all the eggs?" he asked.

"Maybe it's a bunch of 'em," I reasoned.

A snake gang? It sounded so ridiculous I looked down and plucked the feathers from the chicken.

"A chickensnake don't swallow the whole egg," Grandpa said. "It's got a bone in its throat that slices the eggs so it can crush the egg. Then spits the shell out. If it were a chickensnake, or a buncha chickensnakes, you'd see the shell; look like little balls of wax. You see any?"

"No," I replied.

"Then it weren't no chickensnake."

Weren't me either.

"What about a ratsnake? They eat eggs."

"Yeah, but I think they push 'em out the nest and bust 'em so they kin suck the yolks. You see any busted eggs?"

"No."

"Then it weren't no ratsnake."

Weren't me either.

191

"Do rattlesnakes eat eggs?"

"Bird eggs—if that's all's in the nest."

"What about corn snakes?"

"They don't make a habit of it because they can't crush the shell, or digest it. If they do eat an egg, they'll git up in a tree and drop down to bust it up."

Grandpa waited for me to pluck the wings of the fifth chicken. He could clean, skin, and debone faster than I could pluck. It was fascinating to watch.

"So if it weren't you, weren't the dogs, and weren't the snakes," he said, "then what was it?"

"The Twilight Zone?"

"That's for sure."

When he finished with the last chicken, he rinsed and laid the meat in the pan of water; breasts and backs. I pushed the remaining feathers and guts into the fire as he bagged up the bones. Legs, thighs, and wings went together. Boodies, hearts, giblets, and necks. Then breasts and backs were placed in separate bags and secured with rubber bands.

"All I can say," Grandpa said, "is you's in a lotta trouble wit them gals."

"I'll say," I responded.

"Then you betta git to the bottom of it."

Giving me the bags of meat, he said, "Go put these in the blue freezer and come back. Let's see if we can solve this."

If I'd known that solving this mystery meant spending the night in the chickenhouse, I would have gladly suffered the wrath of "them gals." I certainly suffered their humiliations. "See what lies bring!" They laughed and mocked me. Although it ranks high as fertilizer, chicken shit is some stank shit! It runs neck and neck with dog shit and pig shit.

The chickenhouse used to be for pigs, but after a year of breeding them indoors, Grandpa realized it was more prudent to raise pigs out-of-doors, because pig waste turns toxic in a hurry, creating gasses such as ammonia and methane that cause respiratory illnesses and are so corrosive they rot away metal hinges and door knobs. It is less convenient but far more healthy to raise them out-of-doors, a good hundred yards away from everything.

That the chickenhouse was temperature-controlled was due to the fact that it once housed pigs. Grandpa divided it with mesh wire, one side for breeding, one side for egg-layers, with five nest boxes on each side. Two feed hoppers and water vessels were on each side and both sides had free range in a big yard.

We have four breeds of chickens: Rhode Islands, Plymouths, Wyandottes, and Sussex. All our hens are top class that could lay 250 to 300 eggs a year each, but most of them are broody, as Manasha found out.

Grandpa placed a makeshift hammock between the last post and the dividing wall for me to sleep the night. He brought me a flashlight, a frog gig, and he brought in a big plastic bag of dry leaves. We were dealing with snakes, and before he left, he said, "They won't never come out if you keep the light on."

"How will I see?" I asked.

"You won't see, you'll hear—listen!"

"A snake?"

He tossed down the big bag of leaves.

"The signs are all around," he said as he shut out the light. "Listen to them."

Then he left.

I felt foolish, sitting in the dark listening for snakes. The only snake that makes noise is a *rattler!* And the thought of me, sitting in the dark of the chickenhouse, waiting to hear the ceremonial pronouncement of the most sinister reptile in North America, created in me a nagging fear that death was close at hand. A disturbing fear arising as much from a want of good judgment as from a want of courage. A fear born of faith but tightly joined to doubt and despair. The strangeness of everything, including the thick darkness, made everything seem more formidable. I was not at all familiar with the chickenhouse in the dark, much less a dark chickenhouse filled with snakes. I flashed the light over everything, hoping that by familiarizing the unfamiliar even those things that are terrible would lose much of their frightfulness.

This terror and darkness of the mind had to be dispelled. If I were to succeed in this endeavor, it would not be by the rays of the sun, or the glittering shafts of the flashlight, but by the law and the aspect of nature.

"*The Lord is my light and salvation,*" I said aloud, "*of whom shall I fear?*"

A hen screeched! I shrank in fear and put the light on it. She fluttered a moment, then settled down. She'd laid an egg.

"*The Lord is my strength of life!*" I sang in distress. "*Of whom shall I fear?*"

The answer to that came loud and clear: snakes!

There are times when fear is good, and this was such a time! I jumped from the hammock and ran through the darkness to the far end of the building, frantically searching the wall for the light switch. I found the door instead, opened it, and rushed into the cool and welcome dark of the night. And the first thing I saw was Ike.

He was standing at the gate staring in. "Ike!" I called to him. "Jumbo! Jumbo!"

He barked once, and the sound of it, passing over me on into the chickenhouse, filled me with relief. Ike was here; what was there for me to fear? His presence gave me courage, for Ike was courageous.

Unlike Shack, Ike had a healthy fear of danger. That is the difference between fearlessness and courage. Shack had no fear of danger because he was ignorant of it. That made him fearless, senseless, and above all else—feared! His very presence and demeanor enable him to strike terror into the hearts of others. Shack knew no dangers and was not bothered by insults. To call him a shit-eating eggsucker would not have bothered him at all.

On the other hand, Ike had a keen sense of where the dangers lay, and there was danger in being suspected of sucking eggs. The thought of such a thing could rob them of their good name. Our dogs were not shiteaters. We honored them and held each one in the highest regard. To even think that they would sink to sucking eggs would be to rate them so low as to dishonor them. That's why, instead of making him leave, I opened the gate and let Ike in. His honor and the honor of all our dogs, was at stake.

"Can't be a rattler," I said to Ike, as he lay quietly beneath the hammock. "They'll eat the chickens too. A rat snake too."

The thought of snakes didn't bother me now that Ike was here. But suppose it wasn't a snake? Suppose it was the gheechie man? Or the butt-naked man? Or the greasy man?

"Ike," I said, sitting up, "suppose it ain't a snake? Maybe we should go git Shack."

A snake was one thing, but a greasy man?

"Ike," I cried, "let's go git Shack."

Ike responded by standing and releasing a low growl. It took me a moment to realize he was not responding to me but to something out there. And that great fear returned twofold. A chicken cackled. It was different from an egg-laying cackle. Ike barked and moved out into the darkness, and I shined the flashlight to give him direction. The chickens in one shed were awakening. Something was moving through the leaves! Ike grunted. I heard Shack barking outside! We looked. Ike barked again, and Lance and Blackie responded. I zig-zagged the light across the floor, then swept it across the nest on the right. The hens in that shed were in a big commotion. Ike recognized it first and ran to it. It was not all that big, maybe three feet long. It was grey with reddish saddles, nonpoisonous, but I knew it could bite the shit out of you just the same. It was a milksnake, and I climbed out of the hammock and grabbed the gig. Something else was moving through the leaves, and it wasn't Ike.

"Jesus," I cried, "I better cut on the light."

I shined the light on the front wall, saw the switch, and dashed to it. The snake was slithering for cover, clumsily crawling across the nest, sending the chickens jumping. In a moment I had it pinned, with the egg still in its mouth! It was a fascinating thing to see.

"We got 'im Ike! We got 'im!" I cried.

Something fell from the rafters. I turned, looked, and saw another one. Its oversized neck showed it had an egg too. Looking up, I spotted another one in the far corner glaring down on me the way snakes do when they see you, but you don't see them.

"Jeez," I said to my dog, "we betta git outta here."

Keeping the snake firmly pinned with the gig, I grabbed it by the neck, careful not the crush the evidence. Immediately it wrapped itself around my arm and squeezed. I left the gig but took the flashlight, and me and Ike raced outside.

"Jumbo! Jumbo!" I called to the other dogs. "Look what we got! Look what we got!"

Ike barked in triumph, and the other dogs became excited. I

ran through the gate and held it down for them to see and smell. It was a big victory, and the dogs were clearly conscious of our success. There was much jumping and spinning and triumphant prancing as we hightailed it for the house.

"Grandmaaaa!" I screamed coming all the way up from Silo. "I got it! I got it ! I got it!"

They'd scoffed when I'd told them it was a snake.

"I got it! I got it!"

They'd laughed and made fun of me.

"I got it! I got it!"

They'd called me a liar and belittled me unmercifully.

"I got it!" I screamed.

"What you got?" Cody Wayne hollered down from the window.

"I got *it!*" I hollered back.

They couldn't open the door fast enough, so me and the dogs ran around to the side door, hollering, barking, and bamming.

"I got it! I got it!"

Then to the back door.

"I got it! I got it!"

And back to the front, where everybody was standing on the front porch in wonder. I held it and waved it in triumph. "I got it," I said. "See—it still got the egg in its mouth!"

It was just an egg-eating snake, but the ecstatic attention being paid to it made it a rare and beautiful wonder. The egg in the back of its throat made it sublime. Grandma Gert said, "I'll be damn."

Cody Wayne ran upstairs and brought down the glass cage we kept snakes in before releasing them. He helped me get it off my hand while I, in one ceaseless breath, described the fearsome life-and-death struggle Ike and I had fought before escaping with our lives.

"It's a nest of 'em!" I told Grandpa and Daddy Troy. "They're all over the place!"

"What they do?" Grandpa asked.

"Just what you said—droppin' from the rafters."

"Milksnakes," said Daddy Troy. "She raise 'em on eggs. She eats one, goes back to the nest, and spits it up."

"They big enough now to eat a whole egg. They only come out at night; that's why we missed 'em," said Grandpa.

"They must can't git out," Daddy Troy said. "If they could they'd be after the biddies."

"Ya oughtta put them polecats in there," Grandpa suggested. "They'll clean 'em out quick!"

"T'morra," Daddy Troy said. "We'll take care of all that t'morra."

"To tell the truth, Troy, I ain't nevah seen no snake eat a egg like that. It look like a milksnake, but it ain't"

Daddy Troy took a deep breath and sighed.

"Lemme go put on my shoes," he said.

"Y'all go on inside and get ready for bed," Aunt Clara said.

"Ahm goin' take a look at this now," said Grandpa. "C'mon Ike."

As I started into the house, Grandma Gert gave me a look of new respect that was nothing less than admiration—even awe. A look of quiet wonder tinged with a faint transcendental pleasure that rang like a voice from heaven saying: *Lo! This is my beloved son, in whom I am well pleased!*

She said: "Take yo ass upstairs and take a bath; you smell like chicken shit!"

The Good People

Grandma Gert hung up the phone and looked perturbed.
"What do you know about these people?" she asked me.
"What people?" I asked her as I rinsed out the rice pot.
"These Wong people."
"What Wong people?"
"Them Chinese people!"
"Oh. They Rudy friends."
"Oh, I think I know that, but what kind of people are they?"
That I didn't know.

I'd met them only once, at a K-Mart in Eloise, and that was
only for a moment. He was with his mother and grandmother,
and the impression I had of them was that they were nice people.
Chinese people. Good people.

"They good people," I said.

Which meant they had no dirt worth mentioning. Which
settled her, somewhat.

"Well, why they like Rudy so much?" she asked.

I didn't know that either, but was supposed to. Anything
involving any of us was supposed to be known by all of us, especially if it involved strangers. And these people were not only
strangers, they were strange.

They were Asians that lived on the other side of Nash where
a large group of Asians had settled. Peter Wong was in Rudy's

fourth grade class, and, according to Savannah, Rudy was his only friend. That was not too much of a mystery. They made an odd pair, but the friendship worked. Children are like that, but then again, Rudy is good people too.

His mother had called to invite Rudy to some kind of Chinese party. Such an invitation would automatically include Savannah and Linda, or me and Cody Wayne. But before anyone could go anywhere, Grandma Gert would have to know what kind of people they were. And it frustrated her that I did not have an answer.

"Well dammit you betta find out!" she fussed. "Go git Rudy!"

Quickly I hurried out of the kitchen, not so much to find Rudy, but to get away from the pots.

I hate pots. Linda and Savannah didn't have to wash pots. They washed dishes, but they didn't do pots. We did. There are three things in this world that we absolutely have to do. Clean our room, rake the yard, and wash them pots! Having to look for Rudy was a welcome respite.

They were good people; what else did we need to know? I suspect it was the "Chinese" Grandma Gert didn't like. Uncle Brendan was killed in Vietnam, and Unck had been wounded. So it was not unlikely that Grandma Gert was extremely prejudiced toward all Asians. To her, they were all Chinese.

That Unck was wounded in Vietnam had nothing to do with the war and everything to do with an illegal money-changing scheme with a Vietnamese madam. That he'd received a Purple Heart and a Silver Star was due to the fact that he'd double-crossed her and stole all the money. The two assassins she'd hired to kill him missed, but he didn't, and the subsequent CID investigation led to a massive dope, guns, and money-changing operation controlled by the enemy. A trial would have embarrassed the

Corps, so they gave him two medals and a promotion instead.

My Uncle Brendan earned his medals the hard way: recapturing the city of Hue. His medals, his stripes, his picture, and a letter from the president still hang on Grandma Gert's and Daddy Troy's bedroom wall, and I doubt if she will ever forget it was Chinese-looking people who killed him. So what did it matter if they were good people? They were Chinese.

If I was lucky, Rudy was down at Silo. I could deliver the message, get lost, and hope she made him do the rest of the pots.

Fat chance.

She would interrogate him unmercifully, then find some reason to label these people "no good" and forbid their friendship. It was going to be an unpleasant episode. The two boys genuinely liked each other and that made the differences between them incidental, as differences between children are.

Grandma Gert was wary of shrimp fried rice, Chinese checkers, and kung-fu, but that didn't stop us from eating or watching things Chinese. They were good people and Peter Wong was all right. These people did not kill Uncle Brendan, did not shoot Unck, and did not assume any superiority over us. If they did, would they be inviting Rudy to any of their parties? And what about us? Were they going around asking about us? If so, then I, for one, was curious to know what the answers were, because we are too much of an enigma to be resolved with a simple yes or no. Are we good people?

The baggage we carry is a heavy load. First, there's my daddy, who's doing hard time in the federal penitentiary. Then there is Bake the Cake, Linda, and Cody Wayne's daddy—Unck, who people speak about in whispers. Savannah doesn't know her mother. And no one talks about Linda and Cody Wayne's mother; it is too painful and sad a subject.

Rudy, Teenie, and Weenie's father is a mean and violent drunk. And Bake the Cake is HIV positive.

Thank God for Grandma Gert.

What I know of my father's trouble is only what I picked up in bits and pieces from people like Bolita Sam, Jessie Red, Betty Red, and Nick-Nack. Good people who did bad things in the name of good. And greed. But mostly vanity.

That they killed dope dealers in Oklawaha County was good. That they resold the dope they stole was greed. That they made a crusade of it was mostly vanity. That's what confuses me and makes me wonder if the good outweighed the bad.

The drug war in Oklawaha County did not begin when Nasty Brown, Betty Red, and Peter Red began robbing drug dealers. Nor when Joe Head bought the Hill Top Motel and began cleaning it up. It began the day they found the body of Robin Porter in a Dumpster behind the Ebony Bar. The pathologist's report said she died of acute cocaine intoxication. It was not unexpected.

Miss Porter was not always a rock whore. Like Aunt Clara, she was a teacher. She had two daughters and was Jessie Red's only child. All of us, if not all of Boggy, were vexed by her steady descent into dope and degradation. Here was someone well known and admired. Someone we believed in. She went to school with Cat and Paulus. Miss Eva was a friend of her father. They'd found her dead, naked, in a garbage Dumpster in Goodbread Alley.

With her death, the hopelessness hit home, and we felt and suffered a loss of worth. The black people hung their heads in self-pity, like a helpless and vulnerable people. A pitiful people. A sick and sorrowful people. Then someone killed the Cuban boy, his wife, and his dogs. And hope sprang.

There was always dope in Oklawaha County. Marijuana is a cash crop, and we are all about cash and crops. The sheriff's department flew helicopter sorties over the county looking for marijuana fields, but nobody worried about marijuana fields except the sheriff, since that gave them the opportunity to confiscate all kinds of goodies. Which is the reason why they didn't have much interest in street dealers.

Illegal street drugs followed the labor crews; drug traffic confined itself to the labor camps of Augustine Quarters and Porters Quarters. It was never an unmanageable problem until Goodbread Alley got its own big-time drug dealer.

With the arrival of Hector Maldanado, drugs, drug dealing, and everything that goes with it exploded in Boggy.

"I breeng two kilo," he was heard to boast, "and make you mama a chicken head."

Once the appetite for cocaine was created, Haitian drug dealers, Miami boys, and Jamaican dealers slithered in to carve out their own markets in not just Boggy, but all of Oklawaha County.

Police agencies were stultified, overwhelmed, and ineffective, vitiated by the little white rock. After the death of Robin Porter, there was an outcry for a new sheriff, and into the fray walked MacArthur Dill.

He was the police chief of Lemon City. A little man filled with quaint little homilies, which were as practical as quaint once you heard them. He had no financial support and no support at all outside of Lemon City. And since it was such a small place, his entry into the sheriff's race was considered a joke. But he had the attention of the Swaggs.

MacArthur Dill sensed the powerlessness and desperation of the people of Boggy, and he spoke to them as individuals, as a community, and as a group. Eva Horton did not ask him to like us, that was irrelevant, and he didn't pretend he did, but the distinction acknowledged our humanity and indicated that he would stand up for the rights of *all* the citizens of Oklawaha County. That was enough to make Eva Horton throw a big party for him at the Masonic Hall.

Two days after the event, the Cuban boy and his wife were found hanging upside down from the roof beam of their living room. A plastic bag was tied over their heads, and their throats had been cut. They were drowned in their own blood.

The police assumed they were murdered by rival drug gangs. But the county sheriff, feeling a strong challenge from MacArthur Dill and his groundswell of support from black people, hinted it may have been a vigilante murder done in revenge for the death of Robin Porter. Since Eva Horton had adopted her two daughters and was a close friend of her father, the implication was clear.

Once again, Eva Horton—and, by association, us—was in the eye of a storm. An especially killer storm, because a group of Spanish boys from Tampa came looking for revenge. They started robbing and killing the Haitian dealers, and the Haitian dealers retaliated. One morning, two men were found shot to death in a Mercedes with Miami license plates. One of them was the brother of Hector Maldanado. They'd been watching Eva Horton's warehouse.

The next day, a Spanish man walked into Tiny's Liquors and asked Tyrone the barkeeper if he was Jessie Red. "Who wants to know?" Tyrone asked him. And the assailant drew a .38 revolver and shot him six times. But Tyrone was a big man, and the shots did not knock him down, but sent him sliding down along the bar to the very end where he kept a loaded .44. The assailant walked down to the end of the bar and looked over at Tyrone, who, with his last strength, fired one shot in the eye of his assailant, killing him instantly.

Jessie Red and all his brothers gave Tyrone a big funeral and immediately after went into hiding. So did Eva Horton. And dope dealing in Boggy became a very high-risk proposition.

MacArthur Dill found himself having to defend Eva Horton as "good people," standing up for what was right. He refused to disassociate himself from her or the Swaggs. He was now a strong, viable candidate for sheriff. The powers in Olawaha County were ready to back him, and the rabble were climbing aboard. They told him he didn't need the Swaggs anymore and pressured him to cut them loose. That would have been an easy thing to do, but MacArthur Dill had more integrity than they thought, and they just didn't understand *that black bitch!*

Eva Horton had friends. And some of these friends worked for the Oklawaha Public Safety Department. Most of them were women. Clerks, secretaries, aides who couldn't support her publicly, but could and did support her morally and spiritually. One day Aunt Sally received a package at her office in Eloise addressed to Eva Horton. She opened it and found a welter of interoffice and confidential memorandums: arrest records, drug seizures, financial records, employee records, and police action plans. When all of it was analyzed, it revealed that the sheriff's department could not account for $200,000 in confiscated drug money, $100,000 worth of seized property, $750,000 worth of illegal drugs, and one ton of marijuana that was supposed to have been burned and never was, or at least there was no record of it.

MacArthur Dill was losing support among the white people. When Eva Horton gave him this information, he called an immediate press conference and asked for a state investigation.

Actually, the state was already investigating, and had been for over a year.

The sheriff's office claimed it was merely the victim of sloppy bookkeeping. Not so, said state investigators, and to prove it, they seized the chief deputy's airboat, the engine having come from a confiscated drug plane. The governor removed him and the sheriff from office, pending the outcome of the investigation.

The investigation by the Florida Department of Law Enforcement revealed that Hector Maldanado was a cocaine and marijuana trafficker turned DEA informant. He was caught zooming through Oklawaha County with two kilos of cocaine and $22,000 in his car. Hector Maldanado made a deal with the Oklawaha sheriff's office, offering to steer drug-laden planes to secret landing strips in the county. The sheriff would nab at least one out of three, make a million-dollar drug bust, and confiscate another million in property. It was a sweet deal, until Robin Porter assumed smoking crack was probably no worse than smoking grass.

It was widely believed that Hector Maldanado was killed by people he'd double-crossed, and the sheriff's memo was an attempt to polarize the voters and cripple the campaign of MacArthur Dill. But an FDLE memo supported this contention. It said a blanket found behind the house was analyzed and found to have been saturated with the ministrations of a female dog in heat. This suggested country boys. This suggested Unck. Thus, Eva Horton became the focus of an investigation about her romantic involvement with Elijah Woodside. Which surprised no one.

The wiretaps also revealed that Unck was one of the ones robbing and killing drug dealers, and that my daddy was reselling the drugs in New York.

Hector Maldanado was a prized DEA informant, and they

were not happy about the manner in which they'd lost him. Indictments were handed down. The sheriff, the chief deputy, two judges, five detectives, twelve deputies, and nineteen other people including Unck and my father.

What surprised the people in Oklawaha County was the character these men displayed in defending and avenging themselves and their place. They were not soft and weak. They were not cowards. They were not even bad. They were good, the kind of people you would want to be associated with. And that is what people would tell the Wongs if they wanted to know what kind of people we were: good people, and not unworthy of their friendship. Unck held no malice against Peter Wong. To me, he was just Rudy's little Chinese friend, and that's all I knew.

"Hey Rudy!" I called to him, seeing him come down the path from Silo. Savannah and Linda were not too far behind.

Something was wrong. He looked mad, walked mad, and was kicking up plenty of dust. His fists were balled and his face was a mask of wrath and fury as he stomped past me.

"Hey Rudy!" I called him again, vexed that he should ignore me. "Grandma Gert just got through talkin' to your little Chinese friend and—"

He spun around with a crazed look and screamed, "He not Chinese!"

Then turned and stomped on toward the house.

"Well," I hollered after him "he look Chinese t' me!"

"Well," said Linda as she came up, "he ain't."

"Well, what he is if he ain't?' I asked.

"Hmong," said Savannah.

"Mmong?" I asked.

"Hm-mong!" said Linda.

"Oh," I said as if I knew what that was. "Anyway, what's

wrong wit Rudy?"

"He mad," Savannah said.

"Who made him mad?" I asked.

"That duck," Linda said.

And that made me mad.

That duck bothered no one but Rudy. Whenever he saw Rudy, he would attack him with an inexplicable and sudden viciousness. Rudy wasn't scared of much, but he was scared of the duck.

"I'm sick of that duck!" I spat.

"Rudy too," said Linda.

"That's why he killed it," said Savannah.

"He killed it?" I asked.

"Killed it dead," said Linda.

"Choked the dookey out it!" said Savannah.

"Gollybum!" I cried in wonder.

"He here?" Linda asked.

"Who?" I asked.

"Pete," she answered.

"He so cute!" said Savannah.

"He look like a lil' doll baby," said Linda.

"No," I said, "his mama just called and talked to Grandma Gert. They want Rudy to come to some party."

"Ooooo!" they both sighed. "We wanna go."

"Well," I said, "Grandma Gert wanna know why they like Rudy so much."

"'Cause," said Linda.

"'Cause why?" I asked.

"'Cause we good people," said Savannah, "and we the only ones don't call him *Chink*."

Which was as good a reason as any.

"Oh," I replied.

Remembering the pots, I started to go down to Silo and get lost, but remembered there was a dead duck down there that Grandpa was going to want plucked. So I opted for the pots and followed them to the house.

11

The Mamas and
The Papas

The Mamas and the Papas

Eva Horton looked at her son and for the first time in her life was afraid for him.

"I told you he wasn't worth the bother," she told him, and realized it wasn't the right thing to say.

Quickly she picked up the phone and touched out a number. Paulus stood at the inner office window staring from the upper office down onto the warehouse floor. She watched him from behind. He was lost. A bright thing suddenly come to confusion. It was her responsibility, as a mother, to clear up confusion and place the confusing things in the right perspective. If she failed to do that, failed to give him a clear understanding, he would not only be lost and confused, but destitute and broken. Everything depended on the right words.

Self-respect. She'd spent her life weaving it around him until it was like a coat of mail that nothing could penetrate. But then came history, the sins of his father, and the distillation of rumor to assault his soul at the same time with the same skewer.

The history was a nightmare of outlandish lies and so much rumor. Never in her life had she worried about rumor; in fact, she fostered rumor upon herself and used it to her advantage. She needed to teach him that, but for the moment, she needed to get his attention.

"That nigga ain't shit," she said.

He didn't flinch. She thought he would.

"Mama, what's a nigger?" he'd asked her when he was six years old.

She remembered the question because she didn't have an answer, and remembered when she was six and wanted to be a white girl, because her father was always complaining: *A nigger ain't shit!*

With that understanding she'd told him, "It's something you don't wanna be."

Which was more or less confusing. And so complex a word and thing it was exceedingly difficult to explain. So complex and yet so simple. It was simply a matter of self-respect.

Head down, he glanced away from the window and whispered, "I'm sorry, Mama."

"All niggas sorry!" she snapped back at him.

All depended on the right words and she had yet to find them.

"Yes, hello," she spoke into the speaker-phone. "This is Eva Horton. I need your help, dearie. Uh-huh. OK. I need you to look up the birth records of Cathleen Parks. What I need is pertinent information. Mother, father, et cetera. Yes. Yes, that's right. I have all this but I've misplaced it, so you can save me a lot of trouble, sweetheart. Uh-huh, yes, I'll hold."

She kicked off her other shoe, leaned back in her chair, and watched him from behind. He was staring down at the floor. In a mocking voice she said, "I left him—ha! That's the lie he always told."

She walked over to the cooler and got herself a strawberry soda. She lifted a napkin from the cooler top and used it to wipe the mouth of the can after opening it. She sipped and smacked her lips. He looked at her, then looked away. She sipped again and walked over to the other window, the big window which faced the outside and presented a clear picture of their old packinghouse across the street. Despite the number of times she'd stood there, watched and reflected on it from the warehouse window, it always seemed so small, and she always missed her name being there. HORTON. She looked at it and sighed. SILO CITY AQUA-CUL-TURE, it said. It was a fish-processing plant these days. A growing and profitable operation. It was Paulus's first business venture after college, a risky venture he'd claimed would expand the business. A fish farm? He was right on the money.

The idea had come from Elijah Woodside, who, along with Red Brown, raised illegal goldfish to sell to bass fishermen. Now she'd heard they'd gotten hold of some Gulf sturgeon. She didn't know how true it was; maybe it was just another rumor. She hoped so; Gulf sturgeon was an endangered species, and something sounded awful rotten about the deal.

The right words.

"If you knew that lyin' sonofabitch like I do," she said, "you wouldn't be all fucked up like you are now."

He didn't flinch.

"And you wouldn't study shit he's got to say," she said.

He still didn't flinch, but he said, "He wasn't lyin'."

"His whole life's a lie!"

"He wasn't lying."

"Maybe not about that, but there's shit you don't know."

Don't know. Paulus thought of the words that had suddenly rocked his world. *Don't know.* Words from his father. The only words of importance his father had ever told him. Words of utter destruction. A world of despair packed into five easy words that bit him like a poisonous snake and had him awake all night reading the Bible and frantically searching for each case of incest he could find. So far he'd found nine. The most telling being Abraham and Sarah.

But if God did bless Abraham and Sarah, then who are we to pass judgment?

"That girl is your sister," his father had told him, *"but ya mama don't know."*

That girl. Why that girl? Paulus Horton stared out the window of the warehouse office, wishing he were a prophet of God.

That girl was Cathleen Parks. The one daughter of Jeneen Parks. No one ever spoke about the father. Certainly not Jeneen, who'd abandoned the baby girl before she was a year old. Cathleen had been raised by her grandmother and grandfather on their small truck farm on the backside of Boggy. Paulus and Cathleen were the same age, had gone to the same schools, but were only slightly familiar. He remembered her as a skinny little black girl who sneezed funny and always wore bright colors that overemphasized her black skin tone. That is what he remembered about her the most. She had that rich skin tone like his mother. She was shy to the point of shame, and for that reason was never popular.

Cathleen grew into an awkward teenager who never had a close friend of either sex that he could remember. After high school, Paulus went to college, while Cathleen went to work.

He never saw or heard of her until the day Miss Gert asked him to deliver the eggs.

Miss Gert had known John and Olean Parks all her life. When the authorities were looking for Bake the Cake, he'd hidden with his father, but the little girl, Savannah, had gone to stay with John and Olean until the trouble was over. She never forgot them, and she never stopped loving them, and since that time, she and

Linda came every Friday morning with a basket of eggs and fruit and flowers and love.

In the eighty-third year of his life, John Parks suffered a stroke and died. One year later, Olean Parks suffered a stroke and remained partially paralyzed, unable to utter more than a few words and syllables, incontinent and needing a complete change of clothes and bed linens throughout the day. Cathleen quit her job in the courthouse cafeteria in order to care for her seventy-five-year-old grandmother.

Linda and Savannah did everything together. When one itched, the other one scratched. When Savannah got the chicken pox, Linda sulked and fretted until she got them too. But in all their selfish distress, they did not forget Cat and Miss Olean, and constantly worried over who would deliver the eggs. The two girls were upstairs that Friday morning and heard Paulus talking to Miss Gert. Spotted, poxed, and pajama-clad, they rushed down the stairs to plead with him and were immediately rushed back up the stairs and back into bed, but Miss Gert presented their request to Paulus and he was more than happy to comply.

It was early morning the day he arrived at the one-story, wood-frame shack. It was located at the top corner of forty-three acres of brush and scrub. Although she'd graduated high school, Cathleen had never gone to any of the class reunions that Paulus had sponsored—not that anyone had missed her. Looking at the shack, he felt a pang of guilt and sadness, and wondered if the terrible shyness of the skinny little black girl, who sneezed funny, was the result of her terrible poverty. As an illegitimate child, she'd endured humiliating, exclusionary teasing. They picked at her. They called her "jew baby." Paulus had asked his mother what it meant. He got no answer.

He got out of the car and started to take out the basket when he heard the unmistakable sound of chopping wood. He followed the sound around the back of the house and found Cathleen using a hatchet to chop wood.

"Cathleen?" he'd called to her.

She stopped and turned around. He had not seen her since high school, but she'd seen him often. Sometimes with his mother, and sometimes with his girlfriends, some of them white. She'd heard about all his successes. He was a candidate for a Rhodes scholarship, she'd heard, but instead came home and worked for his mother, building and operating a refrigerated warehouse complex in Eloise. She, like most, was surprised that he would even return to Oklawaha. He seemed so out of place, so unreal.

"Hi," she said.

The mysterious God had answered her prayers.

What Cathleen Parks had taken on was a task requiring an effort and an attitude beyond what any employer could ask for, but to her it was nothing out of the ordinary; it was the way she'd been raised. Every morning she got up and warmed one room of the house by lighting a small wood-burning stove.

"This little house has always been cold," she said, stirring the fire to get a good burn going. "Even when I was little I remember it being cold."

Paulus smiled at the thought of her being little. She placed a small kettle of water atop the stove and was trying not to appear shy. She was grown now, past shame; life had become too desperate for shame. Still, when their eyes met she could not help but avert them. Paulus sensed it. She dropped things. Was it shame or was it him? She'd always been a child of shame, but as a child, her beauty was yet unripened. She'd grown up to be sweet, and she was not without beauty. Beauty with kindness.

Beauty with truth. Beauty with innocence. Beauty with virtue.

No woman is without beauty, simple beauty and nothing else.

The beauty of her soul lay bare. She was a woman beautiful, to be wooed and won. A woman to be loved.

Cathleen went into the bedroom to see to her grandmother. In her absence Paulus took in the contents and the smells of the house. Smells of kerosene and lemon-leaf tea. Prince Albert tobacco and burning wood. Old. The house smelled old. Old as in oak. Old as in ancient. Old as in venerable. Old as in green growing vines and leafy ladders and antique high-back chairs. Empty snuff cans, a brown glass Clorox jug and big tin washtubs. All of John Parks's old things were still there. Things that belong. Things that lived long, existed long, been used long, and had stood for a long time. A washboard. A wood-burning stove. A faded photo of John and Olean Parks. A hand-painted sign above the front door that read: "A mother's love can never be told."

After changing her grandmother, Cathleen eased her into a rusty wheelchair and pushed her out into the living room, talking to her all the while. When Cathleen parked her in front of Paulus, Miss Olean struggled to indicate she wanted something. Cathleen laughed.

"What is it?" Paulus asked.

"She want a hat," Cathleen said. "I don't know if it's to keep her head warm or for you."

Cathleen hurried off to find her grandmother's black straw hat. On her return trip, she was matter-of-factly carrying soiled linens and bedclothes that she set in a tub on the front porch.

They had no running water. The water pipes had burst during the extreme cold of Christmas and were not repairable. She drew their water from the well of her neighbor, Mr. Mailer, where she also prepared at least one hot meal a day.

"How are you makin' out?" Paulus asked during the course of their conversation.

"Oh, we get by." She hugged her grandmother and laughed with the aspiring resignation of people who've had to struggle all their lives. "It just got rough about the time Daddy died. They didn't honor the insurance policy, so we had to spend our savings to cover burial expenses." Paulus shook his head in understanding.

"Things are starting to look up now," she continued. "We got mama's S.S.I. up to eight hundred eighty-four dollars a month. And Mr. Sears is intending to clear off five to ten acres and plant something for us."

"He never said nothing to me about it," Paulus complained.

"Well, it's nobody's business, really."

Paulus smiled softly, listening to Cathleen talk to him and her grandmother. Miss Olean heard things occasionally, but rarely responded. It was hardly shame, for shame would have killed her sometime ago. No, not shame, but a quiet reserve of *self-respect.* Nothing benefitted her more than her own self-respect. Grounded in a firm belief in goodness, it gave her a well-managed strength to surmount whatever difficulties or humiliations life presented. She was not as soft as she looked.

Paulus had to go. He had business and businesses to take care of. Clients, customers, attorneys, politicians, and people to meet. He was Eva Horton's son, an up-and-coming mover and shaker in the county, if not the state, if not the country. And Cathleen had things to do, too. She had to wash those soiled linens and clothes. Air her grandmother's mattress. Bathe her grandmother, and herself. Cook food and feed her grandmother and secure a ride to

Eloise for her grandmother's medical appointment in two days. Neither one had time to sit around and chit-chat the morning away. Yet, for the remainder of the morning, they sat around and played a game of "Whatever happen to?" And "Do you remember?" And by the time he did leave, he was wondering why his soul was so glad. She was marvelous! The selfless energy of her spirit was an expression of the harmony in her life, including all the pain and all the deprivations and all the hard luck. She was a fine blend of all the forces of the human spirit.

The small wind that blew the first time he'd delivered the eggs gathered force. So much force that by the time the two little girls had gotten over the chicken pox, they found in the midst of their spiritual bond of feminine faith—Paulus Horton.

Not only did he come every Friday, but Saturday and Sunday too. He took them wherever they needed to go and for long Sunday afternoon rides. He not only brought them baskets of eggs and fruit, but a brand-new wheelchair for Miss Olean. And new linens, and new clothes, and a brand-new hat. Then he arranged for them to lease their forty-three acres of land which allowed her to get the one thing she wanted most in this world: a new trailer to allow her grandmother to be cool in the summer and warm in the winter.

Linda and Savannah felt their worth diminish when Paulus had asked them why they hadn't told him about Miss Olean and Cathleen. And Linda told him because it was none of his business. The two girls did not see Cat and Miss Olean as poor. Broke, but not poor. They always had each other. But now who needed two girls when they had Paulus Horton? He was *the* most desired young man in Oklawaha County. He had money and he had sense. Who needed two little picky-head girls hanging around just to bring some old eggs? Who needed them to brush and scratch her head, like they did their grandmother? Or clip toenails, or pick corns, or thread needles like they did for their own grandmother? Who needed them underfoot giggling endlessly? In the five weeks since Paulus had first taken the eggs, he'd asked them five times to come ride with them on Sunday. And five times they said, "No!" And swung their heads away viciously. This was girl trouble that Paulus did not know how to solve.

It was not like they'd slipped her mind, but so many wonderful things were beginning to happen for her. And she did need them to at least sit with Miss Olean while she went to the store, even though Paulus took her everywhere she wanted to go.

Linda and Savannah came home from school one Friday afternoon to find Cathleen sitting on the porch with Miss Gert.

"Mama want to know why y'all stop comin'," she pleaded, even before the girls were up on the porch.

They had no answer.

"She miss y'all."

They fidgeted and stared at the ground.

"When y'all comin' back?"

"When you want us too?" Linda asked, starting to cry.

And Cathleen started to cry.

And Savannah started to cry.

And Miss Gert moaned, "Ooooh laaaawd!"

Cathleen got up and hugged Savannah.

"He wanna marry me," she cried. "Don't ask me why."

"You say 'yeah'?" Miss Gert asked.

"Yeah," she answered and wiped her eyes.

"Then the hell with 'why'!"

"I want y'all t' help me with the wedding," she said to the girls. And she was crying again.

"Don't cry, Cat," Linda whimpered and hugged her. "You're s'pose to be happy."

"I am," Cathleen sniffed. "We're plannin' a big weddin' at his daddy's church."

She wiped her eyes, turned to Miss Gert and asked, "Is it all right if they come and say 'hi' t' Mama?"

And Miss Gert shook her head yes.

Before they left, Savannah ran upstairs and got the poster she and Linda had painted while they had the chicken pox. It read: "The love of a daughter can never be told."

T he right words.

Eva Horton stared at her old packinghouse and contemplated the right words. The wrong words would make him hate his father and ultimately himself. The right words would give him at least a healthy respect for human nature.

The right words.

"You fuckin' her?" she asked.

Paulus looked at his mother and sighed. He understood the question.

"I know what I'm getting."

"Oh yeah? Well how do you know she ain't got a *swipe?*"

He said nothing.

"A big old *johnson?*"

He still said nothing.

"S'pose you reach down on your wedding night and feel a great big old—"

"Why don't you be quiet!" he yelled, trying hard not to laugh.

She did.

"I know what I want," he said.

"I know—she told me," she said.

"She told you what?"

"Girl talk—she's my daughter now."

"Miss Horton?" the voice came over the speaker phone.

"Yes!" she answered quickly.

"I have what you asked for."

"OK."

"Cathleen Anita Parks. Date of birth: September seventeenth nineteen seventy-two. Mother: Jeneen Parks. Father: deceased."

They both stared at the speaker, listening but not hearing. All that was pertinent had been said. *Deceased.* That was the same thing he'd learned when they applied for a marriage license. *Deceased.* That's what the official records said. She looked at him, he looked at her. *Deceased,* Paulus thought, but what did that mean?

Eva Horton waited until all the information had been given, then she thanked the clerk and asked her when she was coming to visit her.

"Can I come to the reception?" the girl asked as Eva Horton knew she would.

"Of course you can," she answered. "Didn't you get an invitation?"

"No, ma'm."

"Child, I don't know what I was thinkin'—I'll do that right now."

"Thank you, Miss Horton!"

"OK, baby. Bye now."

She hung up the phone and immediately wrote down a name.

"What are we trying to find out that we don't already know?" Paulus asked.

"Who her daddy is," Eva answered.

"We already know."

"Weeeellll, you know the saying—mama's baby, daddy's *maybe?*"

He looked away. There was no maybe in it. Except for her black skin, you could mark the resemblance in her hair, her nose, her mouth, especially her eyes. She and Paulus had the same funny-colored eyes. She was unmistakably Rev. Keats's daughter.

"We can cancel it. She can git sick or I can git sick."

The right words.

"Well," she said, sitting up. "Let us make any changes. Me and Cat's got everything just right—just the way we want it. All you gotta do is show up."

He was staring again. She wanted to make him laugh and not feel so desperate.

"Officially," she said, "he's not her father."

"That doesn't mean anything," he said.

"Officially it means a whole lot."

He looked at her and ran his hand over his head. Unlike Cathleen, he had hair like Herbert Horton.

"She was born in the house," Eva Horton said. "Miss Beck delivered her. She was one of the Yeager Clinic's midwives, so they have birth records. More than likely they have him listed as deceased, too, but that would only be the official record, so let's see what Miss Beck's got to say."

She touched out a number, sat back, and waited. After several rings a little girl's voice answered.

"Helloooo?"

"Hi, this is Eva," she answered.

"Uh-huuuuh."

"Who's this?"

"Bree."

"Hi, Bree."

"Hi."

"I wanna talk to your auntie—is she there?"

"Uh-huh."

"OK, run and tell her Miss Eva wanna talk to her."

"OK."

She waited and watched him.

"Yes," a voice suddenly came over the speaker.

"Miss Beck?" Eva asked.

"Hi, Eva."

"Hi, how are you, Miss Beck?"

"A little rain."

"Wellll, a little rain's gotta fall you know."

Paulus winced.

"Did you receive your invitation?" Eva asked.

"Child, yes, and oooo, it made me so happy! I born that girl—"

"I know."

"Her mama too—"

"I know."

"You too!"

"And half the niggas in Oklawaha."

"Y'know, I had t' fight t' get you to come out!"

"It was a lot better in the womb," Eva said, "more peace."

"Child, I know what you mean."

And they both laughed.

"Eva," Miss Beck said softly, "I got that invitation and I just sit down and cry. It made me think about John and Olean. And Jeneen—wherever she is."

"Wherever," Eva said sadly.

"Everybody was talkin', Eva."

"As always."

"Everybody was talkin' 'bout how he was just playin' with her."

"Hmmmm."

"But I git my invitation and sit down and just cry. It bring me so much joy."

Eva said nothing, but stared at Paulus.

"I think she's a lucky girl," Miss Beck said.

"Hah!" Eva Horton snorted. "He's the lucky one, if you ask me."

"Exactly what I told Cathleen!"

And they both laughed again. After a pause to catch her breath, Eva said, "Miss Beck?"

"Uh-huh."

"Uh, we're trying to get their health histories for, uh, insurance and everything."

"Uh-huh."

"Things to help Miss Olean."

"Uh-huh."

"Well, uh, Cathleen's father isn't listed on any of the birth records and uh—"

"He's dead."

"But who was he?"

There was a pause. The old midwife remembered every child she'd helped bring into the world. She knew the mamas and the papas and their children and how most of them turned out to be.

"Nobody knows," was her answer. "Jeneen said he was dead; she didn't say who; she just said he was dead, and that's what I put in the record."

"And the whispers?" Eva asked. "The milkman? The mailman? The iceman?"

The preacher man?

"Who knows?" the midwife said.

You! Eva Horton thought and knew. *You! You know, and you know you know! You know and I know you know! You know because you are smeared in the blood. His blood. Her blood. Our blood. The blood of our sacrifices. The blood of our sin. The blood of our guilt. You! Who examined the blood. And slept with the blood jammed between your fingernails. The blood of all our generations. Blood so cheap, bursting from his loins, flowing from between her legs, and in our veins, from all our fathers. Blood let from fathers, the father of the fathers, and made thick by the fathers. Nasty, vulgar fathers that you yourself cursed when you last saw them drip from her womb in a terrible burst of blood! You know and you know you know, for we are all born in blood and you did all the borning and the drinking of the sorrow. You know too much, too much of the blood.*

"Well," said Eva Horton, "tell me what you *don't* know."

"Whoever he is," Miss Beck said, "or was, he can be real proud of her. She ain't out runnin' the streets, and she ain't on dope."

"She's with us."

"She did good."

"OK, Miss Beck. I think we can manage with what we got."

"Eva?"

"Yes, ma'm?"

"It don't matter who he is. This is God's doin'."

"OK, Miss Beck, tell Bree and them I'll see 'em at the wedding."

"OK, baby. Bye now."

She clicked off the speaker and rubbed her eyes.

"She's his daughter," Paulus said.

"Doesn't matter," she said.

"I can't ignore it. I can't pretend it's not true."

"You have to learn to live and deal with lies and rumors."

"This is worse than a rumor, and worse than any lie. It's a crime to marry your sister. It's infamy! It's scandalous! It's—it's—it's—"

"An abomination?" Eva laughed at her own joke, but Paulus only stared in anger. It was not a laughing matter. But she laughed.

"Oooooh shit!" she laughed. "Oooooh shit!"

He glared and hissed, "Why can't you talk sense to me?"

"Because," she said abruptly, "I'm evil—remember? Evil Horton. This is my mouth and I say what the hell I want out of it."

But that was a lie, an Evil Horton lie. He knew it and she knew it. Her family circle knew it. Her one hundred and fifty employees knew it. The sheriff, the mayor and everybody else knew it, too. Evil Horton was a myth, an attitude she used to protect herself against any man who could look her straight in the eye. And even Paulus, if she felt evil enough. Miss Gert too, the day she felt big enough, bad enough, grown enough, and rich enough to talk to Gertrude Lillian Woodside any kind of way. And that was the day Gertrude Lillian Woodside knocked the evil out of Evil Horton. And sent her flying across a crate of tomatoes with a single backhand! Five-year-old Paulus and everybody in the packinghouse had witnessed it and everybody else heard about it.

"Bitch, I'll break yo back!" Miss Gert stood over her and growled.

Paulus remembered how Miss Gert grabbed him by the hand and stormed out of the packinghouse. As he weathered his mother's arrogance, Paulus remembered well how her bridge had come sailing out of her mouth as she splat-landed in a crate of squash. Miss Gert, and only Miss Gert, could subdue her arrogance.

"I wanna go talk to Miss Gert," he said, getting up.

And Eva Horton's arrogance faded quickly. Unlike everybody else, Miss Gert equated Eva Horton to a child whose arrogance would not submit to age.

"Sit down, Paulus," she said softly, motherly. "College is a place where you're supposed to learn to think, so let's think this out."

She pushed her hair back and ran her fingers through it, trying to think of the right words. She eyed the big Bible, picked it up, and laid it down in front of her.

"Reverend Keats was the first to call me that," she said, skimming through the book.

Miss Beck could have given her all the biblical justification she needed, if that's what was needed. But it wasn't. What was needed was a guide through the dark corridor of dry bones.

"Called you what?" Paulus asked, still standing at the door.

"Evil," she said, resting her head in her hand.

"Not without reason."

Sarcasm was not good. He had yet to learn how to ridicule without wounding.

"His reason," she said, "was to save his son's reputation by making me the bad girl. He succeeded 'cause you can't stop gossip and you can't stop what people think. And people had a lot to think about, 'cause I came back from Immokalee without him, three o'clock in the morning with Joe Head, Bolita Sam, and Jessie Red."

Paulus looked confused. He knew these men, hoodlums, were close friends to his mother, but he didn't know she'd run with them. Eva Horton smiled to herself.

"You ain't never heard all those stories about ya mama floating around here?"

"Not about Bolita Sam and Joe Head," he answered, "but a lot of other stuff."

"What stuff?" she asked quickly.

"Lotsa stuff. Lies—all of them, not that I listen to them. I made a rule not to listen to lies and rumor."

"Then you made a mistake. You'll never find the truth if you don't know the lies. You've got to understand the lies in order to understand the truth."

"What is truth?"

"You've been reading too much of this, kiddo," she held up the Bible and let it drop back to the desk. "God is truth—then again, God is a lie."

"What is the truth we're looking for?"

"We're hashing it out now. It's hard because nobody speaks the truth when they're talking about themselves."

"What truth?"

"The truth that leads us to believe in lies."

"My father's a lie? Is that what you're saying?"

"I already said that."

She sighed hard and sat up.

"Lies are sweet, Paulus," she said, rubbing her eyes, "and truth is bitter."

"So we take truth and make fiction."

"Fiction is closer to the truth than the truth itself."

"Tell me the truth."

"The truth can never be told."

"Tell me the truth. Tell me who."

The right words, now more than ever.

"All of us—that's who," she said, speaking slowly with her eyes closed and rubbing her temples. "All of us who grew up here. Jessie Red, Peter Red, Betty Red, Dirty, Red Shorty-Poot, Doody-Poot, Georgia Boy, Joe Head, Harriet Baker, Sally, Nasty Brown, Red Brown, too, even though he was a white boy—him and Tommy Green.

"All of us wasn't bad like some of them, but we all know each other, we all grew up together."

She paused. The right words would come, but only with the truth. It was the history she was telling, and history, all history, is but a pack of lies.

"Elijah and your daddy used to run together. That's where this mess started. You can call it bad karma. That's what it was, bad karma for years to come. He was a preacher's son, but he wasn't shit."

"You married him," Paulus said.

"That was another lie—my marriage to him."

She lit a cigarette and blew out a long plume of smoke. Paulus knew she only smoked when she was under stress.

"He was all about the con-game, so . . . "

Her voice trailed off as she realized what she was doing. These weren't secrets, these were closets and a tangle of skeletons. Still she proceeded on.

"Daddy made me marry him," she said. "He was a preacher's son, he was popular, he was rich—at least by our standards. He was bright-skinned, had curly hair and a good future. But I knew him for what he was. It's no surprise to me that Cat's his daughter. He was fuckin' half the girls in the congregation. But he couldn't git nowhere with me. He tried and got his feelings hurt."

"I imagine nobody could," Paulus said.

"Elijah could!" she snapped, "and that hurt his manhood. All the fuckin' he was doing was just the whims of his adolescent ego. Even when we were young, he had the pride of a pimp. That was his secret interest in me. Elijah beat his time and he couldn't stand it."

She paused to draw off the cigarette and reflect.

"Now don't git me wrong," she said in reflection. "I wasn't just another girl. I was 'Little Eva,' Herbert Horton's daughter. My daddy ran labor crews up and down the Eastern seaboard for forty years. The white people deferred to him. The niggers were afraid of him. But they stayed with him because he got them the best deals, and he didn't cheat them."

"That's not how I remember him," Paulus said.

"Well, that's how he was! And that shows how much you don't know."

There was a silence between them. In a calmer voice she said, "In other words, everybody knew and respected him—even if they didn't like him. He had power and he knew it. He was cursed by it, because the growers depended on him and they knew he knew it. So he had to be careful and play the role, even though he could bust a planter simply by going to Pennsylvania instead of Alabama. He got anything he wanted from them, and I was his princess.

"Miss Gert raised me. He stayed on the road so much, Miss Gert took me and raised me with her children. That's the only mama I ever had, the only family I've ever known, and the only people he ever trusted."

Paulus walked over to the window and stared outside. Let her talk, he thought to himself. Just let her talk.

"Only Elijah was bad," she continued. "Daddy liked him but

then Daddy found out how much *I* liked him! He didn't think Elijah would amount to much. But I think it was because Elijah was so black. Come tellin' me Leviticus Keats is the kind of boy I should be tryin' to attract. He was wild, and his daddy wanted him to marry and settle down. His daddy was all right, but his mama was color-stuck too. I was too black for her.

"Well, the daddies had their way and the next thing y' know, he was suckin' up to Daddy, and Daddy was showin' him off, showin' him the ropes. Really, I was amused by it all, 'cause I knew what I wanted, and I woulda had it, if Elijah had acted right. He was just like you see him now. Overalls, big old brogan shoes, and he always needed a haircut. Damn—I love that nigga! And they couldn't understand that, but that's because they don't understand love.

"I don't know what kind of deal they struck, but they invited me to a big dinner one night. It was a special dinner for some big church people from out of town. These were people who would support Leviticus and start him out. Real snotty people. I got the feeling I was being swept along into something I had no say in. This was like an engagement announcement or somethin', but I wasn't impressed.

"Back then, good girls didn't do much without an escort. So if you saw me, you saw Clara and Sally Gal. So to Miss Gert, it was the three of us who were invited to this big dinner. And I decided to use it to make my point. I convinced Elijah he was invited too.

"He got a haircut and bought a new suit, and Daddy got mad as hell when he saw him comin', but it wasn't nothing he could do, unless he wanted to insult Miss Gert and Daddy Troy.

"To these kind of people, Elijah was just a nuisance, and they just ignored him. It was easy for them to make him feel out of place, but we didn't care, we'd made our point, and Leviticus got the message. To me, the only man at the table who was more man than Elijah was my daddy.

"So they played these head games with us. Mama Keats kept cutting her eye at me. I shoulda knowed somethin' was up. You know what they did, Paulus?"

She called his name to make him turn away from the window. He did.

"Lemme tell you what these people did to us," she continued. "When we got to the dinner table, they gave Elijah the honor of saying grace!"

Eva Horton chuckled to herself, then laughed long and hard in remembrance.

"I mean," she said, trying to catch her breath, "we wasn't ready for that. We'd practiced our table manners and etiquette and all that proper shit, but we didn't expect them to give us the honor of saying grace. I mean with all them preachers there, who woulda thought it? Well, his old prune face mammy did! That was the kind of bitch she was. But still that wouldn't of been a problem but we wasn't religious. We didn't give no blessin' or say no grace at home. The food was ours. We said grace to the one who cooked it! We did the work, we reaped the bounty; it was simple as that. We weren't sharecroppers or serfs where we had to beg thanks to the lord of the land—or even to God. To us, God is good. It's as simple as that. There are only two forces in the world, good and bad. And God is good. And that's all he had to say: God is good, God is grace. Ain't that how it goes?"

"God is grace, God is good," Paulus replied.

"And we thank him for our food!" They sang together.

"And that's all he had to say, but he just sat there looking like 'Who me?'"

Eva Horton smiled sadly.

235

"Nobody had nothing to say to him all night and now they want him to give the blessing. The guests had picked up on what was happenin' and was like laughing at him. And Elijah wasn't smart enough to pass it off and he couldn't think of nothin' to say to save his life! Everybody had their heads bowed, hands clasped and were waiting for him to say the grace. And all he could think of was 'Oh Lord!'"

For the first time that morning, Paulus laughed. Not a chuckle, but a deep-chested laugh straight from the heart.

Eva Horton laughed too.

"Oh Lord!" she said and laughed again. "That's all he kept saying. 'Oh Lord! Oh Lord! Oh Lord!' I peeped outta one eye and everybody except Clara and Sally Gal were staring at him. He had his eyes closed, his hands clasped, and his head bowed, talkin' 'bout 'Oh Lord! Oh Lord! Oh Lord!'

"Then your daddy, the righteous Reverend Leviticus Keats Junior, showed his ass! I mean he took a simple blessing and turned it into the 'Sermon on the Mount'! I mean, God bless this! And God bless that! And God save the queen! And the hand that gives! And the eyes that see! And the dead that die! And on and on until the damn food was cold!

"And all them holy rollers sittin' there suckin' that shit up!

"When he finally got through, Elijah's chair was empty. We didn't even hear him leave.

"The only thing I could do to comfort him was to give myself to him. And even that didn't do much good. Three weeks after that dinner, he ran off and joined the Marines. And I ended up marrying your daddy."

Paulus was sitting and listening attentively. This was a room she seldom entered. A dark and haunting place. She was feeling her way through, searching for the right words to lead the way. She got up and lit another cigarette, then walked over to the window and stared outside. Here was the mystery of his mother, the aura and the riddle that was Eva Horton.

"We were married two years," she said, blowing smoke and staring, "but it was a marriage of appearance. He got what he wanted, but he had to marry me to get it. After that, I was just a trophy to him. He kept me cooped up in the house while he bragged around that he 'married the best pussy in Boggy.' I couldn't tell, 'cause all the while I was pregnant, he was gone.

"He was building his reputation as a preacher, going from town to town, church to church hustling religion. He came home right after you was born. He took one look at you and grinned that old shit-eating grin of his. 'But he got yo eyes—' his old prune face mammy kept saying. 'He take after Herbert, but he got your eyes.' She meant you was too black for her taste and she made a point of it because all of them are red, what daddy called 'shit-colored.' But it was important to them because preaching is show business, and perception and appearance is everything in show business. So, for appearances sake, we played the role.

"He got his own church over in Augustine Quarters. Saving souls for money. But the poor souls in Augustine Quarters didn't have much of it, so he decided to take this show on the road.

"Jessie Red had just gotten out of prison and was fulla that jailhouse religion, and the first thing he did was hook up with Leviticus, because *game recognizes game.*

"I don't know where they got that big old circus tent. A big ugly monstrosity they began holding revival meetings and baptizings underneath. You was about a year old then, and I was sick of Reverend Keats and Mama Keats and Jesus this and Jesus that, so I convinced him to take me on the road too. I convinced him by telling him that only a damn fool would trust Jessie Red and Joe

Head and Bolita Sam around that much money, and baby, the money was comin' in fast! Lemme tell ya somethin', Paulus, we was in the money business! The only game where money comes faster is the dope game. I didn't feel right about it, but shit, we talkin' 'bout money, and I handled it all!

"We went south 'cause watermelon season was in, so we headed down around Clewiston and Arcadia. One thing can be said for Leviticus—he could preach. I mean, wherever we put up, they came to hear him preach. He had a rap for your ass! And all I did was play the organ and count the money.

"We swung around the lake. Belle Glade, Pahokee, La Belle, and then Immokalee. That was supposed to be our last stop— Lord knows it was.

"Don't much happen in Immokalee until watermelon season. Then everybody whose got a *game* heads down there. We made more money in that town than anywhere else. We made so much money we got greedy and stayed there longer than we should have. I knew we shoulda left, cause I was pregnant again and showing. But the money was comin' in too fast and too sweet."

She walked to the desk, picked up another cigarette, and lit it. Paulus wondered what she was leading up to and how did all this fit in with Cat. She walked back to the window, stared in silence, then resumed speaking.

"They had a big old nigga named Jabbo White that ran the colored town. That was his section, and let me tell you, this nigga didn't play nuthin'! He didn't like red niggas to begin with. And he didn't like red niggas with processes. And he especially didn't like red nigga preachers with their hair processed coming to Immokalee to hustle!

"He didn't like Leviticus at all!

"That shoulda been a warning to be careful. Leviticus knew

238

it, but it was just like with Elijah, a thing about who's the most man."

She looked Paulus dead in the eye and said, "He's a silly nigga!" And Paulus shifted in his chair.

"He knew Leviticus wasn't nothin' but a crook. I mean, most preachers are, but some have a certain degree of good in them. I mean, they dance with the devil, but they'll cheat the devil too. But not Leviticus. I would give to charities wherever we went. I'd set aside money just for that. But he didn't want to give a penny away. To Leviticus, religion is about the beat. Religion is a front, and he paraded it in Jabbo White's face, because there was nothin' Jabbo could do. The white people know it's a game and they don't give a damn as long as they git a cut. They call it a license fee, and we paid about five hundred dollars in license fees, so they left us alone.

"Joe Head and Jessie Red had a bad habit about runnin' con games in the same town we were in. I warned them about that, but when things got slow, or just for the hell of it, they'd go off and do pigeon drops—assholes!

"That's what they were doing while we worked Immokalee. And one night, somebody from Fort Myers came to the revival and recognized Bolita Sam. And that somebody went and got Jabbo White! And him and his henchmen came in just as Leviticus was doing a miracle on Joe Head. He was washin' Joe Head's head with holy water when Jabbo White jumped up and shouted, "That nigga ain't blind!" And one of his boys shot at Bolita Sam and Bolita Sam dropped his crutches and tried to run under the tent, and all hell broke loose! Joe Head tried to hide his big fat self under the podium, Jessie too, but they got 'em. And they got me too trying to hide under the organ."

Paulus tried to stifle a laugh, but she wouldn't let him. She laughed loudly as she stuffed out a cigarette.

"If there's one thing they're serious about in Immokalee besides watermelons," she said, "it's Jesus. The crowd went crazy! They wanted to hang us—they tried to hang us! And these were black people!

"Jabbo White snatched me from under the organ and dragged me outside! And he didn't care nuthin' 'bout me being pregnant. He didn't care nuthin' 'bout us at all. Soon as we got outside they set fire to the tent and had Jessie Red, Joe Head, and Bolita Sam up on the flatbed wit ropes around their necks! They weren't playing either.

"I don't know what Jabbo had in his mind, but all he kept asking me was, 'Where's ya husband? Where's ya husband?' And all I kept sayin' was, 'My baby! My baby!' And that didn't do me one bit of good. The only thing that saved us was the truck wouldn't start. And the fire.

"It was a big tent, and it made a big fire, and somebody somewhere called the fire department. Now firemen were white, and I thought that would help us. But these niggas was so mad and crazy, they beat up the firemen and ran them off! And Jabbo White wouldn't do nuthin'! He just stood there holding my hand, waitin' for the truck to start. Even when the police came, the white police, wasn't nothin' they could do. There were so many niggas out there they couldn't get through the crowd. And the people was shootin' at 'em! All they could do was block off the road and call in reinforcements. Police came from everywhere and they were scared to come in and git us.

"Except one!

"He drove his car through the crowd real slow. The crowd parted like the Red Sea! He had his light on and everybody could see it was the chief! And let me tell you, I ain't nevah in my life been so happy to see a redneck Cracker as I was to see that one! Baby, he got out of the car like John Wayne! And he walked up to Jabbo White and said, 'Just what the hell's goin' on down here?'

"And before Jabbo could open his mouth, I said, 'Mister, please help me!'

"And Jabbo said, 'Shut up!'

"And I said, 'Suh, suh, they tryin' t' kill us!'

"And Jabbo said, 'You need to be dead!'

"Now for all I knew, this Cracker coulda been the grand dragon of the KKK—they believe in Jesus too, y' know. So, right away I started talkin' money, and that got his attention. Money talks, baby! And that Cracka wasn't listenin' to that shit Jabbo was talkin' because I was talkin' shit like, 'Five thousand dollars! We got five thousand dollars!'

"And Jabbo said, 'Shut up!'

"See, he knew we had that money, and he saw it gittin' away, 'Cause in one breath I went from five to ten to fifteen thousand dollars! And the chief said, 'Jabbo, you ain't got no business doin' what you're doin'. Just who in the hell do you think you are! You s'pose to be keepin' the peace around here. Now don't let them start that truck and I'm holdin' you responsible.'

"He was talkin' tough, real tough! But he was scared too. I felt it when he grabbed my wrist and pulled me away. He led me to his car and put me in the back seat, then got on the radio and told somebody to get their ass in there and help Jabbo git them boys out and disperse that crowd. Then we backed out slowly.

"Me and Leviticus always rented a house. I insisted on it. And I insisted on a nanny and a housekeeper to help me with you. The rest of them stayed in motels. I showed the chief where the house was and we drove there. We didn't talk, we just went there and went inside.

"I handled the money, but Leviticus kept it. He'd give them their cut, take out expenses, then wire the rest to his daddy's church—in his name, of course. But we always had a few thousand dollars around for expenses. It wasn't nothin' for me to send my daddy or Miss Gert a thousand dollars. That's how Sally went to college. I handled the money and took care of expenses, so naturally I took care of myself. If we took in a collection of a thousand dollars, I'd keep at least half. We were pullin' in so much, nobody suspected. I'd squirrel away a good five grand and send it to Sally, and she'd put it away. We have about seven or eight bank accounts around the state. I had fifteen thousand dollars stashed in your crib, and that's the money I offered him.

"When we got inside, Miss Lee, your nanny, was in a panic. She said Leviticus had already come and gone and a woman was in the car with him; she thought it was me. I took you from her, went in the bedroom, and showed him where the money was. There was another three hundred dollars on the vanity, and I gave that to Miss Lee.

"I thought I was safe, but the chief came out of the bedroom and said I had to leave—right now! He said Immokalee wasn't safe and I had to leave town. And he wasn't jivin' either. When he put the money in the trunk, he took out a shotgun and loaded it up. He was dead serious!

"Just before we pulled off, Miss Lee came out of the car and brought me my baby bag, and that was the last time I seen her. She thought I was going to jail.

"I could see why the sheriff was scared when we passed the police station—there was a huge crowd outside. He had his radio on but there was nothing but static and confusion coming over it. They finally got the flatbed started, but the police had Joe Head and them, so they drove it out to the middle of the street and set it on fire. The police couldn't pass, so they had to detour across a cow pasture to get to the highway. They were pretty beat up, but they were still alive.

"The chief drove to Fellson and pulled off the road by a little post office there, and waited. Know sumthin'? You were quiet the whole time. The chief didn't talk either. Wasn't nuthin' to say. We just sat there and waited. And after a while, you could see the lights coming up in the distance. When they got close, the chief turned on his lights and the caravan stopped in the middle of the highway. It must have been fifteen cars in all with Joe Head's big red Cadillac in the middle and fulla bulletholes!

"The chief got out with his shotgun on his hip, and took me over to the Cadillac, opened the door, put me in, stepped back, and waved us on.

"We went straight down Twenty-nine, straight through La Belle. Didn't stop for nuthin'! We went all the way to the Hendry County line and pulled off to the side of the road. One policeman got out, came to the car and said, 'OK. This is as far as we go. From here on out, y'all's on ya own.'

"And he stepped back, and Joe Head hit the gas, and baby, let me tell you, the whole front end of that big Cadillac hawg sat up in the air! We went from zero to ninety in two seconds flat! And we didn't slow down until we got back to Boggy!"

Eva Horton took a deep breath and looked hard at her son, wondering if he could see beyond her woe. If so, then he saw the wickedness we are conceived in and that meant he saw too far beyond his own understanding.

"I didn't have to tell them where to take me," she resumed speaking. "Joe Head drove me straight to Miss Gert."

She moved to the desk, and picked up the phone.

"What they say about the sins of the father is true," she said.

"The sins of the mother too," he said.

"I lost *his* baby that night."

There was silence between them.

"I didn't know," he finally said.

"That's why you're my only child," she said. "They put out I had an abortion."

"I didn't know."

"There's a lot of things you don't know that Miss Gert said you should know."

"Like Cat?"

She sighed.

"Don't you think if I'd known he was fuckin' Jeneen Parks and Cat was his daughter, I would have told you?"

She didn't wait for an answer but picked up the phone.

"What do we do, Mama?" Paulus asked in resignation.

"Preachers come a dime a dozen," she answered. "Let's find another one to do the wedding."

"What about Cat? What about what people say—"

She slammed down the phone.

"You ain't heard a damn thang I been sayin'!" she hissed.

She sighed wearily, closed her eyes, and sat back in the chair.

"I never cared what people say, because people say anything," she said. "It was a whole year before he showed up in Boggy again. And by then, people were saying all kinds of shit. But to this day I have yet to say one word to him, his mama, or his daddy."

She opened her eyes, softened her voice, and added, "It wasn't that I didn't want to. I was in the hospital. I had a hysterectomy. I was waiting for Reverend Keats or Mama Keats to come visit me, but they never did. What they did do was talk about me and badmouth me to everyone. Broke my daddy heart, the things they was saying. Miss Gert and Clara took care of me. And Sally came home from school to be with me—missed a whole quarter.

"And all him and her could think about was his son's reputation. And they were doing it from the pulpit too! Sally and Clara went to church 'cause they wanted to talk to Reverend Keats after the service, but they couldn't even stay, he was talkin' 'bout me so bad. They came home mad as hell. They said he didn't call my name, but everybody knew who he was talkin' 'bout. Well, I was too sick to worry 'bout it, but Sally wanted to know who this *Aholibah* was. I thought she was somebody like Jezebel or Delilah, and them two was always all right wit me. But Sally kept lookin' and lookin', and she went through the whole Bible and couldn't find who they was talkin' 'bout. So she asked Grandmama, who found it for her. And I read that shit and cried."

Eva Horton laughed, flipped open the Bible and gave it to Paulus.

Paulus took the book and began to read: *Son of man. There were two women. The daughters of one mother. And they committed whoredoms in Egypt. They committed whoredoms in their youth.*

Paulus paused, took a deep breath and looked up at his mother. Eva Horton smiled.

. . . thus were their breasts pressed and there they bruised the teats of their virginity. . . . And the names of them were Aholah the elder and Aholibah the sister, and they were mine, and they bore sons and daughters. Samaria is Aholah and Jerusalem is Aholiba, thus were the names. . . .

When he finished, Eva Horton said, "That was the last straw for Miss Gert. She and Sally drove back to the church. And Miss Gert went in. And she went right down the middle of the aisle and stopped right in front of the pulpit. And her first words were, 'Let me tell you one goddamn thang!' And ooooh, Miss Gert stood there and cussed for fifteen minutes! I mean she put it on 'em! She pulled the covers off Reverend Keats, Mama Keats, Deacon Rhodes, Reverend Powell, Mamie Allen, and all of them! I mean she read them like a book! The ushers were tryin' to talk to her, but they wouldn't put a hand on her cause Miss Gert's got four boys that might kill ya for even talkin' 'bout her. Old Deacon Rhodes tried to get the choir to get up and sing. Half of 'em did, but the other half was too busy listenin'. And that's when Reverend Keats and Mama Keats got up and walked out of their own church!"

She sat back with a smile on her face. She started to say something but Paulus asked, "What's all this got to do with me?"

"Plenty!" she answered quickly.

"What're you saying, Mama?"

"What's not easy to say."

"Is he my daddy?" he asked hoarsely.

"Go ask Gertrude."

"Who?"

"Go see Miss Gert."

"Why?"

"Because."

And she laughed.

"Because," she said, "when I first showed you to her, she said, 'Mmmmm, he every bit his daddy.' She was talkin' 'bout your eyes. See, that's what fooled 'em. You got funny-colored eyes, Linda's got funny-colored eyes, and Clara's twins, and Arthur Lee and Melvin. And all y'all got them from Grandmama. Know where she got hers?"

Paulus shook his head no.

"Eloise Parker," she said, "the woman this town is named after."

Paulus looked stunned. "Kin to the Ceelies?"

Eva nodded her head.

"Miss Gert told me," she said, "and she oughta know. That's somethin' ya don't talk. It coulda got them killed in the old days." Then she said, "You are not Leviticus's son."

"I don't understand," Paulus said.

"Well," she said, "that's a lie you better understand."

"I'm not my father's son," he said, rather than ask, against his own understanding. "But he's the only daddy I ever knew."

"No, he's not! He's the only man you ever called daddy. A wise father would have known. Elijah knows, and he never asked me why. He just shrugged and said, 'That's the way it goes.' It's kind of wisdom that's secretly understood. You're Bake the Cake's brother. Cody Wayne and Linda's brother. You're Savannah's uncle and Miss Gert's grandchild."

Her eyes filled, and one big tear dripped down her face, across her lips, and down onto her breast. One long tearful drip of human nature and human frailty. A tear for silence and a tear for joy. Paulus sighed. He didn't want tears; he wanted answers.

"Because!" she snapped sharply, before Paulus could get the why out of his mouth. Then in a softer, sadder tone she said, "Because." She sighed and threw up her hands in a loss for words. "Because, because, because." She massaged her forehead and took a deep breath. She said, "When he came back from the Marines he was crazy. Miss Gert said shell-shocked, but that's just another way of saying crazy. I was in Jacksonville in the middle of a big blueberry deal with Pantry Pride when Clara called and said he was home. I dropped everything I was doing, left the car, left the deal, and flew straight back. I hadn't seen him in two and a half years— that's how long he was over there. My love life was nothing. Everything was business, business, business! I got back and ran straight in the house, huffin' and puffin'. Miss Gert said, 'He in the shack.' And I ran over there and opened the door and first thing I see is this big ole army tent sittin' in the middle of the living room!"

Her head dropped back and she laughed aloud. "I mean it blew my mind. I'm standing there lookin', wondering what the hell's goin' on! And he come crawlin' out lookin' up at me talkin' 'bout 'Hi.' And I looked at him and said, 'Elijah, you pitched a tent in the house.' And he say, 'Yeah.' And I say, 'Why?' And he say ''Cause the roof leak.' And I say 'Why don't you fix the roof?' And he say, 'I dunno, seem like a good idea.'"

She held her head and laughed again, then sat silent for a moment with her head resting in her hands.

"He was crazy like that," she said. "That's why people are a little scared of him. And I didn't know whether he'd get over it. So, against Miss Gert's better judgment, I thought it was best to leave things the way they was, but I was wrong.

"Don't ask why," she said. "Don't ask what. You bring us joy, so much joy. Everybody's happy. There's no blood between you and that girl, only in Leviticus's mind. So go be with her, and be happy."

She wiped her face and sniffed hard. He was still sitting there. She looked up at him and said, "Go! I gotta call Miss Beck and straighten this with her. And then I gotta make some more rumors—start some more shit."

And she picked up the phone and touched out a number, but Paulus knew, as he walked away, all she wanted to do was cry.

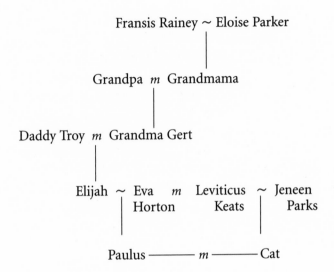

Fransis Rainey ~ Eloise Parker

Grandpa *m* Grandmama

Daddy Troy *m* Grandma Gert

Elijah ~ Eva *m* Leviticus ~ Jeneen
Horton Keats Parks

Paulus ——— *m* ——— Cat

III

The Thang
That Ate My
Grandaddy's Dog

Of Dogs and Alligators

About a mile outside of Lemon City, just off the road and into the bushes, there is a small pond surrounded by cattail reeds. Somewhere inside this pond lives a twelve-foot, voracious alligator.

If you pull up to the path that leads to the pond, the alligator will come charging up out of the water with its mouth wide open, expecting you to toss it something to eat.

The first time we showed it to Manasha, it came rushing up toward the car, and Manasha, believing it was possible for it to jump through the window, hit the gas and cut a new road back to the highway!

It was almost like a tourist attraction. If the county knew it was there, they would have charged a fee to see it and a fee to feed it.

If people had not started feeding it, no one would have known it was there. It just would have been back there minding its own business. But everybody knew it was back there because a fellow went back there to fish the pond and discovered it. It was only about four feet then, but it grew rapidly when this fellow and his friends found it very entertaining to feed it stray dogs.

This has become a big event Saturday and Sunday afternoons, with truckloads of spectators swilling beer and cheering wildly as this ferocious reptile devours some poor mutt.

We were not amused by this, and Manasha was distressed. It was the most cruel and inhumane thing she'd ever heard of, and that is saying quite a lot, because Manasha was raised in New York City. Even in New York she'd had a dog; here she had five, although Poochie was the only one she could hug and pet and pamper and love like the one she had when she was a little girl. Ike and Shack and Blackie and Lance were not house dogs, did not care to be house dogs, and would not let you house-break them. They pissed where they felt like pissing.

But if Manasha went down to Silo, one or all of them would meet her along the way, stay with her until she finished what she was doing, then escort her back.

Our dogs, with the exception of Poochie, did not like the house. There were too many rules and too many chiefs for their liking, for these were dogs, male dogs, always looking to dominate. Each one had his own house in his own territory and did not suffer intruders. Silo was their territory, but all the swamp and forest was theirs, too.

Manasha had a great deal of admiration and respect for the dogs, even though they would not eat from her hand. But still, they would tear you apart if you messed with her. This was a goodness beyond love and not a nisus for self-preservation. Dogs are like that, and in that sense, they are much like us, or rather, the way we should be. *Train up a child the way he should go and he will not depart from it.* Which is the problem with us. Human beings go can astray for the most capricious of reasons, but a stray dog is a metamorphosis.

Dog is "man's best friend," and we abandon and desert them. I wonder if an abandoned dog suffers a spiritual trauma. Does it seek to reunite the bond between it and humanity? I know one thing: It will revert back to the wild.

It takes about three generations for a dog to revert to the point beyond rehabilitation. In that time it is a pitiable, vulnerable, and most often contemptible creature. Like humans, dogs are dependent creatures, needing love, affection, and a sense of worth. If a stray dog is fortunate enough to avoid trucks and cars, the Humane Society, wanton cruelty, and the mange, it will find a pack to run with. This is not unusual, since all dogs revert to pack behavior; it's built into them. Two dogs make a pack, and wild dogs are merely wild as opposed to *savage*. It is this type of dog that is not to be pitied—but feared: the savage *feral*.

These savage predators are the most dangerous threat, besides the elements, to all of us living on the fringes of the Oklawaha Swamp. They are more dangerous and frightful than panthers and wolves. Those creatures are wary of humans; feral dogs are not. A lone wolf will not attack, but follow you until the pack catches up. A feral dog will attack you and cripple you so the pack *can* catch up. You can't poison them because they only eat "fresh kills." And you can't trap them because they know steel.

Packs of wild dogs inhabit the swamp, and occasionally a fire, heavy rains, or some other natural catastrophe will bring them out. Our dogs are exceptional in every respect, but they are no match for a pack of feral dogs. One night they fought with a group of six that had come into Silo from around Sky Lake. The boldness exhibited by the ferals caught our dogs completely by surprise, but they ran out and met them by the hothouse, killing two and driving the rest off. While all this was happening, a larger group was vandalizing the pens where we segregated hens and their broods.

Dogs of any stripe are not automata. They have a keen intelligence. Wild dogs possess intellect. That alone makes them more than a match for people, and that is why the Humane Society, as well as the not so humane among us, fears them and kills them.

It is my sincere belief that our dogs would not revert to their natural state to the point where they could not be rehabilitated. They knew their worth. Dog is man's best friend, but our dogs were family, bound in obligation and duty. My dogs would have searched and sought a master worthy of them, in full knowledge that the social whole of humanity has greater worth and significance than the individual asshole. Some men are worthy, some men are not. Some dogs are worthy, some dogs are not. The difference between worthy dogs and worthy men is sublime, but not indiscernible.

Rudy and Rodney Kemp found an abandoned pup in the alley behind Alberts Funeral Home. Rodney picked it up, shrieked, and threw it down; its underside was covered with ticks and fleas. But all Rudy knew was there was something about the little pup he liked, something faintly perceptible to a little boy who knew that if he didn't do something, the dog would die. So Rudy put it in a box and brought it home, where we dunked and de-liced and picked all the ticks off it. We groomed and nursed it back to good health, constantly fighting to keep it with us and out of the house and ribbon bows. He was a runty little thing, always trying to keep up with the other dogs. The funny thing about him was he didn't bark. He emitted something like a yowl to attract your attention. Otherwise he was silent. It took Red Brown's practiced eye to discern what was special about the dog. It was an African basenji, a rare and valued breed.

Rudy had named him "Runt," as in "you fuckin' runt!" And he was reluctant to part with it. But Red Brown was a worthy man, the dog a prized breed, and Rudy's uncle was a lawyer. Represented by Bake the Cake, Rudy incorporated the dog and received a premium on every ounce of sperm it produced. A high price for a stray dog, but we didn't see strays as other people saw strays. When we look at a stray dog, we try to determine its retrogressive state, that is, if it still believes in humanity. Poochie was a stray. Grandpa got her from the Humane Society. They were going to put her to sleep.

Lance and Ike were wild, born wild. I guess you can say, born free. They were part of a small group the forestry service was trying to run down. When they killed the dominant males, the group joined a larger group that was coming down from the reservoir creating havoc. This started people to shooting any kind of stray dog they came across.

A forest fire brought them out of the swamp, desperate, hungry, and dangerous. They might have been content to raid garbage cans and maybe snatch a few chickens, but people began to hunt them down, and they returned the favor in kind. Mr. Nate was attacked by a group of three that were guarding a bitch that had given birth to a litter of pups in his sunflower field. What saved Mr. Nate was that he always wore a .357, slung low like a gunfighter, whenever he was out in the fields. The dogs, however, didn't know anything about a .357. They attacked him from three sides, knocking him down and tearing at his flesh before he was able to kill two and drive the other one off.

A serious effort was made by the county and various trappers to subdue them, or at least push them back into the swamp, but the pickings around the farms and ranches were good. They pulled down a horse at the Weaver Stables and terrorized Mr. Blanding's milk cows, tearing out udders to get at the milk. They terrorized campers and hunters and foiled all efforts to trap them. The County and Forestry Service used helicopters and night scopes and still met with little success. What they learned was that you can't poison them, you can't trap them, and half the time you can't even find them. They also learned to use automatic weapons and to keep their own dogs on a short leash.

All of this was right down Unck and Red Brown's alley. All they needed was for everyone to get out of the way, and a sick pig.

They took the pig to where the tracking dog picked up the scent. They followed it until they began to find fresh droppings. Dogs are extremely territorial and will mark their space and defend it. When Unck and Red Brown were certain of where they were, they released the sick pig.

Around mid-morning the next day, they went looking for it. They didn't need a tracking dog, because in the wild, dogs are carnivorous predators. They kill their prey and rip open the stomachs, eating the vital organs first. Unck and Red Brown just followed the pig's trail until it became a blood trail. Soon after, they found all the dogs lazing beneath the shade of a big sycamore tree, filled to bursting after gorging on three hundred pounds of pig meat. And the slaughter began.

They killed nineteen and caught six runts. Lance and Ike were among them.

Red Brown said he kept Ike because he was the least confused of all the runts. And he was pit bull and bullmastiff, but not overly aggressive. He was special. The only thing special about Lance was that it took Unck an hour to catch him. The little runt played a game of in and out of the bushes, and Unck admired the vigor of his quick and lucid mind.

The runts of any pack of wild dogs are highly valued, no matter what the pedigree. Lance was a border collie, but his young life thus far had been a struggle to keep up with the pack or die. Like Ike, he was full of fight and keen instincts. To me, Lance was our best dog, and it was he who'd trained Runt.

One breeder came all the way from Virginia and another one

came from Louisiana to inquire about the pedigree of Runt. Both men were like Red Brown, more interested in the quality of a dog. They were two top breeders, astonished to hear that this rare and beautiful dog was once a homeless stray. There were very few in the county, and only one in the Southeast. Red Brown struck a deal with these men to raise and breed them in the U.S. The only problem was, it was Rudy's dog. He'd found it, brought it home, helped train it, and loved it to death. The dog was registered to him.

So all Red Brown could do was represent Rudy. And that is how Rudy became a co-owner in a breeding partnership of basenjis—simply because he could feel the distress and misfortune of a stray dog with tenderness and understanding as well as an urgent desire to aid it and spare it suffering. Thus, he was as horrified as Manasha or any civilized person to learn how these horrid fellows from Lemon City indulged their passion. We did not care to witness what an alligator on a rampage does to a helpless dog—a blood lust cruel, inhuman, and unworthy of us as human beings in an advanced state of culture.

We showed it to Manasha to prove it was there. She didn't believe it at first, even though we'd described it to her in detail upon ghastly detail. We painted a picture of blood and death. She didn't believe it, or want to believe it. Unck believed it, but was stoically amused. Grandmama shook her head sadly. Red Brown didn't have time for it. And nobody really cared until we brow-beat Manasha into pulling off the highway. Her disbelief suddenly gave way to astonishment when those huge jaws with rows of savage teeth came gaping at the car. And it wasn't expecting a baloney sandwich.

It was Manasha's horrified reaction that affected Grandpa so much that he told Unck to do something about it. And that is how

Lance taught Runt to bait an alligator up out of the water.

You must be licensed to hunt alligators in Florida. Unck and Red Brown were unlicensed and therefore were poachers. They were not only alligator poachers, but fish poachers, turtle poachers, bird poachers, and everything else poachers too. They had an illegal alligator farm on the back of Red Brown's ranch that featured two rare white baby alligators.

They paid us five dollars apiece for baby alligators. That made us poachers, too, a secret between us, Red Brown, and Unck. There weren't any gators in the lakes, but five miles down the run in the marshes there were plenty. None of them got very big because we caught them before they had a chance to grow. We caught them using big red-and-white bobbles. If it was over three feet, we cut the line and let it go. A gator that size could easily remove a hand or a foot. A gator the size of the one in Lemon City would gobble the bobble, the boat, and you too. To get a gator that size, first you had to bait him to the surface and get a rope around him. And the best bait for a gator, is a dog.

To our dismay, the gator did not come charging up out of the water when we first drove up, even though Lance and Runt were clearly visible. This meant he wasn't hungry, and Lance had his job cut out for him.

All of us got out of the truck and surveyed the area: burnt-out campfires, beer cans, discarded women's underwear, whiskey bottles, used condoms, dried blood, and bones.

"Put the dogs down," Unck told us.

"Runt too?" Rudy asked.

"Yeah."

Lance knew what he was doing, but Runt? Red Brown had trained him, some, with gators. He knew they bite. He had his own way of ducking and dodging them, but he had no idea of how to bait one up out of the water. All he could do was follow Lance, and learn from Lance, but if he made a misstep, then that was his ass.

Unck eased into the bushes and Lance went up and stopped about fifteen feet away from the bank and sat down. Runt did the same. They both smelled gator and there was no doubt gator smelled them. Lance got up and started toward the water but turned suddenly to move parallel to the bank. Runt did too. They trotted along, a good five yards away from the reeds, ducking toward them from time to time but moving quickly. Runt imitated Lance to the letter, going so far as leaping straight up in the air like a kangaroo rat. Lance was showing himself and at the same time sniffing out the nest. If it were a mama gator, there probably was a nest close by, and a mama gator is never very far from her nest. If not for Runt, it would have been an inspiring thing to watch, but we were too fearful for Runt. He was looking sharp and alert. He knew what Lance was up too, but was he nimble enough to run up under a gator if it suddenly burst up out of the water? This was a big test and the stakes were high. Unck did not have a rifle.

The dogs circled the whole pond in that hainty manner. Up to the water, away from the water, leaping, ducking, gazing, pausing, and feinting until they'd come full circle, where they sat down again a good fifteen feet from the bank.

They got up and started for another go-round, when suddenly a dark and fearsome missile exploded out from the reeds!

"Git!" I screamed.

Lance moved instantly, but Runt only turned. I thought it had Lance, but the dog dropped to its belly, doing almost a gator crawl itself to elude the big creature before gaining its footing. For one moment the gator saw Lance out of this eye, Runt out of that eye, and paused in confusion, allowing both dogs to escape. *That*

was not supposed to happen! They were not supposed to get away!
They never got away! Lance stopped and got clearly in its vision,
and the gator dashed after him. And gators are not slow. In a
straight eight-yard dash, you are as good as caught. Lance didn't
have that much; what he had was presence of mind and *sense.*
Sense enough to know that he couldn't outrun the gator and sense
enough to know the stupid thing could only see out of one eye at
a time. So Lance zipped this way and zagged that way. And the
gator first saw him out of this eye, then that eye, and got all cock-
eyed trying to keep up with him. It stopped to gain its bearings
with a wild shake of its long head as Lance turned and mocked
him. The gator raised up to come again and Unck creeped out of
nowhere, straight up behind it, and did a diving leap right atop it!
You could almost hear it go, "Oof!"

Right away me and Cody Wayne ran to it, he with the loop
and me with the tape. Unck had the gator laid flat out and totally
helpless. These beasts, for all their ferociousness, have no "lift."
Even their mighty jaws, which can crush the hard shell of a turtle,
have no lifting power. You can hold them shut. Unck had both
arms wrapped around it, hugging it close to his chest. He pulled
the head up just enough for Cody Wayne to loop the rope around
its mouth. As soon as he finished, I taped it.

Unck, still riding it, pulled its head back until its whole belly
was showing and he looked as if he would break its back. Instead,
he whipped both his legs around and put a scissor lock on it and
fell straight back. Now Unck was flat on his back, his arms and legs
locked around the gator and the big white belly exposed to us.

"Put 'im t' sleep!" Unck yelled.

And Rudy, with both hands, began rubbing and massaging
the beast's belly.

It didn't take long to sedate it, and Unck eased from under it, got up and called Runt. The dog came up and sniffed at the unconscious beast and Unck patted and stroked him.

"Good boy," he cooed, "good boy."

The only thing that had been expected of him was simply not to get eaten. In that respect he did good.

But Lance did great!

He'd mocked and humiliated the great mocker and humiliator of his species. Here he'd touched the highest point of his greatness, a greatness thrust upon him by his association with and love for man. The greatness lay in the fact that he was willing to expend himself in what to him was essentially a game. In time, Runt would learn the game, which was basically a game of how not to get eaten. After all, they were not lions, they were dogs.

Daddy Troy's Possum

"You should see it, Daddy," I said, holding the receiver as if he could see it. "You should see it."

"I already know what they look like," he replied.

"Looks like a big old rat, don't it?"

He said nothing, but swallowed hard. I sensed his displeasure.

"Don't eat it!" he bellowed in disgust.

"I won't," I cried. "I won't."

"They're horrible! They're scavengers! They eat the dead!"

Although I thought they were pretty good, at times, I had to think about what he was saying. Dead what—people? And the more I thought, the more fascinated I was with the dead marsupial, half-cooked, grinning in death, and laid out atop the microwave with a sweet potato in its mouth.

He'd stopped eating possums after he'd moved to New York City and found them scarce. Not to mention the fact that every other someone in New York City frowns upon the dietary habits of the rest of us. And now he did, too.

My father had become a Muslim in prison, and no longer ate things like possums and pork chops. But I did. I think possums are pretty good, the way Grandma Gert cooks them, and I'll eat them, but only if I don't know it's a possum. If I know it's a possum, it does not matter how Grandma Gert cooks it—I am not going to eat it. And neither will Manasha or Aunt Clara, Cody Wayne or Rudy, Savannah or Linda, Ingy or Cheryl, or Teenie and Weenie.

"Uh-huh," I answered to something my father was saying.

But I could not get my mind off the possum and how I'd seen it crawl up out of the ass-end of the rotting carcass of a dead cow. Now, who would eat such a thing?

It was Daddy Troy's possum, and only he would eat it. He ate them whenever he caught them, wherever he found them. He would see a possum, run it down, and make it play dead. Then he would pick it up by the tail and say, "In the pot!"

Daddy Troy loved possums. I don't see how anyone could love a possum, alive or dead. Possums ain't pretty. They are ugly, repulsive creatures even when they smile. They have sparse, dirty hair showing grubby pink skin underneath, which makes them look as if they have the mange. And they don't like water—they stink! But still, he loved them. He would catch them and cage them and fatten them up, then all of sudden one day, gut one and give it to Grandma Gert, who, if she didn't cuss and throw it in the garbage, would char it and scrape it and boil it before she fired, barbequed, or baked it. And as long as I didn't know it was possum on my plate, it was all right with me. And for that reason I never asked, "What's that?"

"Uh-huh," I answered to whatever my father was saying.

It is difficult to be a father by phone. He called often and talked about God knows what.

"Uh-huh, uh-huh, uh-huh," I answered.

I, on the other hand, wanted to talk about the possum, but my father had caught and eaten enough possums to last a lifetime and did not find them interesting. I, on the other hand, found them very interesting. To me, there is nothing on earth as interesting as a possum, but to my father, they represented extreme poverty, the kind of poverty that seizes the soul, deadens the spir-it, and becomes a state of mind. Possums were the reason why my father left Boggy.

I sensed my father hated Boggy because he never talked about it. So I didn't either.

But Rudy did.

He came into the kitchen, looked up at the possum, and turned up his nose.

"Who dat?" he asked me.

"Daddy," I told him.

"Lemme talk."

My father was Rudy's uncle, and, although Rudy had never seen him, he loved to talk to him.

"Hey, Uncle Melvin," he greeted. "When you gittin' out?"

It was the first thing he always asked.

"Oh," Rudy said, "know what we caught? A possum! Know where we caught it? Inside a cow! A dead cow!"

I wondered what my father's reaction to that was, or what he thought as Rudy went on to describe it.

It used to be that possums and other things seldom got this close to the house. The dogs kept them at bay. But now we had only Poochie. Blackie and Ike were dead, Shack was crippled, and Lance was not good for much.

In this, the night things rejoiced and crept ever closer. So close that now, if Daddy Troy wanted a possum, all he had to do was get up early in the morning and set the lid on the garbage can.

He was ready for a good possum dinner and all that comes with it. It was that time of the month again. I was taking out the morning trash when he burst out the back door with his shotgun and shouted, "Git that spread!" It was one of Grandma Gert's handwoven bedspreads, one of the ones she did not trust to the washer or dryer but handwashed and hung out on the line to dry. It was trouble for sure, but Daddy Troy had commanded me and I did not question or hesitate.

As I took the spread from the line, Daddy Troy dumped one of the garbage cans and placed the lid back on it.

"C'mon," he called, slinging it across his back.

We struck out from around the back of the house, across the Ceelie Road and up the Ceelie fence where he set the can down across it.

"Jumbooo! Jumboooo!" Rudy called from the front porch. "Where y'all goin'?"

Without waiting for an answer, he came.

"Git through!" Daddy Troy hurried us.

Halfway through the fence I heard Grandma Gert shout, "Come with that spread!" And immediately I froze.

"Git through—git through!" he urged us. "Git through!"

He passed the shotgun over to me and climbed through.

"Brang that spread back here!" She came onto the porch and screamed, "Right now!"

"Git the pot ready," he shouted back. "Ahma brang ya back a possum!"

"Don't put no possum in that spread! I don't want no possum! Ain't nobody cookin' no goddamn possum 'round here t'day! Johnny—Johnny! Brang that spread back here!"

The thought of running down a possum excited me, but not as much as Grandma Gert coming down the porch. I picked up one side of the can, Rudy picked up the other side, and we left the spread dangling over the fence as we hurried to catch up to Daddy Troy.

I understood the spread, but I did not understand the can. I know that a good way to catch a possum is to throw a blanket over it. The best way to catch a possum is simply to trap it, but that calls for patience and luck because, despite what people think, possums are not dumb—well, they're not as dumb as armadillos. Possums are very alert and crafty animals, smart enough to open cages. They eat snakes, but are smart enough to leave rattlers and moccasins alone. They come out at night to feed, and hide during the day. They climb extremely well, grip with their tails, and have a hiss so horrifying it will make your hair stand on end. And just because they wind up as roadkill at about the same rate as armadillos, it only stands to reason that they are often the victim of their own survival technique. An armadillo, depending more on its armor than its speed, will roll up into a little ball of armor if it sees an eighteen-wheel, thirty-ton truck barreling toward it at great speed in the middle of the night. By the same token, a possum, if it sees an eighteen-wheel, thirty-ton truck barreling toward it at great speed, will roll over and play dead.

"A possum is a dumbass thang," Daddy Troy said as we hiked across the field. "I drive from here to Canada and all I see is dead possums in the road."

It now stood to reason that the best way to catch a possum would be to go out onto the highway and scrape one up off the asphalt.

"The best way to catch a possum," Daddy Troy said, "is to set a slop can out overnight and git up early in the morning and set the lid on it."

That explained the can.

"Only thang love slop more than a hog," he said, "is a possum."

We were about a hundred yards into the pasture when the putrid stench of rot hit me and I realized we were going to the dead cow.

The dead cow had been dead for three days. It was dead because it had been struck by lightning. The first time we saw the dead cow, it was on the other side of the Ceelie fence across the road from our house. That was not where the lightning had struck it, but where someone put it for the sole purpose of aggravating us. The next morning the dead cow mysteriously appeared in Mr. Ceelie's driveway, which infuriated Mr. Ceelie to the point where he tried to have Unck arrested. He said only Unck could crawl low enough to get past his dogs. Unck shrugged and laughed and said he didn't know anything about the dead cow. And Mr. Ceelie screamed, "You're fulla shit!" And that he knew everything about the dead cow and if he ever caught him on the property, he'd shoot.

The next day the dead cow reappeared at the fence. That night, it disappeared from the fence and reappeared in Mr. Ceelie's hay barn. For a dead cow, it sure was getting around. When it reappeared at the fence the next day, Unck told Daddy Troy that as soon as night came, the dead cow was going swimming in Mr. Ceelie's pool. And Daddy Troy told Unck he was just asking for trouble and maybe it would be best to just burn it.

So, Daddy Troy dragged the dead cow a good ways from the fence and left it.

As we approached the dead cow, Daddy Troy raised the shotgun and fired several rounds to scatter the buzzards. I picked up the empty shells and put them in my pocket.

The stink was so bad my eyes watered. Rudy pulled up his shirt to cover his nose and mouth. The dead cow was stiff and bloated and full of maggots. Where its tail should have been there was a gaping hole boiling with blowflies. Daddy Troy placed the open end of the can against the rump of the dead cow and told me and Rudy to sit on it. Rudy and I straddled the can.

"OK now," he said, "just sit there."

He poked at the belly and the dead cow seemed to tremble all over. Daddy Troy smiled.

"OK," he whispered conspiratorially, "don't let it git away."

Daddy Troy kicked the dead cow in the head and jammed the shotgun into its mouth.

"Hooooldit!" he groaned as if getting ready to snap a picture. "Hooooldit!"

Since we knew what was about to happen, and since it was happening inside the dead cow, the blast did not scare us. What scared us was the sudden impact of rotting matter and buckshot bursting through the butt of the dead cow and slamming into the back of the can.

"Gottdog!" I screamed sharply.

"Stay on it!" Daddy Troy shouted as Rudy jumped off.

He fired again and there was an outward burst of rotting matter up from the side. I held my place, frightened for sure, but curious as to what kind of business was this. Daddy Troy started to fire again, but the dead cow began to shimmy. The haunches trembled, the belly shook, and something fell into the can clawing and scratching across the metal.

"Hold it tight!" Daddy Troy shouted.

I held my place.

"I think we got it," he said.

"What we got?" Rudy asked.

Like a scene from the movie *Alien*, where the infant alien monster suddenly burst up out of the belly of the astronaut, a grisly little alienlike head suddenly burst up out of the hole in the belly of the dead cow.

"Oh shoot!" I cried.

"What's dat?" Rudy cried.

"Another one!" cried Daddy Troy.

And Rudy took off running.

I didn't recognize it at first, not until half its body had wiggled through. It plopped out onto the ground, bared its teeth, and hissed viciously.

"In the pot," Daddy Troy cried in the deepest of glee, "in the pot."

He ran out in front of it, teasing and poking it with the shotgun. The possum hissed and tried to run in another direction, but Daddy Troy blocked it and began playing the matador. The possum lunged to attack and Daddy Troy bonked it on the head with the shotgun. The possum, seeing no way out, raised up, trembled, rolled its eyes, slobbered, lolled its tongue, gasped, rolled over, and played possum.

By that time, Rudy had run halfway back to the fence and was watching us from afar. Daddy Troy hollered at him to get some kerosene, and he acknowledged with a wave of his hand and hurried off.

Daddy Troy picked up his little bundle by the tail and held it up.

"In the pot," he sang.

"What do you want me to do?" I asked.

"Lift the can," he told me, "but don't let it git away."

I tilted the can up quick and looked down on the possum who first looked up at me curiously, then grinned that peculiar possum grin. Daddy Troy dropped the other one in and I closed it.

Daddy Troy ejected the remaining shells and I picked them up.

"Let's go yonder in them pines," he suggested, "and see if we can git up some wood."

It did not take us long to gather enough wood to build a pyre over the dead cow. We finished just as Rudy was returning with a five-gallon can of kerosene.

"Grandma Gert say burn that spread," he said, huffing and puffing as he reached us.

"We left it at the fence," I said.

"I know, but that's what she say."

"What else did she say?" Daddy Troy asked.

"She say buy her a new one, too."

"And?"

"And don't bring no possum in the house, neither."

"Cause?"

"Cause she say she ain't cookin' it, either."

Daddy Troy laughed as he doused the dead cow with kerosene. Rudy cradled the shotgun, I picked up the garbage can, and we walked a short distance, turned and watched Daddy Troy light a match and toss it on the pile. It whooshed up in a ball of black smoke and flames, and we watched it until it got a good burn going, then we turned and started back for the house.

Just as I was climbing through the fence, Grandma Gert ran from around the side of the sto-house with a strap.

"What the hell you doin' wit my spread!" she screamed and took a swipe at me.

"Daddy Troy told me to git it!" I yelled and took off.

"Don't let it git away!" Daddy Troy screamed and lunged for the can.

She must have thought he meant me, because she increased her step and got in a good lick. She never even looked at Daddy Troy, but focused all her wrath on me, and he just grinned.

"Take your behind back there and pick up that garbage you dumped!" she hollered and swung wildly.

"Daddy Troy didit—Daddy Troy didit—Daddy Troy didit!" I cried.

Fortunately I was able to stay two steps ahead of her until she gave up the chase and yelled, "I done told you I ain't cookin' no possum 'round here t'day! Not t'morra neither! Not t'day! Not t'morra! Not t'nevah!"

But she did. In spite of herself, she did. I guess because he begged her and sweet-talked her and took a bath first. But more because each time he brought a possum to her, she was being romanced again. As old as they were, the spirit of romance was not dead—not as long as there were possums around. To Daddy Troy, the best of creation was barbequed possum and the one that cooked it.

Then again, their romance was always young, because the gods of the hunt and the gods of romance were unchanged. The aura of their love was not an illusion; they could reach out and touch it, and it was always where they were, not where they once were.

It was an eternal romance and the possum was a confirming symbol. All was cold and gray without it, because the best portion of their lives was little unremembered acts of love owed to the spirit of adventure.

A good possum dinner was still the desired expression of affection. A good possum dinner and its supposed aphrodisiac qualities were a cluster of mysteries and riddles where two became one and one became two.

I had accepted the long-distance call from my father just after I came out of the shower. By then the possum had been burnt and scraped and was ready to be prepared. Grandma Gert and Daddy Troy were nowhere to be found.

"Uh-huh. Yeah. No." Rudy cried in the receiver. "I dunno."

He held the receiver away from him and asked me, "Where's Manasha? Uncle Melvin wanna talk to her."

"Sleep," I told him. "She just got in from work."

"Sleep," he said to Daddy. "She just got in from work."

"Where Daddy Troy?" he asked me.

"I dunno," I told him.

"Dunno," he told Daddy.

"Where Grandpa?" he asked me.

"Silo," I told him, "I think."

"Uncle Melvin said go find Daddy Troy."

"I dunno where Daddy Troy is."

"Uncle Melvin said go find 'im."

"You go find 'im."

"Uncle Melvin said you go!"

"You go!"

"You go!"

"You go!"

"He said he ain't goin', Uncle Melvin. He said bunk you!" he lied into the phone.

"Ahma beat yo guts out!" I screamed and started after him.

He dropped the receiver and scooted beneath the table. I crawled down after him only to see him scooting out into the living room past Savannah and out the front door.

"You betta run!" I screamed after him. "You betta run!"

"Y'all betta stop that in here," Savannah cried as I burst into the living room, "or Ahma tell!"

Her favorite words.

"Betta not let me catch you!" I screamed.

As I turned back into the kitchen, Savannah held out the phone and said, "Uncle Melvin said go find Daddy Troy—right now!"

Even though he was still in prison, somewhere in New York, he was still my father.

"Shoot!" I cried and stomped my foot. "Shoot!"

"Uncle Melvin," she mocked me, "he say 'Shoot!'"

"Shoot!" I cried and stomped again, but left by the back door before he sent her upstairs to wake up Manasha.

I thought they were in the sto-house; if not, I could say that I looked but could not find them. I walked across the lawn yelling, "Daddy Troy! Daddy Troy! Daddy Troy!"

Just as I started to leave, I heard the faint cry of "Trrrroy!"

It sounded like nothing I'd ever heard before.

"Trrrroy!"

It sounded like nothing I ever knew.

"Trrrroy!"

I sounded like a haint!

"Trrrroy!"

"Who dat?" I called.

"Trrrroy!"

"Daddy Troy?" I called.

"Trrrroy!"

I came down the hallway to what was once the bedroom of Grandma Gert and Daddy Troy. It was now a storeroom but it still held some of their old things, including their old bed.

"Troy! Troy! Troy! Troy! Troy! Troy! Troy!"

It was coming quick, loud and urgent, so I pushed open the door. To this day I am still embarrassed by what I saw.

"Trrrroy!" Grandma Gert screeched like a cat.

Daddy Troy saw me. "Boy!" he panted. "Boy!"

What an awesome cause of wonder! Something far beyond anything I could ever anticipate! Grandma Gert and Daddy Troy—what a mellow surprise.

"Boy! Boy! Boy!" he gasped. "Git! Git! Git!"

And he fell across the bed panting.

"Git yo ass outta here!" she barked.

Only then did I think to move. I closed the door, went and stood quietly in what used to be our living room, forgetting why I'd come in the first place. I didn't think old people still did it! Not old people as old as Grandma Gert and Daddy Troy. Then again, Mother Nature is often full of surprises. But this had to be a surprising thing to even Mother Nature! It was astonishing to the mind! A disturbing thing to the harmony of the universe! What would she say when she came out! Worse—what would she do?

I did not wait to find out. Quickly, I left by the back door and went running to Silo. Caught in the wrath of Grandma Gert the second time that day, it did not pay to hang around the house, but to be as close to Grandpa as possible. God may have sent the possum, but if you asked me, the devil sent the cook, and something did not have to be all that bad to make Grandma Gert get on your ass. And this was bad—very bad! This was momentous! This was something I definitely should not have seen. Something I knew I would regret, because the last time I saw something I should not have seen, it was beneath the dress of Eveleen Baker.

What I Saw Beneath the Dress of Eveleen Baker

Eveleen Baker and her sister Dianne were two flim-flam sisters who lived in Boggy a few houses down the road from Unck. Two empty heads with long, wagging tongues. But Eveleen and Dianne Baker were not as empty-headed as some people thought. The former could con the last five-dollar bill from the hands of a stingy miser, and the latter could play blackjack with a pinochle deck and no one would be the wiser.

These were two sisters who took care of their needs by borrowing the means to do it; in fact, they did the kind of borrowing that knew no bounds, and what was often lent to them was usually lost forever.

They were very indiscriminate about what they borrowed and who they borrowed from. If you were a woman, and not careful, they would go so far as to borrow your man. And if you happened to be that man, Lord have mercy on your soul! Because any man who gave them enough rope often ended up tied in knots.

One morning Grandma Gert sent me to retrieve her big colander, various pots and pans, a heating pad, and a garden rake. Since lenders have better memories than borrowers, she gave me a little note to take along.

Their house was the last one on the Thomas Road, right

where the Thomas Road turns and the Ceelie Road begins. I rode Cody Wayne's bicycle the short distance, crossed the tracks, and found the two sisters sitting on their front porch stripping collard greens. Whatever was said or thought about the two sisters, they were not crackheads and they were indeed beautiful.

"My Gramma say send her stuff," I told both of them.

"What stuff?" Dianne asked.

"The stuff y'all borrowed."

"Like what?" Eveleen asked.

"Like her colander," I said, pointing to it and a pan of freshly peeled sweet potatoes.

"We still usin' it," said Dianne.

"Well," I said and offered her a shrug, "she told me to come get it."

"But I'm using it now!" Eveleen snapped.

"Well," I said falling into the trap of giving her the benefit of the doubt, "what about her other stuff?"

"What other stuff?" Dianne asked with more than a little doubt.

But I was more than ready and whipped out the note. "This stuff!" I said. She read the note, then passed it to Eveleen.

"I don't know nuthin' 'bout no rake," Dianne snarled as if borrowing a rake was somehow beneath her. "I already got a rake!"

"It's around back," said Eveleen. "You can go git it if you want it."

As I turned to leave I heard Dianne say, "I better go wash them pans 'cause she funny 'bout her things."

She then set her bunch of greens down and went inside the house. I found our long-handled garden rake holding up a clothesline of just-washed clothes that held my attention far longer than it should have taken me to retrieve the rake and gave me some insight as to why some folks referred to Eveleen and Dianne Baker as the weird sisters—because they did things that struck most folks as weird, or at least unusual. For instance, it is highly unusual for women, especially young women, to hang their drawers out on the line for everyone to gawk at. Women just don't do that, not if they have any modesty about them. A woman's drawers seldom see the light of day, since most women wash their drawers as soon as they step out of them and hang them on the shower rail or the towel rack to dry—or they just throw them in the washer. But Eveleen and Dianne Baker were anything but modest, and I suspect there were some very ulterior motives at work here, because for one brief moment I felt as if I were standing before the holy of holies! I mean, some of their drawers had holes in them, yes, but at that age I had yet to experience a woman's drawers, holey or otherwise, and the experience of witnessing such a colorful array of the most delicate underthings of two of the most beautiful girls in Boggy was almost spiritual—a sight to behold!

"You found it yet?" Eveleen shouted from the front.

"No!" Dianne spat from the kitchen window, "'cause he back here gawkin' at yo drawers!"

Quickly, I looked for something to replace the rake. Finding nothing adequate, I returned to the front and told her so.

"My clothes gotta dry!" she shrieked.

I sighed.

"Come back when they dry," she said.

"What about that?" I asked of the colander she was packing with greens.

"What about it?"

And I sighed again.

"Here," she said, passing me a bunch of collard greens. "Help me git through."

Reluctantly, I took the greens, sat down in front of her and began stripping the leaves and tossing them into the colander she held fast with her legs.

Eveleen Baker said to me, "Mangoes."

"Huh?" I asked.

"Mangoes," she said. "Mangoes."

"What about mangoes?"

"How y'all grow mangoes when nobody else can?"

"I dunno—Cracka Bill got a whole grove."

"Yeah well, later for Cracka Bill."

Because Cracka Bill did not give them away.

"Y'all mangoes ripe yet?" she asked, watching me hard.

"No," I said, trying to keep from smiling.

"You's a lie," she laughed with me. "Y'all mangoes ripe."

"No they not."

"Well, they almost ripe."

"Almost."

"Well, when they do git ripe I know you'll bring me some—won't you?"

"Uh-huh."

She began humming and stripping the greens, then without looking up at me said, "We use to be able to go down the Sky Lake and fish as much as we wanted, but since Mr. Sears put that fence around it, we can't no more. Why he did that?"

"He makin' it a brood pond," I told her, but not for what.

"For what?"

"Uh, perch and uh, bream and uh, softshells and uh . . ."

"Turtles—y'all growin' turtles?"

"Yeah."

"How?"

"Same way we do catfish."

"That's nice. Lijo brought me a softshell once, split it and cleaned it for me too."

"That's nice," I said, wanting to get off the subject of Sky Lake.

"What would really be nice is if Mr. Sears would unlock the gate and let us fish for a while."

"Y'all can go down to Silver Blue Lake anytime. He won't mind."

"Shit. That's all the hell back there and my car's in the shop; Sky Lake's closer. We can walk right down the tracks and be there in no time."

"Ask him."

"You ask him for me."

She turned and reached down to pick up several leaves from the bunch down beside her and as she did, her legs swung open, her dress raised slightly, and boy did I get an eyeful! But I wasn't exactly sure of what, because unlike her sister Dianne, Eveleen Baker was black, and way down there between her legs was dark. But I was sure of one thing: Eveleen Baker was not wearing any drawers! I'd never seen a big girl with hair and all, and my curiosity became quite aroused.

"Ask him for me," she said sweetly.

She turned to pick up several more leaves and again her dress raised and I leaned forward to sneak a better look. As she turned back to strip them, I leaned back in place.

"Last time we went down there," she said, deftly stripping the leaves, "the breams was just jumpin' out the water. We didn't even use no bait. Know what we used?"

"Un-unh," I answered, not looking up.

"Ivory soap. Mr. Sears taught us that. I musta caught a hundred fish that day."

She giggled to herself, turned and leaned, and I leaned and looked. She sat back and I sat back. She giggled again.

"Y' know he fish wit his big toe," she giggled.

"Who?" I asked, gazing up into those lovely eyes.

"Yo granddaddy!"

"Daddy Troy?"

"No—Mr. Sears!"

"He my great-granddaddy."

"Same thang!"

"Yeah."

"Funniest thang I ever saw."

"What?"

"Fishin' wit his big toe!"

"Oh."

"He got a big old callus on it, too."

"Yeah," I said, forced to think of Grandpa's big toe. "He say fishin' is for relaxin', so he like to lay down and sleep while he fish."

She giggled and turned and leaned, and I leaned and looked and stretched.

"He'll do it if you ask him to," she pleaded, turning and leaning.

"OK," I said, with absolutely no intentions of doing any such thing, but still leaned and looked and stretched. "OK."

And so it went. She would turn and lean sideways to pick up the greens, and I would lean and look and stretch to see what's what. She'd sit back and I'd sit back, and together we looked like a well-oiled machine moving back and forth and up and down and sideways in one smooth and highly synchronized motion. And it may have gone on forever, had not Dianne come from around the side of the house with the garden rake. She stood and observed this peculiar scene for a few moments, then from a distance of less than fifteen feet, hit me square in the back of the head with a sweet potato!

Pow!

"Ow!" I shrieked in pain.

"What you lookin' at!" she shrieked in horror.

"What's the matta?" shrieked Eveleen in wonder.

"He sittin' here lookin' up under yo dress!" Dianne shrieked and sent another sweet potato flying at me.

"No I wasn't!" I cried.

"Yes you was—and don't call me no liar," she disputed me and flung another sweet potato.

It missed, but Eveleen brought a whole load of collard greens crashing down upon my head!

"Ahhhh!" I yelped and tried to flee, but tripped over the colander with both girls flailing away at me unmercifully!

"What'd you see—what'd you see!" Eveleen demanded. "What'd you see!"

"Nothin', nothin'. I didn't see nothin'!"

"Then why you look?" Dianne asked with a double whack!

"I dunno! I dunno! I dunno!"

Quickly, I scooted through her legs and fell from the porch at a dead run with sweet potatoes flying to the left and right of me.

"Git from here—you old nasty thang!" Dianne shouted.

"You too little for me, anyway!" added Eveleen.

"Oh yeah? Oh yeah?" I turned at the fence, just out of harm's way, and shouted, "Well I might be little, but I betcha one thang—I betcha I got a bic-dic!"

"Oh yeah? Well you better take your little bic-dic ass on away from here before I come down off this porch!" Dianne threatened.

"Oh yeah? Oh yeah?" I huffed and puffed and threatened in return, "Well bring ya bad ass on down here—you old hag, you!"

And both girls leaped from the porch and tore across the lawn after me! But they had about a snowball's chance in hell of catching me, because I was fast, fleet, and expeditious! I was so fast I didn't even bother with the bicycle, but took off down the road faster than arrows, bullets, wind, and thought! Faster than a dog will lick a dish.

I told Grandma Gert neither of the girls was home and I was much too considerate to disturb Miss Harriet, but if she wanted me to, I would return and try again that afternoon. Grandma Gert said I was a good boy and it wouldn't be necessary for me to return, she would send Savannah and Linda that afternoon.

But that wasn't necessary either, because that afternoon Eveleen and Dianne drove up and began unloading all the things I was supposed to have retrieved that morning.

"Hi Mister Bic-Dic," Dianne taunted.

"I brought your bicycle, Mister Bic-Dic!" Eveleen taunted.

"Come and get it Mister Bic-Dic!" both girls taunted in unison.

Instead, I crept off the porch and hauled ass for Silo looking for Grandpa. I knew that once Eveleen and Dianne got through lying on me, Grandma Gert's understanding would be zero!

I found him down at the fish farm and quickly told him my side of the story, especially the part about Eveleen trying to pick my mouth about the doings around Sky Lake. All he wanted to know was what I told her about the doings around Sky Lake. And when I told him "nothing," he said, "Eveleen ain't shit! And Dianne ain't shit! And that ain't shit for you to fret about. Bunk them! And they mammy too!"

And that was the end of it. Except that Grandma Gert told me that the next time I did or said something nasty like that, she would beat the black off me! And I believed her, too.

Which is why after walking in on her and Daddy Troy, I was breaking my neck to find Grandpa, pursued by a new shame, an old sin, and the ever-impending prospect of death!

The Ever-Impending Prospect of Death

I found him down by the coops. Shack was with him. This was something I did not know how to talk about. I thought first to ingratiate myself as the idiot son; he didn't think I had much sense anyway. Nobody did. And sometimes it was a convenient excuse, pretending to be stupid. It worked well with Manasha. As I came up behind him, he reached down and clutched the dog by the scruff of the neck and held him firm. I saw the hammer and realized what was about to happen. In one quick motion he brought the hammer crashing down upon the dog's head. Shack lurched and twisted in Grandpa's hand, sat back on his haunches, and died. Grandpa let him go and drew in a heavy sigh. He looked up and saw me. How peculiar, the circumstances that brought me to witness this. Now he had to explain. He stuffed the hammer into his back pocket and said, "He's been killin' chicks again."

He wiped his hands across his pants, looked down at Shack and said, "Take 'im and bury 'im somewhere nice."

And he walked away with the quiet anger of a patient man.

Shack

I wanted to cry, seeing him lying there with two rotten chickens tied around his neck.

"Boy, you fucked me up good!" said Daddy Troy, coming up behind me.

First he saw the tears, then he saw the dog. "What happened?" he asked.

"Grandpa hit 'im in the head wit a hamma," I said sadly.

He looked at the dog, then back to me, and said, "This was best. He got mean."

Maybe so, but this was Shack—our Shack! Why such a vengeful death?

Grandpa came back pushing a little wheelbarrow. As he got close, I saw there was lime and a shovel in it too.

"If I was you," Daddy Troy said, remembering me, "I'd stay out of Gert's way."

"Why? What he did?"

"Fucked up her monthly shot!" he tried to whisper.

"How he did that?"

"I didn't know they was in there," I cried to Grandpa.

"Ya suppose to knock!" Daddy Troy growled.

"Daddy was on the phone," I whined. "He wanted to talk to you."

"Ya still s'pose to knock! She's so mad she took the possum

and throwed it in the garbage!"

Grandpa chuckled to himself. The thing about romance is that it leaves us so unromantic.

"Bury 'im in the fruit field," he said. "Put 'im down with a layer of lime so's nothin' won't dig 'im up."

Daddy Troy reached down and tore loose the rotten chickens around his neck.

"Don't bury 'im with this," he said.

And I picked him up and laid him down gently in the wheelbarrow.

It was not as hard to look at him dead as it was to look at him alive. Crippled in a fight with a wild hog, he'd become a sad and pitiful sight. Shack was the best hog-hunting dog we had, and a hog had killed him. At least that's what I like to think, because he was dead long before this. He was dead the minute he'd grabbed the hog by the head. In fact, he was dead the minute we'd spotted the big boar and Rudy cried, "Let's git it!"

Cody Wayne and I knew better. We had no business going after a hog. They are dangerous, unpredictable, and nothing to play with. But the dogs took off after it and I tried to tell myself it was not my fault. I tried to tell myself it was Shack's own fault because Shack was a bulldog, and bulldogs are dumb.

But Red Brown didn't think so. He swore on the intelligence of pits and mastiffs. He said it was all in the way you trained them. He'd trained Poochie to be a good house dog, and Poochie didn't even bark inside the house. Red Brown trained hunting dogs for a living. He'd trained Shack.

Shack was trained to be a "head-dog," which is almost always a bulldog. This is the dog that charges in square from the front and seizes the hog by the snout or the ear and just holds it. This was Shack. Not the leader of the pack, but the head-dog never the less.

And the head-dog cannot be a dumb dog, because if he seizes the boar wrong, or times it wrong, or loses his grip, or if he grabs the boar by the head instead of the snout, then the head-dog is a dead dog.

People are wrong, and I should not tell myself bulldogs are dumb. At least not ours. I'd seen our dogs working together as a unit too many times. Once, Daddy Troy and Red Brown were hired by Pine Meadows County Club to remove a large family of pigs that had taken up residence and were destroying the grounds. The golfers wanted them shot but settled for having them caught and shipped somewhere else.

My job and Cody Wayne's job was always to hold Shack and Ike. Ike was a bulldog too, pit bull and bullmastiff. He was also an "ass-dog."

And because of the sound and the fury of the hunt, it was a struggle sometimes to just hold them. But you had to hold them! They were bulldogs and you had to hold them until Red Brown screamed, "let the ass-dog go!" And you released Ike, and Blackie got out of his way, because Ike would go tearing after the hog as fierce as ten furies straight for its ass, or if it were a boar, its nuts! He always had a clear shot at them because the hog would be pre-occupied with Lance, who would keep it facing him so Ike could have a clear shot. And once Ike had it by the nuts, the battle would explode with all the blind fury of creation, because that is when the hog is most dangerous—when it is cornered, when it is wounded, and when you've got it by the nuts! Then it will turn and use that huge, powerful head and snout, with tusks that might be five inches long! And it will bullrush the dogs using all its upper-body strength and the relentless ferociousness of a many-headed monster trying to get at whatever has it!

Only a good "chase dog" like Lance does its job well and will

289

continue attacking and nipping from the front, keeping the hog off balance and off the ass-dog until Red Brown screams "Let the head-dog go!" And that was Shack.

They were a team. A well-trained, efficient unit. They were champions. Which is why Red Brown could not understand how Shack, throwing caution to the wind, would grab a hog by the head.

Gallivanting

And in the second place, we had no business with the rifle. We'd told Grandpa we were going out to whistle rabbits, kiss squirrels, and run the dogs, what Grandma Gert calls gallivanting. Which is exactly what we were going to do. You cannot kiss squirrels and whistle rabbits with dogs around. And what in the world did we need the rifle for? It was Cody Wayne's rifle, but we could not have it without permission, and permission was seldom granted.

We could never understand why, until the day Kevin Donehue, his brothers, and two more young fellows we didn't know asked my grandfather permission to hunt on his property. My grandfather asked them who they were with, and when they told him they were by themselves, he sent them packing.

The pine forest and the woods leading away from the reservoir were filled with every kind of game you could imagine. It is a hunter's paradise. But these boys were not really hunters. The oldest was only a few years older than Cody Wayne and the youngest, carrying a sawed-off shotgun, was no older than Rudy. They never saw me and Cody Wayne following them, watching them trespass. We make ourselves *dim*. If there is one thing Cody Wayne and I know, it is how to *be* in the woods. These boys looked as if they didn't know anything. They were creeping and crouching and moving around as if they were on some kind of military patrol expecting an ambush at any moment, ready to blast away at anything that moved.

They were not hunting, they were killing. That is why our people were so strict with weapons, because they have but one purpose: to kill. And at our age, they did not want us to gain any pleasure in killing.

But we were not out to kill anything. We only wanted to shoot, and the desire was so strong we snuck away the rifle and fabricated the lie.

What we wanted to shoot, or shoot at, was rabbits. They are the best thing to practice with. If you could hit a rabbit on the run, then you were good. That is why most people use a shotgun. But you don't need a shotgun for rabbit. They have a very fast respiratory system; you can literally scare them to death. All you have to do is shoot close enough to kick up a puff of dirt and they'll fall over dead. Another trick is to whistle at them. It makes them curious about what they're hearing long enough for you to draw a bead.

Squirrels are the same way, only you kiss at them and they will not only stop, they will come to you, too.

And it was all fun, kissing squirrels and whistling rabbits. There was not fun in killing them, which meant skinning them, cleaning them, and picking buckshot from them, and storing them in the freezers until Manasha or Aunt Clara got tired of looking at them and threw them out, because Manasha and Aunt Clara, Savannah and Linda, Ingy and Cheryl, and Teenie and Weenie did not eat anything they considered wild.

Grandpa said that killing out of anything but need was a waste. What is it to kill a rabbit or a deer for the fun of it? For sport? For trophies? What silly animals we are! That's not sport; that's pointless!

A four-hundred-pound boar hog is sport!

The Thang That Ate My Grandaddy's Dog

A fifteen-foot alligator is sport!

A Kodiak bear is sport!

Some people hunt alligators by shooting them from a distance. That's easy. How Unck and Red Brown hunted alligators was something else: they lured them up to the boat and jumped on them! Now that's sport!

Nature pardons no mistakes. Her rules have no exceptions. Yes is yes. No is no. Dead is dead. There are men who hunt lions with nothing but spears. They will find a lion, approach it, and stare it right in the eye. Of course, if the lion is hungry, they may become sport—for him!

We were not taught to hunt and kill for pleasure. A pleasure to us was tracking and observing. To do this, you first have to consult nature about nature. And she speaks to you, in her signs and in her symbols, often telling you her secret. And you learn there is nothing sad in nature. Nothing grotesque in nature. In nature, there is nothing unbeautiful. All nature is hope.

And the *secret* is only told once.

Tracking and observing is the ideal of nature. It is to feel calm and beautiful. It puts you at peace. It is for the hunter of dreams.

We were tracking and observing, whistling rabbits and kissing squirrels, when we ran up on the big boar. Lance saw him first. Lance was a black-and-white border collie descended from Australian sheep dogs. He was fast, he was a thinker, and he was quiet. Which is why we didn't notice he'd picked up the scent of the hog and followed it. All of a sudden we looked up and saw Lance chasing the hog. Then the hog chasing Lance. Then Lance chasing the hog again. And to the other dogs it looked like a better game than the one we were playing, and they all ran away from us to join in the fun.

Dogs hunt for fun. They think it's a game. It is the serious-
ness of the hunter they adopt, and we were anything but serious.
We were playing. The dogs were playing. Only the hog was serious.

Cody Wayne and I knew enough to know that we should
have restrained the dogs. But it happened so quick, and we had the
rifle, and Rudy shouted, "Let's git it!" And what started as a game
would end in earnest.

We ran across the dry grass and scrub chasing the dogs.
Lance and Blackie were chase dogs. Lance more so than Blackie.
Blackie was a coondog. The best tracking dog I ever saw. He could
pick up a scent and run it all day. What made him a champion was
that he did this at night too, across a myriad of smells, and once
he had the scent, he and Lance would give chase and pursue their
prey until they ran it tired, then they'd circle it and keep it at bay
for the two catch dogs.

But Shack and Ike were in on the chase too, and the hog was
anything but tired. It fought the dogs with an intense and cunning
old fury! They couldn't get hold of it, nor would they let it escape.
As we drew close, our only intent was to bring the dogs to heel, but
even this was beyond our control and ability. We should have kept
our distance, because as soon as the hog saw us it broke from the
melee and charged!

Cody Wayne aimed and fired.

"I got 'im!" he yelled. "I got 'im!"

The shot hit the boar high in the shoulder. It buckled and fell
to its knees, rebounded immediately, and continued its charge
with an even greater ferocity!

"Oh shit!" I cried. And Cody Wayne dropped the rifle and
the three of us scattered.

It was going for Rudy. We ran in three different directions
but the boar stayed behind Rudy.

"Run, Rudy, run!" I screamed, and chased after them with a stick. "Run!"

Rudy fell! My heart jumped! And the boar lowered its head! Lance was the fastest of all the dogs, and the realization that this was not a game made him even faster. He caught the boar from behind and attacked it with all the abandon of an animal protecting its young! Surprised for a moment, the boar recovered quickly, and with one twist of its powerful head, flung Lance high into the air. For one brief moment, it had a choice between Lance and Rudy. It was at that moment that Shack leaped in and grabbed the boar by whatever he could grab. That action saved Rudy and doomed the dog, because the boar shook him off and began goring him.

It would have killed Shack too, had not the other dogs caught up and attacked en masse. Cody Wayne, who'd gone back and gotten the rifle, fired directly into the fray but hit Lance, who yelped and let go of the boar's snout. That enabled the boar to use its head to throw off Blackie and force Ike to turn it loose. It then took off for the bush with Ike and Blackie hot pursuit.

"Ike! Ike!" I screamed running after them, "Jumbo, Ike, Jumbo!"

The dogs were cautious enough to know not to chase the wounded animal into the bush. They stopped but stood guard to make sure the boar was gone.

Shack lay quietly on his side, panting and bleeding. There was a long, ragged slash along his back and a gaping hole in his side. The boar had missed the dog's soft underbelly, but the wounds to his rear haunches were terrible and everlasting. Rudy rubbed his head and tried to comfort him. Lance hobbled about and whimpered in pain. He'd been shot in the rear.

"Oh lordy, oh lordy," I cried.

"Gottdogitt! Gottdogitt! Gottdogitt!" Cody Wayne whimpered in disbelief. "Gottdogitt!"

"Look what we done," Rudy cried hoarsely, his voice strained from screaming, his face stained with tears. "What we gon' do? What we gon' say?"

I did not have the slightest idea; neither did Cody Wayne. In times of trouble we would go directly to Unck, confess, and explain the trouble. And Unck would tell us what to say, what to do, and what lie to tell. If need be, he'd cover for us too.

But there was no cover for this. We were in big trouble.

"Let's just tell the truth," Rudy suggested, knowing they would sweat the truth from him anyway and he'd come clean by saying he was only following us.

Bunk the truth! Only those who lacked courage told the truth! The truth would only get us an ass-whipping! The truth was Lance! The truth was Shack! The truth was we had no business with the rifle and had strayed far beyond the property line. The truth was, Rudy knew he'd be spared.

"Bunk the truth!" I said.

A lie would save us a world of explanation.

"Let's just say we was whistlin' rabbits," Cody Wayne finally suggested, "and, and the hog jumped out the bushes and, and . . ."

"What about Lance?" Rudy pointed out the obvious flaw.

We looked down at our most beloved dog and realized that a simple lie was not going to do it. What we were going to need was not just a good lie, but a red-hot, odious, magnimonious lie with a lid on it! What we realized was that this was trouble only the truth would help.

"OK," Cody Wayne said, agreeing with Rudy. "OK."

"Git the rifle," I directed Rudy.

"Unload it," Cody Wayne told him. "I'll take Lance."

Rudy ejected the remaining shells as I looked for the best way to pick up Shack. He weighed about eighty pounds, about as much as a bale of hay. I eased my arms beneath him and cradled him up gently. He howled once, then rested easy.

Cody Wayne did the same to Lance, only Lance howled all the way home.

An Ugly Fact

It would have been better had Shack died that day. The dog had much too much dignity to go out like some kind of shiteater. His death seemed more like a punishment than a favor. I looked down at him lying in the bed of lime, and my eyes watered with tears: *Death is an ugly fact of nature that nature should hide.*

The fruit field is a square acre of land between the house and Silo. It has a split-wood rail fence around it and it is full of green grass, fruit trees, a big cherry blossom tree, and a hundred-year-old live oak. Sometimes Grandpa would bring the goats up and let them feast off the fruit that had fallen from the trees. And for some reason the ducks had taken to frolicking in the fruit field instead of Sky Lake.

I wanted to bury Shack where he'd have peace, where we could look and think: *Over there lies Shack.*

And when they asked me where did I bury Shack, I could point and say, "On the south side of the cherry blossom."

That night, after they came back from the vet, Daddy Troy broke the rifle over the fence rail. He came upstairs, got Rudy and let him eat, because after all, he was only following us. Instead of eating, me and Cody Wayne were made to recount the whole incident for the third time that day. They'd heard from Rudy, they'd heard from me, and now it was Cody Wayne's version they wanted to hear.

It is a good thing we did not choose to lie. A lie would not have endured. None of our lies ever did. We were not good liars, because the greatest thing in the world for us was to win the praise and approval of our people. To have Grandmama or Grandpa or Daddy Troy smile on you. To have Grandma Gert or Aunt Clara or Manasha hug you. To have Unck wink at you because he liked what you did. Praise was their reward and praise was sufficient, even though their silence, at times, was praise enough, because we imitated them and followed their example. For that reason alone, Cody Wayne and Linda did not live with Unck.

Discipline to them meant training and control; not punishment, but consequences. And the consequences of what we did was the ruination of a good hunting dog. We were to learn that disciplining good hunting dogs and disciplining children were one and the same. It meant helping them learn to control themselves, and it was best done while they were young.

Grandpa mumbled something about "little things." Yes. Little things again. We would always hear about little things. It was not so much one little thing, but one little thing after another and the same little things over and over again. We were children, and unlike good hunting dogs, we were slow to learn from our mistakes. But they did expect us to have at least some sense. Sense enough to know that a .22 rifle is useless against a boar.

Yes, it is the little things that kill you—like the little scar on Grandpa's neck. That, too, was a little thing. An ugly little thing that made you realize that sooner or later all the little things will add up and culminate in tragedy. And for my dog Blackie, it was not long in coming.

Blackie

By the time we'd caught up, Blackie had treed the coon. It was dusk and we were without flashlights. We had to get it before dark. Without a flashlight to spot it, the wily coon would climb from limb to limb, tree to tree, and leave us and the dogs barking up the wrong tree.

Or, it could hide behind a limb and make you miss. If it did that, then I would have to climb up and flush it out, and that was the last thing I wanted to do.

It was that four-year-old bobtail coon nobody believed existed. It was considered to be a myth until the day I'd stumbled across it in a garbage dump rooting through a bag of garbage. It was not expecting me and I was not expecting it when it leaped up suddenly and threw out its claws and bared its teeth menacingly. It was one of the most astonishing things I had ever seen. And frightening! It stood three feet high and wore a thick frizzled coat of yellowish hair that gave it the appearance of a little grizzly bear. It hissed ferociously and fanned its big razor claws. I froze in terror, unable to run, unable to think. We both were down into a little depression and there was no easy way out. It hissed and spat and I was expecting it to attack when, without looking behind it, it began backing up over the garbage. When its back hit the wall of the ditch, it began moving straight up! Not once did it take those fierce eyes off me or lower its claws or close its mouth. Only when it reached the top, in the clear, did it turn and flee.

When Red Brown heard the story, he got his dogs and went after it right away. Even though they'd picked up the trail hot, they'd spent all day and the better part of the night pursuing it, finally catching up to it around midnight. Red Brown trained hunting dogs for a living. He went out with three of them and came back with one.

Unless a dog is trained to fight and hunt coons, he does not stand a chance against one. But against three dogs, a coon is as good as dead. Against three dogs, most coons wouldn't even put up much of a fight, but would roll up into a little ball and, in effect, commit suicide. Against Red Brown's dogs, this coon had first exhausted them, then tricked and maneuvered them away from Red Brown and each other, then fought them in the dark, one at a time, slicing one's belly, cutting one's throat, and slapping the eye out of the one that did survive.

I remained the only one who'd ever gotten a good look at this coon. It was a crafty animal that, so far, eluded all the traps and all the hunters and all the dogs that had ever gone after it.

Blackie was just as crafty, twice as smart, and one hell of a coondog. He'd picked up the scent cold and quietly pursued it until it got hot. By then the coon knew it was being pursued. Long before the dogs began to howl, it started marking trees, and crossing streams, and crawling through old hollow logs in an effort to shake them. If it weren't for Blackie, it would have succeeded. The dog pushed on and pursued it. Even after the coon got into the water and ran a quarter of a mile down the shallow bank, Blackie pursued it. When it crossed and recrossed, Blackie crossed and recrossed, never losing the scent, staying with it until the coon exhausted itself and every trick it knew and went up in the trees to hide.

It was nothing to trifle with. A coon of this size, age, and disposition was trouble for any dog and any bunch of dogs. Even Blackie, a spotted bluetick, was careful with this one, because by the time we finally caught up, the coon had gone high up in the trees and the dogs weren't sure where it was.

Once again it appeared that the coon had outfoxed the coondog.

"Damn!" Grandpa exclaimed.

Not to be outslicked, Blackie began circling the tree.

"Git Lance. Git Ike," he ordered me and Cody Wayne. "It kin shit me, but it can't shit Blackie."

Because that was what the coon was trying to do—trick us into believing it was marking trees again when all it was doing was hiding.

But Blackie would know. The little circles around the tree grew wider and wider until the dog was nowhere in sight. If the coon was marking trees again, it came down somewhere and the dog would know. But it wasn't marking the trees and the dog came back and stood against it.

"He's up there," Grandpa said.

Praying, I thought. Which is what a coon does as soon as the light hits it. Pray. At least that's what it looks like it's doing. Its eyes will shine green and it will close one or look away. For as long as you are there, it will sit very still with its head pointed straight up and its paws covering its eyes. *Hiding.* Occasionally it will ease its head over and glance down, but for the most part, it sits with its hands and its head up, as if it is praying.

No. It was somewhere up there watching, because we had no light and there was no need to pray.

"Think that's a nest?" Grandpa asked of the dark spot in the highest reaches of the tree.

"No," Cody Wayne and I answered.

The shot was sudden, startling, and found its target. We heard the coon dropping through the branches. Even as it was dying it tried to catch itself and hang in the branches.

"Go shake 'im down," Grandpa told me.

I shinnied up and climbed out on the branch it was hanging on. It was bleeding and lying very still. It did not look at all like the demon I'd encountered in the garbage dump.

"It dead?" Grandpa called up.

"Uh-huh!" I shouted down.

Before he could say "Make sho," I began shaking the limb. It fell and landed in the lower branches low enough for Grandpa to reach. Just as he grabbed it by the tail to pull it down, it sprang suddenly and attacked with all the spitting viciousness of a fiendish cat!

Coons play possum too.

The rifle went one way and Grandpa ran the other way, screaming and struggling to get the coon up off him. He fell to his knees and Cody Wayne grabbed it and flung it afar and the frenzied dogs took off after it in hot pursuit.

"Git the dogs!" Grandpa screamed, blood flying from his mouth and face. "Git the dogs!"

I jumped down and ran to catch up to Cody Wayne, who was running to catch up to the dogs, who were running to catch up to the coon. The dogs were excited—too excited to think. The coon was wounded and desperate; with the dogs closing in, it was more dangerous than ever.

We'd been outslicked, but it was no disgrace. It only proved what coon hunters all the way from Georgia had been saying. We should've let it go, but it was imperative, at least to me, to catch it and check it for rabies. Maybe the dogs felt this too. Why else would Blackie pursue it into deep water? It was the wrong thing for the dog to do. The coon had purposely led them to the water. It had chosen the little stream to make its stand.

Coons are at home around water. Find a good water spot, lay your trap, and you'll catch a coon. But it was the coon who'd laid the trap, and Blackie, a tri-state champion coondog, ran right in to it.

This dog knew better! But the water was only shallow and Blackie had it in sight. We could not make him break off. We could not make him quit. We could not bring him to heel. Lance and Ike followed Blackie into the water, with me and Cody Wayne not too far behind. We'd lost control of the dogs and therefore the hunt. It was a classic case of the hunter being captured by the game.

I'd picked up a stick, hoping I'd get close enough to hit it in the head. A coon's head is as soft as paper and it doesn't take much to kill it, but we didn't expect the water. This was its turf and it was using it to full advantage, leading us down the shallows, lulling us into its trap, ever onward until the bottom dropped unexpectedly and what was shallow became deep. Suddenly the coon was swimming, and the dogs were swimming. And me and Cody Wayne screamed for the dogs to come back, because all of sudden they were looking very vulnerable.

And the coon knew it! It gave Blackie its tail and as the dog reached for it the coon turned and shoved the dog's snout into the water. With a nose full of water the dog panicked and tried to step up. The coon climbed on its back and bit the dog in the neck. I threw the stick and Cody Wayne threw a rock. And the coon pushed him down again. The dog surfaced and wheezed. The coon climbed on his head, held him down, and snarled like a mad banshee!

The dog did not surface again.

The coon only had a scratch wound, for it turned and swam

quickly away. It swam strong and victorious, confident that the dogs had had enough.

It is here, in distress, where you'll find great courage and character. Cody Wayne and I were throwing rocks as fast as we could find them. One hit the coon. It turned in time to see Lance directly behind it. The coon swung around quickly and bared its fangs. It snarled and threw up its claws. Ike, after witnessing the death of Blackie, must have sensed the hopelessness of the chase. He was smart enough to know he could not fight and swim at the same time. A coon has a great deal of body fat and can almost float. When it turned and waved its claws, Ike veered away and made a beeline for the bank, which is what we hoped Lance would do. Instead, he maneuvered to get behind it! The coon snarled and spat and slapped at the dog, but Lance circled it and would not come in close. It was either fight or flight for the coon, and it chose the latter. That was its mistake.

It lunged once and turned for the opposite bank, but Lance, having the angle, cut off its escape. Instead of turning away, the coon heaved itself at the dog with the intention of pushing him beneath the water.

And that's when Lance got it!

It was a very quick and unexpected move. The dog swung his head and made the coon miss, then very quickly it seized the coon by the shoulder, forcing its head into the water. And not once did he forget to swim. The coon's only struggle was for air as the dog swam for the bank, where it flung the coon high into the air, and Ike tore into it like the most savage of predators!

If Grandpa had any notion of preserving the skin, it was a wasted notion at best.

"Goddamitt!" Grandpa screamed when he'd finally caught up. "I meant git the goddamn dogs!"

We knew that, but . . .

"But nuthin'!" he raged. "You nevah, nevah let a dog go in the water after a coon! A coon will kill fifty dogs in the water!"

Not Lance.

"Goddamitt! Goddamitt! Goddamitt!"

He called the dogs, and they came across, Lance bringing the coon with him.

A raccoon has no saliva glands. If it has a wet mouth, it either has worms or rabies. Looking into the coon's mouth was futile, but it showed how scared Grandpa really was. He was still bleeding from the head, and for the first time I saw the ugly little scar on his neck. It was just a little thing, not bleeding at all, but little enough to have killed him.

Mistakes. One by one, mistakes. Little things in themselves are not mistakes, but ignoring them is a mistake. It would not have been so bad if we'd confined our mistakes to ourselves, but we persisted in our mistakes to include everyone else.

Some say you learn from your mistakes, but Grandpa said only fools learned from their mistakes. Mistakes are not the best teachers; other people's mistakes are. So he made me carry the dead coon all the way home so Cody Wayne could learn from my mistake and know a dead coon when he saw one.

Fortunately, the coon did not have rabies.

We never found Blackie. A gator probably ate him. At least Ike got buried. We never knew where, because Grandpa and Daddy Troy never talked about it.

After burying Shack, I parked the wheelbarrow beneath the Chinese plum tree and sat down. The sadness multiplied. It would not have been so bad had I not seen both Shack and Blackie die. Especially Shack. Why couldn't Grandpa just take him to the Humane Society and let them put him to sleep? That way, we just would not have seen him again—like Ike. That way, I could still think of him as heroic—just like Ike.

Ike

In every pack of dogs, there is one that is, without question, the undisputed leader.

This was Ike.

He was the leader by consensus, which meant he could whip all the other dogs.

Lance was exceptional. Ike was vulgar.

Shack was fearsome. Ike was cutthroat.

Blackie was intelligent, where Ike was only clever, but all of them deferred to him.

And rightfully so.

The most powerful men and women are the ones with the keenest minds. And so it is with dogs. As with humans, if you put a group of dogs together, the leader will naturally emerge. But unlike humans, the leader had better be able to take on all the challenges if he is to remain the leader.

Which does not mean that Ike was never challenged.

If Shack had been as shrewd as Ike, he would have challenged Ike, and he probably would have won, because he was bigger, broader, and far more vicious than Ike.

Blackie would take on any coon no matter its size or demeanor. He was highly respected and valued for that. But that made Blackie the leader of the coonhunt—not leader of the pack.

That Lance, the border collie, challenged Ike, the pit bull, was perplexing. Grandpa said he knew something like this was going to happen. How? Because dogs will take on the personality of their masters. And since Cody Wayne had taken to Ike, and I had taken to Lance, the dogs adopted the ongoing conflict between me and my first cousin.

Cody Wayne was the one everyone claimed had all the sense. I wanted to have some sense, too. I wanted everyone to think as much of me as they did Cody Wayne. He was a year older, a pound heavier, and an inch taller than me. And everyone said he had more sense than me, too.

To tell you the truth, I did not understand *sense* at all, since I was much smarter in school and played a better game of baseball. Still, none of that seemed to matter. To everyone else, Cody Wayne was the one with all the sense, even though he was the one who thought an optimist was an eye doctor.

One day, Grandpa got sick of all the bickering and squabbling, because the dogs had taken to bickering and squabbling and fighting too. We didn't expect that from the dogs—and Lance, a border collie at that! But Lance was the best dog and that counted for something; if not, it would not have been the fight that it was.

Perhaps it was the fact that Ike was an ass-dog that made the other dogs wary of him. He fought dirty. He went straight for your balls. Which is the best place to attack your enemies.

"These dogs ain't enemies," Grandpa admonished. "Y'all caused them to act that way by always tryin' to best one another."

Lance was smart and knew just what Ike would do, just as he knew what a deer would do, or a hog would do, or a gator would do. He knew Ike would fight low, try to get under or around him and grab him by the nuts. That was Ike's game in a nutshell. So, Lance kept his ass low and fought Ike like a mongoose, which Grandpa said was the damnedest way he'd ever seen a dog fight.

And that only served to further enhance Lance's standing in every-one's eyes, although it did not win the fight for him. For no mat-ter what his fight game was, Lance was basically a sheepdog, and Ike was a pit bull. Lance quit the moment Ike locked down on his hip. The only thing he could do was to sit in such a way as to guard his nuts.

That night, Grandpa burned the sun-rocks.

We burned sun-rocks in the same pit where we burned our garbage. We burned sun-rocks before a hunt so they'd be good and ready by the time we got back. After a hunt, it was a ritual for us and the men who sometimes hunted our property to sit awhile, relax, and sweat.

The sweathouse was just a little brick structure with a few wooden benches lining the inside walls, a wooden water barrel, and a brick fire pit. The sun-rocks were heated and laid out over the ashes of hickory or birch. Water, with minerals added, was poured over the rocks at intervals creating a relaxing homemade sauna. He didn't tell us why he was burning sun-rocks; we had not gone hunting, and none of us had arthritis.

There were people who came to Silo just to sit in the sweat-house. For those people we added to the water whatever relieved their suffering.

All it did for me was make me sweat, and I wanted to have nothing to do with it. I was still angry that Lance had lost and how he'd lost. He'd tried to grab Ike's nuts, then Ike's ear, but Ike would not let go. Lance then cried out in pain and we had to hold his nose and use wedges to unlock Ike's jaws.

After the fight, Grandpa took Ike to the fruit field and chain-harnessed him to a mango tree. I took Lance to the doghouse to let him lick his wounds.

I wanted to go comfort Lance, not build a pyramid of sun-rocks for some old fogey with rheumatism. The sun-rocks had been burning all night. When we began taking them out, they were the color of Epsom salts and too hot to stand over. We picked them out of the pit with tongs and carried them down to the sweathouse in a wheelbarrow. As soon as we had a nice big pyramid of sun-rocks, Grandpa closed the shutters.

"Gimme ya clothes," he demanded, "shoes too."

I looked up at him, not comprehending at all. The last time he demanded our clothes, he left us out in the woods for four days to see if we could fend for ourselves. Cody Wayne began stripping, so I did too.

"Y'all always arguing about who's the best," he said as he poured a bucket of water over the sun-rocks. "Now we'll find out."

He stepped back as a great cloud of steam hissed and spat and rose to the ceiling. He took our clothes and shoes and said, "First one comes out—ain't shit!"

Then he walked out and closed the door.

Already the sweathouse was unbearable. Sun-rocks will hold heat forever. We kept them in the fireplace during the winter and never had to worry about the house going cold. The steam was thick and strangling. Somewhere in the rising steam, as it was in the dark of the forest, there was a lesson to be learned.

"This shit don't make no sense!" I said, panting.

Cody Wayne said nothing.

"I think Ahma throw up!"

"Go outside," he said.

"Go git Grandpa."

"You go. You the one sick."

All was quiet for a moment, then I said, "What kind of shit is this!" And Cody Wayne said, "You caused it!"

"I didn't cause shit!"

"Crybaby!"

"Coochie!"

"Coochie you!"

"Coochie you—back!"

"You look like you wanna cry!"

"That's from smoke."

"So that's why you should go outside."

"So I can look bad in front of Grandpa?"

The door opened, Grandpa came in, poured another bucket of water over the sun-rocks, turned and left. Somewhere in the haze of steam I heard Cody Wayne's heavy breathing.

"I think Ahma be sick," I said. "I feel sick."

"I feel stupid."

"Ahma throw up! Ahma—" I threw up.

"Don't throw up in here!" Cody Wayne snarled. I threw up again.

"Don't say nothin' to Grandpa," I gasped.

"OK," he promised. "But let's go."

"OK."

"OK."

"OK—you first."

"You first. You the one sick!"

"OK, uh—let's go together."

I got up and wiped my face. Cody Wayne was smiling.

"You ain't won cause I throwed up!" I cried.

"I ain't said nuthin'!" he said.

"Yeah, well, just don't be thinkin' you won."

Side to side we walked to the door and opened it. The whoosh of fresh air and steam clashed at the threshold, with the steam winning and rolling out in a huge fog engulfing Grandpa.

"Didn't stay very long," he said.

Cody Wayne faked a move, as if he were going to step out. I pushed him sharply, but he grabbed me. Grandpa looked at us and said, "Neither one a' y'all's got the sense of a damn tree monkey."

And he walked away.

If there was any lesson to be learned, it was lost on us. That is, until the next day. Grandpa called us back down to the sweathouse and ordered us to load the fire pit with pinewood, because "Y'all ain't learned a damn thang!"

"We learned a lot!" I quickly yelled.

"A lot like what?" he asked.

"A lot like a whole, whole lot!" Cody Wayne put in.

And I agreed. I just couldn't put my finger on it. How could I, when I didn't know why he'd made us do it in the first place? But, so that we wouldn't have to do it again, I tried to think of something profound. Something heavy. Something from the Bible. For the first time in my life I wished to God I'd paid attention to all the Sunday school lessons I'd ever heard. Unfortunately, all the Sunday school lessons I'd ever heard went in one ear and got in the wind.

Bake the Cake drove past in the cart. Linda, Cheryl, and Weenie were riding in the back, yelling at us. Suddenly Lance burst from between the silos and took off after them. Grandpa whistled and the dog stopped and turned around. He looked good. Not stiff, not hurting. He came to us leaping and licking, full of energy and joy. I patted and rubbed him.

"If a man bested me in something," Grandpa said, starting to walk, "I would be the first to go and shake his hand."

We were walking toward the fruit field.

"Like a football coach after a game. It don't make no sense to do nuthin' else. Being mad just poisons ya soul and clouds ya thinkin.'"

He stopped and looked at us.

"The thing about envy," he said, "is you start to hate what you envy."

How could I hate Cody Wayne? We were kin, bonded by blood and name.

Ike, still harnessed to the mango tree, amused himself by running in a circle, full speed, until the yank of the chain sent him sailing around and around the mango tree.

"Dumb dog," Cody Wayne said.

He was as excited as Lance, and I wondered if he still had it in for Lance.

"Even if a man beats my time for a gal," Grandpa continued, "I'd still go and shake his hand."

"Why?" Cody Wayne asked, as if he understood such things.

"Because a man is a man, and the better man for it. And it keeps out the green sickness."

"Green sickness?" I asked. "What's that?"

"Envy."

"Oh."

"I'm almost a hundred and I envy no man on this earth."

Lance saw the ducks and took off after them. We sat down at the picnic table.

"Everybody is good at somethin' and can do somethin' nobody else can," he said. "I can't read, I can't write, and I sho can't do that kind of 'rithmitic Linda do."

"Algebra," I said.

"And I can't tell y'all exactly how many acres I got in land."

"Six hundred and ten," Cody Wayne said.

"Listen to me! In this world, what I kin, I can. I can't do everythang, but then again, I can—cause I think I can! I'm as fit and able and capable as any man. And I got sense. Plain old common sense."

He let us think a moment, then he said, "Now it was just plain dumb for y'all to sit in there and suffer for no other reason but stubbornness. No principle—just stubbornness. If it were me, I woulda got up, shook his hand, and walked out."

I was watching Ike, who was watching Lance shepherd the ducks.

"If two men is riding a horse," Grandpa said, "one of them's gotta ride in back—and that one can't do no guidin'."

The ducks got sick of Lance and flew away. He came charging across the field and hopped straight up on the table. He hopped down and wandered into the perimeter of the chain. He hesitated and looked around, glancing at Ike. He started to move, but the other dog came up to him and stopped. Lance did not move as Ike sniffed him. Very quickly, Ike raised up and tapped Lance's back. Standing at Lance's flank, he did it again, holding it a second longer. As the leader of the pack, it was Ike's right to drive him away, or kill him.

Grandpa petted and rubbed both dogs, but he did not unleash Ike. Unlike us, Grandpa was master in more than name, and he was showing Ike and convincing Ike that *he* was the dominant pack leader. Ike was just top dog, a member of the pack.

He couldn't sniff out a gator's nest like Lance, but still he was top dog, because whenever Unck and Red Brown went way back there to take care of their business, they took Ike.

Unlike Blackie, who loved honey so much he'd go right into a beehive after it, Ike wouldn't even consider such a thing. But still he was top dog, because the moment a boar was sighted, Blackie got out of Ike's way.

Shack welcomed a good fight. To him, one animal was as good as the next, but in that, he'd lost his sense of caution and it cost him his life.

But not Ike!

Ike was always aware of what was what, and how to attack whatever he was up against. Thus, Ike knew exactly what he was doing the day he ambushed the lynx.

The Lynx

Conventional wisdom says you do not let your dog run up on a cat, for the simple reason that a cat will kill it. A bunch of dogs might work, if the cat sticks around, which it won't; it will leave in its wake a bunch of dogs that will never in their lives run up on a cat again.

I'm speaking of a panther or a bobcat as opposed to a lynx, for a lynx will stand its ground and make any dog or maybe any group of dogs pull up and break camp.

This usually happens by accident, since the moment a dog picks up the scent of a cat, he will begin to howl. A cat of any kind is a frightening prospect. But if you cross trails accidentally and suddenly there is a cat licking its paws and minding its own business, what ensues would probably depend upon the distance between the dog and cat.

Ike's scrap with the lynx was not an accident or a matter of stupidity. Ike knew what he was doing. He had to fight the lynx because he was top dog to us all.

We'd been gigging for frogs in the drainage ditch, behind the fish plant. When they built the fish plant, they cleared away an acre of woods that at one time or another had probably been the cat's domain. Now he found it shrunken another acre and was more than likely figuring out a way to compensate himself for the encroachment. As we turned down the trail going back to Silo, there he was, sitting in the middle of the trail as casual and relaxed as you please, sizing up the ducks, or something to extract his revenge, like Teenie or Weenie.

"Look!" Rudy had gasped.

The three of us stopped dead in our tracks. We'd never seen anything like it. Seldom do you get this close to a cat. They are extremely rare. It is unusual to see them this close to any human habitation in broad daylight. He was gray and black with a pair of alert little ears that twisted up into a devilish little tuft of black hair. Sitting down, he was waist high to me.

We stood there staring, each to our own individual and collective wonder. To us it was nothing less than a Siberian tiger!

After several moments, the cat, very casually, looked back at us as if it had known we were there all along. He looked back up the road to Silo, then, with an air of indifference, got up and moved toward the bushes. When it did that, its nuts and ass were facing Ike, and the nuts and ass were Ike's best business! The cat was intending to ease into the bushes and continue its surveillance, but Ike put a crimp in those plans. He shot across the trail so quickly the only thing the cat had time to do was try and get up a cedar tree off the edge of the trail. Sensing the cat's move, Ike did a Michael Jordan from ten yards out, snatched the cat, and bounced off the tree! Any other dog would have been content to chase the cat away, but any other dog was not Ike.

He'd been upwind at Silo and saw the cat before the cat saw him. With a great deal of stealth, he'd come easing through the bushes on the other side of the path and waited for the cat to turn its back. Ike was indeed a dirty dog.

He would have been a dead dog if it weren't for Lance. He had the cat down by the lower extremities which made the cat fight with the kind of ferocity only cats have, using all fours and the most terrible fangs in the animal world. It was tearing Ike to pieces in a frenzied state of madness. In fear and awe we screamed, "Git 'im, Ike, git 'im! Git 'im, Ike, git 'im! Git 'im, Ike, git 'im!"

Any other dog would have let it go. If Ike had any sense, he, too, would have let it go. But the pit in him, that never-say-die impairment, made it a fight to the death.

"Go git Daddy Troy!" Cody Wayne screamed an order at Rudy.

"Go git Unck!" I screamed one, too.

Cody Wayne ran a few steps forward and threw his gig at the cat; it missed.

"Gimme that!" he demanded mine.

"I got 'im!" I shouted, as I ran a few steps and with all the force I could muster, threw mine—and missed too.

Cody Wayne looked for something else to throw.

"Go git somebody!" I screamed at Rudy.

I shoved him and he turned to run, stopped and screamed, "Sic 'im, Lance!"

And there he was, tearing down the trail at lightning speed.

"Sic 'im, Lance, sic 'im! Sic 'im, Lance, sic 'im! Sic 'im, Lance, sic 'im!" the three of us cheered hysterically.

The cat had one eye on us, the other eye on Ike, all the while trying to get its nuts up out of the sand. He never saw Lance coming. Rudy hit it in the head with a rock and Lance struck it like a thunderbolt! And the battle became a fierce tussle of ear-piercing screeches, ferocious growls, and flying tufts of hair and blood rolling in a ball of dust!

It was a desperate situation for the cat that got more desperate when suddenly we heard the long low wail of Blackie! We looked up and saw him and Shack racing down the trail. Like a desperate animal caught in a steel trap, the desperate cat leaped up with a violent twist of its body, tore itself away from Ike and rocketed off into the bushes with Lance, Shack, and Blackie and a trail of blood behind it.

The woods were too thick for the dogs, but not the cat, and for a good little while we could hear it screeching and raging as it got farther and farther away.

Ike looked all chewed up. His right ear was gone and there were deep cuts and slashes all over him. We carried him as far as the old hay barn when we felt the need to lay him down.

"What's that in his mouth!" Rudy asked.

It looked like a twist of bloody hair. I tried to pull it out, but Ike would not let go. It was not until the vet put him under to stitch him up that his mouth dropped open and Ike became a legend. Inside his mouth were the testicles of the cat.

Little Griefs

Lance wandered along the road from Silo with his nose to the ground and his tail hanging down. He was looking for Shack. After the death of Blackie there was an emptiness the dogs had shared. The death of Ike left Lance and Shack completely destitute of all purpose. The lime was not so much to keep critters from finding and digging up Shack, but more to keep Lance from finding him and howling in sadness all night. *When dogs are sad they sing, and make everyone sad along with them.*

My dog was sad. My dog grieved. My dog was becoming well acquainted with grief. And so was I.

A little grief will make us tender, a lot of grief will make us hard. So we honor the dead with remembrance, not grief, because it is infamy to die and not be missed. I feel most good about Ike when people ask me about the dog that fought with the lynx. I tell them he died. And I tell them how he died. And they smile sweetly and praise him in death.

That was Ike.

But Grandpa didn't think so. He would rather have had Ike. He found no value in the dog's legacy, no matter how rich it was. A living dog is better than a dead legacy. Tommy Green knew this and avoided Grandpa for a month.

When leaves fall they flatten out, and underneath the many layers of flattened leaves, snakes burrow and nest. It is something

I can identify even at a glance. If one is shown to you, you will not forget it. Daddy Troy said Tommy Green had to be drunk to wander into a nest of rattlers. He'd come to this conclusion after they found Ike and saw the number of times he'd been bitten. Backtracking, they found the 'shine camp, and further back they found what the Sheriff's Department, the Florida Department of Law Enforcement, and the DEA could not. They found Unck, Red Brown, and Tommy Green's marijuana crop.

That they blew up the shine camp and burned the marijuana made Unck, Red Brown, and Tommy Green sick. But it demonstrated what we felt about the dog, and Unck, Red Brown, and Tommy Green were made to feel the weight of their folly.

Although he could avoid Grandpa, he could not avoid me, Cody Wayne, and Rudy. Grandma Gert said Tommy Green didn't have much sense, but we looked up to him so much that every time he saw us he had to wonder and fret over our opinion. Our presence annoyed him so much that his conscience became a fence, confining him to the trailer between the fish plant and the fish farm. We were like a thousand witnesses—a thousand accusing witnesses.

The death of Ike was like an open wound until he realized that he was his own redemption. The glory that was Ike's and the grace that was his—even in shame. So, one day as he was checking brood boxes for hatchlings, he called me and Cody Wayne to give him a hand. And he told us how Ike died.

He said yes, he was drunk, but he didn't know how drunk. He said he didn't begin to feel drunk until he'd already started for home, which is how people get themselves killed in cars. He said when it began to hit him, he just followed Ike. The dog knew the way home. Then all of a sudden he wasn't following Ike. He was lost. Then all of a sudden there was Ike, following him. Then Ike was barking, and pulling at his pants leg. Then there was Ike out in front of him. And that's when he saw the snake! Ike was out in front, trying to draw the snake's attention. He didn't see the other one, coiled and ready to strike. Or the other ones, the hundreds of little ones that came slithering up out of the nest. He said it scared him so bad, all he could do was back away.

For a long time the three of us sat in silence at the edge of the brood pond watching a group of redtail hawks and thinking about Ike, in all his glory, his final glory, death, taking some of the enemy with him.

The Reason Why We Never Run Out of Pork Chops

If a dog trots around long enough, eventually he'll find a bone, but Lance was trotting around looking like an untrained dog who'd lost the scent. He was now alone. *It is not a good thing that a dog should be alone.* I whistled and called to him.

"Here Lance! Here boy! Jumbo! Jumbo! Jumbo!"

His ears perked and his tail shot up. He came to me, climbing into my arms and licking my face. I held him and squeezed him and rubbed his neck. And he licked my face and licked my face and licked my face. Grandma Gert doesn't like for dogs to do that on account of they're always licking at themselves. But I loved my dog, and my dog loved me, and I let him lick my face and lick my face and lick my face as much as he wanted. He looked over at the cherry blossom.

"It's all right boy," I whispered gently. "It's all right."

He lay quiet with his head across my lap.

I tried to imagine his sadness. Lance without Blackie, Lance without Shack, Lance without Ike. There was still me. But it wasn't quite the same. I tried to imagine myself without Cody Wayne and Rudy. There would still be Savannah and Linda, Ingy and Cheryl, Teenie and Weenie, but it wouldn't be the same. I'd still have Manasha and my daddy, Unck and Aunt Clara, Grandma and

Grandpa and Daddy Troy. And probably still feel alone. Only when I thought of Grandma Gert did I feel what Lance felt, because I felt as if I didn't have Grandma Gert anymore. Not after this morning. I looked up toward the house and wondered what was so bad about what had happened. I mean, Daddy Troy didn't think it was so bad. The only thing he was mad about was his possum. I mean, what was so shameful about the act if the participants didn't think so? I mean, I was not thinking shame, she was thinking shame! And shame on her for thinking shame! This was a case of the hen crowing harder than the rooster.

I mean, it wasn't like something I'd never seen before, although I do admit, human beings are a bit more discreet. If only because they find so much shame in the act. Shoot, I see chickens do it all the time. And goats too. And none of them seem to care whether you see them or not. Even though Tommy Green explained it to me a hundred times, how fish do it is still quite a mystery to me.

But not pigs!

If there is one thing pigs love more than eating, it is screwing! It is the reason why their peters are all screwy.

It is the reason why we cut the balls off the boars.

It is the reason why we never run out of pork chops.

And the main reason why it is not ladylike to hang around Silo and why Daddy Troy will always shoo Savannah and Linda and their friends back up to the fruit field.

Pigs have some very bad habits. I don't think you can pick up a bad habit from a pig, but you can become very sick and disgusted watching them and be not inclined to eat pork chops.

One day, Manasha ventured down behind Silo to watch them. Since Manasha was from New York, she was not inclined to eat pork chops anyway. But nothing made her hate a hog more than the day she witnessed a big boar stomp and gore a small sow because she wouldn't let him do it. It upset her so much that even though she was afraid of pigs, she climbed through the rails and tried to help the sow. But the boar bum-rushed her and chased her out. As frantic as if one of her own children were in mortal danger, she ran for help. By the time she got back with Grandpa, the sow was dead.

More as a consolation to her, Grandpa said, "It's about time I slaughtered him anyway."

And Manasha screamed, "Lemme do it! Lemme do it! Lemme blow the muthafucka brains out!"

So, Grandpa set a bucket of feed inside the rail, and when the boar began to eat, he steadied the rifle in Manasha's hand. And when she pulled the trigger, the hog was staring her right in the eye.

Other than that hen, it was the first thing Manasha had ever killed. And how she enjoyed it.

I petted and rubbed the dog's head. He nuzzled me with his chin. His ears perked and he looked around. Cody Wayne was coming over the fence.

"Jumbo!" he called, cupping his hands over his mouth. "Jumbooo!"

The dog leaped up and ran to him.

"Jumbooo!" I answered.

Jumbo. Manasha taught us that. It meant "Hello" in the African languages. Jumbo was our secret. Our secret call, our secret greeting, our secret warning. A secret we used to calm or excite the dogs and to announce ourselves. Everything to us was "Jumbo."

And only the dogs understood.

He knew about Shack, but he hadn't seen it like I'd seen it.

"Grandpa want you," he told me.

"For what?" I asked him.

"I dunno."

It was the kind of "I dunno" we fed adults. The kind of "I dunno" you told them when you knew you were going to get an ass-whipping as soon as you stepped through the door.

"What he want?" I asked again.

He said, "He want Lance."

Lance

"It's like with lions," Grandpa said as we made our way through the pine forest. "The females are better hunters. They're lighter, faster, and they have that maternal instinct."

He was carrying a Winchester pump and I was carrying two boxes of shells. He did not tell me what they were for, and I knew enough not to ask, but to listen and act as if I had some sense.

"I had Poochie since she was a pup," he said. "She woulda been a good huntin' dog, but since she couldn't breed, I kept her in the house."

Poochie came from the Humane Society, and like everything else that came from the Humane Society, she'd been neutered.

"You should always keep one or two females that'll breed," he said. "That way you'll always have good, smart, huntin' dogs."

He stopped and cradled the rifle in the other arm. He said, "That was something I forgot to do. So now, instead of some good huntin' dogs to work with, all I got is a big mess."

Which meant Lance.

"He a good dog," I said, almost pleaded.

He said nothing.

He was more than a good dog. In fact, he'd surprised everyone because they didn't think much of him when they first got him. He wasn't a pit bull. He wasn't a bluetick. He wasn't a mastiff. He was a shiteater. A sheepdog that had never been around sheep, which was probably the reason why all the bubbling intelligence went into doing other things—like catching gators.

Because they didn't think much of him, they'd made him a gator-dog.

Gator-dogs don't last long; sooner or later a gator will get it. But no gator ever got Lance, and in that sense, he'd fooled everyone, the same way he could fool a gator up out of the water thinking it could get him.

"He a good dog," I said again, but mostly to myself.

"He was a good dog," Grandpa said, "until somebody shot 'im in the ass."

I cringed.

"I'd be the same way too," he said, "if you shot me in the ass."

You would think what happened to Lance would only happen in human situations, since it aroused so much pity and sorrow. It did not happen all at once, but began after he'd been shot and gradually progressed with the death of each dog.

I'd noticed it after the death of Blackie. I'd first thought nothing of it, because a lot of people were afraid of thunder. At the sound of thunder, the dog would leave whatever it was doing and find a safe place to wait it out. Sometimes he'd hear it before we did and slip off and hide. I did not want to admit something was wrong with the dog. I would say he was only warning us about the weather. I thought he would get over it, and he would have, too, if it weren't for guns.

Some dogs are trained to take off the moment a shot is fired. Lance, depending on what we were hunting, was that kind of dog. But it wasn't long before the sound of gunfire made him cringe and duck and try to get out of the way, which is a smart thing, considering what had happened to him; but on the whole, it rendered the dog worthless.

Which this dog was not!

This was the dog that ran down the hog to save Rudy!

The same dog that charged the lynx to save Ike!

The same dog that outfoxed the big bobtail coon in deep water. The coon that killed Blackie.

This dog was something special. He would go into the brush, come out and bump you five times, and that would be the number of quail or grouse. He meant as much to me as Cody Wayne and Rudy, and it broke my heart to see him the way he was; at the mere sight of a gun, Lance would run and hide.

And that was why the dog was somewhere else with Unck and Cody Wayne.

"I need y'all to do somethin' for me," he said.

"Uh-huh," I replied.

"I know y'all was lookin' forward to ridin' wit Troy this summah, but I need y'all t' put aside this year and train some dogs for me."

I sighed audibly, but nodded my head yes. What he was asking us to do was spend the whole summer with Red Brown, which was asking quite a lot, because you had to have sense around Red Brown; he expected nothing less. We were who we were and were expected to know what to do without being told and what not to do until we were told. Life around Red Brown could get pretty complicated because of the psychological and emotional bonds between man and dog. You sometimes get to thinking the training will take of itself, but it does not; it is the owner who makes the dog what he is, and he has to understand the dog and his role in the dog's life. If he doesn't, life gets pretty complicated.

"Life ain't complicated," Grandpa said, reading my thoughts again. "Seventy-five percent of it ain't nuthin' but common sense. What Ahm askin' y'all t' do ain't no chore and should be as much fun as ridin' t' Canada wit Troy."

Maybe so. But what he was askin' us to do was not so much to train dogs, but to start growing up.

"Life wasn't meant to be complicated," Grandpa said. "God meant for life to be easy, but things can get pretty complicated if we ain't got no dogs."

"What about Lance?" I blurted.

"We'll fix him," he responded.

"He a good dog."

"Course he is. C'mon, Ahma learn ya something."

Rudy and Cody Wayne were in the boat, out toward the center of the lake, rowing in circles. Lance was with them. When Unck saw us coming, he waved them in.

Grandpa took one of the boxes of shells from me and began loading the shotgun. As the boat got closer to the bank he fired off several rounds. Lance began to cower.

Rudy and Cody Wayne got out and steadied the boat on the shallow bank.

"Stay! Stay!" Unck commanded Lance.

Lance looked around uncertainly as Unck got into the boat and held him by the collar. Grandpa got in and Unck began rowing away. I looked at Cody Wayne. He shrugged.

"Let's go up the trestle," Rudy suggested.

They left, but I stayed and continued to watch the boat, as it moved farther away, and Lance, who was watching me, fear chalking his face—the kind of fear that is ten times more dangerous than the danger itself, the kind of fear that cannot be avoided, the kind of fear that kills.

The trestle across the back part of the lake offered a clearer view, but I could not leave him; he was looking to me with too much fear in his eyes.

I could see Rudy sitting down across the tracks, his legs dangling through the ties. It had taken him some time to get over his fear of the trestle; even now, he was still on the lookout for oncoming trains even though there were no tracks leading to the bridge.

The booming report of the shotgun snatched my attention back to the boat in time to see Unck pick up Lance and toss him over the side.

"Oh no!" I gasped.

Then Grandpa stood up.

"No!" And raised the shotgun.

"Noooo!" And fired.

"Laaaance!" I screamed. "Laaaance!"

The dog had turned back for the boat, but when Grandpa began firing he turned away in panic and began pedaling for shore. Only his head was above water as Grandpa continuously fired directly over him. This was torment, nothing but torment!

"Lance!" I screamed, "Lance!"

Grandpa stopped and reloaded, but Unck kept rowing, keeping up with the dog, passing him and moving out in front of him. Grandpa got up and began firing again. The dog turned sharply and began paddling back out. Every ten yards or so, Unck would row out in front of him, and Grandpa would fire over his head. The logic was painfully clear. Lance would either overcome his fear of gunfire and get back in the boat, or he would get tired and drown. It was a terrible thing to do to a dog. After a while you could see how desperate he was. And tired. And finally he began to falter.

"Git in the boat, Lance!" Cody Wayne and Rudy were hollering from the trestle. "Git in the boat."

He paused and dipped and I held my breath as Grandpa fired in rapid succession. No longer was he moving forward, but treading the water in an exhaustive effort to stay afloat.

Grandpa reloaded and the dog turned.

Grandpa fired and the dog stopped.

Grandpa paused and the dog began moving *for the boat!*

Me, Rudy, and Cody Wayne let out a great cheer! He was so close, Unck could've reached out and pulled him in; instead Unck began rowing away.

And Grandpa kept firing.

And Lance struggled to keep up.

"C'mon, Lance!" They shouted from the trestle.

The dog was tired. They'd been in the water for more than an hour. His body began lurching, trying to keep his head up. Then he stopped. So did Unck.

Grandpa fired until the gun was empty, then he reloaded and began firing again. Lance pushed himself up against the side of the boat and remained there until Unck reached over and pulled him in.

Tears of joy were no outlet for my relief. The dog was the best thing about us. He was brave, and more than brave; he was courageous! His natural instinct taught him to discern what was good and courageous. A true nobility that exempted him from fear. This was just one more fight for him, one more big adventure. By virtue, Blackie, Ike, and Shack had all earned their deaths, and how bravely they died. By that same virtue, they still lived in Lance, and Cody Wayne, and Reuben Joseph, and John Calvin. We were the fruit formed by the prodigality of their nature. And we were not unworthy in their eyes, the eyes of those who knew us and the eyes of the world. Lance was a sheepdog, and a deer-dog, a coondog and a bird dog, a hog-dog and a gator-dog. And gator-dogs don't last long. But Lance did! He not only lasted, he'd triumphed too.

Unck pulled the little boat up on the bank and the dog jumped out and ran straight to me. His big heart had been repaired. His great spirit had returned.

Grandpa fired several shots and the dog stiffened alertly, his nose to the ground, his tail in the air. He was looking for the target. He saw Rudy and Cody Wayne coming from the trestle and he slipped past me and ran to them.

"Box up those shells," Unck ordered. Quickly, I climbed into the boat and began gathering up all the spent shells.

Dark Thirty

Dark thirty.

Most people say dusk dark, but Grandpa says dark thirty.

Dark thirty, the best time to fish.

Dark thirty, a genial emergence.

Dark thirty, the onset.

Dark thirty, when the bass bite.

"Look at 'em jump," cried Cody Wayne in wonder.

For the first time I noticed it. Shad, shad fry, and striped bass.

"Let's git a net full," Cody Wayne suggested, "and go sell 'em."

"It's almost dark," I said, closing up the box of shell casings.

"Yeah," he said looking at the sky, "but they sure are jumpin'."

Lance was standing at the water's edge looking alertly across the water. Dogs are not good at fishing, but I think they understand it, and why it's important.

"They tryin' to git away from that Loch Ness monster," Rudy said.

"Shut up wit dat Loch Ness monster shit!" I snapped. "You still seein' things."

I snatched up the two cases of shell casings and headed up toward the truck where Grandpa and Unck were. Unck was leaning across the hood of the truck and Grandpa was talking to him.

"Think he'll still sniff out a 'gata?" Grandpa asked Unck as they walked toward the trestle.

"Sounds challenging enough," Unck said.

"No, I mean find out why them fish jumpin' like that."

Unck looked across the lake, then he looked across the sky. "Dark thirty," he said.

"My ass," Grandpa said. "They's jumpin' like they's tryin' to jump out of the water."

"'Gatas?"

"Let's ask the ducks."

"Ain't no 'gatas here. 'Gata woulda got the dog."

"I wonder 'bout that."

It was another little thing and another little death. Cody Wayne and I had laughed at Rudy and convinced him it was not a gator he saw. After all, gators didn't come up this far. Gators stayed down the run and it was just little ones at that. Big ones, four feet or more, were caught and taken to Unck and Red Brown's illegal alligator farm. Besides, gators only went from gator hole to gator hole.

Rudy said it was a gator, but he wasn't sure it was a gator. He only saw it out the corner of his eye when he'd dived off the trestle. He'd hollered in midair and was trying to get out of the water before he was in. We laughed at him and convinced him that the big splash we'd heard was him.

Gators were way down by the marshes. And even Rudy said it wasn't a gator. Even if it was, Lance would have sniffed it out a long time ago. Especially one as big as Rudy said it was.

But even so, we were supposed to report anything that was not right. We were supposed to go to someone and say, "Rudy say he saw a 'gata, but I think he's seeing things." That way, even if he was just "seeing things," they would have checked it out. They would have questioned me, questioned Rudy, questioned Cody Wayne, and questioned the lake. Then they would have investigated it thoroughly. And it would have prevented another little death.

We were walking along the edge of the bank when Unck whistled to us. They were atop the trestle waving us back. It was the urgency that made me think about what Rudy thought he saw. They would want to know why I hadn't said something sooner and I was trying to think of something other than, "because we were playing hooky."

None of us, especially Unck, were so good and faultless that we didn't deserve an ass whipping ten times over. We could be as bad as the worst and sometimes, as good as the best. They did not expect us to know what we had not been taught, but they did expect us to know what was right. The worst thing we could be was hardheaded, and that covered a world of sin. They respected us as children. We were taught to keep ourselves busy and not waste the treasure of our time. So busy, we learned how to derive fun from the most mundane task.

It is said there are no children nowadays, that children learn too fast, and grow up too fast. That is how some people want their children—to grow up and get out of the way. But to us, the process of growing up was a process of learning what to do with life and living.

And to be content.

And to be at peace.

Life is not a complicated thing.

"Listen," Grandpa would say before giving us some rotten job. "Ahma learn ya something."

There was no one on the earth from whom we could not learn, and we were expected to learn even though we might not like being taught. Life was more than fun and games. Life was learning. A lesson in humility. A lesson in little things. A lesson in little deaths, for at the end of life, yours or someone else's, you learned about death.

The death of Lance was a lie in learning.
The death of Lance was the lie in life.
The death of Lance was the secret of nature.
The *secret* of nature is death.

We were going down the edge of the lake, going back to them. If they were thinking gator, Silver Blue Lake was an unsafe place until they knew for sure. Unck caught gators for sport. We'd seen him do it, and we did it with him. Sometimes he'd use a dog for bait. *A dog is a gator's best business.* He liked to use Poochie, because Poochie was so frisky. It was a game to her. The moment she hit the water she would bob and splash, and no gator worth its salt could resist her. They would come right to the top for this tasty little morsel and all Unck had to do was see it.

A gator was Unck's best business.

And Poochie was his favorite bait, until Savannah found out what he was doing with her. Now all you have to do is mention gator, and Savannah or Linda or Ingy or Cheryl or Teenie or Weenie will run and hide Poochie.

If not Poochie, then blood. Gators are like sharks when it comes to blood. If not blood, then something little, like a little duck, or a little fish, or Teenie and Weenie and Rudy. Or Lance, walking along the edge of the bank. His splashing around is what attracted it. Still, a gator is not likely to attack unless you provoke it, or you're close to its nest, or it is hungry. And it is impossible for a gator to go hungry in Silver Blue Lake. No! What it did to Lance was out of meanness and spite, and gators are not mean. They're not nice, but by nature they are not mean creatures.

This was not a gator!

It had stalked us. It had watched us and followed us. A gator, if it was not hungry or aggravated, would have watched us out of curiosity, then it would have gone on about its business. But this was not a gator! It burst up out of the water so quick and so sudden that I only had time to gasp. So quick I did not think to run. So quick, Lance had only time enough to look, and die. It came up out of the water with its mouth open, and opening wider, dripping with seaweed and death!

"Git away from the water! Run!" Unck screamed as he ran to us. "Run!"

And Rudy did run! And Cody Wayne did run! And they both had the presence of mind to run in different directions. But I could not run. All I could do was stand there and witness the horror of those terrible jaws crashing shut! And Lance's guts bursting out through his mouth! And the blood gushing from his nose! And that thing, rising up and up and up! And the big arms enveloping me and snatching me up and carrying me away.

Unck did not put me down until we were away from the bank, and even then he did not let me go. The truck skidded to a halt in front of us. Unck opened the door, lifted me in, and climbed in beside me. Cody Wayne and Rudy were in the back.

"I knowed them fish weren't jumpin' for nuthin'!" Grandpa shouted.

"Well, you didn't know it soon enough!" Unck shouted back. Both were excited and shouting.

"That weren't no 'gata!"

"What?"

He swung the truck around and sped for Silo. I sat quiet.

"How in the hell can somethin' like that be down here," Grandpa asked, "and nobody seen it!"

It was not a direct question, but an accusation and a chastisement. I trembled and Unck felt it.

"The ducks," he said. "The ducks shoulda told me."

Yes, the ducks and the fish and the otters and the dogs. The dogs would have definitely told us, because they didn't bark for nothing. Lance would have sniffed it out a long time ago, because he was never really shepherding the ducks, he was finding out why they'd abandoned the lake.

"That ain't like no 'gata to come all this way up against the flow," Unck said.

"Weren't no 'gata. Goddammit—you should know that!" Grandpa cussed.

What he knew was that Unck would take up for us no matter what.

"When's the last time y'all seen a 'gata come close to being that big, huh?" Grandpa asked. "Y'all woulda caught and skint it by now!"

It was bigger than anything I would expect to see. I'd looked down its gullet and saw its big blunted tongue. And the dog's eyes bursting out the sockets. Rudy was right this time: it wasn't a 'gata—it was a dragon!

"A crocodile?" Unck asked.

I trembled again at the thought and the sound of it.

"A crocodile?" he said again, not as a question, but as a wonder. He too, had never seen anything like it. It was unique and the thought of it, the *sport* of it, was exciting. "A damn crocodile—goooodamn!"

He'd seen a lot of things around the swamp, but how did a crocodile come to Silver Blue Lake? They'd been hunted to extinction in North America, and only those people who feel we have a moral responsibility to nature saved the alligator. There were saltwater crocodiles, but they wouldn't come this far inland.

It was another great wonder, like the thirty-foot boa that fell atop a tractor while they were dredging a canal through the swamp. Bake the Cake recovered from the shock quick enough to empty a .44 magnum into it, but it still scared him half to death, because he never expected to see a snake that big. Which only proved there were things back there no one ever saw, or wanted to see.

Cody Wayne and I had once gotten lost back there, but not *way* back there, and certainly not *way, way* back there to see any boa constrictors. *Way, way, way* back there was where Unck and Red Brown found the two white baby alligators.

"Somebody shoulda seen it, and that's all I got to say," Grandpa said, with the finality that made it the last word.

And that somebody said nothing. That same somebody sat perfectly still and stared straight ahead, because that somebody noticed he'd pissed his pants.

When we pulled into Silo, Grandpa got out and Unck took the driver's seat. Rudy and Cody Wayne climbed into the cab and we pulled off.

"I toldja!" Rudy exclaimed.

He looked past me and asked Unck, "We gon' catch it?"

"We gon' kill it!" Cody Wayne shouted. "It killed Lance—we gon' kill it dead!"

"Lance coulda got away," Unck said.

I looked at him and wondered how; the dog never stood a chance.

"I seen a-plenty 'gatas come up out the water for that dog," Unck said as he drove. "He was trained to make them come out. Best 'gata dog I ever seen."

He looked at Cody Wayne and said, "That weren't no 'gata."

"Then what was it?" Rudy asked.

"A crocodile."

"A crocodile!" Rudy gasped, putting in the emphasis and awe the word inspired.

341

"A 'gata ain't shit compared to this! I'll jump right on a 'gata! But I don't think I'll mess wit one of these."

But what did that mean to Lance, if he could've gotten away?

"If Lance hadda ran," Unck said, "the croc wouldn'ta chased it—too big. It woulda turned and got one a y'all."

Cody Wayne looked at the big wet spot in the front of my pants. I looked at him. *One a y'all.* Meaning me.

You would think that we are the only ones that make bargains, that one dog does not bargain a bone with another. But Lance did bargain. He'd bargained me. He'd bargained death.

The Thang That Ate
My Grandaddy's Dog

The moment Rudy hollered "crocodile," Ingy ran from the porch, grabbed Poochie, and ran back in the house.

"A big one!" Cody Wayne yelled.

"A real big one!" Rudy added.

A gator was no big deal. We had a freezer full. A gator in the lake was only a small cause for concern. But a crocodile was something else! A monster crocodile that had snatched the dog and scared Johnny so bad he'd pissed his pants! It was an alarming fact that made Grandma Gert get out her shotgun.

"Where's Daddy?" Unck hollered from the truck.

"What wrong?" asked Grandma Gert, coming down from the porch.

"Crocodile in the lake—it got the dog."

She looked at me standing there looking lost.

"He all right," Unck told her. "It just scared him."

She came to me and, with one hand, pulled me to her.

"This thing is big—a real monster," said Unck. "Where's Daddy?"

"Took off somewhere. Said he'd be back d'rectly," she answered.

"Soon as he come back tell 'im to come down to the lake. Bake the Cake and Tommy too."

As he backed out of the yard he yelled, "Call Red and tell 'im t' come help us wit this thang!"

He spun the truck around and sped back to Silo.

She looked at me for any sign of hurt, and I strained to keep from crying. We had yet to gain experience to guard and protect ourselves. If Savannah and Linda went to the store, Poochie went with them. It was comforting to know the dog was there. They loved us. They loved us more than they loved themselves. And the loss of all that love was much cause for grief.

"Go bathe and change," she said gently.

She understood the love, and she understood the loss. And the harder I cried, the tighter she held me.

"Hush," she whispered, "hush."

So much gator bait. So many stumbling blocks and pitfalls. So many little things causing so many little deaths. And all the dead were calling unto me.

"Y'all go wash and get ready for dinner," she said to the rest of them.

A little common sense may have avoided all the little deaths and all the ugly facts and all the little griefs. In that sense, common sense is a very uncommon thing. Common sense, as I don't understand it, is a gift. Grandpa's got it. Aunt Sally's got it. Grandma Gert's got it. Red Brown's got it. Unck's got it. And Miss Eva's got it, too. Common sense in the uncommon degree in which they have it is what the world calls *wisdom*. And seldom are men and women blessed with common sense to such an uncommon degree. They have good sense, and sound sense, and some sense, and a little bit of sense. They have a seventh sense, and technical sense, and a whole lot of wonderful, and not so wonderful, nonsense. But what we lack, and what we want, and what we need, is plain old common sense. And where common sense is wanting, everything else is wanting, too.

Even Rudy had sense enough to run. Common sense is what makes men; it is what makes life endurable. So what could they expect of me? I could go to college and earn a degree, but I still wouldn't have any sense. Like Bake the Cake and Tommy Green, I'd have "book sense," and they still wouldn't trust me to do the kind of things that took plain old common sense.

A thick head can do as much damage as a hard one.

Once, I remember teasing Linda with a vulgar rap song.

"Pop dat coochie!"

"Pop dat coochie!"

And Grandma Gert heard it and hollered, "Who dat singin' that?"

"Johnny!" both Savannah and Linda pointed.

"Ahma pop his coochie, if he don't cut it out!"

"He think he cute!" Savannah said.

"Where at," Linda asked, "on the bottom of his feet?"

"Look like the thang that ate my Grandaddy dog!" Grandma Gert snapped.

Savannah and Linda laughed, but Grandma Gert only looked at me without expression, wondering whether I had, or would ever have, any sense.

The room door opened and Savannah looked in.

"Johnny," she called softly, "Grandma Gert say come eat."

I sat quietly on the bed and did not turn around. More than likely she'd told her to close the door and leave me alone if I didn't want to eat. She came in and sat down on Rudy's bed.

"Don't cry," she whispered.

"I ain't cryin'!" I snapped.

Savannah had a strange way of knowing. A strange way of getting us to confide in her. Which was a very dumb thing to do, because Savannah told Grandma Gert everything.

Except everything that involved her.

"Well," she said, "don't think about it. You can git another dog."

"Dogs," I said.

"Huh?"

"Dogs—all of 'em are dead."

"Poochie not."

"She yo dog."

Savannah sighed.

"I tried to save 'im," I said, turning to look at her, tears slipping down my face.

"Who?" she wondered.

"Lance. That's why I didn't run."

It was not fear that had gripped me, not a total fear and not at first. I did not wet my pants until Unck had grabbed me. I was scared, but there is no courage unless you are scared. It was the helplessness. I'd turned, crouched at the ready, fist balled, prepared to fight. But the size of it! Mean and outrageous, it rose up out of the water and kept rising until my ability to react was lost by the sheer enormity of it. And in my defense, the dog looked it right in the eye and uttered not a sound.

"Don't cry," she whimpered. "You makin' me cry."

"It was just so big."

"That's what Rudy say. He say he saw it once before, but y'all didn't believe him."

"Yeah. They mad?"

"Who?"

"Grandma Gert. She mad?"

"She ain't fussin'. She just wanna know why y'all ain't had sense enough to say somethin'."

"'Cause that's the day we went and got the marbles and played hooky."

She wiped her eyes and understood, because for fifty cents from me, and fifty cents from Cody Wayne, and a quarter from Rudy, she'd written the permissible excuse that was never questioned because of her excellent, adultlike handwriting.

"Don't worry," she got up and said, not wanting to dwell on anything that involved her. "Grandma Gert say if you don't wanna eat, just lay down and go to sleep."

She eased out and closed the door.

Low Twelve

The difficulty of sleep was reconciling myself to dreams. I slept and I dreamed. Like a dog, I hunted in my dreams, which is not dreaming, but more of a change over the spirit.

I dreamed of the night. And the eyes of the night. I could see and identify them all.

"See, that's a coon."

It closed one eye, and the other one shined green. And Grandpa smiled, and shined the light across the yellowish eyes of "a deer!" And the greenish eyes of "a cat!" and Grandpa smiled again and shined the light across the lake, and the eyes shined a sinister red.

And I said, "'Gatas!"

And Cody Wayne said, "'Gatas!"

And Rudy said, "'Gatas!"

And Grandpa said, "Unh-unh."

One by one they began disappearing beneath the surface until only one was left. And Grandpa said, "That ain't no 'gata." and Unck raised his rifle and fired.

"Go git it," he said.

I took the rope and climbed into the water. And Grandpa said, "Make sho it dead."

"Ahm sho," I said.

"He sho," Cody Wayne said.

"We sho," Rudy said.

And I tied the rope around its tail and pulled it to shore. And the eyes opened. It wasn't dead. The eyes opened and shined a sinister red. And one by one they began rising to the surface, watching me. Fear has a thousand eyes. All of them are red. And all of them are watching me.

And watching me!

And watching me!

And watching me!

She is forever watching me. That is the way she is. In her mind's eye she is forever watching me. She used to call home every night at break time, and all Aunt Clara had to say was something about a crocodile and Johnny in the same breath and she had to come home. I was sitting out on the roof of the porch when I heard her coming. Me and Savannah were sitting out listening to the doings around the lake. There had been three explosions, and something was still burning. An ambulance had come and gone, and the three sheriff's deputies that had gone down there were still down there. Savannah went to bed moments before Manasha drove up. I climbed in off the porch roof, got in bed, and feigned sleep.

I knew she would come.

She came, quick and in a hurry, she came, just like she came the day she came looking for us after we'd gone gallivanting down the run. All by herself she came searching for us in a no-man's-land of snakes, sinkholes, and dire consequences. Grandpa had opened the lake to everyone during Cat and Paulus's wedding.

John Calvin Rainey

There were more than a hundred children to watch that day, but she was watching me, and when she didn't see me anymore, she came down the run where the land gets low, and the water runs swift, and bass are in abundance, and the gators come for bass—she came.

Where moccasins are as big as your arm and nests of brown eagles line the bank, and bear tracks line the trail—she came. Further than we'd ever gone before. Where she'd never gone before. Where everything's got rabies and industrial sludge pits abound. Where a man must know what he's doing before he goes back there because there were no mistakes in nature, only consequences.

"Gimme your belt," she'd asked Unck the minute she didn't see me.

And Unck said, "I'll go find them."

She went to Daddy Troy and said, "Gimme your belt."

And Daddy Troy said, "They'll be back d'rectly."

She went to Grandpa and said, "Gimme your belt."

And Grandpa said, "Quit frettin'. They ain't gone nowhere."

So she went to Grandma Gert and said, "I need a belt!"

And Grandma Gert asked, "Why? What's wrong?"

And she said, "They gone where I told them not to go and did what I told them not to do!"

And Grandma Gert said, "Git a stick! A big stick! And if they gone way down there where they ain't got no business, beat they ass all the way back up here!

"Beat they ass till it rope like okra!

"Beat they till it jam like jelly!

"Beat they ass like you mean business!

"Beat they ass!

"Beat they ass!

"Beat they hardheaded ass like it ain't never been beat before!"

And that is why I never found out where the sweet crystal clear water from Silver Blue Lakes flows. To this day, the farthest I've been down the run is where it drops suddenly, creating a little waterfall, and big rocks turn the water white. Where water-snails are as big as your fist and bigmouth bass think moccasins are worms. Where the banks rise ten feet high and the current is fast and unforgiving. Where peat moss, brewing for over a million years, bubbles up from somewhere deep inside the earth and if you struck a match the water would catch fire.

Where Manasha finally found us.

The three of us and Lance had climbed down the bank, undressed, and were just about to challenge the fast-running water when Lance started barking and we looked up and saw her coming. She had a stick, all right—a big stick! A belt too! She was not smiling and she didn't look at all like Manasha.

We thought the stick was for snakes. The belt was for show— or so we thought. It was the only time Manasha ever did anything like that, and to this day, I have never gone back down there because that day, Manasha whipped my ass all the way back up to the lake. I learned something about my mother that day, mainly how fast she could run. She'd started with Rudy because Rudy just stood there playing innocent, as if he wasn't at fault, as if he was only following us. But Manasha didn't give a damn! She made sure that he would never follow us down there again. When she started on Rudy we knew she meant business and what she had in store for us. So me and Cody Wayne, still in our drawers, flew past her, confident that she could never catch us. But Manasha was not just fast, she glided over air!

When she got through with Rudy, she caught up with me,

and when she got through with me, she caught up with Cody Wayne, and when she got through with him, she caught up with me again and good God a'mighty—Gail Deevers ain't that fast! When Lance finally snatched the belt from her and ran, she broke a stick from a limb and took off after him, too.

What I learned about Manasha that day was that she was faster and cleverer than me.

What I learned about my mother was that I would never quite be a man to her. I would never quite outgrow the child. I would always feel her presence and she would always be watching. No matter where I was, Manasha would be watching. No matter how fast or clever I thought I was, Manasha would be cleverer and faster and always watching. Not God—Manasha! God could not be everywhere at once, so he sent Manasha.

She tucked my blanket and smoothed it out from where she'd been sitting for almost an hour. She tucked and smoothed Cody Wayne and Rudy's blankets, then went over, closed the screen, and locked it to keep out the bats.

It used to be mosquitoes she worried about, but despite the lakes and the swamp and the reservoir, there were not many to contend with. As Grandmama explained it, the fish ate the larvae of the ones in the lake, and the ones out of the swamp never made it through the wood because the bats ate them.

"Bats?"

"Just little old fruit bats," said Daddy Troy.

"Bats?"

"They eat mosquitoes by the ton," Grandma Gert told her.

"*Bats?*"

"They don't bother nothin'," said Unck.

"*Bat's—there're bats around here?*"

"We know where a whole cave full of 'em at!" Rudy told her.

Manasha was from New York; what did she know about *bats?* To her they conjured up dark, gothic visions of fog-clouded London, Jack the Ripper, Igor, vampire blood-sucking—*bats?*

Why worry about mosquitoes when you've got—*bats?*

And crocodiles!

And wild boar hogs!

And boa constrictors!

And rabies!

And your dogs are dead.

She made sure the screen was secured, and had turned to leave when Rudy sat up in his sleep and said, "Unh-unh! Unh-unh! Don't let them scare you!"

And she laid him back down and sat at the edge of this bed to further contemplate this batty and crocodilian world.

Providence

They'd been coming all morning to see it. A TV crew, several photographers, two reporters, three game wardens, an agent from the Fish and Game Commission, two researchers from the University of Florida, and a bunch from Gatorland.

Mr. Ceelie even came!

Miss Eva, too.

And MacArthur Dill, high sheriff of Oklawaha County.

I looked out the window and saw Eveleen and Dianne Baker driving back up the Ceelie Road. They honked twice. The sun was up, what Grandpa called "high twelve." Noon. I'd slept all morning. I put on a pair of pants and hurried downstairs.

"Where everybody?" I asked, stepping onto the porch. Manasha and Grandmama were sitting down talking to another woman.

"C'mere," Manasha called me.

She reached out and pulled me to her.

"Where's everybody?" I asked again.

"Still down there lookin' at it," Grandmama said.

"Oh."

"People been callin' all mornin' offering me condolences and tellin' me how sorry they are and—"

"Sorry for what?" I asked.

"For you!"

"For me? Why?"

"They think you got ate," Grandmama said.

"Not me!"

"That's what I keep tellin' 'em," Manasha said.

"You saw it?" I asked her.

"Yeah," she said, and shuddered to think what something like that could do. I knew then that it was still alive.

"Is it dead?" I asked anyway.

She wet her finger across her tongue and rubbed the matter out of my eyes. I cringed.

"Go wash the yuk out ya mouth," she said, "and put on a shirt. She wanna talk to you."

The woman smiled.

"Who she?"

"She's from the newspaper. Her name's—uh—what's your name again?"

"Loukia," the woman said. "Loukia Louka."

"Oh," Manasha said. "She wanna talk."

"'Bout what?" I asked.

"'Bout what happened," Manasha said. "Talk to 'er."

"I'm from the *Tampa Tribune*," the lady said.

"Oh," I said.

"We were over in River Rise when we heard about this."

River Rise. That meant Gulf sturgeon, and that explained the presence of the Fish and Game Commission, who were restocking various Florida rivers with thousands of two-month-old caviar and good meat-producing Gulf sturgeon. In an even greater effort to help bring it back from the brink of extinction, Unck, Red Brown, and Tommy Green had already trapped at least eight hundred of them, and that explained the reason for the fence around

Sky Lake. No one knew it, but we were in the caviar business.

"It must have been a terrible experience," the reporter said.

A truck we didn't recognize passed and honked twice. It was Red Brown. We didn't recognize the truck because it wasn't his. His truck, four-wheel drive and all, was still in the lake.

"It's Red Brown," Manasha said to Grandmama.

His arm was broken and in a cast. He was driving with one arm.

"Look at 'im," Grandmama said. "He just like a little boy. All this right down his alley."

"Yeah," Manasha said. "Him and Lijo gittin' a big charge outta this."

"Maybe we should charge people to see it," Grandmama suggested.

"I assumed that's why they didn't kill it," the reporter said.

"They shoulda killed it," I said. "It killed Lance."

"The dog?" the reporter asked.

"Yeah."

"You were very lucky," she said. "A little girl was killed by an alligator in Charlotte County last week."

"I heard about that," Manasha said.

"But this a crocodile," I said.

"That's what makes this interesting," the reporter said. "What's a crocodile doin' here?"

I shrugged.

"Believe it or not, there used to be a lot of crocodiles here and abouts," Grandmama said, "but they's all been hunted out."

"Maybe they didn't get them all," Manasha said.

"But why here," the reporter asked, "in the lake?"

"Fish, I suppose," Grandmama said.

"Y' know," said Manasha, "it's a big old swamp back there."

"Fulla God knows what," Grandmama said.

"I guess they gotta have some place to go," said Manasha.

They could go to hell as far as I was concerned.

"Sometimes," Grandmama said, "people take things back there and leave 'em."

"That's why a lot of wild dogs are back there," said Manasha.

"Ferals," I said.

"Bake the Cake killed a big old snake back there," Manasha said.

"A boa," I said.

"And one day a big old lizard fell out the pecan tree and scared the piss outta me!" Manasha said.

"A monitor," I said.

"Scared the piss outta everybody," Grandmama said, "before the dogs ran it off."

And a little wave of sadness came over me.

"Uh—is that a skunk?" the reporter asked hesitantly.

Cleo came from around the side of the house and up to the porch. Since none of us seemed excited, she remained somewhat calm.

"Cleo," I called to her. She came to me and hopped in my lap.

She wanted a picture of me, the little boy who was almost eaten by a crocodile, but was made to understand I was not particularly interested in going down to the lake for a nice little picture. So, she had one taken of me right where I was. Me, Manasha, Grandmama, and Cleo. And it appeared two weeks later in the *Tampa Tribune*. It was a big feature story about a little girl who was killed by an alligator, and a little boy almost killed by a crocodile. There was also the story of how they caught it, how they used pig's blood and a live chicken connected to a five-hundred-pound

357

test line with milk bottles attached to it. As soon as the croc snatched the chicken, they had a fix on it and threw in a stick of dynamite. Now that's sport! It knocked out the croc and brought it to the surface where they got a rope around it and dragged it to the shore. They were just in the process of tying it when it woke up. In one picture, you could see Red Brown, arm in a cast, Tommy Green, and the sheriff, standing atop the trestle looking down at Red Brown's truck, four-wheel drive and all, still submerged in the water. You could see the tip of the motorboat where it sank, too. And the John Deere tractor lying on its side on the edge of the bank.

There was another picture of Grandma Gert and Aunt Clara, Linda and Savannah, Ingy and Cheryl, and Teenie and Weenie among the ducks down by the lake.

Grandpa and Daddy Troy were standing next to the Ford pickup, gaily pointing to the smashed-out back window and the dangling tailgate.

Unck, Cody Wayne, and Rudy were in the big picture standing next to the croc. In comparison to them, the world could witness the awesome size of it. Even though it was tied, chained, roped, taped, and staked to the ground, it was still a picture of sheer terror. I shuddered at the sight of it. I had not seen it since that day, nor had I seen it when they caught it, or when they brought it out. But I looked at it now, and fearsome was the word for it. And frightening.

But was it evil?

It killed Lance.

But was it evil?

It killed my dog!

But was it to blame? An evil thing to be punished for its villainy?

It was mean!

Yes, it was mean, mean enough to produce great anxiety and fear, but was it evil? Was it evil from within? Did evil proceed from its thoughts? Could it commit murder? Could it commit adultery? Could it steal? Was it deceitful? Could it cast the evil eye on you? Did it curse? Was it proud? Was it foolish? Was it all these things, or was it but a hungry stomach?

It was my enemy! I could not blame it for being mean and vicious and ugly, but it killed my dog and would forever be my enemy.

The picture that bothered me was the picture about me. What bothered me was Manasha and Grandmama. They were sitting directly behind me looking very grim, looking like mothers of four dead dogs and three rash little boys who might survive on luck and pluck.

Boys will be boys, I guess, but they seem to be wondering, would boys be men? Would we ever grow up to be men, or just children of a larger size?

Not without practice.

Not without patience.

Not without experience.

Not without protection.

Certainly not without sense.

And not without the dogs.

The dogs were dead, but by their deaths, we gained much strength, courage, and confidence, which gave us more of a fighting chance at life. They were grim because they could not see ahead of us, as if there might not be any tomorrow.

But I knew that in eight years, I would be eating caviar, because that is how long it takes Gulf sturgeon to mature. Two years for eucalyptus trees, fifteen for pulpwood, and forty for big pine.

It takes approximately ninety to a hundred and twenty days for a crop of alfalfa to come up.

Twelve hours for a hen to lay another egg.

And eighty-nine days for me to wear out another pair of tennis shoes.

But that is the hope, and the magic, and poetry of rash little boys depending upon luck and pluck and dreams.

That is providence.

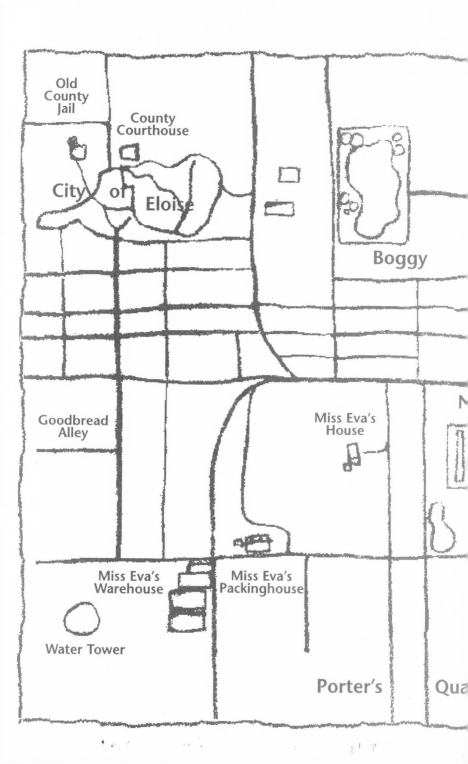